NEEDLES & SINS

To Charlie! Enjoy these Sins!

JOHN EVERSON

NEEDLES & SINS

JOHN EVERSON

NECRO PUBLICATIONS
2007

first edition
NEEDLES & SINS

book design & typesetting:
David G. Barnett / faT caT Design

assistant editors:
Amanda Baird • C. Dennis Moore • Sean Woods

a Necro Publication
5139 Maxon Terrace • Sanford, FL 32771
www.necropublications.com

trade paperback: ISBN: 1-889186-74-0
This book is also availabe in a limited edition hardcover of 100 copies.

Printed by
Publishers' Graphics
Carol Stream, IL

For Shaun
Who Loves a Good Bedtime Story

TABLE OF CONTENTS

Introduction

This introduction to *Needles & Sins* will be less literary and more informal than some introductions. This is because John Everson's latest collection pulls such a diverse range of emotions from me.

I couldn't have been happier or more honored to be asked to write the introduction for one of my favorite modern horror authors…not to mention one of my best friends. This doesn't make me biased. Just pissed I hadn't written these stories myself.

John Everson has produced a variety of tales which will neither bore nor grow stale with the telling. His prose is whatever it needs to be for the piece: raw and shocking, bitingly tender with traps, rich yet always believable. His knowledge, feel and love for the work shows in every line, like the brush strokes of a painter. Yet it is most definitely of the 21st century and hurray for thus. Writers should step up and create from a new millennial gut. Times change and good writers aren't sheep…no matter how wicked they pretend to be while attending a convention. If you write RAW, you aren't shy. You know rules were made to be broken—unless all you want is a cozy buck. John says what he means and means what he says. Ought to have been born a Texan. (Oops. Sorry.)

And to see him, he's so adorable. A true gentleman. He is a Renaissance man: author, musician and composer, critic and artist. But the gentleman in the right shadow reveals a delicious flint in his eyes, suggesting a well-healed surgeon out slumming in London's old East End.

I don't know anyone who doesn't like John Everson. Well, there is this one creep who is ostentatiously jealous of John's many talents. May this varmint rot in a bilge stew of vomit-feathers and excreta-caked love beads found crammed into either end of a dead tramp cut in half by a rodent train in the meth back alleys of Dallas.

(Um, let me shake myself a little. Whew! That feels better!)

Now let me make a few comments about the book, *Needles & Sins*. I won't mention every story. I want you to explore for yourself. Bring waders—it can be treacherously deep in Everson waters.

The first is "Needles And Sins." This hurt me in more places than I thought I had. It is about suffering and abuse, and either you've been there or you haven't. Either way the story is moving...dreamily, nightmarishly toward a spot in the soul that never quite gets filled.

John uses "Bloodroses," a reprint I still love. It is a touching story, some of it in places you would never want to be touched. Depends, I suppose, on your tolerance for kinky. This story makes me cry (probably due to 13 prescription medications and an opioid patch—ain't modern science scary?) and still gives me nightmares. It also makes me cringe at the sight and scent of roses.

Then there is "The Char-Lee." What can I say as I blush? I love a tale that turns me into a real...

Sacrifices. They are like candy and flowers. Just not roses. "Her flesh wept with the tears of a thousand fickle knife-kisses..." Ouch! Oh! My...

"Mutilation Street" is just too much grisly sinful fun for anyone one nostril short of a good blood-red line. I laughed pounds off. I love Stupid Bitch.

"Warmin' the Women" sure ain't the Boy's Town Spencer Tracy knew. Not so sure about Mickey Rooney.

"Mary" I don't know if I would have dared. But I wish I had: "...Mary panicked, struggled against the lulling torpor of his sensual valium."

I have done many stories about circuses and/or special people. This book derives almost a quarter of its content from the final five interwoven stories under the big top of LOVE & ROPE & SEX & SCREAMS: A CIRCUS IN FIVE ACTS. This is a wonderful quintet, especially to close such an amazing collection with.

The Big Death is popular now, full of religion, end times, and all its big hair. Because we have just done the last century and millennium and have girded our loins for the next, perhaps we feel it in the air, a sense of change. Death is change, the ultimate maybe, not necessarily the finale. Here is where writers, fools, and seers enter the picture, giving us shivers with options, maybe even a message wrapped in a rattlesnake speaking in tongues. As John writes in the first page of "Letting Go": "Death was like that. A land of unintended consequences."

Perhaps the meek (and sheep) shall inherit the earth. But who will get the lands beyond it?

—Charlee Jacob
Texas, 2007

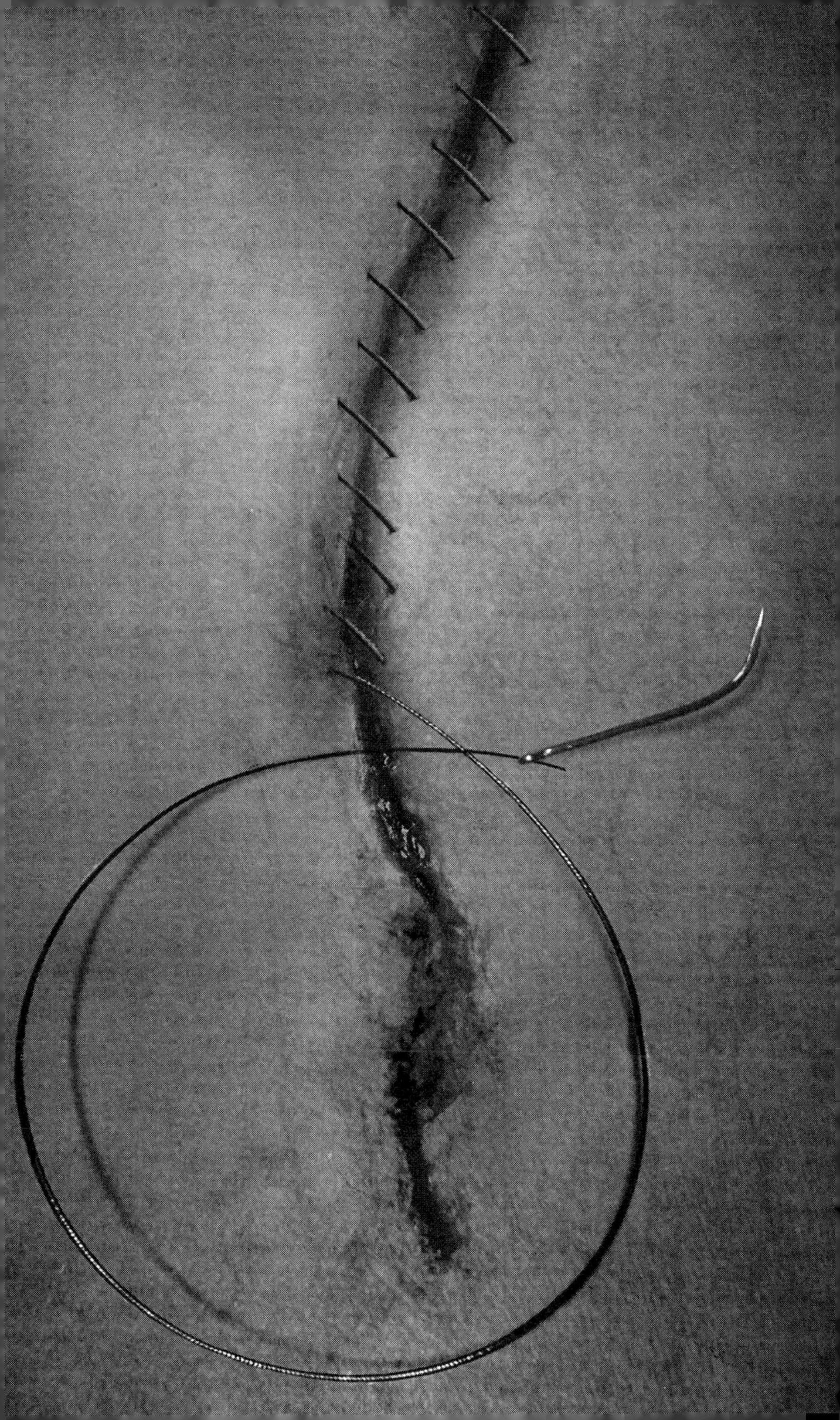

Needles & Sins

He heard the song before he felt the pain. Just a whisper on the edge of wanton breath. A woman's breath, light and sweet. She moved in the shadows beyond his head, and the melody lurked just behind the heat of her earthy scent as his eyes struggled to open. To wake to this new place.

That's when the piercing began. That's when his eyes snapped open—no longer able to just drowsily think about it—and his body convulsed, and in a flash he saw:

...His chest laid open, a red, gory river snaking its way from somewhere below his neck to his belly button...

...His ribs glittering like a pearly cage of broken bones in the yellow lamplight...

...His gleaming, helpless organs revealed like a deli tray of cannibalistic delights...

...His genitals lolling like broken meat across a slack thigh, spattered with spots of crimson...

...His toes, purpled and bruised, spasming at the end of the table he lay upon...

...A white hand, fingers long and thin, pulling a long, hooked needle through the far end of the fatal gash near his belly and trailing an almost invisible fleshtone thread in the air behind it...

Charles screamed.

The song stopped, and a warm wetness slid across his forehead. Her tongue. A kiss. "Shhhhh," the liquid voice intoned. "We've only just begun."

"What happened?" he moaned, biting his tongue harder and harder until he felt the warmth of blood pass his lips as the woman's thread passed lower, through his torn flesh. He struggled to remember, but nothing would come. "Why am I so torn up?"

She whispered two words in answer. "You lived."

The needle dipped into a bowl of liquid near his ribs, and came out dripping golden rain in the weak light. Then it moved to touch the hamburger of his abdomen again. "Remember your wife?" the voice coaxed, and in a flash, he saw Sharlene circa age 32, just as she was trying her damnedest to make it work between them…

"Whatever you want," his wife moaned in the shadows of 2 a.m. He grinned, a lust-shark in the blood-scented water of twilight and pushed her face down, down to the place where he knew Sharlene hated, where he knew she would feel defiled and humiliated, to the place that would haunt her dreams with feelings of self loathing and inadequacy. He knew all about her inner demons, but at that deep-sea moment he didn't care, not then, not when he knew what could come, or cum, of it… "Yes," he grinned. "Suck it good."

The pain jolted him from the memory, an electric cattle prod.

He tried to push away from the table with his arms, but nothing moved. He was helpless beneath her song, and her needle. "Goddamnit!" he cried.

"Oh…he did," the whispering woman agreed with his curse. Again her needle left his torso, trailed blood-slick thread high in the air and descended to the bowl to be baptized with a splash of…something. And once cleansed of the stain of his gut, the needle hooked through his skin once more.

"What about your son," the perfumed breath whispered over his eyelids. "Did you love him?"

««—»»

Barry looked up from the hole he'd dug in the yard in panic. "Dad, I didn't mean to ruin the grass, honest, I was just looking for locusts, you know, that might have nests that got buried..."

His hand slapped the boy's face almost without thinking. The boy needed to learn. Learn to respect property, people. How dare he just start digging a hole in the middle of the lawn that had just been resodded a month ago? Barry had to learn...

Charles' hand came down again, clipping the boy in the lip and cuffing his head. In that moment, the sweet, wet-lipped infant he'd once cradled in his arms metamorphed into a foul stain on his white sheets. In Charles' heart, Barry became nothing more than a nuisance, a delinquent, a problem, problem, problem child that had locked him down to a life he never wanted...

"Dad, I'm sorry, I won't do it again," Barry begged, tears already staining the dust on his face as he scrambled away from the pile of broken grass and muddy earth and launched his feet in a scramble for the house where mom and safety lie. But Charles' hand caught the hem of his shirt and yanked him off balance.

Charles right hand came down. "I'll show you sorry..."

"He needed to learn to respect property!"

"Of course he did," the woman whispered. "A broken arm is a good lesson. One he'd remember."

"I didn't mean..." Charles started to say, but then broke off to scream as the hook dug into the tight part of his flesh, just above the sternum.

"Why are you doing this to me?" he cried.

"Your life is one long thread. I'm just making you whole," she said. And she began to hum. He could hear the words in her melody, words about pride, and tears and needles.

"Ohhhh," he moaned. As the tip dug into the space above his rib, he looked down and saw slack, dead white flesh and sickly black hair curled atop it like leavings. The remains of his day.

"Why did you live alone at the end?" she asked.

The glass was cool against his lips and he smiled in the golden light of its love. Okay, it didn't love...but it was what he *loved. What he needed. He remembered the last time he'd had a woman here, in the tiny space that he'd carved out for himself just off the broken pavement of 8th Avenue. The complex was a last stop for most, but he'd covered the uneven walls of his purloined space with a $10 can of beige paint that he'd watered down to make it go farther and thus had hidden most of the cracks in its distressed drywall. He pretended that he lived in a home and that the soybeans he ate tasted like filet. He'd stuffed blankets in the draughty cracks that separated the walls from the floor and the windows from the walls and most of the time in the winter, he kept the place above 50 degrees. With a bottle of Jack Daniels a day, he could make it feel like the place was warm, while his flesh shivered unheeded in the cold.*

The phone rang, and he almost dropped his glass. The phone never rang. Probably just another creditor or solicitor, he thought, brain buzzing with the metallic jolt of whiskey. Still, he answered it, pressing the cool plastic to the scratchy whiskers of his chin. Idly he scratched at the dry skin there as he said, "Yeah? What can I do you for?"

"Dad," a voice said from a faraway crackle. "I need help."

"Buy me a beer," he answered, and laughed as he dropped the phone between two couch cushions. He looked for it squirting in the shadows, but his hand didn't seem to have the energy to dig between the seams to retrieve it. Instead he fell back and closed his eyes. From somewhere far away, he heard a voice calling his name, but he no longer felt like answering...

The needle dug closer, and his eyes shot open, wider than wide in agony. A jet of crimson spurted like a geyser from some lost artery near his heart, and he gagged on the bile that gathered in the pit of his throat. "Stop," he gagged.

"...the tears I gotta hide," the woman's voice whispered, singing along with the tune she'd been humming with every stitch. "Needles and sins," she laughed softly, and completed the stitch as his body jolted against her hand. "Needles and sins."

Charles was 16, and glad to be away. He crept through the cattails holding his BB gun like an army rifle. He was ready to use it. That's when he saw the mouse scurry down the trampled path to disappear into the crumpled mass of stalks and dirt. He kicked off the top of the mound and laughed as momma mouse bolted away from the nest, leaving four pink, hairless babies to sniff and paw at the air, blinded by the unnatural light of the day. He cocked the air socket of the gun, aimed and blew tiny ball bearings through the thin skins of those helpless rodents. One, two, three, four. Tiny circles of blood blotted their purplish bodies, and the mice shuddered and clutched each other as they collapsed onto the matted grass of their once comfortable nest. They couldn't understand the sudden change in their lives from warmth to pain, but mercifully, they died in seconds, just like the...

The needle plunged deep, drawing its thread tight.

...love that died as Charles lifted his hand for the first time when Gwendolyn told him in the back seat of his Chevy Citation to cut it out, that really hurt and maybe he should try learning some manners the next time before he touched a woman as if she was just another piece of trash for the curb, but he didn't listen and her spit and blood coated his hand as she turned away in hurt and shame just like the way...

««—»»

The needle dipped into the bowl, and dripping cool sting, slipped inside his flesh again.

...happiness died as Charles looked at his daughter in her prom dress and laughed, saying "who do you think you are, the

freakin' Queen of Siam? Do you think the other kids are going to go out looking like that?" And as Rachel's face crumbled into a black hole of betrayal...

The needle dripped and stitched, washing his flesh clean of blood as it closed his exposed organs back up within.

... Trust died as Charles promised that he'd be home on time tonight, and instead stopped off, just for one nip, just one, just one more, just a quick last taste...

"Stop, please stop," he begged.

But she only whispered from behind his head, her voice sweet as spring lilies. "Still they begin," she said. "Needles and sins."

...And Ambition died as Charles watched the next hotshot and the next and the next walk past his cube over the years atop the soulless grey carpet to take a manager's office at the end of the hall. An office with a door. And at last, one night he walked into that envied office and sat himself in the chair of his boss, 10 years his junior, who had left for home and cocktail parties two hours before, leaving Charles to work alone, pulling the weight for both of them. Charles sat in that leather-backed chair, and leaned back to stare at the framed poster on the otherwise sterile wall that featured the block letters spelling S-U-C-C-E-S-S in a black bar at the bottom and at long last, years in the making, he began to cry.

«« — »»

The needle now closed the livid tear near his throat, the end of a long scar of twisted, bloody, knotted flesh. "They say not to sweat the small stuff," the woman whispered behind his head. "But that's what it's all about..."

"I wasn't like that all the time," he said, and then moaned, "It hurts."

Images clustered in his mind's eye of his wife and kids and broken dreams mixed with the memories of dying mice and the spider-webbed glass of the car his parents last drove in and the pink slip that sent him from a broken home to the apartment where the liquor drove away the cold. And then his memories fled like dandelion seeds in an angry April breeze.

Dad?

Charles?

Baby?

Son?

The voices reverberated from inside, first louder, but then muffled, as the woman pulled the last skein of thread through his suppurating skin.

"It will hurt," she whispered, humming softly into his ear. "It will hurt forever."

"But why?" he moaned, trying without success to lift his arm to touch the horrible stitching that held him together and formed a knot at his heart.

"Because you lived."

At last she moved so that he could see her. After tying off the thread that wound and bound inside him, she picked up the bowl of liquid. Her chin thrust into the dull shadow in stark, bone white, heavy eyes shone black as night water. She drank the deadly liquid from the bowl and grinned, her teeth stark in bony sockets stripped of flesh.

"Every stitch soaks my poison into the flesh," she grinned. "Just like every sin poisons the soul."

"So this is the end," he whined. "All of my days done?

She only laughed.

Behind her, Charles watched the black shadow of wings unfurl in the wavering amber of the room's deadly light.

"Still they begin," she whispered and gathered him to her to start again…her needles and his sins.

Something Inside

"There's someone else hidden inside me," the woman whispered. She seemed adamant. "She has been trapped inside me forever, and I want you to set her free."

I had heard it before. Sometimes, I felt like I'd heard it *all* before. Hidden within every big assed woman was a skinny beauty queen dying to be "set free" for her tempestuous moment on the runway of dreams. Or so they thought. As a surgeon, I have a firm and well-founded belief in the innate ugliness of some people. No amount of surgical intervention is going to change the summation of a gene cesspool. But still they came, false dreams in their rosy lenses and checkbooks in hand. They wanted their water balloon slack tits to defy natural law and stand up straight as B-52 bomber cones, or their cellulite-striped bellies not to stretch like beached and rotting whale blubber over their shiny, tight-cinched steel belts. They especially wanted to obliterate that saggy, baggy line that stretched from the pubis to the ribs and which rippled and shook every time they moved. No regimen of weight loss could completely erase the sagging quicksand slippage of skin that said "once there used to be a big vat of fat—or a parade of babies—that nested here."

The latest in a long line of women who wished that I worked in miracles and not scars sat in my examining room and pointed at the spiderweb of lines on her face, and then gave a general gesture to the rest of her flesh. It was not unattractive, but it was also not a look-twice-at-on-the-street body. An objective assessment said that she clearly wasn't one of the genetic cesspool derelicts that was beyond salvaging. With a bit of cutting, stitching, nipping and tucking, I could set free the more beautiful woman that the years had walled up inside her.

But there was a look in her eyes that I couldn't place. I'm not sure how to describe it really. Desperation? Yearning? Obsession? It was the kind of overly intense look that, five years ago, would have made me send her packing without a second glance.

Surgeons can't take a chance on potential crazies. People think doctors make cartons of cash, and they do. But what people don't know is that most docs have 10 years of student loans to pay off, and that as soon as you hang up your shingle, you've got to sign up for malpractice insurance—which instantly saps half your revenue. You operate on a couple nutjobs and get some outrageous lottery judgments against you from a bleeding heart liberal jury, and your malpractice insurance goes up and up; you might as well take up baggin' groceries to earn a living.

Which I was close to doing now. I speak here from the deep deep well of experience. Ironically, because of my desperate situation, I listened to the desperately strange woman longer than I would have not so long ago when things were better for me—back when the local newspapers used to write articles about my surgical prowess, not ineptitude.

"I want you to cut me open," she continued to explain. Her finger traced a line down the center of her forehead, across her nose and down in between her breasts. I noted, purely professionally, that she had no need of augmentation or reduction there…her chest looked provocatively obvious and well-rounded. No sags or deflated bags there. She was of a higher caliber than most of the patients I'd seen in the past two years. Not that there had been very many of any quality.

"There is certainly cutting involved," I said, ignoring her crude directions which basically would have had me cut her in half if I carried them out to the letter. "But what is it that you want to achieve?"

She looked at me with the kind of seriousness that I imagined impassioned serial killers display as they approach their victims with single-minded purpose.

"I want you to cut me from my forehead to my toes," she said. "I want you to set her free."

I nodded and wrote something in her chart. "Nutcase," I believe, is what I wrote. Then I stood up and said, "Wait here just a minute."

I opened the door and ducked into the hallway.

"Wait doctor," she began, leaping off the paper-covered examining table. "I know this sounds crazy but…"

I was already at the receptionist's station. " Carrie," I said. "I can't operate on Ms. Phoenix. Please give her the name of someone at the Artgeld Clinic."

I always used to give Carrie the shit jobs. After all, she ran the desk. She was my front line protection.

The problem was, when you're on the way down, nobody is all that keen to protect you and help you back up. Especially when your checks bounce. And when you turn down cases when your payroll checks are bouncing…

Well…that's why, the next time Ms. Phoenix—"Please call me Janis"—came to my office, I was the only one there to receive her.

She rang the buzzer at the front desk and I had to answer. She roused me from a reverie of worry that involved the winner of the next NCAA pool among the medical building tenants, the fleeting concern about my overdue mortgage and the thought that maybe, just maybe, I might get laid if I went down to Billy's Tavern tonight and mentioned that I was not just a surgeon, but a doc who had given "breast lifts" to the stars. It was a weak dream, but it was better than the thoughts of the repo men coming to cart all of my furniture back to some endless, Orwellian warehouse.

I knew the stains on my office carpet were really the visible comments on the lackluster spark that had been my brief career. I probably would have failed as a vet. I was probably best cut out as an accountant. But here I was. A skids surgeon who had gotten his degree in an offshore program because my grades weren't quite up to par to make it into a medical school here in the states. A guy with a scalpel, a mediocre degree, and an office that cost too much, even though it shared a zip code with the slums. While at first I had charmed a few well-connected patients—and the press—I had, in the end, not done particularly well for myself.

Nor for others really.

The carpet of my office was as stained in blood as the legal proceedings against my name were saturated in ink. I got into this business to help people; really I had.

Yet here I was, in an empty, beaten-down office, with a crazy woman asking me to flay her open. Filet her like a trout.

And there wasn't a nurse to be found to back me up. Normally, doctors always had a nurse in on a consultation, largely to make sure that if any litigation followed the surgery, there would be a) a witness, and b) another woman to refute it. Put a man in court against a woman with a spit-on-command eye faucet…and the man lost every time, regardless of the circumstance. Estrogen always triumphed over testosterone in our courts of law. Call it primordial. Call it unfair. It was what it was.

And right now, there was a woman in my broken down office, for the second time in as many months, asking me to cut her open.

Only this time, I was within five days and $250 of losing my lease. I had no staff salaries to pay because I had no staff. But Janis Phoenix was potentially the only patient between me and bankruptcy. And I didn't even have a heroin habit to blame on my decline.

"You remember me," she said, when I came out from the back room and raised an eyebrow at her stance behind the nurse's station. She had rung the tiny "call" bell ten times in as many seconds.

"How could I forget?" I asked. "You want me to cut you open…but to gain what?"

"To release the inner me," she said.

"What you've proposed will only release your blood and put you in danger of dying," I said.

When she smiled, I almost believed that letting out a little blood on the table would make her sing. But that wasn't the end of it. She wanted me to trim her flesh to the bone. To cut her from stem to sternum and then some…until her skeleton was set free to dance in a kaleidoscopic celebration on my fucked-up bones. Because if I did what Janis wanted, I would have no office or career, or life. I would be locked up forever, for first degree murder…with a violently violated corpse as gruesome evidence that provided no potential defense. Nobody cut open a woman for a procedure the way this woman wanted me to.

"You can release your inner you without my help," I said finally, after listening to her insane demands. "Watch Oprah."

"I have," she said. Her wide lips curled up higher in a sneer. "But this isn't a fake bourgeois 'I need to go to the mall' problem that I have."

I shrugged in curiosity. I'd like to say disinterest, but frankly, this woman fascinated me. She was not bad looking. She was close to my age. And she seemed to be fixated on having me put a knife to her flesh. I assumed she was some kind of extreme masochist. Not my kink, but fascinatingly perverse, regardless.

"Listen," she said. "There is a better *me* inside me that needs to be let out." She ran a finger up my arm, as if to suggest…sensual reward for my work. This, I was well-versed in dealing with.

"Janis," I said, "I can help you to realize the goals you have in your surgery…"

"Spare me the surgical-psycho mumbo jumbo," she cut me off. "I don't have any goals other than that you cut me open and let the real me out."

I laughed.

She slapped me.

"I'm not fuckin' kidding," she said. "I want you to put a scalpel on my forehead, draw it down to between my breasts, and then open my belly, my thighs and my calves until the blood flows out to the floor like a bad plumbing leak. I want you to slip your hands inside the open wound, and lift the flesh like a door until my body is truly 'open.' Only then, can she be set free."

"Assisted suicide is not legal in this state," I whispered.

"I'm not talking about suicide," she insisted, her eyes blazing wide. "I'm talking about rebirth."

Color me stupid, but I just didn't feel that desperate yet… I turned her away, a second time. And as the door to my ramshackle office rattled itself closed, I sank to the stained carpet and held my face in my hand. She had been my only potential patient for days, and I'd turned her away for …what? Morals? Ethics? She was crazy as a loon but who was I to deny taking money for doing what she wanted? And I was at the end of my own hang-noose rope. I could have insisted on cash payment up front and disposed of whatever remains remained efficiently, after the fact. Beggars can't be choosers, or they die. I stood up after a while, walked to the back office, and poured a tall glass of Maker's Mark bourbon. No other patients rang the receptionist bell that day to interrupt my drink. It was the last I was likely to have of the good stuff. When I finally left the building, it no longer looked lost and rundown to me. It only looked blurry. Like the focus on my life.

I imagine that she went to other doctors in her mad, self-abusive quest. I imagine she was turned away. I imagine that's why she spent some time on research when she found that my medical practice had closed, and turned up at the door a few weeks later to my one-room apartment. It was hard to pull myself away from the buzzing glare of the hypnotizing lights inside my head to answer the door. I had been drinking cheap whiskey and sometimes cheaper vodka for much of the month, and sound was occasional. Cognizance optional. The lightshow was phenomenal though.

"I've been looking for you," she whispered, when I finally staggered to the door. I responded with something intelligent to that, like "huh?"

"I want to live," she said. "I can't take being bottled up anymore. But you have to set me free."

She pressed a boxcutter into my hand, and began to unbutton her blouse in full view of the still-open hallway door. "I want you to help me."

How could I dare to touch her? She was a more handsome woman than the bitch who had married me, drained me of all my free cash and then divorced me with a large alimony anchor. Her eyes were hazel and mysterious in their refusal to choose a color. Her breasts were full and alluring, despite being hidden behind a fabric that never showed cleavage. Her waist was not thin, but was also not fat. I could imagine being lost in the midnight mysteries of her and dreaming of returning. Why would I cut her?

She waived a stack of green hundred dollar bills in my face. The stack was thick. At a glance, I guessed that it amounted to three or four thousand dollars. Maybe more.

"There's more if you'll just perform the procedure," she promised. I laughed at that.

"If I cut you the way you said, you'll be dead within 10 minutes. There will be no more anything."

"No," she insisted. "I will be reborn. And I'll pay you for that." She pulled up her shoulders to stand straight and declare with laughably dramatic posture, "I will pay you handsomely for setting me free."

"Why don't you just cut yourself open?" I asked. I looked pointedly at her visible scars. "You've clearly played with knives in the past."

"I didn't say the procedure wouldn't hurt me," she said. "You're right; I've cut myself plenty." She pointed at the ghost-white lines tracing history across her face, her neck and her arms. "I've seen the real me, my beauty within. When I open myself, I can see her slip around and knot and move beneath the skin. But it hurts too much for me to do it myself. I need your help."

She pressed her hand against my chest, and the pressure almost tipped my inebriated derelict body over.

"I need a surgeon," she said. "And you need the money."

The idea of the money in her hand transferring to my bank account flitted through my blurred mind. It was a fine idea. Buying bottles to hide in was growing increasingly difficult.

"I need anesthesia," I declared, wobbling just a bit. "Not for me," I added.

"No anesthesia," she said. "No drugs of any kind. If you put me to sleep during the procedure, you'll put my inner self to sleep as well. And then it all will fail. I need you to strap me down, and cut me open. Fast. You must be quick."

She looked hard at me, and there was a glint in her eye that threatened to dissolve into tears. "Can you do that?"

What she asked of me was barbaric. To be filleted alive. Without relief. It was worse than murder. Yet the crime didn't daunt me in my desperation.

I nodded. Yes, I could be quick.

"We need an operating suite though," I said. "I need a table to strap you to, and scalpels. And no one can be around."

"They haven't emptied your old office yet," she said. "I stopped there today. The door was locked, but the furniture still was inside."

"Why…" I began. But she put a finger to my mouth.

"Don't ask questions," she said. "Just cut me open, and let the real me out."

There was a chain around the door of my old office, and a yellow sticker that declared it an off limits place. A scene that had been deemed criminal…or at least, *unpalatable* by local authorities. I had been evicted. But from the look of the door, you'd have thought that I had murdered patients and stacked them like gory firewood against the rafters inside.

Maybe tonight, I would perform an act that would give those stickers some remote credence.

"We can get in a side window," she suggested.

"We'd have to break one," I said. "They didn't open easily from the inside, let alone from the out!"

"It's not like anyone's monitoring the place," she pointed out.

I looked at the urban avenue around us and had to agree. The pet supply house across the street had bars on the windows and doors, and a pawn shop two doors down also was well sealed. A few cars slipped through the intersection two blocks down, but nobody had passed through the sighing wind on our street in five minutes. It was desolate. And lonely. More than a little creepy. The wind felt empty as hopelessness, and tasted hot and end-of-day stale as broken dreams. When I had moved into this office, this had been a vibrant section of the city. Now it had about as much going for it as I did.

"Let's go in through the alley," I suggested, not quite ready to bash in a window in full view of the empty street. I picked up one of the paving stones from the front walkway, and then we walked around an unkempt browning evergreen shrub to slip into the shadows of the alley. There wasn't a light on in any of the buildings nearby, and in seconds, we were literally feeling our way down the wall of the building to a window.

"This should be the window in the hall near the first waiting room," I said, raising my hand to bash the rock through it. She pulled a t-shirt over her head and held it out to me, while standing in the alley wearing only a bra and pants.

"Wrap this around your hand," she said. "We can't afford for you to cut your hand now."

Appreciating the irony, I used the shirt to wrap and protect my hand, and then brought the rock down on the glass.

In the movies, glass smashes like so much electric tinsel. This glass was tougher. My hand bounced off it on the first try, and again on the second, though this time the edge of the rock made a chiseled, white-crusted mark.

On the third try, after I exposed the edge of the rock better, and swung my arm harder, the glass gave way with a crackling splash of sound. My arm slipped into the warmth of the inside of my old office, and jabbed painfully on a shard of glass still stuck in the base of the window. But the protection of her shirt paid off, and I pulled back my operating hand unscathed. In moments, using her shirt as protection, I had cleaned off enough of the ledge of free form glass that she could help me up and into the office.

Once inside, I found a chair and handed it through the window to her. In seconds we were both inside. I pulled the window shades on my old small surgical center room to close out prying eyes, and flipped the switch to turn on the lights. The electric still worked.

Another bonus. My ex-office was on a deserted street in a shady side of the city and was locked from the outside…but still had electricity. Janis had surely chosen her surgeon well.

I almost cried as I looked around at my old operating table, equipment drawers and red-stickered bodily waste disposal can. I hadn't performed an operation in weeks now. And I missed it so bad. It had been my life…when I had a life.

Janis didn't look around. She wasn't here to reminisce. She stripped off her bra and pants, and laid down on the table in the center of the room. "I'm ready," she announced.

I wasn't. I asked for her to wait a moment and walked out of the bright room back into the black of the hallway and into the shadowy grey of my old office. The furniture was still there as well, and I pulled open a drawer of my desk. It was empty.

But I felt with my fingers to the way-back of the drawer until I found a small steel stub. I pushed it, and a small door opened. My fingers slipped in, pulled out the glass container, and held it up to the dim light.

A small secret stash of Maker's Mark. Half full. I twisted off the stopper, took a long gulp and held it in my mouth, enjoying the burn as it settled on my gums and strained at the back of my throat.

I coughed when I swallowed, and said "Fuck yeah" to a vacant room. Then I stalked back to the OR, to do what I was being paid for.

To kill a woman.

A woman who was paying me to kill her. My only saving grace here, I figured, was the fact that I would be wearing rubber gloves. I pulled on a pair as soon as I got back to the room with my bottle.

"Care to share?" Janis asked.

When I cocked an eyebrow at the question, she said, "Hey, I didn't say I couldn't have a drink. I just can't be knocked out like a log."

We shared a couple swigs, and I marveled at the color in her eyes. They were brown, but that dark light veiled a flicker of fire. And desperation.

"What do you want me to do?" I said presently.

She pointed the way. "Cut here. And here," she said.

"And here."

She pointed to her forehead, and breastbone and belly. I retrieved a marking pen from the surgical drawer and drew lines across her in the places she marked, which grew to include slash marks on her arms and legs.

"Why do you want to die?" I asked at the end. "And why do you want to do it in such a painful way?"

Her chin trembled in a deliciously frightened but determined way. "I don't want to die," she said. "I want to live. Finally."

"This operation, without anesthesia, or instant stitching up, which you say you don't want, will kill you," I declared. As I said it, my leg gave out and I clutched at the table she presented her naked body on.

"So says the drunk," she tittered, and lay back on the table, exposing breasts I could never hope to suck between my pale, lost lips without induced anesthesia. I'd been there before, and the legal aftermath hadn't been a feather pillow. She didn't really need surgery to look good. But she was going to use an ex-surgeon to make her look bad. Really bad.

I pinioned her hands in the straps, and then locked down her feet.

"They'll arrest me," I said. But I'm sure she could tell from my voice that that wouldn't stop me. Desperation breeds fatalism.

"Do what I paid you for," she insisted.

I pulled a scalpel out of the surgical tray and held it up to make sure there were no stains on its shiny surface. I needn't have bothered. I knew that if I started cutting this woman, I was going to kill her, so postoperative infection really wasn't a concern.

"Start on my face," she said.

I took another slug of bourbon, and brought the blade down to her forehead. Slowly, I pressed the blade into the skin of her head just above the nose, and began to bring it down. She moaned, slightly, as I broke the skin, but then, before I'd cut an inch, she yelled at me.

"Deeper you fuck. Don't just make me hurt…Cut me *open*, you lazy no-good hack of a butcher!"

She pissed me off.

The blade seemed to slide through her flesh of its own accord, dividing her nose in half right down to the skull, and creating a cleft in her upper lip that not only severed the outer lip but dipped deep inside her oral cavity to open her gums to the bone.

She began to scream, bubbling bloody spray and air all over my hands, but I laughed in a haze of violence begat by empty loss.

"You want me to cut you?" I said, as I drew the blade along the smudged marker line on her throat. The wheeze of her gurgling wet breath instantly filled the room.

"I'll cut you to the bone you stupid crazy bitch," I said. The blade slipped into the chest cavity, and I could see the white of her sternum as I slit and pressed hard. I was no longer performing an operation, but a desecration. I wanted to cut her open from tit to spine. From belly to coccyx. I would lay this stupid cunt open to the core. She had badgered and stalked me and offered me the glimpse of green that could save my pathetic life, at least for another month or two. And I wanted to give her exactly what she'd asked for.

Customer service indeed.

"Does this feel good?" I asked, as the lining of her belly parted with a warm rush of iron breath and I could see the inner bags of her uterus and stomach lying like fruit to be plucked and crushed in her cavity.

A rage had taken me, and I couldn't stop.

"Stupid, stupid, fuckin' crazy cunt," I howled, and dug the blade into the delicate pink folds that led from her esophagus to her belly and again from her belly to the wrinkled, tightly wrapped folds of her intestine. The room filled with the rich organic scent of blood and the foul retch of shit. And an acid, back-of the-bar smell of puke. Her insides opened like tissue paper to my knife, and I cut through them indiscriminately. On the table she thrashed and screamed but once begun, I didn't look back. I continued to follow the lines I'd drawn at her direction, and opened the flesh of her thighs to the yellowing muscle near the bone, and to the calves, and to the bones of her shaking, convulsing, last-seconds-of-life arms.

I cut the tendons at her wrists last. She had stopped screaming, though her howls were still an echo in my ears. Her blood had spilled like water from a broken dam to the floor, and her shit and piss and blood mixed in a foul odor that colored my world in a red haze of horror. A horror that I had created, bathed in, enjoyed. I was crying as I traced my blade along the last lines of marker to sever the tendons of her fingers.

I stepped back from what was left of Janis Phoenix and looked at the ruin of her body. She had not been so bad to start. But now...*now* there was nothing pretty left. White flesh speckled with the radiant blood of murder. Blue eyes bulged with the pain of unmitigated brutality. Guts opened to spill like slaughterhouse waste to the ground.

I hadn't needed to pry her flesh open as she'd asked to let her "inner self" out. Her flesh had parted to the violence of my knife without resistance. Her life was an open book, and I was the sole reader. But I could not see any story worth studying now. She was a testament to death, and an accusation to me. How could I have fallen so far?

After years of carving people open to change and shift and stitch them into another—a hopefully better— form, I looked at Janis and felt violently ill. My stomach lurched uncontrollably and I dropped to my knees on the operating floor, the bourbon a hot flame in my gullet that threatened to join the blood and offal of Janis on the floor. Accusation indeed.

But as I fought off the sickness of my own pathetic life's decay, I looked up at the body of Janis Phoenix. She shook and trembled on the table, clearly in her last death throes. I had cut her as she wanted. And her last words were to call me a butcher because I wasn't cutting enough.

I stood, grabbing at the table for support, and stared down into the hole I had dug in the poor woman.

Something moved inside her.

Something pink, and long and agile. It shook and rattled against the confinement of her flesh, shifting folds of tissue and gut and then, finally, punched through the suffocation of her intestines. A hand.

The fingers were small but perfect. They waved in the air like a flag of victory. Or denial. I can still see the shiny needles of their white, blood-streaked nails in my minds' eye today. First one hand, and then another emerged into the empty air from the brutalized gore of her chest, and then a small but delicate leg pulled free of the flesh of her thigh to point like a cheerleader at the blinding glare of the operating room light.

A head finally slid free of the mush I had made of Janis' not-so-terrible face. It had skin of porcelain, and eyes of ocean blue.

It was sexy and ethereal at the same time. With a grin that showed teeth no newborn nymph should ever have, it slid like rubber from the bloodbath of her broken core and then, dragging all of its newly born body with it, fell in an uncoordinated tangle to the bloody tile of the floor.

"Oh my fuckin' god," I whispered, looking at the thing I had released from Janis' body. Sirens were screaming outside, but I didn't even notice.

Its mouth opened perfect, pointed teeth to laugh, and then the creature I had set free from Janis Phoenix stood up for the first time on its own two feet. She wrapped two bloody hands around my waist, looked up into my eyes with deadly piercing orbs of her own and with a strangely garbled squeak, laughed at me. I swear it was a laugh of thanks, not of meanness. As she pulled away, in a high, breathy voice she gasped three words. Maybe they were just nonsense. Syllables of the damned. I don't know. But I could have swore she said, "Free, at last."

Then she stepped back and walked, nakedly— and almost human— to the broken window out in the hallway that I had entered with Janis less than an hour before. With a single, strangely liquid wave, she slipped over the sill and into the alley to disappear into the night.

"What did I do?" I whispered, as I looked back at the mutilated body of Janis Phoenix. "What DO I do now?"

The room was filled with the shifting light of red and blue as the sirens I'd been hearing grew closer. You can't strap down and flay a woman alive and not expect someone to hear the screams if you lived within 50 miles of...*anything*. And this was the city. A backwater slum, but still the city.

The wrecked, split face of Janis looked back at me and smiled. Smiled in the wrong direction. A vertical smile of murder.

I was fucked, whether she had left hundreds or thousands of dollars in my pocket. Whether they found my fingerprints or my rubber gloves. I knelt to pick up her pants and her shirt, running my hands through the pockets to look for whatever money might be hidden there. Maybe I could still follow the strange creature who had slipped free of Janis like a wraith. Like a prisoner set free from a lifetime in a cage. I found a pocketful of green, but the spotlights already splitting the black shadows of the ceiling said they wouldn't help.

"I did what you wanted and set you free," I whispered to the dead remains of a not-so-crazy woman in what had formerly been my operating suite. "I let something inside of you out."

From the hallway of my office, a smash, and then a voice.

"Put your hands in the air."

Somehow I knew that it wasn't in the cards for me to have the same kind of transcendent, phoenix-like rebirth as the corpse on my table.

Bills fell from my hands like confetti, and I stood to meet the start of my own new life. I suspected that it would be far more confining.

The Strong Will Survive

The petals slip lazily down like bloody autumn leaves, spattering the glass above his face. I put the unbreakable window there to protect him. Not from decay, he'd done that already himself, but from the children, the pilgrims. They come from near and far. Hundreds of them. Thousands. They continue to pass through this corridor and still, they do not cease to come.

They do not bring friends. Certainly not lovers. Their pilgrimage here stems from the hidden depths of love.

And hate.

Some wait in salvaged pews that I dragged here weeks ago from an abandoned church on 11th Street. Often the pilgrims wait in this damp, concrete warren for hours or days before leaving. Some arrive wearing three-piece blue pinstripe suits, and some appear in sweat pants and Reeboks. Still others are dressed for the season, in layers—flannel draped over cotton shirts and T-shirts and Marine-green Eskimo coats on top of it all. I thought they should have some place to sit and sleep besides the blackened floor.

Time seems to stand still here, deep below the steady pound of the city. Trains are the only clock, breaking the chill silence periodically with their rhythmic clicking and clacking and braking screeches. The room rumbles and shakes with their passage, but leaves us otherwise unchanged. Untouched. Our attention rarely strays from the dead man beneath the glass. He also, untouched. And we…untouchable.

A middle-aged man kneels before him now, the gift of crimson roses shivering slightly between his clenched fingers. His almond hair is already silvering, his wide, faintly Irish face furrowed with the early cat scratches of time and heartache and worry. His ears look chafed and protrude somewhat from the cut of his close-cropped hair. A dark mole guards the entrance to his right ear, the one facing me. A tear glistens there too, and the slow rain of curling petals turns to a storm as his praying hands begin to pound on the glass above the face of the dead man.

I leave him be for awhile; that's why I put the safety glass there. There are others seated in the shadows of the room, waiting. Some for their turn at the glass, some for…even they couldn't say. None move during the newcomer's outburst. This man was certainly not the first whose mingled and conflicting emotions drove him to try to annihilate that which was already dead. But, like any monument, I felt this one needed preservation, so that all who were summoned could have the chance to witness.

And yes, I mean summoned.

This is no open exhibit. No wake for friends. We were all called here.

I was the first.

I called the rest.

««—»»

I almost didn't open the envelope. Karen's funeral was still a thorny crown around my eyes, constricting my ability to see beyond the most selfish moments, and most of my mail was going straight from box to trash. I had no time for junk solicitations. I had no time for much of anything besides nursing a parade of golden longnecks on my couch while staring at the goose-feathered dreamcatcher she'd given me just weeks before. It hung, a manmade mystical web of feather and twine, in the living room above my television, where it was likely to stay empty. No dreams there. Only regrets.

While the return address in the upper lefthand corner was pre-printed with a doctor's name and street, this envelope was hand-addressed to me. When the day's refinancing offers and car wash coupons and CAR-RT-SORT vacation offers slipped unread into the paper recycling bin, I held this one out. Absently slipping my thumb beneath the loose endflap, I opened it.

Inside was a small piece of stationary, emblazoned with the same return address as the envelope. Upon it, a hastily scrawled, cryptic note:

I need to see you. It's urgent. Come at once.
—Dr. Chavis

I stared at the address, and the name, trying to make sense of it. I hadn't been to a doctor for myself in years, though I'd certainly sat with Karen in several crowded reception areas. But none of her increasingly desperate appointments had occurred in the area of town that this office was in. And I didn't recall any Dr. Chavis from our medical travelogue. We'd been from one specialist to another, looking for the miracle cure to her chronic disease.

We hadn't found one.

I began to crumple the note up, and then stopped. Tucked it in my pocket. Maybe she had seen him at some point. Or a partner. Maybe he had something to tell me about her.

The phone rang. It was my mother, who now checked up on me every day, reminding me that she had withstood the passing of my father, and that my life had just begun.

Her pain made me feel guilty, but no less lost.

"Remember the good things," she told me again, for the hundredth time. "And leave the pain behind. Karen would want you to move on with your life. You know she'd want you to be happy."

"I know, Mom. I know. But I've got to go now, I've got an appointment."

I pulled the note back out of my pocket, smoothing the wrinkles on the yellowing countertop. "Do you remember a Dr. Chavis?" I asked on a whim.

She thought a moment, then replied. "It sounds familiar, but no, I can't place it. Why, hon?"

"No reason," I said. "Just some junk mail I got today. Gotta go, 'K?"

I closed up the house and started my beat-up Honda. It choked away from the curb with all the warning signs of pneumonia, but I ignored its coughing. My mind was wrapped around the memories of Karen. And mystery of Dr. Chavis. I had become instantly convinced that he must have had something to do with her. Some news of her sickness to tell me. And while she was gone now, I was still collecting and filing away every sad detail I could find of her life, and death, and tucking them into a mental file marked: heartbroken.

The sign read "Rennsalier Chavis, MD, Obstetrician/Gynecologist." It was a small sign, a quiet bronze placard the size of a piece of looseleaf paper, hung near the door. The building was small, an out-of-place brown brick dwarf on a street of paper warehouses and parked construction machinery.

"I don't have current patients, so there's no reason to keep up an office in the nicer part of town," he would tell me later. "I'm really just tracking my old patients now. And I can do that from any address."

I stepped through the outer door into a foyer of scuffed red tile, and then, without knocking, tried the next door. It was open. There was only one person in the office and he looked up from a file.

"Can I help you?" he said, his voice a reedy pitch that matched the bone-thin fluting of his physique. His hair had retreated to a pair of snow-white drifts around the ears, and his skin was the color of aged parchment. Liver spots freckled his deep forehead. His eyes alone betrayed the strength of the will I would get to know so well, so quickly. They flashed like the blue arcs of a welder as he talked, while crossing the room to shake my hand.

I introduced myself, and without further explanation, pulled the piece of paper from my pocket with his name and address on it. And the note.

A thin smile spread across his lips as he looked at the letter. Then a flash of uncertainty, a furrowed brow. He seemed at a loss for how to proceed.

"Is this about Karen?" I asked, breaking the pause.

"Yes," he agreed. Then, "No."

He took a breath. "In a sense, I suppose it is. Please, come back with me and I'll try to explain why I called you here."

««—»»

After the man had pounded his roses to ruin, I finally put my hands on his shoulders, and coaxed him away from the casket. He had had his turn, and others might wish to look upon the doctor themselves today.

"It's not fair," he whispered to me, tears still streaming from bloodshot eyes.

I nodded.

What was there to say? It wasn't fair at all.

From the back of the shadowy room, a blur of motion. Coat and scarf falling to the floor, heels clicking on the cold stone. A flurry of long midnight hair, the raccoon hint of shadowed ebon eyes. And then the pounding that fills this room on an almost hourly basis. The pounding that finds an anvil in all of our hearts.

"Why?" is all she cries.

The answer wouldn't make her feel any better or worse. There is only the pain of loss. The pain of identity. The pain of predestination.

There are no answers for that.

I settle the rose man into a pew as another man steps from the back to place a calming hand on the hysterical woman's shoulder. I wonder if he knows her, or is only taking this opportunity to meet her with the offering of empathy. His face is younger than the man I have calmed. His skin is unlined, his shock of blonde hair undiminished. He has a mole by his right ear, but that is the only blemish on a strong face steered by shocking blue eyes.

His eyes remind me of the intensity of Chavis.

««—»»

"I'm 94 years old," he told me, offering a cup of steaming coffee. We were in a small kitchen area behind the front office, a room of white tile and white walls. In his white lab coat and white hair, Dr. Chavis almost seemed to melt away into the room itself. I felt blinded.

"Do I look 94 to you?"

I shrugged. He looked old. After a certain point, it doesn't really matter what decade the wrinkles had been brought on by. You just looked old. He could have said he was 80 or 100, I wouldn't have been any more surprised.

"You did good in school, didn't you?" he asked.

"Yeah. What's that got to do with anything?"

"Been sick much in your life?"

I shook my head. I'd always been pretty healthy.

He nodded; a secret smile flickered behind his lips.

"Ever think about having this removed?" he asked, touching the mole on my right cheek.

I shook my head no.

"Good."

««—»»

Most of the pilgrims are between the ages of 10 and 40. Chavis had more or less given up active practice a decade ago and begun work on other projects. One of which, a body petrification serum, has ensured that he will be with us for as long as I protect his remains from abuse. Everyone should have at least one chance to see him, I think. After his death, according to his wishes, I injected the serum that keeps his face as stern and frozen and composed in death as it was in life. So I remain here, a sentinel, his caretaker at the grave.

A punk wanders into the room and I can feel the handful of pilgrims freeze. You have to try pretty hard to get here; down the stairs of a locked and abandoned subway station, past the old boarding platform and into the dark tunnel of the constricted underground tube that serves as the bullet sheath of the trains. Just beyond the first curve is this room, a pockmark in the otherwise smooth subway wall. Perhaps it was intended as a mechanical storage area, or an engineer's room. Whatever it once served as, it was now a tomb. And our meeting hall. Very few would ever stumble upon it aside from pilgrims with determination and clear instructions. But delinquents and roughnecks and punks…they might seek this out-of-the-way hideout for their own.

Twelve eyes followed the boy as he strode cockily down the aisle beside the four pews. Chains jangled against the zippers of his black leather jacket and a knifesheath swayed from his belt. His hair was spiked and greased to attention, his mouth chewed animately on something—gum, tobacco, human flesh? Who could say?

His jaunty steps slowed, however, when he reached the front of the room. He didn't kneel, as so many did, but instead planted his hands with a solid thud on the frame of the casket and stared deep down into the crypt.

Long.

I could feel the breath of the room still held, but I released mine, because from my vantage point, I could see that he wasn't just any young punk here without a calling. His demeanor still said he might try to tip the display and scatter the remains of the perfectly preserved dead man within. But like the rest of us here, he has the right. He didn't look back at anyone in the room, but I could see the glint of tears starting down his face. One of them shining atop a darkened spot on the right side of his face.

Near his ear.

««—»»

"I devoted my life to helping women," Chavis explained to me. His hands shook as he poured me a second and shortly thereafter, a third cup of coffee. But his eyes never lost their shine.

"I started out as a research scientist in embryonics and genetics. Trying to cure the common cold. We never will, you know. The common cold isn't common, it's rare. It exists for a few months maybe, and then mutates into something different. All this time we've sought for one answer, but there is no one answer. There is only change. Evolution. The strong survive."

He sipped his cup and looked at me over the rim.

"We can't cure mankind from sickness, but we can make him stronger. With all of our medicines and hospitals and expensive isolation units, we've been reactive though, rather than proactive. We've been preventing the very thing necessary to our survival—mutation. Change. That which doesn't kill us makes us stronger. Well, if we don't allow anything to kill us and cull the weak…we'll never evolve. We'll never get stronger."

"What does this have to do with Karen?" I asked finally, three cups into a conversation growing increasingly theoretical, and without any grounding in why we were discussing it at all. Overlaid on his deathly pale mouth, I kept seeing her pert, pink butterfly lips in my mind. Discussions of Darwinistic theory were increasingly difficult for me to focus on. I wanted to drift away with the comfort of her image, not concentrate on his esoteric theories.

"It has to do with you," he announced. With that, he stood up and left the room.

He returned a few seconds later with a fat blue binder.

"What's your birthday?" he asked.

"April 22, 1998," I said and he smiled as he flipped through the early pages of the book, passing picture after picture and finally coming to rest on the reddened, blanched face of an infant. He stopped on an ugly baby, a shock of black hair pointing every which way atop a fat blotchy forehead.

"Here you are," he announced.

I looked closer at the picture and saw the scrawl of vital statistics across from it. "Delivered 4/22/98, 3:45 a.m., 21 inches long, 6 lbs, 4 ounces. Black hair, blue eyes."

"Mother ever mention that you were a test tube baby?" he asked.

My stomach seemed to ice over. Why should I care? I wondered, but something in the way he said it....

"No," I answered.

"No, they never seem to. Don't want to admit their infertility, I suppose. Doesn't support the whole myth of feminine fertility goddesshood."

He winked at me.

"But that's what I was here for. To help these good little women become good little mothers for their good little husbands. Just call me the babymaker. I made sure they became fertile. And I made sure their kids would be strong.

««—»»

The punk didn't push over the casket. He stared up at the ceiling for a few seconds, no doubt batting back the unmanly tears, and then went to sit in the first pew.

Right at the front.

Where no one could watch his face.

He sat near a young woman in a conservative brown business suit, very little makeup. I wondered if they'd leave together.

Stranger pairings had come from this room.

It was almost time for me to make my daily announcements. Another woman entered from the back, hesitated before starting forward in that inexorable procession to stand near death himself.

I took her faltering as my cue and stood, turning to the growing assemblage to announce:

"If you haven't been here before, please sign the book at the back. We'd like to keep a count going so we can track who has made it back here, and who has not."

««—»»

My mother had never mentioned that I was a test tube baby. But I was an only child. No wonder Dr. Chavis' name had seemed familiar to her. He had never been my doctor, or Karen's. He *had* been my mother's, 30-odd years before.

"I wanted to make sure my patients had strong, healthy children," he said presently. "I wanted to have children myself. And I wanted to make sure we escaped the tyranny of false preservation that the waning age of antibiotics had given us. How much sickness do you hear about today?"

I rolled my eyes. Disease seemed almost rampant anymore. New ones were named every week.

"More than when you were a kid?"

I nodded affirmatively.

"I could see this was our future—and this was no secret. They talked about it on the radio and TV all the time. Every year a new strain of killer flu. Vaccine shortages. But I could also see that there *were* genes in the population that were naturally resistant to bacterial infection. I had these genes myself; I never took flu shots and never caught the flu. Unfortunately, I was also unable to produce offspring myself."

"You weren't married?" I asked.

"Unable," he reaffirmed.

Later, in making his body ready for "burial," I discovered the reason for his "inability." Sometimes, size does matter, no matter what they tell you. Thankfully his deficiency was not a gene he had apparently passed on.

"I began to experiment with utilizing my own genome, and that of some other unfailingly healthy, intelligent patients. Mixed with the mother's genetic design to ensure a variant gene pool, I began to birth children who I knew would make their parents proud."

My mouth dropped wide. My father wasn't my father?

He could see my discomfort and rested a hand on my shoulder.

"It's a lot to take, I know," he said. "But regardless of who raised you, or who contributed your genetic material, you are who you are."

"How do I know what you're saying is true?" I asked, fishing for a way out.

He pointed to the mole on the right side of his face. And then touched my own.

"You are my son. And as my son, I need your help. I don't have much longer. I'm dying."

"Why should I help you?" was all I could think to say. I was angry. Betrayed.

"Not for me," he said softly, leafing through page after page after page of pictures in the blue binder. Each side with a dozen baby pictures on it, each picture showing the tearful, scrunched up faces of infants. White infants, Chinese infants, black infants. Babies with hair as fiery as a carrot, and babies with no hair whatsoever. But every tiny face betrayed one signature trait. A mole.

His mark.

"I need you to help me notify them," he said. "All my children. There are things they need to know."

«‹—››»

"You're here because you received my letter," I said, looking out at the small audience. There were 11 today. Not a bad turnout for a rainy night. A few I had seen before. There were always a few that I knew. We rarely spoke, but nodded in passage. They were waiting for someone. And when they found that someone, they would leave for good and not return.

"It answered some questions you've had, but certainly raised many more. I will answer what I can for you, what I know. I, too, received a letter of calling. Only mine was from Chavis himself. Our father. He told me of his researches, of the genetic experiments that led to us."

"You all have a mole on the right side of your faces," I said, and several newcomers reached up to touch their right ears. "This is his mark. A way for us to recognize each other, and he, us. It's certainly no guarantee of brotherhood, but it is a clue.

"You were drawn here by death; someone you loved has passed away. In the future, the only safe love you can think to have will begin here, in this room. With your own family. If you love an outsider, they will die."

«‹—››»

"The only way I could make sure that these genes stayed pure," he explained, "was to put in a failsafe mating recursive."

We had moved to the couch in his outer office, and he had locked the entry door.

"What?" I didn't understand him at first.

"A mating guarantee," he said. "If you have sex with anyone who doesn't bear the mark of my children, you will pass them a virus. They will become ill and slowly dwindle away. A wasting sickness. You saw it with Karen."

If the knowledge of my parenthood hadn't been enough of a slap, this was a thunderbolt.

"*You* killed Karen!" I screamed and launched myself at him, grabbing him by his white lapels and shaking that wizened head so hard it should have snapped off.

"No," he wheezed, between shakes. "*You* did."

««—»»

This night, as I do every night, I explained to the newcomers just what Chavis had done. And how that evil act must remain hidden, lest we be hunted by our marks for the death we bring.

I told them of how he found a way to preserve himself, so that he would remain an icon for us in death, a saint of his own cause. And I told them of how I brought him to this place, so that they could all have a chance to see their father. And meet their family.

"In his last days he charged me to go through the books that he kept. There were records on all of us; he tracked us quite well. I sent you all letters bringing you here."

After the explanation, the room was always heavy with an injured, shocked silence, even though much of my talk had been detailed in the letter that brought them here. It was like that now. And so, as I did every night, I told them, "You may stay as long or as little as you like. Good luck to you."

With that, my brothers and sisters slowly rose and walked to the front of the room, even the punk in the leather jacket. As if by instinct, we joined hands, and cried again together.

As we did every night.

We cried for the loved ones we'd killed, unknowing. And for each other. And for the loss of our childhood dreams of romance. And for the hope that we'd find another that we could love. One who wouldn't die from our kisses. One who bore the mark.

All of us come to the crypt alone.

But not everyone leaves that way.

The strong will survive.

The Beginning Was the End

The beginning was...
The end.

Angel spit in my face. Holy water sizzled on my skin, ice to flame. I didn't brush it away. I lived for the pain she gave.

"Don't you get it?" she screamed. The blue of her frenzied eyes was chilling. "We have nothing in common. Nothing! We never did. All we do is hurt each other. I won't listen to you tear me down for doing the right thing anymore."

"And I won't listen to you calling me a liar, a demon and an asshole," I whispered. I never raised my voice at her, even in anger. If I let those fires loose...who knew what hell a creature from heaven could withstand?

"But you *are*," she insisted.

"Come here," I soothed, arms outstretched to enfold her. She batted me away with wings of gossamer white.

"Don't touch me," she hissed. "Ever again."

"Have you looked at yourself in the mirror lately?" I challenged. "It's not seemly for a child of grace to spit and screech so. You might find your privilege in the City of Light revoked."

"I'm only like this when I'm around you. Can't you see? *You* do this to me. You turn me into this, this...witch!"

"If I'm not mistaken, we are all responsible for our own actions."

"You bring out the worst in me."

"Opposites attract."

"Well you repel me."

I bent forward to kiss those pale pink cupid lips and felt a knee in my groin.

"I warned you," she said, and slapped a creamy palm across my face. I felt her cottony flesh catch and scrape against the blackened barbs of my stubble. I hadn't shaved today.

"I love you," I countered.

"You are incapable of love."

Angel turned and fled. Probably to her mother's, the Saint of all Solace. No matter what good deeds that mother's tongue supposedly suggested, I found her an intolerable gossip.

««—»»

It had all come down to the simplest truth. No creature of gentle heart and heavenly virtue should dally with a beast of blackened lust and perverse pursuits. She knew that going in, and so did I. But when I'd first met Angel, she was just a lonely spirit, yearning for something to brighten her nights and darken her days. Life in the City of Light was too constant for her, too predictable. She relished the shadows I cast on her path and the flames of temptation I wore like a robe. She adored me. She yearned to strip my temptations from me and explore my evil. She probably thought she could save me. A lot of City of Light girls are like that—always wanting to redeem someone.

My excuse? Lust. Of course. And something more. There was a particular sweetness in her, a softness, a beauty that I'd never seen in the hard girls of the Dark Carnival, where the mirrors of seduction were ever-present but the curve of a true heart could never be seen. The day that I slipped through the caverns of the Carnival and recklessly stole across the forbidden ash of the Grey Lands, I received my just punishment.

She was bathing, alone, in a crystal brook. I crept through

the brush unseen, and spied on her from behind a rock. Her beauty took my breath away, and a strange pain bloomed within my chest. I grinned and considered all the ways that I could soil that perfect skin. I imagined her chained in a basement warehouse, breasts flogged bloody, flanks gored by the rabid teeth of a thousand starving rats. I smiled at the image of her downy wings tarred with pitch, and her thin legs spread in a spider's crooked stance, pinned to a board by my hooks of iron. In my mind I hung her from rafters on meathooks and drank her blood like rain, my mouth open wide below her thrashing feet.

But then another image came, one more horrible than any that went before. In this vision there was no blood, and no bonds. I saw my head lying cradled in the cushion of her glowing lap. I felt her silken hands caressing the burnt furrow of my brow. I tasted the honey of her kiss smoothing and filling the bitter chap of my lips.

I laughed out loud at the foolishness of this dream and she heard. My naked Angel leapt from the water, darting into the woods beyond. Dazzling starbursts swirled to pop like soap bubbles on the still water in her wake.

It was the last day of my corruption. And her innocence.

The middle was...
The Between.

I won't bore you with the details of our dysfunctional courtship. Of how each day I braved the Between, the forbidden limbo of The Grey Lands, to cross over to her. Of how she failed to appreciate the purity and ingenuity of my gift of three crucified, gutted virgins (one in each color—blond, brunette and redhead!) or of how she nearly poisoned me with her offering of a rosary made from the ivory-bone beads of St. Theresa and incense cultured from the leaves of a Golgotha olive tree on our one-month anniversary. She said it was symbolic, but it took me a week to wipe the blinding sheen of purity from my eyes. That was a week I almost didn't survive, since you need your darkest vision to survive in the fetid bowels of the Dark Carnival.

Somehow, our love overcame these and other missteps. We leapt together past the boundaries of good, evil and propriety to merge with force and fury, my foul heat offset by the chill of her holiness.

Oh yes. We came together. We fucked wilder than demons or angels. And when she came, the air grew so thick with the heavenly musk of lavender that my own foul carrion scent was expunged. When we coupled, it seemed as if the universe imploded and exploded at the same time, as the pain and pleasure of the forbidden shot through our bodies in equal measures of exquisite excess. We drank in each other's barred beauty and survived to suck down more. We should have been thrown out of both hell and heaven, but somehow, our liaison struck the perfect balance, and neither God nor Devil troubled us.

And then the balance shifted.

Entropy is the law of all life, and it proceeds much the same in afterlife. Or to quote the lyrics of lost rock star P. Rockrohr, "Nothing stays forever, anymore."

The seven deadlies somehow came to play on our page in Scheherazade's stories.

One night as Angel's grace-embued sweat poisoned, burned and evaporated from the hellish furnace of my chest, she stared at me, blue eyes piercing as nails, and said "You fuck devils when you go home, don't you?"

I was a little taken aback. I mean, I had never suggested to her that while I was gone to the Dark Carnival, she was swallowing the oily, holy crism of the cocks of angels, did I? Never did I even consider that she might be taking it up the pristine ass from the prong of a snow-white heavenly sheep!

But once heaven's eye or hell's middle finger is trained on a quandary, there is no looking back until it's solved. Or dissolved.

I laughed at her probe, showing yellowed, pointed, deathly

teeth. The teeth that had fed on the vile entrails of the lost, and the dead. Dangerous teeth that had touched her teats but tenderly.

"What do you take me for, Angel?" I begged. "I've given myself to you. Isn't that enough?"

"I will not be soiled by the prod of a devil who's carrying the oil of a hell-whore on his scepter." She had a way of renaming the anatomy so that it sounded more exalted. Cock would have suited me fine. But I joined in the act.

"And I suppose you haven't been spreading the chapel wide for the flock of the holy shepherd to graze upon."

Her cupid lips drooped. "You know I've always been true to you, though I shouldn't be."

I laughed. "How could an Angel be anything but true? Unless, of course, she was fucking a devil?"

That earned me a slap that burned for hours.

And so the descent into our own private maelstrom began.

While in the past she had ignored my habit of hanging stray angels on coat hooks in her utility room to bleed poisonous holy salve from their wounds (the blood of an angel was worth a million bribes in hell), now she insisted that I put away my toys before they were fully fruited. She claimed the stench was murdering her meditations.

And I, for my part, took stricter notice of the relics and various translations of the Bible that seemed suddenly to multiply throughout her house. And in taking such notice, I shat upon them.

Uncouth, I know. But even devils have their pride to uphold…or unload.

She answered by spiking my beer with the mead of St. Michael. I nearly choked to death on my first honeyed draught. "Bitch!" I screamed, my throat hissing with holy smoke. The icy broken glass tinkle of laughter shattered from above.

"You should take more care with what you put in your mouth," she warned.

After that, before I sucked them, I rubbed down her breasts with the effluence of an Etruscan whore I knew from the Carnival. Better safe than sorry. Angel shivered at the pollution, but her distaste still turned to ecstasy when I put my fevered lips to her.

Until the final line was drawn.

"Come to the Dark Carnival with me," I said. She was frying a snow white fish in the balm of etheria. Angel looked at me with eyes wide and frozen blue, and simply said, "No."

"Come with me to see where my strength lies," I begged once more, and she only shrugged.

"Will you step with me into the light of the City?" she said. "Will you kiss the brows of refugees and coddle the concerns of the just with no thought for yourself?"

I admitted that I could not.

She flipped the fish in the invisible grace of its oily etheria.

"Then I cannot accompany you either."

And so the division was stated.

From there, it only grew combative.

She lined my shorts with the dust of chaste and dowdy Dominican nuns. And I filled her bathtub with the curdled blood of suicidal goth girls.

Our skins prickled at the thought of each other.

No more did our lovemaking bring ecstasy. Now we only brought each other damnation and salvation…the opposite of whatever the other wished.

Her loins joined to mine like the iceberg to the Titanic…without frenzy or favor, just relentlessness…she dragged me down to desperation, just as I burned her saintliness to a hairs-breadth of damnation.

««—»»

I was walking though the barrier of the grey lands, when the messenger found me.

"Devil," she said, prostrating herself on bloody palms and wounded knees before me.

"Rise," I instructed, and enjoyed the strangely rolling arc of her eyes, and the wrinkled crimson signature of her broken jaw. Her head and shoulder twitched every few seconds in a catatonic rhythm.

"If you visit the heaven whore again," she said, "you will live in the wastelands of loss forever." She hiccoughed, and a stream of blackened blood spattered the ground at my feet.

"And you are?"

"I am Benevi, whore of the last dick-tator."

"Fuck him," I suggested, and stepped away.

"Wait," she begged, clutching at my bony heels. But I did not stay.

I knew, nevertheless, that my time with Angel was almost up. We were at war, hell was upon me for my indiscretion, and the hole in my chest could not widen much farther. Heaven and hell should only come so close.

««—»»

"I bring you the heart of a virgin," I announced amid the pristine coral white of her bedchamber. In my hand, dripping crimson blood, I did, indeed, hold the naked organ of an earthly innocent.

Angel fainted.

I held the heart above her mouth and squeezed, until the blood dripped down her lips and eyes and stained the sheets like faded lipstick.

"Drink, my darling," I begged.

Instead, she spit.

"Bastard," she said. "Who was she?"

"You would have preferred a him?" I asked.

"I would have preferred your balls in a blender!"

I had no response to that.

"I sacrificed her for your honor," I explained.

"And I piss in your mouth for her memorial," she returned.

An arc of dismissal did indeed emanate from the area where, formerly, we had coupled. She peed steaming holy water in my face. Hardly heavenly.

I grabbed her around the neck and squeezed with intent, but she only grinned purity, and kneed me in the groin.

"You should control your temper," I suggested.

"You should control your deceit," she returned.

"You ignorant bitch," I screamed.

I'm sure the scream was the key. For the first time in our relationship, my damnable anger overtook me and fire literally poured from my mouth to limn and blacken the beautifully angelic face of my love. Her scowl was rimmed in the light of a puritan moon. She didn't take it well.

She never even touched the ravage my fury had made of her face. It would rebuild itself in eternity. "Damn you to hell," she cried at last.

"Too late."

"Ahhhh!" she moaned, frustrated beyond words. With five heavenly nails she gouged hard at the well-traveled scars of my face. And with holy spit she burned the light from my eyes.

"I hate you!" she proclaimed.

"I love you!" I returned.

We were both wrong.

No creature from heaven can feel in the right way for a creature of hell, and vice versa. God and Satan must have laughed in tandem. Whatever we felt, it was anathema. We were doomed by our attachment.

I threw her to the ground and cackled. Imagine the worst horror movie villain giving a chilling warning of esoteric humor. It was ghastly. Frightening. Subversively sublime.

She seemed nonplussed.

But I kicked her in the head repeatedly until her iceberg eyes fluttered back and closed.

Angels should never fight with demons. We're so, so much more desperate.

I left my Angel's home at the outer edge of the City of Light and fled, as if a criminal, to the Grey Lands. Not that I had to worry…regardless of who succumbed in this round of violence, we were both eternal.

I spent many hours there, walking in desperation…wondering if I had crossed, not the line, but the very border of existence.

But a demon can never escape the bounds of his prison, and so I was only punished more for my transgression; not by Satan, but by my Angel's own desperate deeds. Desperation is our calling card in the Dark Carnival. We one-up each other with every desolate day.

I never wished to take her heaven from her. I envied her that salvation.

After I left her in her tomb of light, I wandered the twilight of the Grey, and kicked in the heads of those who came in my path. They came to me in obeisance, since my aura still reeked of the scent of salvation of the City of Light, and as they kneeled before me, begging my aid, I put a razor-edged boot to their foreheads and grinned like a sickly clown. "Zombo to you," I spat.

Their souls fled to the next level of damnation as ethereal brain matter spattered the ashes of the ground.

But my destructive glee was short-lived. Our fight had driven Angel to another form of destruction. Self.

On the horizon, I spied a shooting star in the deep blue of night. It's always night in the Grey Lands. The heavens spat out a star, and it fell. It fell angrily, sputtering purple and white light in a whirl. I hurried forward, eager to see the pit of its death.

My feet pummeled the earth in pursuit, but I could not beat its path to the lost land of the borderland. By the time I arrived at its impact zone, it had already arisen.

It was a she.

Fire still bled from her hair and limbs, but I knew without a doubt whose soul had fallen from heaven.

Her white hair still flared a taunting challenge, and her lips puckered red at my gaze. Her once beautiful snowy wings were ruined; two blackened, spiny limbs were all that remained. My Angel shook her head once, twice, and then her ivory legs pumped hard and she ran, ran, ran away from me to hide deep in the caverns of the Grey Lands. But no matter how fast she ran, I knew that she could never outrace my love. And at the same time, I knew that my love could never offer her the solace of heaven.

I hurried to meet her burning soul.

The end was...
The beginning.

Letting Go

She was newly born; her face gave it away. The shadows of death hadn't marked her yet. The smudgepot glow of the stagelight flickered bloodily on lily pure cheeks as she gaped, aghast at the spectacle. I moved to intercept before some other eater caught the scent of her naiveté. She was angelfood. Pure vanilla-spun sugar.

"Just another Saturday night," I said, slipping an arm wreathed in the ink of demons and skulls around her shoulders. She didn't shrug me away, as I'd expected. I chalked her acceptance down to shock, not invitation.

"I don't understand," she said. Her voice was a whisper of sadness. The lovers before us mortified her. I didn't know how she had ended up here. Maybe she was reborn right there, in that spot, and opened her eyes to see the depraved sex show as the first vision in her new home; it happens. Regardless, she remained utterly disconnected.

Angelfood indeed. Innocent and clueless.

"It's just sex." I squeezed her bird-thin shoulders. I hesitated in pulling her closer, worried I would snap her in half unintentionally. Death was like that. A land of unintended consequences.

"But they're…they're…"

"Bloody?"

She nodded, unable to verbalize the horror that coupled in

front of us as the entertainment for an audience of shadowed thousands all around.

On the stage, a man and a woman did, indeed, rut without regard to the spectators. But unlike an underground sex show hidden just off the Times Square police beat, this couple were not, in any way, pretty to see. The woman was thick in the waist and long of burnished bronze hair. It was impossible to tell her age, not that age meant anything here anyway. But if she had wrinkles or grey hair or sagging breasts…it was all moot now. The scroll of her life had been skinned off, leaving only her true self. A skein of veins and slippery muscle leavening shape atop ligaments and bone.

The man, gangly with silver hair and an odd, spastic jerk in his lovemaking rhythm was in the same, blood-slick state. His teeth were bared from the loss of his lips, making him appear apish, inhuman. He had mounted her missionary style on the bare stage, and the floor around them was slick with their sweat and semen and mostly, blood. The scent of their bodies bled from the stage like the perfume of the slaughterhouse—warm, rich, and redolent of iron. Both screamed with every thrust of penetration, as their stripped, shining muscles shivered and shimmered together. He took her close, wrapping bloody, meaty arms around her. Their raw muscles slapped together wetly, unencumbered by hair or skin, an abomination. They flowed together into a single large, writhing travesty of exposed, twisted sinew and shrieking pleasure. My new friend turned away and buried her face in my chest.

"Why do they keep doing it?" she cried. "Who skinned them?"

I shrugged. "It just happens. The exaggeration of balance. With ultimate pleasure comes the ultimate pain of scourge."

"But they're screaming! Where is the pleasure in that?"

"Look at their fingers grasping at each other," I said, pushing her gaze back to the stage. "It's as if they want to climb inside each other; with their skin gone, they almost can. They can also feel every touch a thousand times more intensely. Look at their tongues. Watch the urgency of their fucking, the desperate way they pull closer even as the equal and opposite force of pain drives their throats to scream. They feel it *all*. They are in ecstasy as much as anguish."

She shook her head, completely disgusted. I saw her eyes light as she took in the room behind me, around us. "Where are we?"

"The Amphitheater. Love given and broken every hour. When they finish, some of the crowd will dine on their remains until they are born again. Come on, I'll show you around."

She followed me out of the crowd, but when we stepped onto the street, she looked up into my eyes, and no doubt saw the hunger there. The blood may already have been beading on my forehead and face; my body thirsted for the heat of her, the sweat of her, so close, so close.

She pushed against my chest with her hand and then squealed something, before turning to clatter down the alley in a panicked, staggering dash. I started to follow, but then relaxed. There'd be other food inside tonight, and she was, maybe, too green to choose yet. As the click of her heels faded, I thought that the first thing she needed to do was to get herself some sensible shoes. This place was bad enough without having blisters on your feet.

««—»»

God knows how she survived her first night without getting flayed. But I saw her again, a day or two later, still unblemished. She was picking through a produce cart in the market square, looking for an apple. I saw her lift one, hold it up to the light and press it to her face to inhale the scent. Her eyes sparkled in the dull, wormy fog of morning for a moment as she breathed in the ripe tang of the fruit, but then her brow wrinkled, and two things happened almost at the same time.

The first was that the apple collapsed into mush in her hand, its thin exterior giving way to the slight pressure of her clutch. The meal spattered her face, and her hand was suddenly a mess of brownish paste, and squirming, twisting, yellow maggots. They spilled from her hands like confetti.

The second was that she screamed, a horrible, high-pitched, trapped-in-a-burning-vehicle kind of wail.

She shook her hand wildly in the air, maggots and apple meat flying in all directions. Her scream turned to a tight hiss, and her breath came in short, fast gasps. I stepped up and wrapped her befouled hand in the fold of my shirt, taking the corruption to myself.

"You again," she said finally, when she'd calmed somewhat. "Thank you."

I grinned and bowed. "No problem mi'lady. Happy to help a hysterical angel in need."

"Angel my ass," she snapped. Her pale brows creased together and moisture gathered at the corner of her dark-outlined eyes. "Clearly I didn't make the cut." She pointed around to the market square, where screams erupted nearly every minute and children and their dogs lay gutted and convulsing on the sides of the road. Patrons walked hunched, in thrall to beast-like men of ebon skin and crimson eyes. Some dragged cages on wheels where other men and women were whipped and kicked and raped in full view, while still more marched locked in harnesses of steel chain and leather spikes. A gang of thrashers walked along the curb, razors moving rhythmically. With each slice, the gang pocketed long slabs of meat peeled from the flanks of the kids and animals and men who lined the gutter, trying to heal from whatever their last abuse had been. Instead they screamed and bled anew.

As I watched, two men dodged in and out and around the crowds, murder in their eyes and long rusted field scythes in their hands. When at last the man in front turned to confront his tail, the second man took off the first's head with a clean swipe of the scythe. The spray of blood from the riven soul's neck spotted the fruit and vegetables all around and the cries of the merchants' anger rose in a howl that superceded the screams of anguish all around the market.

"Why am I in hell?" she whispered, and before I could answer, she was gone again, running hard through the carts of half-rotten potatoes and kicking up clouds of carrion flies and sewer bees in her wake. I thought I might slice myself a meal from the weakened souls in the gutter, but first I reached down and found a healthy apple, and took a bite. Its juice was pure and sweet, its pulp hard and crunchy in my mouth. I enjoyed several bites, and then spit the last one out, and dropped the core of the fruit on the ground to rot.

Balance.

««—»»

It took me a long time, I remember, to become acclimated after being born again, so many years before. My skin was flensed the first time I fell in love after death, to a black-haired girl named Rhee. My heart tore to shreds when she bore us a baby with cloven hooves and a rattlesnake tongue. I couldn't believe that such a beast was mine, yet, how could she have endured the pain and disintegration of sex with anyone but me? I would have known if she'd had another; skin doesn't grow back in a day.

One night, as Rhee kissed our twisted child goodnight, its newly sprung rattlesnake teeth poisoned her, offering death even here beyond the grave, and she took the bait and faded before my eyes. I took the beast up from its steel crib with tongs from the kitchen and flushed it down the toilet. I still wake to the echo of its hideous, accusing screams in my dreams.

I never fell in love again. Too dangerous.

There are ways to live and ways to die. I keep to myself and don't bleed much that way. The physique I died with doesn't hurt my chances of being left alone; I stood six feet four when the reaper, dressed in the grill of a green Ford took me down on earth. Here, I find my steroid-enhanced forearms, embellished in a living artist's depiction of the depravities of hell, serve me as well as they did in life. My tattoo artist could have really found some inspiration here, I often think, but he did ok. No one fucks with a guy who looks like a killer.

Never mind that the worst thing I ever killed was a dog that had two broken legs. Don't ask me how long I had to hold it underwater before it stopped kicking with its good ones. I'll go through eternity with the scars from where its desperate toenails cut into my gut. The damn thing would never have run again, and still it struggled desperately to stay alive. It wouldn't let go. Stupid beast.

I live now in a tiny room just above the Chinese grocery. That doesn't tell you much; there's a Chinese grocery on every corner here. But that's where I live, just the same. I keep some things there to write, to eat, to drink. But never much.

Corruption here comes fast and unexpectedly. I only had to clean up once after a scourge of roaches descended on my canisters of flour and cereal to know better. One night, I went to bed with a fridge full of milk and meat and fruit, the next, I was spraying ammonia on every surface of my kitchen, drowning thousands of tiny black roaches, smothering the maggots that looped and leered at me from the fouled mess that had been a raw slab of soul meat on the top shelf of the fridge. When I opened the milk, my stomach released itself instantly, hot acid dripping over the hair of my hands and into the opening of the gag-inducing jug to join with its spoiled contents in a stew of sour. When I poured the foul mess down the sink, it gathered at the drain in clumps so large I had to pick the clotted remains up and throw them into a garbage bag with the meat and the dustpan piles filled with skittering, dying roaches.

Corruption here comes without reason or warning. I keep my house empty. Like my heart.

««—»»

I saw her next at the Wall of Life.

I don't normally go there; I'd advise anyone against it. Nothing good can come of spying on the living. All that it brings is disappointment and bleeding. And once you start bleeding, you're prime prey for the thrashers, and eaters like myself. Food is food. Here, you bleed whenever an emotion stretches itself out of balance.

For some reason, on that day, I took a longer walk than usual, and found myself at the edge of Death. There, against the invisible glass that reached to the sky and into the subterranean depths, I saw her again. My heart leapt at the sight of her short-cropped hair, almost white in the ever-twilight that is our day and night. Her waist was narrow as a girl's, and her hands clutched helplessly against the transparent, but impassable wall between life and death. Her fingernails pressed against the invisible, white with tension. I wondered what she saw. The window, vast as it seems, is individual; one sees the places and people one's soul begs to see. Its view then is different to every eye.

"How could he?" she whispered to herself, as I walked closer. She was crying.

I put my palms over her hands, and pried her from the wall. "Come with me," I insisted. It was like moving a statue to drag her from the precipice of eternity.

"With my best friend," she said after a while. Her voice was raspy, as if she'd been screaming at a sports stadium for hours. "I trusted him."

"You're not there anymore," I reminded her. "Life goes on."

She flipped around in my grasp and beat a fist against the iron of my chest.

"Well what did I do to deserve being here?" she yelled. "Why was I sent to hell, what did I do wrong? I took care of my husband for more than 30 years. I never complained when he stayed out late and didn't tell me where he was. I washed his socks and cooked his dinner and bore his children. I lived for him and our family and never asked for anything back."

"Did you love him?"

She shrugged. "I guess so. What's love anyway, after the lust is gone? I did what I was supposed to do, that's all."

"What about your children?" I asked, leading her away from the edge and towards the square. A brief smile lit her face. "We had two. Jonas and April." Her face clouded again. "But they grew up and moved away. They had families, but never brought them to visit. I loved them more than life itself, and they walked away from me and never looked back."

"There's something to learn in that," I said.

She put two bony arms on her hips. Her nostrils flared. "What—to spurn those that love you? That's not what I taught them."

"No," I said, and patted her shoulder. She bristled and pulled away. "Sometimes you have to learn to let go."

"I did let go," she said. "I felt the pain in my chest for months, but I didn't take the chemo. And now I'm here."

She was crying.

"You're not in hell," I said.

She laughed. "Well it certainly isn't heaven! There are people murdering in the streets, the food turns to poison in your hands and people watch bloody skinned corpses fuck for entertainment. I didn't read about that in Revelations."

"No doubt. Nevertheless…look at that."

I pointed to the Gossamer Cathedral, one of the key landmarks of Irish Square. Its base was built of perfectly glossed white granite, and golden towers rose from its four corners, with a final fifth glimmering with blinding beauty atop the center of the structure. All of the stonework was wildly etched with amazing filigrees and designs. As we walked towards the church, I pointed out the intricate detail of Christ's passion, told in Technicolor beauty via three-story high stained glass windows spaced along the main wall of the building.

She wiped the tears from her face presently, and stared. "It *is* beautiful," she admitted. "How could they raise a church in hell?"

"There is no hell," I corrected. "There is only here. If you sit watching long enough at the Wall of Life I just pulled you away from, you'll realize pretty quickly that every soul that dies on earth awakes here. You can see them coming."

"So this is limbo," she said. Excitement beamed in her eyes as the idea bloomed. "This may not be my final stop. There's still hope."

I didn't want to say it. But I couldn't help myself. "There is no hope," I said. "There is no other place."

"But what about God, the angels…"

"Lies," I said. "Feel-good fantasies. You'll hear rumors even here. People like to talk about a light that opens up sometimes, and souls slip into its spotlight like moths to a porch light. But it's just talk. This is where the strong souls come, after the body dies. This is the abode of the stubborn, the willful, the greedy and the needy. This is where people who will not go quietly, end up. This isn't hell," I said. "This is forever."

"If there is no God," she said, "than why is there a church?"

"I told you, this is the place for the thick-headed and hard-willed. Some still believe in a higher power. But come around here, I have more to show you."

We walked around the flower gardens of beautiful tropical flowers and bougainvillea and as we stode past, the leaves of mimosa plants closed behind us, as if they were rolling up the welcome carpet. A thousand shades and scents lined the walk up to the glowing golden wood doors of the most beautiful church in creation. A fairytale castle sprung to form in the afterlife in honor of something that never existed. Dreams inside of lies inside of illusions.

As we approached the far side, I felt her body stiffen.

The walls of the church on its far side had given way, or been blown away. Instead of granite and stained glass, there was a ragged hole through most of the long wall. It was ringed in soot, as if a great fire had destroyed half the church, yet somehow left the other half completely untouched. What she gasped at was not the destruction of the architectural miracle, but rather, the line of gallows and nooses that hung from every peak where a stained glass window had once been mounted. There were 13 in all, and from 13 thick rope nooses hung 13 skinned and bloody corpses, faces twisted in a communal rictus of anguish and insane pain. Every now and then, they would twitch and swat with swollen, ropy arms at the flies that buzzed with a vacuum cleaner drone through the air, biting and sucking at the flesh, fresher than fresh. The hanged men were still alive; or rather, animatedly dead. The flies ate their skin off as soon as it could regrow itself, an endless cycle of rebirth and death.

"Oh god," she cried.

"For every good, there's a bad, for every love, a hate," I recounted. "We live on the razor's edge of balance. This is heaven *and* hell, together in a yin-yang ouroboros. There is no pleasure without equal and opposite pain here. No beauty without horrible ugliness. No angel without devil."

I wrapped my arm around her again and pulled her from the scene. A scream, horrible and ululating, rang out behind.

"I don't believe you," she said, but the emptiness in her voice said otherwise.

««—»»

I was falling in love. Still, I had never asked her name. It was better that way, a means of keeping distance. But now, distance was receding. I found her again and again by the Wall of Life, crying about Jonas, her son who had molested his own child, and April, her daughter who was snorting enough white powder that it was only a matter of weeks—or even days—before she joined us. Still, she insisted on following their lives and seeing all of the bitter mistakes and hidden sins that a mother should never be allowed to witness in her children. She cried blood every morning, and I sweated it as I walked her home.

I was well-established here, and she only fumbling her way. I rented her a small room on the corner of Efluvium and Serenity, and I held a key. I used it now to let her in, and then closed the insanity out behind us. The place was clean; I had quickly instructed her on the proper ways of avoiding a corruption episode when I saw a counter full of bananas and oranges on my first visit.

Now the counters were clean, and the single couch offered us a sterile respite I dared not indulge in. I knew all about the yin-yang of pleasure/pain that love caused in death. And I liked my death quiet, and with little blood— little of my own anyway. At least, that's the thought that crossed my mind as I wiped a pink smear on the cuff of my shirt. I was falling in love. We were doomed.

"Come, sit with me," she begged.

I followed, and my blood began to boil beneath my skin as I smelled the lilac rich scent of her. She handed me a goblet of purple nectar, and told me to drink.

"The grocery downstairs had this," she said. "Transcendence Nectar. I have never tasted anything like it!"

I inhaled its fragrance, and knew then that the lilac smell was not her, but the drink. It made the brain reel just to take one sniff. I gingerly tested it with my tongue, and nearly choked at the heaven of its taste. "Oh my God," I gasped, and she giggled like a girl, hitching herself up on her knees to lean in and whisper in my ear.

"I thought there was no God," she laughed.

I tossed back a shot of the thick purple elixir, and the room disappeared in a spiral of fireworks. A thousand hands rubbed and traced each nerve of my skin. I think I passed out for a moment. It was amazing; just what heaven should be about.

"No," I said finally, minutes later. "There is no God, but Transcendence is definitely from heaven."

"You said sometimes souls here do die…or at least they fade away," she said. "If they are not going to a heaven, where do they go?"

I stroked her cheek, and when my fingers pulled away, her skin was slick with blood. Hers, or mine, I wasn't sure. But it had begun. When we touched, our hearts bled. The pain was soon to follow. And the flensing. I shivered.

"Perhaps they are recycled and reborn again to life," I said. "That's what the Buddhists would have you believe."

"What do you believe?"

"I believe there is a time and a place for everything. And when yours is done, you should let it be done and stop holding on to past and memory. I think that those who disappear have finally stopped holding on to nothing."

"Letting go," she sighed.

I nodded.

"The shopkeeper told me to buy the Transcendence in small doses, because it is as vile when it corrupts as it is exquisite when it is fresh. Should I run downstairs and get some more, for both of us? He also said it gives you an awesome buzz if you have more than a shot or two."

I laughed and said sure, I'd have more, if she was buying. Then I opened my wallet and gave her a slip of currency so that she could actually afford to buy some. Even in death, we continue to live by the false principle of valueless paper equaling valuable goods.

She slipped out the door and down the stairs, and I leaned back on the couch and felt my heart pound. What was I doing? Just days before I had scouted her out as a worthy meal, someone whose fear and flesh I could feed off of, for a while at least, until she either faded or flew. Now I was almost playing house with her, and surely about to indulge in the ultimate act of sacrifice—love kissing lust in a bloody twine of razor wire and delirium.

From outside the small room, a scream broke high above the din of traffic, and then another. Fear gripped my heart. I ran to the window, and saw the body lying just outside, in the middle of the street.

It was her.

I dashed out the door and into the night to save her. Once on the street, I saw her tormentor was still there, taunting her with unknown words, and thrashing her back and face with the lash of a long leather whip. Its end was threaded in wicked barbed hooks, and my love's face was already all but torn away after what I supposed was only a handful of blows. The white of one of her eyes looked doubly large, as he'd ripped the eyelid off with his hooks.

But it was the sickle in his left hand that had truly done her in. He'd swiped a clean, deadly sweep right across the line of her knees, and the street was heavy with the pools and splatter of her blood. Her legs lay separate from the rest of her; they looked like gore-tipped prosthethics amid the crumpled newspapers and trash of the gutter.

"Serves you right ma," the man laughed. "You should have known better! This is all your fault!"

He brought the cruel whip down on her again, this time it caught in the flesh of her side, and he yanked it back to open a three-inch rip in her white skin.

"You fucking bastard," I screamed, and drew back a fist to deck him.

"Exactly," he said with his last breath. When my fist made contact, it hit him so hard that he lifted from the ground and stumbled across the pavement to land in a motionless heap a few feet away. I hit him so hard that two of his teeth were left embedded in the flesh of my fingers. I flicked the teeth from the wound and knelt at her side.

She tried to speak as I leaned down to kiss the bloody mess of her mouth.

"Shhh," I said. "Save your strength."

"It was Jonas," she said. Her voice gurgled with a gargle of blood. "Why?"

"I don't know," I said. I looked to where he had fallen, but there was nobody there. Had I punched him clear to oblivion?

"I'm sorry," she hissed, between pants of pain.

"Don't be. Consider this a payment to balance a nice afternoon."

"What…will…happen to me?" she said. Already her jaw and cheeks were swelling thick, and I could barely understand her. "Will I…die? But I'm already…"

"Shh," I said again. "You'll heal. We can get us some more Transcendence in a few days and you'll be right as rain again. Only…"

She screamed then, as the pain overcame her, and I looked hard at her, covered in her deathblood, the street slick with her stubbornness. At her legs, so lifeless and strange, as they lay disconnected from her body. A trail of tears bled through the ragged red gore of her flayed cheeks.

"…Only, maybe it's time for you," I concluded.

She grunted, a questioning sound.

"You're fighting hard to stay here, in death. You have never learned when to let it all go," I said. "You've told me how you stayed in a loveless marriage for 30 years. Of how you stayed in a thankless job that you hated, bullied by a sadistic boss for equally as long. You've cried over and over again of how you tried to bring your children closer, only to have them move farther away. Maybe it's time for you to stop trying, to stop being so dogged."

"But, I want to be with you," she gurgled, dark blood spilling from the side of her lips. "I…I love you."

"And you'll pay for that for the rest of eternity if you stay here," I said. Now I was crying, and red tears bled and ran down my face to fall and mix with the ruin of her soul. I kissed her, and the sensation was electric, amazing. When I pulled back, I could feel the skin of my face degrading, the pain spread like a sizzle of acid across my mouth and nose.

"Look at me," I said, and she struggled to open her right eyelid fully. Her left was gone, but the skin around it had puffed and swelled. "Do you want to watch me decay every time you kiss me? Do you want to scream every time we make love? I don't want that for you."

She was crying harder now, and I knew it wasn't from the pain. "Jonas' father raped him, and he blames me," she whimpered.

"Do you really want to wait around for April, to see what venom she's held for you all these years?"

The blood seemed to have slowed its torrent from the stumps of her legs, and I knew what that meant. Soon, her ethereal body would begin to pull itself back together. She would heal, and in a couple days, be good as new, so that someone else could scalp her or rape her or beat her.

That's what happened here. That's what happens when you put the most stubborn, self-centered, maniacal souls together for eternity. Oh, there was beauty, sure. But the horror lurked so close. Too close.

"The secret of life, and death, is letting go," I whispered, and with a finger, pressed her right eyelid closed. "Whatever happened to Jonas, it wasn't your fault. Stop hanging on to the past. Open your arms, open your heart to whatever will come. Accept oblivion."

She struggled a little, pressing to open her eye against my finger, but I held it closed, and with my other hand stilled her mouth.

"Don't be afraid," I whispered. She jerked as if in a seizure beneath me, but I held her firmly and in a moment, her breathing slowed. In another, it stopped.

Her face just…relaxed. Her whole body settled against the ground; you could feel the tenseness, the energy, the stubbornness that rooted her here, dissipate. When I took my hands from her, the skin of her face was already healed. The soft, tight lines of her cheekbones, and that thin, proud patrician nose were, again, perfect. She was beautiful in death after death. Stunning, actually.

And fading.

One moment, and the beauty of her quiet face wrenched at my heart, which screamed for me to call to her, to rouse her, to bring her back.

And the next, she was just…gone. All of her. Blood, legs, body—it was as if she had never been. Was the sky above us just a little brighter as she passed?

I cried so hard that soon my blood pooled in the street as much as hers had. I don't know if I did the right thing to send her to…wherever she went. A new life? Annihilation?

And what kind of coward was I, to push her away, when I had always been afraid to let go myself? Why else was I still here, living in an empty room, eating the pain of others, too afraid to live. All I did in death was hide.

Something clicked then, with that cold self-realization. After a century of denial, I decided to take my own advice and follow her. Still crying and shaking with the horrible, ever-tragic pain of love, I lay down in the street amid my bloody tears and closed my eyes.

A hypocrite no more, I took a deep breath and released it slowly, forever. Finally, letting go.

The Char-Lee

1. A Sacrifice at Dawn

There's no time like the early morning, just after dawn has slid its fingers under the sheets of night, but before the heat of the midsummer sun has really taken hold.

I was enjoying that perfect time, the dew still glinting diamond prisms off the grass on the side of the road, the birds still swooping the swaying emerald fields ahead, looking for the worm that hadn't already fallen to breakfast for some earlier riser.

I ignored the gagging, grunting, animal sounds in the back seat and watched the road ahead. It demanded attention. There was more grass than pavement to it anymore, and at times, the broken asphalt seemed to disappear altogether. No tires had seen this pavement in many years.

We'd already been on the road an hour or more, creeping through the backside of the country towards the caverns of the hills. It was shaping to be a hot one. You could taste the threat of sizzle on the air, as well as the thick, cottony honey of clover. The white cones of it rose above the rough tufts of grass like the spume of the ocean, rolling up and over the gulley to froth onto the road. I breathed it in and sighed, savoring. It was going to be a good day, I thought.

Then I swerved to avoid a huge pit in the road, and lost the back tire in the hole. The car shuddered as if it been hit by a missile.

"Shit," Rick swore in the back seat, and in a moment, that's exactly what I smelled. That sweet morning air was suffused with the odor of sewer, and I looked over my shoulder to see Rick's white hair dotted with crimson.

He gave me a lopsided grin and shrugged, holding up a gore-streaked bowie.

"Knife slipped."

"Great," I said, catching a glimpse of the girl's glistening entrails that instantly ruined the peace of my morning before turning back to watch the road. "Where are we going to find us another sacrifice just standing there waiting to be picked up?"

I looked at him in the rear view mirror as he licked the blood from the razor-sharp edge of the knife and shrugged again. "Someone'll turn up."

"You're disgusting," I said.

"Just drive."

We'd found our first "someone"—now dead on the back seat—on the side of the road a couple days before, just outside of Hillside. She'd been walking along, duffel on her back, long chestnut hair blowing in the breeze. When she heard the engine, she'd turned to stare at us in surprise, then put out a thumb and jumped up and down just a little bit. She had on a yellow tank top, and it bobbed with her in a soft swishing rhythm that I quite enjoyed.

"Thought hitching was illegal," I said idly to Rick, who was riding shotgun.

"Lotta things was illegal," he nodded, looking away. "*Was*... Pull over."

I stopped the car just beyond where she stood, and watched as she jogged over. She was young, maybe 20. Her skin was brown as tobacco with no apparent lines, and I guessed she'd been a farm worker, outside under the sun all the time, before she'd taken to the road. In a place like Hillside, where the center of town held nothing but a granary, a small general store and a bar, you didn't get brown by lying out in the sun. You worked for it, or you starved.

"Hi," she said, when she leaned into the window on Rick's side, her face flushed and dotted with freckles just a shade darker than her tan. "I'm Jackie. Mind giving me a lift?"

"Depends where you're going," I said. Rick didn't say a thing, just looked her up and down with obvious intent.

"Anywhere that's not here," she said.

I nodded at the back seat.

"There's room."

Rick cocked his head to watch her as she opened the back door, and then turned to me, eyes glinting with fire and violence.

"She'll do."

Turned out, Jackie *had* been a farm girl, I'd pegged that right. She tossed her duffel in the seat ahead of her, slid herself across the worn vinyl and began to regale us with her life story before the door had fully slammed behind her. She'd milked and picked and tilled and loved a boy from down the acres before he'd taken up with a widow 10 years his senior on a bigger spread and damned if that didn't set Jackie to the road once and for all to seek something just a little bigger than the hard grey earth of the back forty and eventual marriage to some other local mudfucker who could offer her a house of hens as well as cows.

We'd only been driving an hour when she asked to stop to take a whiz in the scrub at the side of the road. When she got back in the car, Rick was in the backseat waiting for her.

"I thought we should get to know each other a little better," he explained.

She smiled, and put a long hand on the white stubble of his cheek.

"That's sweet," she said. "Did you know, you look just like one of those old movie guys? You know, the ones that were always in the action adventure flicks."

"Did you know," Rick asked, "that you talk a lot?"

She laughed, which really was a poor choice on her part, because that's when Rick grabbed her by the hair, yanked her backwards and stuck his Bowie into her open mouth to slice off her tongue.

It didn't really cut down on the noise level much for awhile. Though I couldn't make out any words, I knew exactly what the high-pitched wails emanating from the back of the car meant.

Tongues bleed a lot, by the way. Every now and then, I felt a warm wet drop sponge down the back of my neck as I drove. She didn't settle easily.

"You really fucked up the seats," I said later, using an old shirt to try to sponge up the mess.

The girl was gagged and tied and lying on the side of the road by the car's back tires. I'd had enough of her whimpering and had stopped the car to get out and take a breather. The sun was going down, and we were still in the middle of god-fuckin'-nowhere. The grey line of asphalt, broken by waist-high stands of grass and Queen Anne's Lace, stretched out ahead as far as the eye could see. We'd only passed two towns in the past four hours, and both had been empty, doors flapping like lost laundry in the wind. I'd found a dusty bottle of whiskey in the broken down shop of one, and gotten Jackie to suck down half of it. I figured it would kill the pain and the germs at the same time.

"Had enough for one day?" I asked.

Rick nodded and moved to the trunk to get his gear. I followed, pulling out a beaten grey sleeping bag and a one-man pup tent.

We set up camp just off the road. I scouted around and found enough twigs and dead branches from a few small bushes to get a fire going for a couple hours, at least. There were still some cans of beans in the car, and I didn't fancy eating them cold.

"I'll take the girl for the night," Rick announced, after polishing off a can on his own.

"Suit yourself," I said. "But I'm guessing if she used to be a screamer, she ain't anymore."

He cuffed me in the shoulder and dragged the girl by one arm into his tent. She was beyond resistance by then. I stayed up a little longer, and looked out at the stars coming up over the prairie. Life's in the journey, not the destination, they say. And this journey was one fuckin' strange one.

Behind me, the whimpering started up afresh, and I smiled as I thought of the first time I'd met Rick.

2. A Sacrifice at Dusk

I was walking down by the Old Plank River after dark. A stupid thing to do, really, but I had won my share of the county's testosterone matches, and wasn't worried about the neighborhood. There weren't more than a few hundred left in Shawnee, and I'd bested my share of the musclebound. The moon was on the horizon, casting a low spotlight across the cattails on the shore, and the crickets creaked a racket like thunder on thorazine. High-pitched and loud.

But not as loud as the shriek I heard suddenly from a few yards away.

I didn't run to the rescue. Nobody's ever accused me of chivalry. But I was curious. I crouched lower to the ground and slipped through the brush towards the noise. The night had quieted with the force of the scream, and I stepped carefully, not wanting to crack a branch or lose my footing in a gopher hole.

When the waist-high grass disappeared, and I reached a stand of willow trees, I saw where the scream had come from.

White as a scraped oyster and laid out on the loam was a dying girl. She was pale but painted in fire, liquid pain drenching her in a shower of mortality. Her own. Her flesh wept with the tears of a thousand fickle knife-kisses, while between her naked legs a man thrust his own deceptive spear. He laughed with a welcoming grin as my face slipped free of the weeds.

"Welcome to paradise, my friend," he said, never slowing his rhythm. Blood coursed down her ribs in spurts with his orgasm.

"She doesn't have much gas left," he announced. Then he groaned before pulling free and gestured with equanimity at her body.

"But she's all yours if you want a piece."

He stood, gore dripping down the hair of his chest like perspiration.

"I guarantee you, she's worth the price of admission…which, in this case, was her life. And I already punched her ticket."

He stepped back from the shuddering girl while his manhood mocked me with its nodding, knowing gaze there beneath the sardonic moon. I didn't buy its tears as those of pity.

The girl locked eyes with me, a brief glint of hope in her tortured gaze. But I could see it was too late for her. In minutes she would be gone, regardless. I loosened my belt buckle, and nodded at the stranger grinning beside her.

"Don't mind if I do," I said, kneeling down to it.

That's how I met Rick. If he thought he was going to shock me with his offer, he had another thing coming. I was a realist and an opportunist. I didn't kill if I didn't need to, but I didn't shy from the act either. And I never looked away from a good thing. Life was short and brutal. You took what you could and then you were gone. And someone else got the goods. So I fucked Rick's sacrifice moments after I met him, and then she was gone, eyes rolled back in her head as her breasts wilted with the stilled pound of her heart. As her body cooled beside us, Rick told me about his plan.

"You've heard of The Char-Lee?" he asked after we'd tendered our introductions. I nodded. There was no one who hadn't heard of The Oracle. In the west, beneath the bleeding heart of the blood-red sunset she lived. Since the start of the long fall she'd been there, waiting for the pilgrims, answering their questions with both riddles and direction, a Sphinx of obscuration.

There were those rumored to have left her bloated in her gifts of magical power, but just as many whose fat bubbled yellow and frothy from their bellies as their shrieks of terror melted with their greed into the stone ground at her feet. The Oracle suffered fools none at all. Hence her second name, The Char-Lee. She was yin and yang, life and death. Her benevolence was matched only by her brutality.

It was a dangerous journey to find her, and still a more dangerous gamble to gain her audience. Still, Rick never wavered in his studies of those sacrifices, rituals and devotions that supposedly set one on the path that assured that they would be granted the powers of The Oracle.

"As many as find her, are lost," I said, when he finished telling me his goal.

"And as many are lost, gain their answer," he replied, thrusting a finger into the hard bone of my chest.

With that, he reached behind him, into a pile of discarded clothes and belongings, and pulled out a mouthharp. With a wink, he began to play a blues scale, and somehow, under the light of a rising moon, it felt right. Naked, I swayed along to the call of his instrument.

He didn't best me with muscle, he beat me with devil music. And mind.

Sometime before morning, we set the body loose in the current, and walked unsteadily back to town. Rick had brought a bottle of whiskey with him to the sacrifice, and I had no qualms with helping him quaff it.

When we lifted the body from the earth to take her to the river, a stream of blood and kidney rained on the ground beneath her and at last I blanched, turning my face away.

"The Char-Lee will require a sacrifice for her knowledge, you know," he said. "Are you man enough to make it?"

I shivered at the mounds of flesh still quivering on the earth and said yes.

"Blood doesn't bother me," I said. "People do."

3. A Sacrificial Lamb

When the moaning ceased, I kicked dirt into the fire and crawled into my tent. This time, I wasn't interested in Rick's seconds. Sometimes a man just wants to forget the screaming regret of death's valet for a night. And having sex with the mute baggage stowed in Rick's tent would only remind me of how close crept the worms. I crawled back to my tent and tried not to think of her blood flowing down my wrists, as I knew it must when we brought her to The Char-Lee for sacrifice.

Or so I thought.

Until the next day when I looked up from my enjoyment of the clover to see Rick's blade dripping with her life.

"*Se la vie*," he pronounced, and I looked away, disgusted.

"They're not just standing around on every corner, waiting to have their necks cut," I said.

A part of me could still hear her chattering on about her ex, aghast at the perfidy of his infidelity. She never had even imagined the brutality of life as we knew it. Despite having been a child of the fall. She should have known better. Still, I had an unnatural sympathy for her ignorance.

Let it bleed, a voice in my head whispered. *Let it all bleed away.*

She was buried without ceremony. Rick threw her out of an open door as I maneuvered around pothole after cratered pothole. I didn't realize she was gone until I heard the back car door slam, so intense was my concentration on what was left of the road.

"We'll find another town," he said, when I caught his eye in the rear view mirror.

The road turned to ash three days later.

The heady honey of clover dried to the brown leaves of thistle. And then, there was only the scraped orange of dead clay. The hills rose away from the road, and the weeds blocking our path frayed to naught but fissures in burnt asphalt.

"We must be getting close," I said, when the sky slipped from blue to brown at high noon.

"Not yet," Rick promised, pointing at the leached earth.

"The Char-Lee lives where no life dare press," I quoted. Rick had shared any number of books and articles about the elusive Oracle with me over the past weeks.

He pointed at sparse bunches of green amid the clay and sand.

"Still, life strives here."

"And our sacrifice?" I ventured.

"Will turn up," he promised.

I didn't feel so sure, but I kept quiet. I didn't think there were going to be any other towns.

As night crept down over the barren earth, a single spot on the horizon kept its dull orange glow. I navigated the increasingly deep holes in the pavement with as much speed as I dared, praying to cover the ground in time. We could have walked as fast.

The glow meant fire.

Fire meant humans.

Humans meant fodder for sacrifice.

It didn't cross my mind that they might not *want* to become sacrifices.

"Leave it here," Rick said a short while later, and I turned the key in the ignition. It was a long walk to the dot of fire in the distance, but we couldn't afford to alert them to our presence. We didn't know if there were five or fifty ahead.

The walk was long, and mostly silent. Night gathered around us surreptitiously, an inky fog, and by the time we were near enough to see the creators of the campfire, it was almost too dark to see each other.

I reached out to touch Rick's arm, to slow him, and he shoved my hand away.

"Don't get fresh," he whispered. "I hardly know you."

I punched him, and pulled him down into the weeds. We were on a knoll just north of the campfire, and below us, I could see two figures leaning in to catch the heat of its blaze. One of them had long hair, the other, short. More than that, I couldn't make out.

"Looks like a couple," I hissed in Rick's ear, and I could see his teeth gleam like moonshine in the shadows.

"You can have him, if you want, but she's mine," he announced.

"You're the one with the oral fixation," I retorted, patting the bulge in his shirt. He always carried a carton of cigarettes tucked into his shirt.

"Make you a deal," he whispered. "I take him out while you hold her down. You can feel her up all you like, but I get to break her in, deal?"

Who was I to argue? We split up, him circling the camp to the east, as I went west. Rick had perfected a pretty convincing owl call, and we agreed that this would be the signal to strike.

I got as close to the camp as I could and waited, watching the two as they talked in muted tones across the crackle of the fire. Where they'd found the wood, I didn't know, but they had a blaze that would last well into the night, and seemed to have already cooked a dinner on it. The scent of burnt flesh still lingered on the night air and my stomach rumbled so loud I worried they would hear.

They looked young; the man was still freckle-faced and smooth-skinned, a shock of blonde hair jumbled like a weed patch across the plane of his scalp. Maybe it was love, or just the fire, but I could see the gleam in his eyes when he looked at her, nodding all the while, and never looking away.

She, too, looked barely a woman. Bone-thin but willowy, her long fingers fluttered over his biceps and thigh, as she animatedly told him a story of some kind. My stomach dropped when I heard the cry of an owl in the distance. I hated to break their moment. To break them.

But my hesitation lasted only an instant, and then I was launched, barreling down out of the brush, the shock of surprise still fresh in her eyes as I crossed the fire, stepped over his crossed legs and grabbed her by the shoulders dragging her backwards out of harm's way.

Harm came from the other direction, and drove a long knife through the boy's back before he was even partway to his feet. I caught the bloody glimmer of its tip parting the kid's chest and shirt just before he toppled forward into the flames, the haft projecting from his back as if he were a newly pinned moth.

The girl screamed.

I couldn't blame her. The man she loved was shuddering spasmodically in the middle of the romantic fire they'd shared moments before. And a madman was now lifting her from my grasp to hold her upright in front of him, eyes aflame with a look I knew only too well, but one that must have scared the fight right out of her. She released her bladder, in any case, and I stepped back from the puddle at her feet.

"Do exactly as I say, and you'll survive the night," Rick announced. He had a growl to his voice like a chainsaw trying to be coy.

"Who…why…" she stammered.

"I'm Rick, and because I wanted to," he said. "Now sit down and be quiet."

We tied her hands behind her back, and then I dragged the boy's body out of the fire and into the darkness. It was beginning to smell deliciously cooked, and I didn't want the temptation.

"Get my knife," Rick called as I pulled the dead boy out of sight.

Her name was Annabel, and she and her boyfriend had been on their own expedition.

"Where the hell were you going out here in the middle of God-fucking-nowhere?" Rick asked and her lips drew taut and thin.

When she remained silent, I raised an eyebrow at her and she shrugged.

"It doesn't matter now."

"Got any food left?" Rick asked, already up and moving towards their tent.

She didn't answer. This one didn't say much, something that made me feel better. She'd live longer. After splitting the remains of a stew Rick found still warm in an old covered pot inside, he disappeared with Annabel into the tent.

"Gimme 20," he said, and winked.

I gave him an hour, but I'm not sure that he needed it. I didn't hear a sound besides the occasional pop of the wood beneath the flames.

She *was* a quiet one.

4. The Upward Spiral

The next morning we broke camp at dawn, taking anything that looked useful and throwing it into a couple of canvas bags. Annabel asked me to carry a backpack with her things, and little more was said as we filed back through the grasslands to the wreck of the road, and then on a mile or two farther to the car. For a moment or two, I panicked that it would be gone, and we'd walk for hours down this road without finding it, but then when I saw it in the distance, I began to worry about getting it started again.

It started and three hours later we were far from the latest in Rick's long string of murders.

We were also at the end of the line.

I shoved the gear into park, killed the engine, and the three of us stared out the pitted and bug-stained glass at the spectacle ahead.

The asphalt of the road itself had disappeared some time ago, but a faint path of grey continued to lead through the almost equally grey parched and empty landscape. It was as if we'd entered a valley of the moon; the earth all around was chalky and dead, its surface featured only with boulders and stones. It was arid and alien, this wasteland, but for miles and miles, a faint path had continued on, leading ever upward, as the ground around us dropped off, and the path in front drew ever closer to the dark shadow of a single rocky spire.

Mountains do not simply burst into ascension; they sort of grow, slowly, the earth gently rising until at one point you say to yourself; *hey, I'm halfway up a mountain.*

This mountain was not like that.

Our road ended at the foot of a 40-foot incline of vertical rock. When I shielded my eyes from the pale sun above, I still could not see the peak.

"Looks like we walk from here," I announced.

"Do I look like a goat?" Rick asked. I ignored him and got out of the car.

"There's got to be a way," I murmured to myself, and began to scout, walking along the base of the jagged limestone pillars that seemed to wall the mountain off from the powdered death at its feet.

The way didn't become apparent. We split up, Rick heading one way, and Annabel and I going the other. We agreed to meet back at the car, one way or the other, in a half hour.

The walk was treacherous. Our path had apparently been a slowly ascending ribbon of land that had grown increasingly distinct from the surrounding plains. As we walked along the unscalable wall of the mountain's foot, the ground to our left dropped off with increasing rapidity, until within a few minutes we were walking on a thin path between wall and deadly drop.

Annabel walked single file in front of me, so I could keep her in sight.

"Did you love him?" I asked at one point, instantly kicking myself. If I'd wanted to break the ice, there were less crass ways.

"No." She didn't elaborate.

I didn't know what to say to that exactly. It wasn't what I expected.

"I'm sorry Rick had to kill him," I finally spit out. Equally dumb.

"Me too," she said.

We walked in silence a bit more, single file, and then she stumbled, cursing as she began to slip off the edge of the path, rock crumbling beneath her foot to fall into open space below.

I dove forward, aiming to grab her about the waist, and instead, hooked my arm into hers, which was tied in a tight loop about her wrist to her other arm, and thus made a convenient hook point.

"Fuck," she screamed as her arms twisted above her head and she hung suspended from my grasp.

The gravel clicked and rained around her feet, which dangled above the grey featureless earth below.

"Try to wedge your foot in the rock," I begged, my own strength quickly giving way. I could feel my body, flat on the ledge, slipping toward the edge.

She swung from my grip, screaming as much in anger as pain, and I pulled with all my strength. I felt her skin sliding through my grasp.

"Come on," I begged, and she shouted back.

"Pull, you bastard!"

I did, and she hooked an elbow onto the rock at the path's edge. I reached out and grabbed a piece of her shirt with my other hand and pulled again, and this time her hip cleared the ledge. With a scream and the twist of a gymnast, she flipped a foot up onto the rock. I pulled hard, and both of us rolled back and away from the drop.

"Fuck, fuck fuck," she breathed, tears streaming down her face.

"Are you alright?" I gasped, and she shook her head.

"Untie my wrists, please," she whispered, and then let out a long scream of anguish.

When she was done, she took a breath, and looked at me with wide, blue eyes that couldn't be ignored.

"I think you broke my arm when you grabbed me," she moaned. "Oh, God."

"Stand up," I said, and helped her to her feet.

Her right arm was hanging limply and I pulled out a knife.

"Promise you won't run," I said, holding it for her to see.

"Where would I go?"

I cut the ropes and then traced her left arm from shoulder to wrist with my fingers. When I got midway between her elbow and wrist, she gasped.

"Okay," I said, and continued on. "Move your fingers?"

She could.

"I don't know if it's broken," I said. "I don't feel anything jagged. When we get to the car we can wrap it."

She nodded.

We started back, her in the lead this time, and then she stopped.

"What?" I asked.

"The path," she said.

"Yeah?"

"We're going down."

I looked back, and then ahead of us again. She was right. The incline was slight, and I hadn't really noticed it on the way, so intent was I not to slip or lose track of her behind me.

"This is the way up," I pronounced.

She nodded, long hair swishing ahead of me, but didn't say a thing.

We started back to the car to meet Rick.

He met us on the way down.

"I heard a scream," he huffed, clearly out of breath.

"Was it your conscience?" Annabel said.

Rick looked her over and then gave a pointed glance at me.

"I can understand wanting her arms around you during the act, but shouldn't you tie her back up now?"

I explained what had happened, and he performed the same test I had. She didn't scream this time when his fingers touched the spot on her forearm, but I could see the swelling there now, and her face pinched as he felt it. Her breath shuddered.

"Let's get it wrapped then," he said.

We used strips of towels to wrap her arm. Whether it was broken, fractured or just badly bruised, it seemed best to immobilize it and tie it up in a sling. Then we lunched on some left-over crackers and cheese from the stash we'd found in Annabel's tent. Finally, as the sun moved towards 2 o'clock, we packed up our things and began our ascent.

The path had looked like a level walk around the base of an unclimbable mountain, but actually, it was a slow corkscrew, leading gently but unquestionably upwards. The sun was hot, and the sweat bled all of our backs into Vs of dark exhaustion. After an hour of silent plodding, I called for a rest, and we sat on the edge of the path, looking out.

We'd circled the mountain. Straight down and to the right, I could see the rusting wreck of our car, and off in the distance, the pale ribbon of the path we'd driven faded lighter and lighter into a horizon bleached of all life.

The wasteland surrounded us, and we were winding inexorably into its very heart.

Surprisingly, it was Annabel who finally broke the silence.

"After you kill me, what will you ask for?"

Rick stared at her. He hadn't expected his lamb to know she was being led to the slaughter. She had not asked where we were taking her, and that made it easy for us. But she'd known all along. Not too surprising, I supposed. Where else could this road lead?

"Mastery of the power," he answered presently. "I've studied and practiced and sacrificed. But I can't get there without her help."

Annabel nodded, as if she completely understood what he was talking about. I barely grasped what he was after myself. I'd participated in his rituals, and helped him clean up the messes afterwards. But while he insisted they were means to an end, it seemed to me that it was just an excuse for the ultimate in debauchery. He enjoyed the flayings too much. And while he'd shown me a parlor trick or two, I really didn't believe, deep down, that Rick was more than a two-bit magician with a kink for blood. Truth be told, up to now, that had suited me just fine.

She didn't speak again, but looked out over the endless ocean of death with faraway eyes. I realized then that her eyes were grey, like the earth below. They held a stillness too, and the proud line of her nose seemed chiseled from the hard ground we walked on. She was a quiet core of strength, not a silly girl, as I'd expected when I pinned her to the ground the night before. Her eyes shifted, caught me staring, and I averted my gaze. But not before I'd seen the spark in those steely pools and the slight smirk in her smile.

She was not broken yet, I realized. She'd seen her boyfriend brutally murdered, been violently raped, maybe broken her arm and knew she was on the way to be sacrificed, yet she wasn't afraid.

Annabel was dangerous.

When I looked back at her, she was still staring at me, and my stomach shivered.

"How's your arm?" I asked, eager to break her concentration on me.

Her smile twitched.

"Hurts like a mother," she whispered.

"You didn't know my mother," I said.

"All mothers are the same," she replied. I opened my mouth to retort, but Rick intervened.

"Enough chatter." He slapped my shoulder and stood. "Time to meet The Oracle."

The path continued to wind up and around the mountain, steeper and steeper. Annabel didn't complain, though I did. She walked in the middle, and I huffed along behind, too out of breath to say too much. I just watched Annabel's lower back, swaying side to side in front of me, an enticing, if untouchable carrot.

And then she stopped abruptly, and my face met her spine for a split second. It wasn't the kind of kiss I would have liked to have given her.

I looked over her shoulder and saw the reason for our stop.

The path had ended.

But not quite at our destination.

Four feet ahead, it picked up again, and I could see the dark shadow of a dwelling at its end.

But where we stood, barely able to lean away from the side of the cliff for fear of tumbling off the far side, the path ended in a jagged cut of rubble.

Rick tapped his toe on the edge of a spiky looking rock, and the ground beneath it slipped away like sand. We all craned our heads to watch that rock fall, and it seemed like it would never touch the ground. I lost sight of it long before it hit the earth, and if it made a sound, the noise was lost in the distance.

"Anyone do well at the long jump in high school?" Rick asked.

Nobody replied.

The cliff's face was sheer and offered no handholds. The only way across was going to be a jump. It wasn't that it was a long gap—it was that there was precious little room for error.

Rick pointed at me, "You first. Then Annabel, then me."

"Um, I think maybe…." Was all I got out before Rick flashed his Bowie in my direction.

"No arguments," he growled. "The strongest person needs to be on this side to make sure our little package makes it across."

He put his back to the cliff and slid along the wall to get behind me.

"It's not far," he coaxed. "Even a lardass like you ought to be able to do it in one try."

"One try's all you get," I noted.

"Well, then I'd suggest making it a good one."

Annabel slid behind me then, without a word, and I stood alone, looking at the deadliest pothole I'd seen on this trip.

"Ah fuck," I swore, backed up three steps and took a running leap across the gap.

I made it without incident, though I nearly lost my bladder in the split second my feet were both in the air. Then I was down on the other side, and falling forward, coming to rest on my hands and knees.

"Graceful as always," Rick taunted from across the gap. He put his knife to Annabel's throat, and whispered in her ear.

"She's coming over," he announced. "Get ready to catch her; it'd really suck if she fell over the edge 'cuz she lost her balance because you broke her fuckin' arm."

"*I* broke?" I complained, but shut up quickly. Annabel was already backing up to make her run.

It was over in a heartbeat, but for me, it seemed as if she came to the edge in slow motion. I could see every muscle on her face tighten, her eyes open wider as she kicked off at the edge, sending loose gravel to litter the ground a mile below. I could see the concentration carving her brow as she hurtled towards me, one arm bound tight to her chest, the other waving above and behind her in the air as she flew.

And then she was crashing into me, and I grabbed hold of her with both arms, dragging her back and down, pushing us both towards the rocky face of the cliff and away from the edge. My head cracked hard against the rock and stars rimmed my vision, but still I held onto her as she fell into the cliff face herself, ramming her injured arm hard.

That stumble broke Annabel's silence, as she let out a tight scream of pain, but before I could pull her up and away from the wall, Rick was there with us. He grabbed her under both arms and lifted her up and away from me, dragging her with him to where the path finally began widening out again; the final approach to the citadel of The Oracle, The Char-Lee.

5. Into the Darkness

I walked up behind Rick and Annabel, whose face was still wet, and followed their gaze to the dark entrance just a few hundred yards away. It was little more than a black doorway carved into the mountainside, but it was hard to imagine what else it could be. A door to the knowledge that transcended. A door to what had been before, and could be someday.

A door to The Oracle.

"Do you think that's it, then?" I asked.

"Who else would live on the top of a mountain in the middle of a realm of death?" Rick answered, not looking at me.

"You a freakin' poet now?" I asked.

He didn't answer, but shrugged off his backpack and knelt to rifle through it. Annabel turned to me and nodded.

"Thanks for catching me," she said.

I felt my face flushing and couldn't think of what to say.

"Take her hand, Romeo," Rick said.

I didn't move, and he repeated the command.

"Grab her arm, man. We don't need her starting to run now."

I reached out and took her arm, though still a little tentatively. It occurred to me suddenly that Rick might want me to sacrifice her myself, and as I looked at those cool grey eyes, and quiet profile, that I might not be up to the task.

"Stand still kids," he grinned, and slapped the silver clasp of a handcuff around Annabel's wrist. The other half, he cracked across mine.

"Hey," I complained.

"You make a good anchor," he said. "You're slow and heavy."

"Yeah, and I'd kick your egotistical ass in a heartbeat."

"Later studboy. Let's go get us some oracling, first."

He struck out in the lead, and I looked in apology at Annabel, and began to follow. Her lips pursed into a tight line, and then she held back, locking her feet.

"If he doesn't do me, it'll be you," she said. "You know that."

Rick was already 10 steps ahead and I shook my head at her.

"We're pals," I said.

"You're meat," she hissed. "And this is a game about power. Pals don't mean a thing."

"Let's GO!" Rick bellowed from ahead, and I yanked Annabel forward. But something in my belly quailed at her warning.

The door was farther away than it had looked, mainly because it was so large.

When we finally stood in front of it, I realized it stretched the height of two tall men, and was nearly as wide. It was fashioned of a dark hard wood, unpainted. I could see the deep old veins of its character, yet its hue was so black it appeared to have been burnt in a flash fire.

"Do we knock?" I joked as we stood at the giant door, looking up.

"I suppose that would be the polite thing," Rick laughed, and raised a fist to pound on the door.

"And on the fourth day of the expurgation, they learned the black lesson of recant," Annabel whispered. I looked at her, but she only stared back, without explanation.

We waited then, and I shivered as the wind whistled by, its kiss barren and cold. I hadn't felt it as much when we were climbing, but now that we stood still, I realized that the air was bitter here. Cool and dry.

The chilly kiss of death.

Rick reached out and grabbed the huge metal handle on the door, a metal drawbar burnished almost as dark with neglect as the door itself. It twisted down with a squeal under his strength, and then the door itself opened outwards with a shriek as he pulled.

"The welcome mat is an unlocked door," he said, and

stepped inside. Annabel and I followed, and as the door clanked shut behind us, Rick asked, "Did anybody think to bring a light?"

"You packed," I reminded him, but it didn't matter. We didn't need a light. As our eyes adjusted, the room revealed its own natural luminescence. Pale green strips shone along the walls, and I soon saw we were standing in a narrow vestibule, that led into a single hallway ahead. You either went in, or you went out. Rick chose in.

The walls were rough, hewn with little artistry into the bone of the mountain, but at some point, the lack of craft had been covered with ornate displays. The remains of a tapestry hung like a burlap sack on one wall, the colors of its ornamentation hidden beneath the thick webs of countless spiders. And along the same wall I could see a series of broken spikes and hooks, as well as the remains of a torch holder.

It had been some time since dances were held here by the light of sconce fires, I thought.

Our steps echoed overloud, like small gongs to my ears as we walked down the dim, eerie corridor. Rick pushed me ahead of him as soon as the entry foyer was behind us.

"I want to keep her in view at all times," he growled, but I knew better. He wanted a guinea pig ahead of him in case things got suddenly dangerous. Annabel didn't say a thing, but I didn't miss the long sidelong glance she gave me.

I pulled on her arm and led our little party deeper into the mountain. Ahead of us, I could see the night grow lighter, and hurried our pace.

At last the corridor ended, and we stepped out into the source of the brighter glow I'd seen.

"Wow," Annabel said.

"Yeah," I agreed.

"Now that's a fuckin' throne room," Rick announced.

The dark, decaying rock hall had opened onto a vast round room that was the antithesis of everything we'd seen since entering the mountain. The floors had been carved seamlessly in smooth pink quartz, and the brilliant white stone walls reached high and smooth, and were lit by dozens of flaming torches pinned just above eye level. Before us were several burgundy couches and sitting chairs, with a clear path between them leading to a dais cut and raised from the quartz.

On the dais, backed by brilliantly woven purple and gold tapestries painted or stitched with the likenesses of hundreds of open-mouthed, tortured, bloody victims, was a lone chair.

Throne rather.

Its back rose six feet tall, and from the rich dark wood of its taloned feet to the caricature of a skull carved into the peak of its head, this cruel seat was clearly a one-of-a-kind work of art. Etched into its wood were screaming faces, bulging eyes and grasping fingers. This intertwined cacophony of pain and terror culminated in a series of grasping armbones that wound and twisted to razor edged fingernails. These were what supported the gruesome gaping eyed skull at the top of the throne.

And that throne was filled.

"Welcome," a voice said. It was soft, but seemed to come from all around us. "Welcome to the center of the abyss. You've seen the suppurating cancers that call themselves men, stalking the pure like deadly syphilitics in those few cities that yet live. You've braved the barren lands of death and climbed the corkscrew of heaven to be here in my chamber. Approach now, and tell me why."

Rick's fist prodded me in the back and I led Annabel forward, studying the woman and her ghastly throne as we walked.

Long white slender fingers curled around the wooden skulls carved into the armrests of the throne; fingernails blackened and sharp tapped gently against the devil's wood. Gauzy black lace hid her arms all the way up her shoulders to curve outward to kiss the jut of her chin. Except for the cool ivory of her hands and face, she was hidden behind filmy, shifting ebon. A slight smile peaked the corner of her pale lips; so caught up was I in staring at this legend that I stumbled over my own feet, nearly dragging both Annabel and myself to the floor. A spark lit the dark pools of her eyes for a moment and then was gone, leaving only the faint flush that marked her cheeks as a sign of life.

As we reached the final step to wait at the foot of her dais, I finally gathered the courage to speak.

"Are you really…her?" I mumbled.

Silvery laughter echoed through the cavernous room, as the woman shifted, ripples of starlight glinting and fading in the cloud of her long death dress.

"Most certainly I am her," she answered. "But which *her* do you seek? If it is the her called Oracle by some, keeper of vision, then yes, I am she. But I am also the Char-Lee, if it is she you seek, font of power, fire and desolation. Be warned, sometimes what you seek brings more, and less, than what you hoped to find."

A palm slapped against the back of my head and Rick said "Duh."

He stepped around us and bowed before the dark lady, the frayed tail of his shirt hanging nearly to the floor, a bum's train.

"I am Rick Lyons," he said, straightening. His voice sounded hollowly formal. "And these are my companions." He didn't bother to name us. Instead, he launched into a speech I knew he had been practicing in his head for weeks. "I have studied the passages of Elysian, and the sigils of Cedar. I have named an apprentice and set out across the wastelands to seek—"

The Oracle held up a hand.

"You have traveled far, I have no doubt," she said. "I receive so few visitors. I cannot offer much, but please accept my hospitality."

A razor thin fingernail cut the air to her right, and something seemed to shift in the shadows at the edge of the cavern.

"Down that hallway you will find rooms. I'm sure you'll want to freshen up and rest a bit after such a trip. Take whichever rooms suit you. Later, I will call you to dinner and you may tell me how things go in the outer world. Then you may make your request, if you still desire it."

She stood, an elegant figure of night. As she passed, she looked hard at Rick, and then Annabel, and finally me. I could see the veins of age cracking the porcelain near her eyes. She was bound by time, just as we were, I thought, and she passed by, leading us across the stone to the dark hallway.

Once our eyes adjusted, the hall was the same as that we'd walked in by. Its walls glowed with the genie light of emerald fungus, and tall dark squares interrupted at intervals.

"Inside, you'll find whatever you may want or need," she said, waving at the dark doorways. And then without another word, she slipped away, a shadow played out against the green glow for a moment, and then fading.

"You think there's a light switch somewhere?" Rick joked. Nobody laughed.

"Stay with her," he ordered, and then stepped into one of the rooms. As he did, a sudden flash lit the hall and the room "turned on," shining with twice the brilliance of the corridor.

"Not bad," he called. "A magical clapper."

Annabel pulled me by the arm and we stepped into the room next to Rick's.

It was a fairyland of light. Tiny pinpricks of green and gold flickered and swayed all around us like gnat-sized fireflies.

"It's just like standing in the center of the galaxy," she murmured.

"Have you done a lot of standing there?" I asked, and she rammed my shoulder. Seemed like I was everybody's punching bag today.

"What I could really use is a bathroom with a hot shower," she said. "Think we might find one of those?"

"Try that," I pointed. We stepped toward an interruption in the shimmering walls and as we passed its threshold, a dozen candles sprang to life all around us. Their light shimmered and licked at the ivory walls, and reflected off the spigots of a huge marble tub. The candles were spaced about the room in crystal cups along the edges of the tub, on the back of a porcelain toilet and atop a long white vanity. Flames also guttered from two wall sconces set on either side of a full mirror above the sink.

"Just what I needed," Annabel whispered, and pulled me forward. Pulling my arm along for the ride, she opened the faucets in the tub and the ghosts of steam swirled into the air. Then she looked up at me.

"I need to do this alone." She stared pointedly at the handcuffs which held our arms together, and I shrugged.

"Rick said to stay with you," I said.

"I don't think you want to stay for this," she replied, walking towards the toilet.

"I don't have a key," I said.

"Suit yourself." Annabel deftly uncinched her pants, dragging my hand uncomfortably close and squatted down on the toilet, pulling me to kneel on the floor at her side.

I'm not sure this was what *I* needed.

6. Wants, and Needs

Later, after undressing, washing and drying off in some awkward choreography that could have made us both winners in a game of Twister, Annabel and I both emerged clean and moist from the bath. I was just about to say that it would stink to have to put our dirty clothes back on when Annabel pointed at a rack to the left of the doorway. Several items of clothing hung from its many pegs, including a man's white shirt and black slacks, and a silky green dress.

Annabel pulled the dress down and stepped into it, and with my help eased her injured arm through one sleeve, which flared at the wrist. The back buttoned with glossy round stones, and I closed as many as I could, leaving her shackled arm exposed. She helped me pull up my pants and socks, and I slipped one arm into the shirt.

She fumbled with the button on my sleeve, and then patted it with satisfaction, tapping a finger to my chin.

"All buttoned up, sire," she grinned. "Now let's find the keymaster so we can finish the job."

As we stepped back to the main room, I could feel the blood warming my cheeks, but she seemed nonplussed by the experience.

"Thanks," I said, a little too soft and a little too late. But she heard me. She didn't say anything, just turned and stared for a moment into my eyes, and then nodded.

I could feel my heart shudder, and the recent image of her in the tub, water glistening on her breasts and streaming down the crevice between them came unbidden to my mind. She'd run her hand—and mine—over her chest unselfconsciously, and I'd felt a torturous mix of desire and discomfort in the moment. The stream of water down her chest turned to blood in my mind, and a tear welled in my eye. I suddenly couldn't imagine that the woman we had just seen, the gracious and noble Char-Lee, would want or require Annabel's throat to be cut in order to grant Rick his request.

Annabel pulled me forward.

We found Rick lying back in his room on a four-post bed, rings of white smoke issuing from a deeply crooked wooden pipe. It didn't smell like tobacco in the bowl to me.

"Que pasa," he grinned, eyeing us and then staring upward to blow a heavy cloud of smoke at the ceiling. He narrowed an eye and turned his head to me.

"I said watch her, not wash her."

"Could you undo this so I can finish getting dressed," Annabel asked, holding out the cuff.

"Apparently it didn't stop you from getting *un*dressed." He stood up and trailed a finger up her exposed ribcage to touch the base of her breast. Then he slid it up to circle her neck. My heart stopped again.

"I don't recall this being what you wore to the party," he said, his hand slipping down to grip the thin material covering her breasts.

"Rick, I don't think—" I began, but stopped with the familiar ting of a knife slipping free of its scabbard.

The hooked barb of Rick's Bowie was at my chin in a heartbeat.

"Back off junior," he warned. "You've had your fuck for the day. If I want to handle the merchandise, I will. In fact—"

He pulled a silver chain from his pocket, and deftly released the cuffs with its key.

"Wait for us outside," Rick said to me, and pointed with the knife at the door. Then he turned back to Annabel, and instead of helping her finish dressing, he pushed the glimmering material off her shoulder and down, until the dress slipped across her thighs to wrinkle like shed skin on the floor.

Knife at her heart, he forced her to the bed, and I slid unnoticed from the room.

Something had happened. The landscape had all changed, I thought. When we had started, I was Rick's right-hand man. Confidante. Friend. But over the past couple days, he'd grown rougher. Not that he hadn't always been a bastard. He had. But now he was ordering me around like a slave, and I was apparently falling for the girl we'd brought along to kill.

Not a good chemistry. Not at all.

I walked back to the fairy dust room thinking that Annabel had gotten what she wanted, just as the Oracle had promised (at least while she'd been in our room), and Rick was now getting what he wanted.

But what about me?

There was a bed now in the center of the room, where I was sure there hadn't been one before. I pulled on my hanging shirt sleeve and buttoned up, and then lay down on the pile of silken pillows at its head. I thought about Annabel in the bath again, and shut my eyes, focusing on that thought, imagining myself in the tub with her, soaping her back…

I must have drifted to sleep, because when I heard the gong, my whole body jolted. I rolled to the side of the bed, and as I pushed myself upright, a pain shot through my left hand.

I pulled back as if burnt, and looked. A thin red line stitched across my palm, tiny beads of blood already at the surface.

The reason was readily apparent.

The business end of a wood-handled straight razor glinted in the dull light on the edge of the bed. I picked it up to study, when I heard Rick's voice from the corridor.

"You ready Romeo? I think that's the dinner bell."

I slipped the razor into my pants pocket and tucked my shirt in. Rick was looking around in irritation in the middle of the hallway as Annabel tried unsuccessfully to button up the back of her dress with one hand.

"Let me," I said, and finished the last three for her.

"Where are we supposed to go?" Rick asked, and, as if on cue, the light in the hall that led back to The Oracle's chambers faded out, and the hall beyond seemed to brighten.

"I'd say this way," I said, and began to walk.

The light led us to a dining hall. A table with enough places for 40 men stretched from one end to the other, and at its head, The Char-Lee sat, resplendent in black lace. She was grace, mystery and death incarnate. Her lips were painted a deep red for the evening, and her silvering blonde hair rode in a wave to the back of her neck.

"Welcome," she said as we entered, and gestured to either side of her. "Join me at my table."

Plates of beef and chicken steamed in the center of the table, and bowls of corn and beans and sauces I couldn't identify led halfway down its stretch.

We sat, Rick on The Char-Lee's left, with Annabel at his side. I sat on her right, alone.

"I trust you found whatever you needed in your rooms," she asked. Rick smiled widely, nodding. Annabel looked uncertain, but nodded as well.

"I receive fewer and fewer visitors these days," The Char-Lee said quietly. "The way grows more dangerous, and my legend, perhaps, less known."

"Your name is yet known," Annabel said.

"Perhaps it would be better if that were not so."

We filled our plates with food, and I stuffed my mouth with creamed spinach and Arabian olive salad as Rick answered the Oracle's request to talk of how things went with the world of men.

"The police states of Irving and Darien have fallen to the gangs of Oakbrook and Willow," he related, "and the cult of Moonrise continues to spread throughout the western towns that remain alive."

He told her of the plague towns and the roving bands of mercenary armies, and of the drought that turned many a small burg into tombs of desiccation. When he began to speak of finding the book of Aurica, and studying the scribes for spells of protection, The Char-Lee turned to Annabel.

"And you, child. What of you?"

"I'm of no consequence, ma'am," Annabel said, barely looking up from her plate. "Like everyone else, I've looked for love and found its taste bitter. I have worked beside the beasts to till the earth and bled enough ground to spare my life. No more than this."

She turned to me next, and though I'd had time to prepare, I had no answer.

"I've had to do a lot of things to survive," I said. "I'm not proud of it all. But I'm still standing."

"You're sitting," Rick laughed.

I considered throwing my roll at him, but out of propriety, declined.

Instead, I looked at The Char-Lee and amazed even myself.

"I've also found the taste of love bitter, but I know in my heart that it can be sweet. And I would give my life to earn such a love."

Rick made a gagging sound. "I'm going to lose my dinner," he proclaimed.

"Then it is time for dessert," The Char-Lee announced.

I saw shadows move out of the corners of my eyes, and I turned to catch them, but saw nothing but the stone walls of the chamber.

However, when I looked back at the table, the plates and bowls of food had disappeared, replaced with pastries and cookies and a cake of darkest chocolate.

There was little conversation during this final course, and even I had to smile in amusement as Annabel pushed bite after bite of cake into her mouth, smearing chocolate on her lips as if it might disappear were she not to get it all inside her quickly. Perhaps it would have, I don't know. I contented myself with stuffed dates and a rich zucchini-honey pastry. When at last, the group of us pushed back from the table stuffed beyond memory, we all looked at The Oracle.

A sad smile crossed her lips, and she nodded.

"It is time," she said. "You have come with a purpose, and I will hear it. But not here."

7. THE ORACLE, THE CHAR-LEE

The Oracle rose, and bade us follow her, back down the hall to her formal chambers, where she mounted the dais and sank back into her demonically encrypted throne.

Rick turned to me and hissed, "Hold her," as he pushed Annabel's arm into my grip. Then he turned to face The Char-Lee, to plead his case, and offer his sacrifice.

"You have come this far, and claim to have studied the ways, so surely you know the duality of my gifts and power," she said, eyes unblinking and cold. "Like the lycanthrope, it changes from cool skin to claw, a symbiotic dance of desire and death. You may leave my chambers now, with my blessing and gratitude for an evening of companionship. If you begin the path of request, at least one of you must die. Perhaps all of you will find dread and claw, not kiss in my answer. Consider carefully, before you speak."

My hand held Annabel's wrist, but somehow, it slid down as Rick began to speak, and I felt her fingers clench around my own.

"In the book of Elysian, it states that the Oracle not only has the gift of sight, but of power," Rick said, and The Char-Lee pursed her crimson lips and gave an almost invisible nod.

"Likewise, it states that this power can be conveyed to those seekers who offer sacrifice, both heroic and brutal to earn it."

Again, she nodded.

I felt the heavy weight in my pocket shift as Annabel's hand gripped mine tighter, pulling me closer. The moment was nearly here. Rick would take her from me, and open her neck with his Bowie, so that he could gain the magic to rule the gangs of madmen that ruined our homes, and haunted our nightmares.

In my pocket, my fingers found and clenched the wooden shaft.

The shadows of the hall seemed to move around us, a twirl of shifting light and darkness that could not be seen, only glimpsed. Forces were moving.

"I have studied the teachings and made the sacrifices of Odun and Nothfair," Rick said, his voice growing louder and more sure as he spoke.

"I have traveled the paths ordained and brought to you an acolyte, and a sacrifice, so that I may be imbued with the power."

Annabel's grip felt as if she would crush my hand, and her lips suddenly brushed my ear.

"Love is *always* bitter," she whispered, as Rick turned, grabbed her by the arm and yanked her from me.

"For you, I dedicate this life," he pronounced, drawing his Bowie and holding it high in the air as he crushed Annabel to the floor with his other hand tight around her neck.

On her throne, The Oracle observed but said nothing, her face expressionless.

"May this blood rinse the room with life and set your generosity free," he intoned, and brought the knife to Annabel's throat.

In my mind, I saw the water trickling down her breasts again in the bath, and felt her hand, chained to mine, a binding that was, at its end, not unwelcome. I felt her hand pinching mine just moments ago, and felt her breath in my ear.

I felt the razor in my palm.

I felt my throat constrict in utter fear of my next step.

But still, I took it.

I pulled the razor from my pocket and stepped forward at the same time, grabbing Rick by the hair and yanking his head backwards. Taken by surprise, he fell back into my arms, a heavy, deadly burden that almost instantly began to struggle.

"I dedicate this sacrifice to love," I said, and brought my razor down across his throat. I could feel the flesh give way, and felt the hot spray of his blood and saliva as I dragged it down deep and severed his throat from ear to ear.

Rick's eyes bugged out wide and white; his brows clenched in shock and anger. His lips struggled to speak as his blood washed my white shirt. Red, the color of death. Red, the color of love. A sharp pain ripped through my side and I heard Annabel scream "No!" as Rick fell away from me and I tried to stand. But there were teeth, blades, acid fire in my gut and I staggered backwards, falling down at the feet of The Char-Lee.

Annabel knelt and pressed her hand to my cheek.

"Be strong," she said, and a new blaze, ignited by her words ripped from my belly to my groin and back to my heart. A blaze that almost staunched the wound.

She kissed my lips then, gently. “Strong,” she repeated and drew back. The world seemed to be growing fainter. Hazy. I pressed my hand to still the screams in my side and felt the heat, the wetness there. Flowing fast.

In the distance, I heard Annabel.

“Accept this sacrifice from your handmaiden,” she said, and I heard something, it had to be Rick, squeal and sputter. “I have brought him to you,” she continued. “He has strength for your strength, and life for your life. May I beg of you the power?”

8. Sacrifice

I awoke in a sea of fairy green, in a bed of down and air.

When I started to sit up, I felt the blades bite my side, and I collapsed instantly.

“You’re awake,” a familiar voice cried, and then warm hands and lips were on my face.

“She said you would wake, that it would take time, but I’ve been here waiting for so long and sometimes it seemed that your breath would stop for minutes at a time and I would kiss my breath to your lips and pray that you would hold on, that you would come back for me once more but I was so afraid because…”

“Whoa,” I gasped, grabbing her by her shoulders and pushing her back, just a little.

“Slow down,” I begged. “What’s happened. Where’s Rick?”

“I finished him,” she said. “He was my sacrifice.”

Annabel’s face filled my vision and her eyes looked sad, scared. Her mouth trembled as she told me.

“When you found me, us, I was already on my way here to find The Oracle. I know the teachings; I have studied the power. And I had a quest, too. When you slashed Rick’s throat and set me free, I used the knife to cut out his heart.”

“And The Oracle?”

"She granted my request," Annabel said, her face suddenly serene and calm.

"Are you going to try to rule the world?" I asked, incredulous that this quiet, beautiful woman could have practiced the same rituals and followed the same paths I'd found Rick wallowing in.

"Rick was studying the path of the powers of death," she said. "I sought the power of life. The sacrifice I was bringing The Oracle had volunteered for the honor. Then you and Rick showed up."

She ran a finger across my chest and smiled.

"The Oracle accepted my new sacrifice and said I should practice the power she granted on you. So you're my first patient!"

"Can you do something about the pain?" I said, wincing.

"Maybe," she smiled, then looked at my face. "Did you mean what you said at dinner and when you cut Rick?" she asked. "About love?"

"You got your bath and Rick got laid when we went to our rooms," I said. A shadow crossed her face.

"The Char-Lee told us that the rooms would provide us with whatever we needed."

She nodded, but looked confused.

"I needed a razor," I said. "To gain a love that doesn't taste bitter."

The corners of her mouth raised and then bent to kiss me.

Love wasn't bitter at all.

Bloodroses

Tanya loved the roses; she only wished she could look at them.

Every morning, her husband Mel guided her down the stairs from her bedroom, through the house, and down the rocky steps to the rose garden.

“Let me help you with that, he’d say, and tenderly lift the shirt over her head, undo her brasierre and slide her pants to the ground. With a kiss and a pat he sent her forth, into the tangle of thorns and leaves and sharp, rocky earth.

Tanya loved to run naked through the rose garden. She loved to feel the roses’ feathery touches, their sharp bite. Once she had been able to smell the humid sugar of their perfume, and see the vibrant smears of crimson across their petals. But that was long ago. Now Tanya could only experience her rose garden by touch, and so she drew the prickling bushes to her bosom and bled with every kiss of their stinging boughs.

She’d been 16 when it happened. Skin of virgin vanilla, cheeks blushed bright cherry, eyes like sapphires glinting against the stark satin of her raven hair. The boy had been called Marshall then, and she met him late each evening—a mute moon the only spectator to their urgent, exploring gropings.

They whispered and laughed and lay down on the bricks to stare out at the stars. “I wonder who’s out there,” they said aloud, but inside they thought, *I wonder who’s in here.*

She had ached for the taste of his tongue as the tickle of fallen rose blossoms caressed her neck. Each night after 10, she would climb down the trellis beneath her bedroom and wait on the brick patio by the fountain. She always heard him before he arrived, heavy shoes clicking like flint strikes against the stone. She was smoking inside; nearly ready to go up. Each night as they kissed and necked, he was tender with her and warm…at first. But as their meetings lengthened, as the moon waxed, his fingers strayed from tremulous sneak attacks beneath her shirt to bolder thrusts under her skirts. He grew insistent. One night, as the moon blinded the owls with its full searchlight shine, he pressed for more.

First he stripped her favorite blue T-shirt from her completely—a bold move being just yards from her father's back door.

"Wait," she whispered, but not too convincingly. Soon her jeans were gone too, and his own flesh fully exposed to the pale tan of the moon, and open to the massage of her hands. A tremor ran through her belly at this unfamiliar territory, but still, his flesh felt soft and delicate, yet solid as wood. She could feel herself warm and grow under his watering kisses, her tight bud engorging with first passion, unravelling in a satin-slick flower of invitation.

But then with the pass of a cloud over the fairie light she shivered and whispered "no."

He seemed not to hear and pressed himself tighter to her. She felt the rose of passion wither and scorch and she pushed with tight fists against his shoulders again, "No."

"Yes," he answered this time, through gritted teeth. "I can't wait anymore."

A pain shot through her like the sting of a thousand thorns, and Tanya at last opened her mouth to scream, only to have it filled with his thick, sour tongue that suddenly tasted not so delicate and fine but fat and base and ashy with the flavor of cigarettes. She panicked then, and struck him in the ear with a fist, but he didn't relent. In fact, her struggles only seemed to encourage him.

Replacing his mouth with a gritty palm, he held her to the brick as he took her, impervious to her cries and wiggles and wide eyes. Finally, she bit down on his hand, hard, so that she felt the skin give way. The hand yanked backwards, but rather than nurse his wound, her sweet and gentle Marshall brought that hand back down in a closed fist and struck her mouth ruthlessly.

And again.

With his hands on her neck then, he kissed her, but not with the blending of a lover, rather with the penetrating jabs of a conquerer savoring his bloody victory. Then he pulled back to ride her in animal fervor, lifting her head with each thrust and slamming it back to the brick with each release.

Tanya felt the warmth pooling beneath her head, at the same time as it slicked and gathered beneath her buttocks. Her heart was screaming as her flesh cried in pain. How could this be happening? How could she have been so wrong about this boy, this wicked young man? She swam in a sea of black filth, every light touch and kiss of the past nights seen now as a violation, a betrayal. There were stars of hurt in her eyes as the heady scent of roses engulfed her like a savior as Marshall came to climax. She breathed it in and savored it as if to blot out the knowledge of the situation, eyes closed, mind seeking another world. And then its sweet perfume turned sickly in her nose, icy sharp in its character. Distantly she felt him remove himself, heard the rustle of his jeans dragged across stone. Heard him murmur, "Shit." She kept her eyes closed as he scurried away into the night.

««—»»

When she woke next, Tanya strained to see through the blackness, but could not. Her nose felt itchy, but she could not smell the roses.

"Marshall," she called.

Then, "Mom?"

The nurse's hand on her brow was cool. "You're in the hospital dear. How do you feel?"

"Could you turn on the light?" Tanya asked. "I can't see."

There was no answer at first, and then she heard the nurse talking to someone at the far end of the room. Whispers, and the tongue clicks of pity.

"It may pass," she heard a woman say.

But it didn't.

Her world remained a black void where only sound could enter. Tanya was alone in a room without windows. Her food had no taste, the roses had no smell. And no color.

But she could feel them. It became her only release. To press the world against herself in a smothering embrace. "You're there," she sometimes murmured. "You're there, I can feel you."

««—»»

Tanya met Mel at a special education class. He was the teacher, and she loved to listen to the melifluous tones of his voice. It was caramel and chocolate. Molasses and cream. She already loved him when he told her she was pretty one night, as she stood in the foyer, waiting for the familiar step of her mother who came each night to drop her off and pick her up. She felt her skin flush, but at the same time, shrugged away his compliment.

"No," she said softly, "...but thank you."

He took her hand in his—wide, leathery, strong—and pressed it tightly.

"Yes, you are. Do you like coffee?"

"I can't taste it," she deflected.

"You can feel hot and cold, can't you?"

Within a month, her mother was no longer driving her to school. In six, Tanya was standing against the wall in their kitchen, listening as piece by piece of her 25 years were carried past, landing with thuds and rattles and grunts in the bed of Mel's van.

"I'll take care of her," he promised her mother. Tanya imagined the wrinkles playing like braille across her mother's falling cheeks.

"Do," was all she said.

Mel fed her ice cream and coffee that she couldn't taste, but could feel. He massaged her feet. Mel read Sylvia Plath and Jackie Collins to her. Mel seemed to smile with his voice at every move she made. But most importantly, Mel took her to the rose garden.

"I can't," she insisted, the first time they drove to the conservatory. "It's where...I...just can't."

"Taste the air with your tongue," he advised. "Feel the scent in the humidity on your skin. It's healthy, even if you can't see them or smell them."

In the end, she gave in, and walked with him tremulously on nearly even flagstone steps. Once she stumbled at the rough rise of a heavy stone and he held her upright by her elbow. She shook with relief and fear. But as they wove deeper into the strange maze of muffled glass houses, she realized he was right. Each house was like a special pressure chamber; the air changed its feel, growing Florida muggy and Phoenix arid and Oregon cool damp with each whoosh of the doors behind them. Its flavor eluded her but she could *feel* its taste. The heat of the sun through the glass panes warmed her head and neck and the clasp of his hand on hers led her to explore the more ethereal aspects of the garden, if not its view.

"Touch this," he commanded, moving her hand by encircling her entire wrist, and placing it in contact with ferns and foliage, buds and stems.

And then.

"Touch this," he said, and laughed when she drew back in pain.

"Every rose has its thorn," he said then, and hugged her to him.

"That wasn't very nice," she pouted, pushing him away. But he kissed her and apologized.

"If you don't feel the pointed things in life, you'll soon take the soft ones for granted," he said. This made sense to her and she found she loved him more.

"Can I feel your pointed thing," she giggled, running a hand up his thigh.

"Yes," he promised, but instead led her to feel the bark of a sequoia tree. It was rough against the back of her hand and she pressed against it, drawing its detail inside herself until her hand was raw. Her blood flowed hot through her arms and she knew that she had crossed a precipice. A divide. She had spent years learning how to avoid bumping into furniture, years hiding from the sharp edges of the world. Years hiding from Marshall.

She wasn't hiding anymore.

"Let's get married," she announced, and in a house filled with unseen armies of roses, she listened as his voice trembled and he said, simply, "yes."

««—»»

"I'm going to grow you a rose garden," Mel said one day, as he lightly ran a knife along the bottom slope of her cleavage. It was a game they had developed. She had taken his message to heart: *every rose has its thorn.* She would not try to savor the rose without first feeling its thorns. It made the end pleasure of the petals so much more intense. Likewise, she would not make love to Mel without first snipping her nerve ends raw.

He would carve sweet nothings in her skin or decorate her with forests of twining, twisting pins. Each sharp prick of her flesh made her face contract, and yet, the rush of the blood through her heart made her beg him not to stop. Each week, they played the game anew, the goal changing with every implement Mel used. The pain made her feel alive, broke her out of her black detachment from everything around.

"Can you stand forty pins?" he would ask.

"Yes," she answered, in a tiny voice. "Forty-five."

If she cried "uncle" before reaching the number, she lost. If she let him go further, she won. Either way, when the game was over and his kisses finally swelled her lips and tightened her nipples, she ended in ecstasy.

"I *would* like a rose garden," she admitted. "I could feel their petals against my skin every day, then."

"And their thorns," he added.

"Yes," she said. "And their thorns."

««—»»

The first time they walked together in the garden, the rose bushes had no buds. Tanya ran her hands up their thin stems and winced as the blood ran in rivulets down her arm.

"They're all thorn," she complained.

"Give them time," he said. "First come the thorns, and then the flowers."

And they did come. The garden grew with the breadth of her belly, which Mel had seeded with a child. And in her fifth month, Tanya felt the first perfect, satin-smooth bloom.

"Oh, Mel," she praised. "It feels wonderful. It's softer than a feather, and more velvety than velvet."

He laughed and promised, "Soon, it will all be in bloom. Just like you."

««—»»

When the contractions racked her body with feral bites of pain in her sixth month, Tanya cried for her baby, and for herself. She felt alive with the fire, and yet shredded near death at its kiss. It was over quickly; Tanya writhed and sobbed in the endless darkness and her pregnancy rushed out of her in a flood of bitter, heated acid. The bed was sodden, soaked in an empty broken promise.

She didn't blame Mel, and yet… His knives seemed sharper

of late, his games more intense. She wondered, as her wracking pains slowed, could his long needled probes have killed their child? Just yesterday, he had brought her to screams with his penetrations.

No, unfair, her mind railed. That was her fault, as much as his. She craved the blades, encouraged their attacks. The pain made her *feel.* Its intensity almost made up for the senses long lost, but still imagined. Sometimes the ghost of a peppermint stick washed painfully across her tongue making her mouth water, or the scent of her father's aftershave before church on a Sunday smothered her to coughing for a second before disappearing, leaving behind an emptiness deeper than the black sea her eyes swam in, day after night. She wished more than anything that she could part that cruel curtain, and see the man who kissed her and held her and kept her safe, as he indulged her twisted needs.

She wept then with guilt at her lack of trust in him. Guilt at her own inadequacy. She had lost their baby. Even in this she was only half a woman.

Mel only made her feel worse as he waited on her carefully, patiently, over the next few days, bringing her soup and toast and helping her to the bathroom, watching to make sure her bleeding didn't continue.

"I love you," she told him, "I'm sorry." And he hugged her tightly.

««—»»

Two weeks after her miscarriage, Mel came into their bedroom and announced, "The roses are in full bloom. Do you want to go?"

"Yes," she answered, and he took her hand dramatically, like a knight come to escort the princess to the ball.

The stairs seemed endless, her legs weak and trembly; it had been almost two weeks since she'd left her bed.

"Are you sure you're ready?" he asked, as they walked through the kitchen.

She nodded and took a breath.

"I'll be fine. I need to walk."

Step by step they descended to the garden, the air teasing Tanya's hair in a ghostly kiss that made her sigh.

"I've missed it out here. Show me the prettiest ones."

He took her hand and guided her to a bush of thick cushiony buds. Tanya held the thorns to her palm and brushed the petals across her cheek to tickle her nose.

"Tell me how it smells," she begged.

He laughed. "Like life," he said, his voice heavy and delicious. "It smells like the breath of the sun and the kiss of life."

She left his guiding hand then and twirled her way through the garden, stopping at each scratch of thorn across her flesh to kiss and rub the bouyant flowers on top, laughing with a giddiness that had seemed lost to her just an hour before.

"My roses are beautiful," she laughed. "Thank you."

"There's just one thing," he said, his voice close in her ear, startling her. She'd thought he remained by the stairs.

"What's the matter?" he said when she jumped at his voice. "Did I scare you?"

"No," she said, steadying herself against his shoulder. "I just didn't hear you there."

"I can be very quiet," he agreed.

"What one thing?" she asked.

"The garden is not quite complete."

Something stabbed at Tanya's back and he yelled "wait, stand still," as she shrieked, backpeddling into a razor sharp tangle of thorn and flower.

"Something bit me," she cried out. "Mel?"

His hand reached out to her elbow to steady her. But she was still off balance; she felt the blood running down her back and she twisted, lashing out at the bite, finding her hands punching, not some stray dog at her feet, but hitting Mel's face.

"Take it easy," he soothed, voice of chocolate tinged with bitter lemon, but she was tumbling away from him, tripped by the slash of a rose stem and sudden vertigo.

The world exploded in a rainbow of fireworks across Tanya's black horizon, and with the light, her thoughts blinked out.

««—»»

Her first thought was that her right leg was broken. A stabbing, red-hot scald ran up and down its length.

Her next was that something had died.

"My god, what is that smell?" she exclaimed, not realizing what she had said until she opened her eyes and *saw* the man bending over her leg, using an instrument resembling a cheese grater to remove slices of skin from her thigh.

Without thinking she kneed him in the face and pulled herself backwards, crablike.

"What..." she began to ask, ignoring the blood running in slow dribbles from her leg and looking around her.

"...is this?"

The man was rubbing his chin with his hand. He was the ugliest man Tanya had ever seen. His left eye was glazed over with white, his cheeks were sunken and grey. Her hands had always known that his arms were somehow misshapen, but now she could see the breadth of his deformity; odd tufts of hair matched with twisted cords of muscle to produce a manged and mangled appearance. His chin jutted sideways and his nose was just a blob of wide-pored clay. His face and arms were covered with a network of discolored scars, a pink and white crosswork of snip and stitch.

"You can see!" he exclaimed. His grin grew wider, dragging his cheeks into eclipse with his eyes. He scrambled to his feet, and lifted his arms.

"I've built it all for you," he said, gesturing around them at the low ceilinged heat lamps beating down orange and bare between the wooden beams just a couple feet above them, and the quiet, slowly oscillating wall fan. There were no windows, only four concrete walls. All this time, she'd thought it was a spacious garden of open breezy air beneath the warmth of the sun.

"It's your very own private garden," Mel bragged. "It will never fade or wilt. It will always be here for you to touch."

Tanya stared at the basement maze of winding paths amid twined branches of barbed wire. She was surrounded by the glint of metal, some barbs rusted, no doubt from the spray of her own blood. At the top of most of the barbed wire bushes were the pale flowers she had brushed her face against so many times these past months. Intricate blooms of layered petals, painstakingly pieced together by her husband and mounted, somehow, on these bushes of unforgiving cruel steel.

"I started with my skin," he explained, pointing to a misshapen rose of brownish black. A strip of Tanya's own bleeding flesh still hung, seemingly forgotten, from his clenched hand.

"It took me a few tries to learn the best way to cure it without it rotting or turning hard. After that, it was easy. Just harvest and cure, assemble and mount. Your mother gave us this whole section here," he gestured to a group of pasty bloomed bushes, adding, "And I did this whole bush here just last week."

He pointed to the devilish twinings of barb and peach-fuzz fine flower next to her.

"That's the culmination of our love, honey."

She looked at the pinkish buds, tightly woven petals seemingly bursting with the need to open and shower their scent to the world.

"That's our baby," he said, nodding, white eye glinting like the moon on a grey day. "Isn't she beautiful? She was delicate to peel, but I think she's the most beautiful rose here."

The tears coursed in heated rivers down her face as she touched the baby soft skin of the rose crafted from her lost child. Then she kissed it and breathed in the scent of her daughter.

"How could you?" she whispered, stomach contracting in horror and despair. Her senses attacked with an intensity sharper than any knife Mel had ever wielded. She could smell the gagging stench of decay of her mother and baby all around her like a palpable thing, a blanket of death. And everywhere…the glint of steel and skin made her want to close her eyes again forever.

She looked down, unable to face the remains of her baby. Or her husband. She saw the sheen of electric red blood slicking her leg, and saw the scars that pitted and poked their way up her thighs, turning to criss-cross trails like a city road map gone mad on her belly. Her once taut and beautifully creamy skin was a wrinkled mess of tears and mends, slices and stitches. There was no more beauty there; her youth was carved away, one pore at a time. Left behind on the points of Mel's pins and knives and barbed wire roses. There were spots discolored, like the stretched skin of a wax figure that was slowly melting and stretching, taffy in the ghastly machine. Idly, she wondered which of the roses here was made of her own tortured flesh. Surely some of the gouges she'd thought to be innocent wounds of passion at the time had been meant to make harvests for Mel's twisted garden.

"Are you okay, honey?" he asked softly. "I know it's probably a lot to take all at once."

She nodded, unable to answer, eyes drawn again and again from her own ruined torso to the tender sculpting of her baby before her, every petal paper thin, yet still a rose grown thicker than most in life. There were bare stems next to it still, barbed branches waiting patiently for their own bloodroses to bloom, and Tanya closed her eyes and said, "it was better to be blind."

She closed her hands around the barren stems until blood dripped brightly to the ground below. She brought her face down as if to sniff the sharpened barbs and then with a wrench, screamed as their tips scraped out her sight, a violent abortion, fake thorns carving new scars in the broken pits of her eyes.

Dimly she heard Mel's usually honeyed voice turn to broken

glass as he screamed "no," but it didn't stop her from twisting the rose stems this way and that, twirling them deliberately all around until the red fire of pain and betrayal slipped from nausea, to numbness, to final, freeing black.

Made for Each Other

A heart never empties in one night. It bleeds itself dry over a period of days and weeks and years. In a best case, the heart is connected to another, and as its blood drains away, it is replaced by transfusions from the other. They become a synchronous structure, both bleeding and refreshing the other. Unless one springs a leak.

The true test of any structure—whether a heart or house—is how it weathers not just summer's storms, but winter's ice. Regardless of conditions, it shouldn't spring a leak. I'm a carpenter by trade and know of these things. Let me tell you a story of hearts and houses.

While a journeyman learning my craft, I purchased a small plot of land for the future. I lived in a small apartment, and put away my earnings until I was ready to build. I was smart. I had a blueprint.

I laid my own foundation, married each beam to each concrete piling. My level was honest. My hammer true. My friends helped me, on weekends, and after a time, I left my lease behind to live beneath the roof of my industry. I followed my plan, worked hard, and knew where I was going. In fact, I got there.

And then I met Regina.

It was at an upscale bar downtown. The only electric lights beamed the room in blue and gold, while candles shadowed every table and corner in flickering mystery. A saxophone's tale slithered between the table legs, while a drum's tongue licked the mirrors behind the bar. The jazz was overpowering, intoxicating. Just like her.

My friends said later it was love at first sight. I looked up at *rap-tap-snap* of her heels clicking in time to the beat across the hardwood floor as she moved in exaggerated rhythm from a table near ours to cross my vision on her way to the bar. It wasn't the red boots, spitting candle tease back in my eyes, or the short black mini, flapping provocatively close to the edge of where her derriere must round. It wasn't the way her filmy white blouse cinched tight to her waist before ruffling out again, lazily, or the point of her red lacquered nails tapping in countertime to the bass drum on the black slate of the bar as she waited for the tender's attention.

No, I was watching her face, captivated by her reflection in the mirror. She looked ahead of herself, unfocused, searching. I stared like a prisoner on first parole at the glinting blue of her eyes, and the glossy promise of lips so full, she might have been pouting, not playing with the napkins while nodding to the sudden rise of the saxophone's sinuous neck.

I could bore you with the painfully embarrassing details of my first approach that night, both of us a little farther into the bottle, the alcohol raising my courage while lowering her resistance. Both of our foundations tilted at a less than steady angle as I patted her shoulder, while she batted her eyelids. From such foundations are relationships built. No wonder the rate of marital attrition only grows.

"You were made for each other," our friends said, gaping in awe as we danced our way from bar to promise bands to wedding, each social event a new brick in the ever-growing masonry collection that was *us*.

In actuality, we didn't have much in common. I was a tradesman; I made my living with my hands, every nail's bite a bond of solid truth. When I finished a job, there was something solid to show, something that couldn't lie about its core, regardless of the amount of paint slapped on its surface.

Regina, on the other hand, thrived on ephemera and illusion. She worked in an advertising agency. She wrote copy that sold millions of people on products they didn't know they wanted or needed.

She wasn't a real blonde.

It was months before I realized that the luscious globes of her naked breasts were not her own. At least, not completely.

Nothing of her was what it appeared on the surface. Still, when she told me she loved me, I never questioned her. A house can be inspected, its joists tested for strength, its walls squared and leveled. A heart pumps away its love blindly, hoping that the flow returns and never knowing until too late if it does not.

Regina's goal in life was to improve things. Or, at least, to sell them as more than they were.

When I undressed at night, she ran her hands over my chest, cool, needy and exciting. I shivered from the sensation and despite my goosebumps, she told me I was perfect. That must have been very frustrating for her.

When she moved into my house, she sighed and spun around the wide hardwood floors of my living room and put her hands on her head.

"It's perfect," she pronounced with a catch in her voice, just before hugging me. I didn't realize, at first, that this was not a good thing.

Perfection never lasts, if it exists at all.

Regina's last husband had not been perfect. Ned was a slacker, she said. A biker in a leather jacket with a perpetual sneer and the tattoo of a naked woman on his arm. It was like she had to compete with his biceps, she told me. Of course, after the bike accident, he'd been missing most of what hung below the biceps. Not to mention his eye. I had started to wonder if that unaddressable imperfection had been the real reason behind their marriage's disintegration. Not that he couldn't have had those issues addressed today, in the new age of body mod.

Regardless of Ned's obvious shortcomings, I was coming to realize that Regina wasn't satisfied with anything for long. Even perfection.

"I love your skin. So brown, so perfect," she whispered one night, trailing her fingers from my belly across the wiry hair of my chest. Her face shifted then, and she looked up at me, bright-eyed. "Let's get tattoos of each other's names," she said.

"Only if you get a dragon tattoo right here," I said, running the tip of my finger from the delta of her thighs to the dark pit of her bellybutton.

She rolled on top and snaked a tongue between my teeth. Wanton.

"Deal," she whispered, coming up for air. "It will be like showing the world that we belong to each other."

"I thought that was the point of this," I responded holding up the gold wheat twine of my wedding ring.

She snorted. "That just says you're married. But not to me. I want something of *me* on you."

"Your brand," I said, and she raised an eyebrow, but didn't answer.

One weekend as I sipped my coffee, enjoying the quiet of early morning, she said, "Let's add a sunporch off the kitchen. It will shield us from the light in the morning at breakfast, and give us a protected porch in the afternoon."

"But the whole point of having an eastern breakfast nook is to have the sun in the kitchen at first light," I argued.

But logic never counted for much in Regina's world. After all, in one of her most celebrated ad campaigns, she sold mortgages with billboards depicting lip-licking braless coeds barely wearing business jackets. Loan applications at the sponsoring bank went up 57 percent during the first week of the campaign.

I built a sunporch.

The new sunporch threw off the planned balance of the house, and strained the furnace, since I hadn't originally structured the ductwork to incorporate another long room. Our bedroom was cool in the winter, and warm in the summer. Once it had been even-temperatured.

"Paint the house white," she suggested, "to reflect the sun better." I preferred its gentle blue and black accents, but still, I did. And found while I brought my brush across the siding that there was a crack in the foundation just to the left of the new sun porch. When I checked the basement, I discovered its previously perfectly smooth concrete work was splintered and leaking. The patchwork took an afternoon, but my house was ready again for winter.

And soon, so was I.

"Look what I got for you," I said one day, beaming (and wincing slightly) as I strode into the now-gloomy kitchen. Regina was sorting the mail, and I rolled up my shirtsleeve to reveal the new blood-red heart pincushioned into my biceps. Across it, in black, was an arrow. Riding the arrow, were the letters R-E-G-I-N-A.

"That's so sweet," she grinned, and kissed me, hard, on the mouth.

"I got a two-for-one special," I bragged. "We can go back and do you, too."

"How about if you just come do me now?" she coaxed, pulling me backwards into the cold bedroom.

Afterwards, she suggested that, while the tattoo was nice, there were other ways in which I could improve.

"You know, the latest body mod fashion is to go one-armed."

"Might be hard to swing a hammer that way," I laughed, flexing her name so that the G jumped like a heartbeat.

"You can have it put back on after the winter," she said, shaking her chest below me. Her breasts barely rippled. She'd had her breasts resized to hard white shields over the summer, at the same time as she'd had the gene modification to color all of her body hair to a bronzed orange. I'd barely recognized her in bed that first night.

"You have to keep reinventing," she'd explained. "Otherwise… well, you wouldn't want to be the same forever, would you?"

"But I thought I was perfect?" I joked, biting playfully at the tiny nipple now held so close and hard to her chest.

Regina had an amputee fetish.

I guess she wasn't that odd; one-armed men were the fashion that year. But I'd never experienced the intensity of the warm, wet explosion of her lust that my first night home sans arm brought. I'd had the left one removed and put in cryo-storage, since my tattoo was on the right. She couldn't get enough of the smooth skin that ran from my shoulder blade around the curve to meet my breast. The ghost image of my arm was troubling; mentally I kept reaching out to grab things that I couldn't touch and I found it difficult to maintain my balance; from then on, she was on top.

In December, the upstairs bathroom began to leak, but not in a place I could reach easily. The leak was somewhere hidden, behind the wallboard. I knew this because a dark brown circle formed on the ceiling of the living room. Before I could get a friend over to help me fix it (I was fairly useless at such things with only one arm) the whole ceiling gave.

Regina was smothering me in bed when it happened, shaking herself in my face and crushing me with a meaty arm across my neck. We both stopped when we heard the noise. A long, slow, grinding that escalated from aching moan into a necksnap crack and disintegrating crash. Her eyes blinked and she pushed off of me, stumbling from the bed to the floor, and I lay there, catching my breath for a moment before staggering erect myself. When we both shambled into the frontroom, I could see a rain of molding, rotted wood and wallboard littering the floor in front of the couch, and the joist I'd laid in so carefully years before with my two hands was now undone, warped and leaning from ceiling to floor.

Regina waddled over beneath the hole to stare up at the dangling tiles from our bathroom. She'd put on 100 pounds this winter, because weight was suddenly the fashion. The perfect point of her chin now waved hello to itself, and the points of her breasts were lost in the surf of her belly. We rarely made love anymore. I couldn't lie beneath her for long without an arm to protect myself and live. Yet still, I held out hope for us. I remembered the waist and wiggle of that girl at the blue-lit bar.

"You really are made for each other," my friends still said, though they didn't sound as sure as they once had. I began to suspect that Regina was made—and remade—for herself alone.

"You'd make a great one-eyed bandit," she said one night, as I tried to slide between the folds of her second belly to find the hidden entry of her sex. Her flesh sloshed beneath me, hindering my explorations with doughy obstinance. It was then that she pushed me away from her thighs and begged me to give up my eye.

"Do it for me, baby. You can always put it back if you want later."

It wasn't lost on me that her ex- had lost both an arm and an eye in a motorcycle accident before their divorce, but I booked the body mod surgery anyway and came home to be almost crushed in her gratitude.

It didn't take long before she was bored again.

"Open it now," she said, thrusting the brilliantly wrapped box into my hands. I had just returned from a walk and hadn't even taken off my jacket. She pulled it off me and led me back to the bedroom.

"What's the occasion?" I laughed, and pulled at the velvet ribbon with my teeth. I couldn't very well hold and open it easily with only one arm.

Impatient, she reached over and pulled the lid off herself. Digging through the white cover of tissue, she pulled out a flesh-colored, rubbery bag of skin and held it up to my face.

"Try it on," she begged. I could hear the water from the upstairs bathroom dripping in steady splats on the worn carpet of my frontroom. My will to build seemed to have been lost with my arm and my eye, and so the hole in the ceiling remained. The water had taken to draining steadily through the ceiling, onto the floor and running in a black wet stain to the corner of the front room, through the drywall into the flowerbed near the driveway. The wall was covered with the thin fuzz of mold, totally rotten. It would soon no longer support the french windows I'd installed.

I'd fix it, I promised. Just as soon as I'd had my arm put back on.

Not yet, she begged. Another month or so.

I stood still, blinking blearily at her through my one good eye as she pulled the rubbery mask over my face. My flesh tingled as my new face found its comfort point and settled tightly on my skin. When she was done, there were dark rims around my field of vision, but I could see her through the hole that settled over my one good eye.

It seemed to grip and mold almost perfectly to my face; I could feel its eyebrow raise when I wrinkled my own.

"What do you think?" she asked. "It's the latest thing—custom facials."

She leaned back on her elbows and appraised me, orange eyebrows raised like peaks of flame. I responded with an arch of my own; she had removed the weight this week, anticipating spring, and seeing her lounge lasciviously supine on the bed was almost like seeing a stranger naked for the first time.

"I think I look like your ex," I said, noting the wart on the right upper cheek and the swarthy complexion of my new face. I'd seen plenty of pictures of her with him. In some of them, he even had all his limbs. My stomach lurched.

"Don't be silly," she cooed and pulled me from the mirror to the bed with my good arm. "You can still walk."

She stroked my cheek.

"It's made from permaskin, the stuff they use on burn victims. If you leave it on for a day or so, it will fully bond with your skin and actually use your own blood supply to survive. "I had this one made just for you."

"For *me*, huh?"

"Kiss me," she said, spreading herself wide for me and pursing cupid bow lips dyed red as plums. A trail of newly pocked bellybuttons arrowed from her revitalized breasts to her burning bright pubes. Bellybuttons—lots of them—were to be this summer's fashion statement.

I leaned forward, favoring my armed side and trying to avoid clumsily falling atop her as I pushed my tongue through my strangely puffy new lips to meet the fruit of her mouth.

Her eyes sprang open at my insertion between her moist lips, glittering with the telltale seagreen starbursts of Seduction Surgery. They sparkled in the dimmest of light like a prism. I had tried to tell her that she didn't need that to seduce me…I'd fallen for her—for *her*…but she hadn't listened. Maybe it wasn't me she wanted to seduce. She pulled me down to her and ran her fingers along the smooth skin of my severed arm.

"Oh Ned," she whispered, staring into my mask, forgetting herself as she ran desperate hands from my new facial wart to the empty socket of my eye to my limbless shoulder. "I've missed you so."

She pressed me to the bed and I cried as she made love to a man I had never met. I cried for a long time when she finally pried the mask of her first husband off my head.

That was the year they revealed the sham of Sallee Regeneration Technique, much to the dismay of thousands who'd removed arms, legs and eyes for fashion. A class action suit helped, but certainly didn't undo the damage. I have my arm and eye back again, but the arm hangs like limp rubber, and the eye rolls to left and sees only shadows. The ghosts of truth.

I kept the tattoo; I am forever now her creation, and wear her brand like a symbol. A symbol of selflessness, for I have truly lost my self.

I left Regina the house; her modifications had destroyed it just as thoroughly as she had ruined me. But I can't lay all the blame at her feet. She called me perfection but asked me to change. And I did. Without thought. Without thinking about what support beams I was breaking inside my bones, and my soul.

I live now in a small apartment, and struggle to find the means to survive. I may never again be ready to build. I was made for her, but she was making another.

I was a carpenter with a full heart and a head of plans.

But now my heart is dry, a fluttering shrapnel-shorn skin.

My house lies in ruins, its beams rotted and broken.

I was a carpenter.

But all of my blueprints have faded.

And Regina…

She's building a new man now, and lives in his mansion up the valley.

She's had the Metallion Treatment. Her skin gleams like polished brass and her hair is now truly made of spun gold.

She says it's perfect.

And he's perfect.

They're made for each other.

But perfection never lasts, if it exists at all.

Spirits Having Flown

It was never so sterile. So polished.

So bereft of life.

The old frame house once sighed with his tortured breath, spoke with his aching lips, stumbled from thunderstorm to snowfall with his unsteady feet.

No more.

I move from one room to the next, noting the forest green granny-square afghan folded neatly on the back of the second-hand couch, its cushions, (for the first time?) perfectly fitted together. The thick, dripping grease spots have been wiped away from the small orange and brown tiles above the Donna Reed-era Amana gas oven range, the sloppy spaghetti stains painting the wall by the garbage can scrubbed down to faded shadows. I can see the patterns in the yellowed linoleum. Bundles of daisies. Given Mac's and my inattention to housekeeping, I'd never seen the flowers before.

The family has come, has cried, has cleaned, has gone.

Leaving me. The caretaker. The tenant.

For now.

And there is only one more thing to do.

Mac said he was only lying down for a nap on the perpetually rumpled couch. Those were his last few words to me. His breathing had been labored all week, and I worried. "Go down to The Last Chance later?" he whispered the question, and I nodded. He grinned a small grin and slipped off his heavy glasses as he curled into the cushions and afghan on the couch.

Nodded at me.

Caught his breath.

Wheezed.

And was sleeping.

I left the room, figuring to wash the car. While it was a gloomy shade of overcast in Mac's living room with all the heavy hand-me-down curtains drawn, it was 85 and sunny outside. Out there, life was dancing. In Mac's house, life moved slower, if at all. Maybe it was the smoke, or the low light. Or Mac. But sitting in his living room was like being trapped in a bubble of amber. Everything was still, and stained in sepia.

When I came back into the house an hour later, wet with sweat and stray hose water, Mac didn't stir. I went to the bathroom, rinsed my face and arms, combed back my hair, and then pulled on a fresh shirt. The house was quiet. Nothing too strange there. Mac didn't go for loud music, and only clicked on the TV at night. But this felt different, even so. At first I put the sense of stillness down to the absence of the screams and laughter of the kids outside, running through sprinklers and shooting at each other with water guns that looked like they'd come from a SWAT armory.

But no, that wasn't it.

The absence, the stillness in the house was a missing constant—that sighing whisper of air trickling in and out of Mac's lungs. The ever-present wheeze that meant Mac was at home. It had been the background soundtrack to my life here these past six years, for if Mac wasn't with me, drinking away the pain at The Last Chance, he was here, wondering how it had all come down to this. From a gentle mother's arms to the edge of the hard Chicago streets to the arms of another woman and her kids and then, not. Loneliness. Only this small house at the edge of a roughed up and left behind farm town with a migrant worker as a roommate and a minute-to-minute struggle just to breathe.

"Life is a bitch," he'd often said to me in a low voice at the edge of a slanted smile.

"Then you die," I'd answer.

He'd squint back at me, take another sip and nod.

"Then you die."

The first time I met Mac was on a barstool at The Last Chance. He was emptying a tall can of Old Milwaukee, and flirting with the bartender with the shadowed eyes. Those shadows came from lack of sleep; she put in time as a receptionist at the Feed Store to make ends meet for her three kids. Still, she humored him, laughing and patting his hand as she emptied the ashtray that had filled up near his right hand.

"In your dreams," she answered some off-color comment of his, rolling her eyes.

"And what exciting dreams those must be," I said, edging my way into the conversation with a compliment to her. Never hurts to flirt with the barkeep—she'll pour better for you.

"What do you know of my dreams?" Mac growled and turned away.

Strike one.

"You're a man. You have the same dreams we all have."

A glare from the evil eye. He started talking to the woman on the other side of him, a haggard thing with long painted nails and a mouth that stretched from ear to ear. She looked 70 but was probably really only 45. He showed me his back and said nothing more.

Strike two.

I finished my whiskey in two slugs and left the bar—and Mac—behind.

I was new to town then, having slowly worked my way down from well-paid insurance suit in Chicago to minimum wage bag boy at the last two-horse town 20 miles north. Seemed I couldn't cure the itch in my soul, and neither could the bottle.

I began seeing Mac almost every night at The Last Chance. Where else was I gonna go after a day working the fields? Sweat and forget, that was my new motto.

One night not long after my first brush with Mac, I pulled up a stool next to him and ordered a Seven and Seven. Mac turned his head to gaze up at me sideways, one eye open, the other squinted near-shut.

"What you wanna do with a highbrow drink like that," he said. "You gonna drink at this bar, you order some Jack Daniels straight up, or have Ginny pull you a beer."

Ginny had stopped to see my reaction, and I shrugged. "Is a Jack and Coke acceptable?"

"Suit yourself."

From that day on, I was Mac's barstool buddy. And eventually, housemate.

There was no funeral.

Mac wouldn't have it. He wanted cremation with no ceremony whatsoever. The family compromised and laid him out in a box to wake for one night. Some people probably wanted the chance to say goodbye, they felt; and they were right. The family was amazed at the turnout, but not surprised when the bulk of the bodies walked straight down the street to The Last Chance afterwards.

I found one of my old Chicago business suits that almost still fit for the occasion, and stood sentinel by the casket as nurses and waitresses and rummies and friends from his growing up days in Chicago streamed by the body. An old flame with a fake eye that was downright creepy if you looked too long probably cried the most. Word is a knife fight with the man who'd been with her before she'd came and went on Mac had taken half her sight. I wondered if she still had phantom sight on her right side, like when you lose a finger but still feel its presence on the end of your hand. A high school buddy holding 40 extra pounds in his belly who probably wished he could slide his beard up *above* his forehead helped her away from her increasingly loud casket-side conversation with the dead body.

But mostly, none stayed too many minutes, or cried too hard. Many were amazed he'd lasted so long.

His face looked like softly brushed wax, his fingers molded in plastic. That thin brown mustache made him look a downright dapper mannequin lying there in his brother's suit. He'd never owned one of his own. You don't need a suit to drink at The Last Chance.

"It's so sad," his family members murmured, talking in whispers in the back of the room. "But it's for the best," they reasoned. "What kind of life did he have? When you're that far into the bottle, what kind of dreams can you have left? He'd drowned them all out."

I stifled a sad smile and turned away. If they'd only known; it was the dreams that sent him to the bottle, not the bottle that stifled them. And no matter how hard he tried, he'd never managed to drown them out.

Nobody sent flowers to Mac's wake. One plant sent over by the local Christian church marked the head of the casket, and I watched it walk down the street with the family, when they left Mac's body to be burned. Their cars were packed with salvaged items from his dresser and cupboards. Memory holders, keepsakes, pictures. The solid imprint of his life on the world, dispersed with more transience than his dreams.

As the funeral parlor locked its doors, I realized that all that I had now of him was a piece of glass and the empty shell of a house. And even that would soon be denied, once the family sold it. Even his ashes wouldn't remain; those would be shipped north for burial once the cremation was complete.

I have to laugh as I think of the reactions in those first hours after his death. The phone calls. The tears. The shock. The first hurried clearing of the house. When his sister arrived late in the afternoon from up north, she barely said a word to me, but instead performed a silent reconnaissance of the house. She peeked into all the cupboards, knelt to peer under the couch and felt between his mattress and box spring. Finally, she got up the nerve to just ask.

"The guns, the knives…?"

"He left me instructions," I said. "I disposed of them all."

A troubled smile, and a nod. One less detail for her to worry about. The last thing the family needed at this stage was police interest in Mac's unlicensed hobbies.

If she'd only known of the one important thing I had yet to dispose of. But, I suppose, she wouldn't have understood. Hell, five years ago I wouldn't have understood. Just a few months ago, I wouldn't have been ready.

It's time now though. For me. I have to be ready.

In his bedroom, I shove aside the ancient metal frame of his single bed, and with a screwdriver pry up the loose board beneath. There's an echo of a child's scream as I lift out the small wooden box buried there, under the dead man's bed. Is the echo from the children outside, down the block? Or is it from the delicately filigreed box, from the faces peeking out there amid the slim vines and trees embossed in its lid? It too, had lacked for a funeral.

I replace the board and the bed, and returned to the kitchen. On the strangely clean table, I lay them out. One violent glass frame after another. They are small things that the box divulges. Country housewives hang similar glass shards from strings above their windows to catch and bend the sun.

Mac used them to catch and bend dreams.

Bad ones.

Nightmares.

I spread the myriad shards of mottled glass until the entire table was covered. The fake woodgrain surface came alive with twisting, writhing shades of flame, of blackness, of blood. Reaching to the middle, I lifted one that I recognize as mine. An ancient face stared back at me through the slender trap of glass.

An old man, by the look, and gentle. But I knew better. This father figure was a haunt who'd chased me through back alleys in the night, all teeth and black nails and rusted razorblades thirsting for my neck. It had been years since he'd plagued my sleep. Mac had trapped him here, along with so many others.

There was the malformed, hideous child that his sister had never borne. There was the grisly red-smeared traffic accident that once woke his niece up nearly every night, shaking and sweating with fear and grabbing at her belly to see if it was still whole. There was the nephew's family dog, dragging its twisted body away from the road, trailing its lifeblood and back legs behind it. And there was his other sister's late husband, a cold thin greying man with a tight fist that beat and beat and then stopped, as his leg sprang to motion, dealing out his love in sharp hard blows to the ribs. Monsters and madmen and murder.

Hard dreams to handle.

These visions and so many more Mac had captured and held from his family and friends over the years, until his box was full and his power stretched thin as an old man's skin.

Only his will held these dreams here, and that will was gone now. Already some of the dreams had discovered that the cage that had bound them for so many years was gone, and I could see the shape and color of the woodgrain pattern through the clear glass they'd left behind. As I surveyed Mac's collection, his life's work, I began to cry. It wasn't the emphysema, or the Old Milwaukee, or the cigarettes that had killed him.

It was the dreams.

Wiping the water from my face, I hefted the screwdriver and considered. The dreams would escape, no matter what I did. Dreams can't be killed; can only be stopped for a while. Mac had taught me this: dreams are forever.

But if they can be trapped, can they be maimed? I wondered. Hobbled?

I looked down at the table and saw a miniature Ginny, being raped after hours at The Last Chance by a thug with long black hair.

"No," I cried, and brought the heavy end of the tool down to crush that vision. It shattered and sent other dreams flying off the table to crack and litter the floor. In the air, a scream, and a sparkle, and then … nothing. I repeated my attack on glass holding a monster intent on rending the limbs from a blond boy I recognized from last night's wake; he'd grown at least a foot since this dream was captured. A slight flash, like the faintest slide of a prism, and he was gone. Again and again I brought the screwdriver down, shattering nightmares and adding crumpled dents to the fake grain of the plywood table. The air filled with the angry twinkle of freed visions, and I felt my heart stumble as they surrounded my head, a chattering, screeching host of untouchable teeth and talons. When all the glass was shattered, I spun about the room and swung the point of the tool like a dagger at the air, alive with nightmares and dream deaths. Tears ran down my cheeks as I begged the dreams to follow their catcher.

"Die," I begged.

"Die."

At last, the room was quiet, and I rose from where I'd fallen on the floor, surrounded by empty, clear shards of glass.

I left it all, and went back to my own room, far down in the shadows of the long hallway.

From beneath my own bed, I pulled out a single triangle of glass. I'd fashioned it from a broken attic window, smoothing its dangerous edges carefully with sandpaper and spit. It was the first talisman of my graduation from apprentice to dream catcher. I lay back on the bed, wondering how I could ever be as strong as Mac, to steal and seal so many dark visions. It was up to me now to carry on his work, to lighten lives of 3 a.m. heartache and sleep-stealing succubi.

I held up my one shard of glass to the light, and felt the weight of its pull on my heart.

Mac's gasping face met my own.

"Let me die," his dream whispered. "Please just let me go."

Just days ago, I had captured this shade as he gasped and trembled in a troubled sleep.

Now I hold his dream to rue and remember forever.

It is the first weight in what will become my own collection of imprisoned dreams.

And I think that it will always be the heaviest.

—For Jerry

Warmin' the Women

I read in an old book once that you can't choose who you love and I guess it's so. I want to have Trent as my own always, to have and to hold and all that, but the council goes and gives me Marta. Some nights she squirms beneath me like a handful of nightcrawlers, but I keep her pinned. It's no effort really. I'm a half a horse heavier than her—she ain't going nowhere. She lays there next to me afterward, mouth openin' and closin' like a fish caught up in the weeds by the tide. She complains then, squinting lids across black marbles in slits of pearl.

"You're too heavy and you make me too hot," she hisses, but I just smile.

"That's my job—that's the job of all men," I retort. "Warmin' the women."

She always shuts up quick then and rolls away. I can't wait 'til her seed week is over and Trent can come back for the nights. This is the sixth month I've had her during her seed week and she's yet to get big. If she don't after this time, we can finally put her to some good use. Meanwhile, I just miss Trent. He never complains I'm too heavy. And he doesn't squirm, he pushes right back. But I got to admit, the council is right. Women have to be got pregnant or there wouldn't be no Trents. Fact is, there ain't many women 'round these days to get a child in. And most just can't seem to hold a kid in their bellies.

I wish I could give Trent a son. We've talked, and he wants to give me one too. Maybe this time his trip will pay off.

Trent's out now on a fuzzhunt to the city. Never know what kinda fuzz you find in those tumbledown ol' towers. Council gave me one a couple years back that they found up there and after her first week I got to itching my own fuzz and pole like they was on fire. I thought it was cuz of all the pictures on her skin—dragons, snakes—boogie stuff. I went 'fore the council and showed 'em what she done to me—got some whistles too when I dropped my pants. I didn't pay the courtin' no mind, just pointed 'n' screamed 'bout the fire she laid on me. I said it was probably poison from the pictures on her skin. Dragon bit me, I says, and council laughed. But doc say it's just an itch, rub this on, and it goes away. But cuz o' the itch, now I get the worst women—'Last stop before the drop is Jack's crop,' the council says when they assign the women. Don't wanna spread the itch. And Trent now got the same fire from me. Well, we give that fire right back to that picture girl, that's for sure. The council sends more guys right back up to the city looking for more. Trouble is, most of the ones they bring back got something wrong with 'em. The skin falls off 'em when ya slap at 'em, they got sores 'n' walk crooked. And they never git kids.

Most o' the guys 're saying now we should stop the city runs. Ain't none of us want to take the women home, and they don't amount to nothing but a rash and a pile o' bones in no time.

My fathers had it better. Twice as many women to warm back then. I remember waking up in the night and hearing both of them slapping and laughing as they worked on getting the latest ones' bellies full. They liked to work at it together, then they'd leave the women all snuffling and whimpering and go back to their own room together. Had us a dozen brothers and sisters 'fore the sick winter. That's when it all started going bad. Council still shake their heads over it, blamin' bad women, bad animals, somethin'. But the long 'n' short is, half o' Boystown died that winter, all screamin' mad, feverish and pus-y. Some had stuff fallin' off of 'em by the time they died. And the ones that didn't catch it 'n' die wish'd they did, 'cause we had to live the winter on roots 'n' bark. Throwed out all the meat—didn't know if it caused the sickness or not, but no one was chancing. Weren't very many women to warm after that winter, I'm telling truth. Out o' my three brothers and nine sisters, there was four of us left. Now there's just me.

Last year 16 men—big chunk of our pop.—left Boystown. Said we was wasting cuz of the water or poison in ground. 'The death and sickness is in the earth,' they yelled and tried to make the council move Boystown. But we been here too long. My fathers and their fathers lived in this same house. Great grandads built it. Other men are the same. Their grandfathers and fathers went through the fires of hell to found our heaven, the council said. We ain't leaving their legacy. Truth—I think the 16 were right and this ain't no heaven, but I ain't left neither. They didn't take no women with them, said they'd find some that hadn't had their jeans polluted. I thought they was stupid not to just wash their women once in a while, but hey, whatever. They'll probably die out before they get a new town going. Maybe poison's everywhere. We sure don't find many women anymore.

««—»»

Trent came home the day I finished Marta's seed week. Trent and I made some new fire that night, I tell you. And the council was licking each other's balls too when Trent and his boys got back from the city—they not only found two scraggly girls, they fell upon a stash o' canned vegetables. We haven't had a good store of cans fer winter since I was a boy. Old ones say the cans from before is healthier 'n what we can grow now. I dunno 'bout that, but I remember they taste sweeter.

Council's sending another group out tomorrow to bring back the rest of the stash. I'm going with this time, while Trent finishes a week with one of the women. She's a lost cause, I know. She been through nine other guys and ain't once got big.

And she stinks. Trent say it's cuz o' the sores on her, but I say she's just rotten inside. "Wouldn't even use her fer compost," I say. She'd poison the garden.

He laughs and says, "Well that Marta ain't much better, all teeth and ribs."

I gotta agree.

««—»»

Two weeks it took us to get to the city. Scary lookin' place, I tell you. My father Dan used to tell me people lived there who liked to do the deed with women, but I think he was just telling stories. What he don't lie 'bout is that almost no one lives there now. Ones ya find there all seem to be broken and fallin' apart, like the city itself.

We walk up to the first of the towers and they's just leaning into each other like evil arches waiting to suck us in. Clouds hang over this place like that thick fog in the early morning; everything is grey—and quiet as death before dawn. Some buildings are tumbled flat on the ground, and we gotta walk for hours to git around 'em.

There's rusted hunks o' metal all around, things called cars, points out Mike, our leader. Cars used to go up and down these paths carrying people places, he say, but I'm not buyin'. With all the crevices goin' cross the roads and all the trees and funny looking yellow creepy plants growing out of 'em, how would the cars be able to move? We gotta cut through 'em with knives sometimes just to pass single file.

We was in the city three days 'fore we found the stash. Don't know how Trent and his guys found it in the first place—we had to cut in and around half a dozen fallen buildings, and walk 'neath a bunch that kissed each other in the sky and looked about like they was gonna come down on our heads before we got to the place. And then, it turns out, we gotta crawl through some thorny bushes into a flight of cracked and broken stairs. The stash is underground! Turns out, must a once been a food store here, and this big skyscraper crushed it into the dirt when it tumbled. But there's still a bit of the old store not totally caved in that we kin get into through these stairs.

Stinks bad inside, and I hear lots o' rats and who knows what else movin' around as we squeeze in through a door stuck half open and crushed near in half by the weight the dead skyscraper's a' levering on the topside. Mike points us to a dark pile lying on the floor. It flashes in the light of his torch, blinding me a moment, and then I see it's a spill o' cans. We all load up our sacks fast to get the hell out of there. No telling what kind of diseases those rats are waiting to give us if we stick around. *And maybe that building ain't done settlin' yet*, I think to myself as I'm loadin' my pack.

Something shifts in a rusty squeal a few feet from my head and I nearly messed my pants. We got outta there in a hurry—cussin' and pushin' at each other when we jammed up in the doorway a moment.

Sighted someone in the street on the way back. Mike got spank happy and started running after yelling back at us: 'We get us another woman and the council let us off a seed week fer sure!' But wasn't a woman. Mike got a blade in the arm when he tackled the "woman" and it took three of us to get the thing off of him after.

It was so dirty and covered with long mangy grey hair that we had to cut its clothes off 'fore we was even one-hundred-percent sure it was a man. Weird looking pink-ended knobby pole 'tween its legs, but it was. It screamed and babbled at us, called us faggots and freaks and Mike finally used its own knife to gut it while we held the arms and legs. Stunk inside as bad as out, and we figured it wasn't even worth carting home for fertilizer. So we left it where it lay, steaming red guts seeping across the weedy concrete, and set for home double speed. Mike needed some medicine for that arm.

«««—»»»

Council was happy to see the cans, and Trent was happy to see me—we'd had only one night together in two months! We was kissing and groping right there in front of everyone, turned 'em on so much some of the other men started in too. But just as pants began to drop right there in the middle of the Boystown square, Councilman Troy come out of the food house and yells fer listenin'.

"Okay!" he bellers, "put yer rods away and come to the Food House. We gonna celebrate with filling our stomachs before you go fillin' whatever else. And we got not one, but two women to do it for us tonight. They can't fill their own bellies, so they goin' to fill ours."

This was met with cheers all around and the men whose pants were already on the concrete was grabbing and hobbling to get 'em up. Everyone in Boystown piled into the Food House, but it still didn't look near as full as when I was a boy. Troy called Trent and I up to the boilers. Food's scarce these days.

"As the last men to fill these women, you have the honors," Troy announced with a ceremonial grab at our crotches. We smiled and accepted the trussed women delivered to our arms. Trent didn't look as if he even wanted to get his hands soiled with Gret, the stinky woman he'd last had and proved barren, but I wrapped my arms tight around Marta, who squirmed and twisted as she always had beneath my pounding groin.

I crushed her pointy boobs against my chest 'til I heard something snap, all the while miming a good in-out boff with my hips. The men were cheering me, and those black holes in her head stared at me in a vicious hate like a wolf caught with its foot in a trap. I laughed, and held her suddenly limp body out from my own.

I heard a splash and a squeal behind me, and I knew Trent hadn't wasted a minute. It was time.

Silverware banged in a tribal rhythm against the Food House tables, and I whispered one last rib in Marta's ear. For just a second I felt funny, bad about it.

Then I thought better about dinner and having Trent to myself and all, and I pushed her into the boiling cauldron. She sunk like a rock at first—disappointing the crowd some by makin' no sound—and then floated back to the top, her normally pale skin an amazing red.

Later that night, as we moved together in bed, I ribbed Trent that while there was plenty of meat left untouched on his Gret, my Marta had disappeared like lobster. I was rightful proud of her. He rammed me pretty hard for that, but it felt good. He asked what I'd said to her before pushing her in.

"Just a little joke we had between us," I hedged, subtly urging him on.

"So spill it," he huffed, sounding as if he was about to do just that himself.

"I just reminded her that I was doing the job men have to do."

"What's that," he said, nipping my neck.

"Warmin' the women."

He groaned then and gave me his warmth. Maybe the book that said you can't choose who you love was only half wrong. I didn't choose to love Marta, but Trent I'll love forever. Through fire itch, seed weeks and all. And maybe someday I can even give him a child. *Won't be by Marta though*, I think.

And I don't quite know why, but in the heat of passion, I shiver.

Mary

"*Hail, Mary!*"

The voice came from somewhere behind her. Or in front of her. She wasn't sure. Mary looked up from the well and squinted. The sun bleached everything beyond a few feet to a wavy blur, and she couldn't see anyone who appeared to be looking for her attention. People moved by the village square quickly, dust kicking up in hazy apparitions with the speed of their travel. Nobody wanted to stay out under the blaze of a noonday sun for very long. Mary shook her head, feeling the sweat staining the veil on the back of her neck and hoisted the water jar to her shoulder. She didn't intend to stay out here any longer than she had to, either.

"Hail, Mary!"

The voice again. This time from her left, by the carpet-maker's tent. What would he want with her? The carpetmaker nodded his tapered black beard at her, but showed no untoward interest. Mary nodded as well, and walked past him, into the alley. It stank of urine and camel dust. She stepped slowly, but still saw no one. At last, she turned and looked back the way she'd come. The back of the carpetmaker's tent seemed small now, and the alleyway long and tight. There was nobody here, and if there was, it certainly wasn't a very good spot to be meeting them, midday or midnight.

"Mary."

The voice startled her and with a slight shriek, she fumbled the water jar. It slid from her delicate balancing grasp and crashed to the packed dirt of the street, cracking into shards of jagged clay and spraying water across Mary's robes and face.

"Who…who's there?" she cried, equally afraid of the unseen voice as of her mother's wrath for a broken jar.

"You can't say my name," the voice answered. "But you can call me any time." Its tone was rich and deep like silky chocolate, with a sly note of humor. It caressed her ears with velvet and warmed her belly with its promise of sugar.

"What is this riddle?" she asked, turning slowly in a circle, staring at the clay of the bare walls on either side of her and still, seeing no one.

"Why would I riddle my future bride?" he said. Mary's eyes went wide. What game was this? Why, oh why, had she stepped out of the public square?

"Leave me!" she exclaimed and turned to run back to the well.

"Love me!" he replied, and suddenly Mary's feet went out from beneath her, and her spine was pinned by a bullish weight against the cool clay of a house.

"Wha…" she cried, her voice escaping in a surprised whoosh, and then something warm and wet pushed against her chest, her neck, her lips and then…she was lost in him, oh him…too much sensation and not enough. With each of his touches she could taste sweet fragrant violet flowers in her head and syrupy golden bee's nectar on her tongue. Searing rainbows of too-perfect perfumed lust flooded into her mouth, her eyes, her spirit. She could fly a caravan's journey in an instant and feast on the entirety of the king's finest banquet in a blink. He overwhelmed her and filled her, and then emptied her and made her beg for more.

He awoke in her an all-consuming appetite, an endless unsated hunger for all things sensual. Her arms raised above her chest and the invisible yet heart-stopping beauty of him pinned her in a tight prison to the rock but she couldn't fight him, wouldn't, because he tasted of heaven and smelled like the spring of life. His touch sent chills of ageless ecstasy through her bones and her startled "no" turned into a lax childlike circle as her body sucked in his ethereal probing tongue and penis.

And then, all at once, he was not there, and her arms were released from their ridiculous stretch high above her head and instead of nursing on the teat of nirvana she was nursing on dry hot air, her body open and exposed to the distant stares of the marketplace.

Tears streaming from her face, Mary ran from the alley and the square, ran home to say she had tripped and dropped the water, ran from the fear of what demon had possessed her…and the more tingling fear that she wished he'd return.

In her bed that night, Mary lay awake, still feeling the marks on her back of her mother's wrath. And imagining the feeling of the demon's tongue. What sweetness could be wrong, but what sweetness that no eye could see could possibly be *right*? Oh, she wished for him, and her legs tensed and bent at the thought. Her stomach fluttered at the memory of his stroking touches and she whispered to herself, "Oh god, please, come back." Then she shook the lust from her head and pledged "No, never again. I cannot do such evil. Will not. He is no god, but the devil, a tempter. He will ruin me for men."

Mary's eyes widened like black moons in her head as her body was suddenly pressed hard into the threadbare woolen blanket beneath her.

"I'm so pleased that you wished for me, Mary. I told you to call me anytime."

Something brushed a lock of dark hair from her forehead and the voice, so thick, so heavy, so crushingly beautiful told her, "Oh Mary, you are one of my finest creations. And together, we will make another."

Her robes writhed like snakes and began to undo themselves, and Mary panicked, struggled against the lulling torpor of his sensual Valium. She pulled the rough material back over her full, exposed olive-skinned breast and shook her head at the demon's strategy.

"No," she whispered. "No, I'll not be the concubine of a demon. They will stone me. I am unmarried. I have no man. You cannot take this from me."

His laughter was like music in her ears and the fear was pushed from her by the feel of his hands slipping beneath her tunic.

"You are mine to take as I please, Mary," he said, his voice menacing, and yet, with an edge of bright butterfly to it. "And I do please. I please very much."

His hand slipped beneath her robes again to caress one taut nipple, and she shuddered in ecstasy at his touch. Her nerves were electrified beneath his hand; torrents of pleasure shot from her chest to her groin and she moaned aloud.

"Yes, my pet," he soothed. His lips then brushed hers, and, mouth open to his tongue, Mary swam just beneath the sea of oblivion. But a part of her strove to see through the darkness, to see what face this being had that could break her defenses so easily, that could make her normally staid person melt with need. She could see nothing between her face and the dark ceiling, but she squinted into the shadow anyway, hoping for some glimpse. Reaching up a trembling hand, she tried to touch the space where his body would be, if he were mortal. Her arm passed through the air and he broke his invisible kiss to laugh.

"Mary, if you wish to see me, why didn't you just ask? If I am to be your eternal husband, I can certainly allow your eyes to pass over me."

With that, he swam into existence, a golden-skinned god of shining oiled muscle and perfect skin. He seemed to bring his own light into the room, and she could see the warm glow of his chocolate eyes and the glossy sheen of the coiled curls that dropped from his head to tickle her neck. His chest was bronzed and taut, the nipples delicate and chased by a light carpet of dark curls. Her eye followed those curls past his bellybutton to the long, heavy stem of his manhood—or if he was to be believed, his godhood rather.

He was beautiful. If she had had a doubt before about giving herself to this creature, it was gone as she drank in his perfect body. His lips pursed in a knowing, pouty smile, and he asked, "Do you find it to your liking?"

Tears streamed down her face from wanting, and wanting to resist. Her garments fell to dust and he rolled to trap her beneath his godlike form, and traced a sigil of power across her breast with his tongue.

"The son of god shall suckle here," he told her and she cried out, in pleasure and fear. She wished that he would stop, begged him to, her hands clawing into his silken steel shoulders. But his need poured over her in unstoppable waves that left her helpless to resist. Through a haze she saw each thrust inside her as a stream of blinding color.

"Hail Mary," he said presently. "Filled with grace."

Every nerve convulsed and her orgasm lit the room with a fireball of lust fulfilled.

Mary blacked out.

She lived thereafter in fear.

Would he corner her again in the market? In her bed? Could she stand him to rape her again? Could she stand him not to?

Mary grew quiet, avoided her friends. Her mother's concern brooked shrugs and avoidance, her friends found better company. She spent hours prostrate, praying to God to forgive her sin. Her hands strayed often between her legs, trying in vain to bring on even a *hint* of the orgasmic intensity he had effortlessly given her, but in vain. She should have been strong enough to stop him. But she had lain with a demon. What would become of her soul? And how would anything ever complete her body again?

Days passed of this silent—sometimes angrily thrusting—agony. And weeks. The inner voice that cried forlornly in the empty nights grew louder as she knew with a prescient certainty that she was with child. She sensed the difference in her body. A thickening. A difference in appetites and tolerance. The heat made her grow nauseous on occasion. Once in the market she heard his voice from far away.

"Hail, Mary."

But she ran and he did not pursue her.

Sometimes she dreamed of a small, perfect golden-skinned boychild, fingers small as bean seeds, eyes wide and innocent as pools of freshly rained water. But then her fear took over and that innocence dried to the hard kernels of the sand beneath it, leaving in its wake a flat malevolence. A boychild that glowed with the power and force and dangerously irresistable charm of its father.

After a time, Mary came to her mother following the morning meal and announced that she would take a trip. She needed to get away to shake this dreariness from her, and her cousin would be happy to receive her company. Mary's mother nodded; her heart sang a song of relief. Perhaps a trip was indeed the thing to shake the darkness from her daughter's soul. As luck would have it, the opportunity presented itself on the very next day, and Mary packed a few meager clothes and left home with a family friend whose caravan was to pass near the town of her cousin Elizabeth.

The heavy blood of sunset stained the doorway of her cousin's house as Mary, trembling with fear and hope, knocked. The door opened, and a dark portly woman, in stained saffron robes received her.

"Mary!" she exclaimed, holding her arms out to embrace her cousin, at the same time pulling her inside. Elizabeth was just 10 years Mary's senior, but already her face betrayed the wrinkles of age, her black coiled hair the thin twinings of grey. When she smiled, her cheeks filled with river valleys for tears.

"It is so good to see you," the older woman said, holding Mary back at arm's length to study her up and down.

"Something of you has changed," she observed instantly.

Mary nodded, but said nothing.

"And I'm certain that this something is behind your visit to me tonight."

She threw her hands up, stopping herself and Mary from answering.

"But there is time for such talk. First, come in, come in. Let me get you something to drink, you must be thirsty after a day in the sun with camels and cameldrivers. Did they treat you well?"

Mary grinned and nodded yes, and the two women retired to the kitchen.

There passed drinks and cakes and a dinner before Elizabeth held up a hand again and stared hard into Mary's watery brown eyes.

"Enough pleasantries, cousin. I've known you since you were in swaddling clothes. This is no social visit. Tell me who, what and why."

Slowly, haltingly, Mary began to describe the voices at the well. Her voice grew in strength as she told of his entrapping kiss and condensed the events of his subsequent nightime visit to her bedroom.

"You are with his child, then," Elizabeth concluded, staring harder at Mary. "I thought as much when I opened the door to you."

"I have heard that you have access to potions that might help me," Mary replied, hanging her head and not daring to meet her cousin's eyes. Elizabeth did not answer, but instead, rose from the table and walked from the room. Mary' heart raced. Had she just insulted her cousin and made sure that she would never be welcomed under this roof again?

Presently, though, Elizabeth returned, and set a vial on the table.

"You must be sure," was all her cousin said.

"I have thought about nothing else for weeks," Mary said. "I am without a husband and pregnant with the issue of a demon. What good could come from this?"

"You will be sick for at least two days after this, perhaps more. We should begin tonight if you are able."

Mary nodded.

"This is very powerful," Elizabeth warned. "A drop or two will not kill you, but will smother the life of a child."

Elizabeth's face betrayed no emotion as she uncorked the vial, and allowed three ruby drops of liquid to fall from the vial into Mary's tea.

"Drink and from this, at least, you will be safe."

At that moment, a fierce wind screamed through the room, and the cup upended from Mary's hand of its own volition.

A violent tornado streamed about the room, its sound shrieking louder and louder as it drained from the sides to the center of the room, shattering every loose bit of pottery in its path. A golden light grew bright from its center, and with a slurping snap, the wind imploded into the shape of a man. A golden, angry man with piercing eyes and a stormy smile.

He put both of his perfectly smooth, long hands down on the table and glowered at each woman in turn.

"You would kill my child?" he asked, incredulity drooling from his lips. He shook his head in amazement. Neither answered.

He looked at Mary. "You disappoint me, girl. I think it is time for you to sleep."

Mary felt her eyes instantly growing heavy, though she struggled to stay awake. Her back relaxed and her body slipped down in the chair.

"No…" she heard her voice mumbling as if from a mile away, when the storm incarnate turned its attention to Elizabeth.

Her last vision was of her cousin's eyes watching, frozen and wide, while her hand moved slowly, shaking—as if it were a great struggle—picked up the vial of poison and drained it into her own mouth, held open by the long golden hands of the demon.

"Drink deep of your own medicine," he whispered, and then Mary's world was gone.

So, shortly thereafter, was Elizabeth's.

"Hail, Mary!"

Her belly cringed at the greeting, daggers of ice spitting her with hatred and fear. He had taken to walking with her through the center of town since her disastrous return from Elizabeth's. The two women had been found collapsed on the floor the day after her failed abortion; only one of them remained alive. Food poisoning, the wisemen had declared, and Mary didn't dispute their divinations.

So she had returned home, and now the demon watched her closely, determined to make sure she made no other terminal attempts on their child's life.

Within her, she had begun to feel his spawn kick.

He fell into step beside her. It seemed as if the ground around the two of them lit a degree or two brighter than the surrounding desert glare. *Didn't people notice the gleam that came not from the sun, but from this man?* she wondered.

"How is the lord's mother today?" he asked solicitously, touching a hand to her belly.

Something within her leapt, and her groin and breasts threaded with heat from just the brush of his fingers.

"Praying for death," she answered in a hiss.

"I'm not answering," he said.

She scowled at him.

"What would make you happy, Mary?" he begged, a haze of sepia lazing from his eyes to her neck and chest.

"Not to be having a bastard child for a demon."

"Mary, the child you carry is no demon, but the son of God," he soothed.

She laughed in scorn.

"And, as for the bastard part, you're correct, we should do something about that."

"Who would have me now?" she said. "I'm obviously ruined. Only my parents are so blind that they do not see."

"Mary, Mary," he said, stroking the back of her head. Her brain seemed to take flight and hover above clouds of orgasmic peach at his attention. "Your body is a temple. We will find a man to worship it."

They were passing a small tent filled with ornate carvings and claspings of wood when he pointed to a withered grey man sitting crosslegged on the ground in its midst.

"How about him?"

Mary laughed. The old man looked up at her, his one good eye widening in appreciation. "He's ancient and crippled and disgusting," she spat.

"Perfect. He will guard you like a precious jewel while you refuse his attempts to polish you. In this way, I can be sure you will always yearn in your heart for me."

He led her to the man, who clung to a table to raise himself to his feet. His voice launched into a well-rehearsed, "Can I interest you in some…"

With a wave of his hand, the glowing man cut short the sales pitch.

"You are Joseph?"

The old man nodded, his bad eye seeming to bob like a yo-yo with a trick string.

"This is Mary."

He propelled her forward into the body of the ailing carpenter. The man clutched at her to prevent himself from losing balance and toppling.

"Would you marry this girl and take her home as your own?"

Joseph looked confused a moment, and then nodded eagerly.

"You can't make me do this," Mary complained. "Such a marriage would not be holy in the eyes of God."

He leaned into her and whispered so that only she could hear:

"It's about time you got used to it, Mary. I AM God."

Something within her broke then, as looking at him, she realized that his glow, his power, his jaunty ease, the purity of sensation that she had gleaned from his touches…could only belong to that of God. She recoiled in horror from the realization.

"And this," he announced, "shall be your mortal husband, Joseph. I expect the ceremony soon. Don't make me come back again, Mary."

With that, he vanished.

Joseph fell to the ground.

And Mary began to cry in the full light of day.

On the following day, Mary rose from her bed, retrieved a cleaver from the kitchen, and brought its edge down across her wrist. The pain was excruciating and she cried out as a spray of blood warmed her face. She grinned as the weakness hit her, cold nausea rising from her stomach to choke her throat. Let this be her answer to the wedding. If the old man would have a bride, she would be a dead weight in his bed. If God would have a child, then let him get it on someone else.

Strong hands gripped her from behind, pulled her upright. It was God and he was angry, his eyes seething with fire. She could feel his rage like waves of heat from a brick oven. He slapped her hard across the face so that she lost her already shaky balance and fell to the floor. Her brain spun with stars and haze and she could feel a warm wetness spread from her arm to her belly where her wrist lay. She blacked out for the second time in his presence.

When she awoke, God was gone.

And so was the cut on her wrist. She was at the kitchen table, dressed in her best robes, and next to her was the old man, Joseph. Her parents were seated across from them, nodding at the older man's words. He sounded cultured, learned in his dissembling, and Mary sought in vain for a resemblance to the decrepit merchant bum God had led her too before. This silver tongue could not belong to that man.

What had happened? Oh God, she cried inside, what have you done?

A voice whispered in her head in answer.

"What I told you to do, stupid girl. You will be married in a fortnight. And you will live to bear my son. What you do with your wrist and your kitchen utensils is up to you after."

Some months later, on the eve of the census, Mary arrived in Bethlehem on the back of a wheezing, stolen donkey, ready to deliver the bastard child of God. Joseph hobbled along beside. The innkeepers laughed in secret at their sad plight, and in public shook heads and shrugged shoulders. Their fleas were not welcome in the crowded city's hostelry. Some keepers with insight to the spiritual made warding signs at Mary's face. As door after door closed to them, she shivered with cold but laughed inside. Perhaps she would get sick and die, taking the baby with her. Joseph reached out a hand to comfort her and she reeled with disgust. The old man was vile and smelled bad. She sensed that his mind was nearly gone. She had never again heard the silver tongue that won her father over once their troth was pledged, and wanted nothing to do with him.

At last, one innskeep took pity on the two and offered his stable for a resting place. As Mary slid from the back of the donkey, she felt a shooting pain, and a warm rush of water down her thighs. Tears streamed down her face, gleaming like falling stars in the night as she realized her plight. On this very eve, in a dirty stable in a town far from home, she was to deliver the spawn of Satan. Or God. She still found it hard to believe that the beautiful tempter could be the eternal. And yet, who else could be so desirable, and so cruel?

She lay down on a bed of straw and pushed, wishing with all

her might that the child would leave her. Wishing that everyone would leave her.

Joseph brought water and rags from their saddles and before the dawn broke, the cries of a newborn babe echoed through the drafty boards of the stable. Joseph cradled the tiny babe, a boy-child, in his arms when Mary refused to hold it. But eventually, she relented and he laid the babe at her breast. It attached itself to her immediately, and she stared at the child in fear, searching its eyes for some sense of its bloodline, its future. Try as she might, she couldn't identify their color. They seemed to glow and yet at the same time were wetly black, fathomless. His head was a mass of deep charcoal hair too, and his face a fat pad of soft pink skin. He looked like any baby, she determined, and at length, let him feed.

Four nights later, as Mary's strength slowly began to return and Joseph had finished the business of registering them with the census, they laid down to sleep for their last night in Bethlehem. The child was strong and Joseph was eager to return home to show off his new son.

But at midnight, as the beams of a strong moon lit the stable through cracks in the roof, a door opened from the yard, and a man, clothed with strands of golden swirling starlight, stepped into the quiet confines. The horses threw their heads and cows lowed their excitement as he stepped forward to peer down at Mary.

Her eyes opened and met his.

"You!" she accused.

He bent to peruse the sleeping babe at her breast.

"He will grow to be a king of humanity," God proclaimed.

"And how will this happen?" she hissed back at him. Mary pointed at the slumbering old man in the adjacent stall. "The man you've tied me to doesn't exactly have high standing in the royal courts."

"I will provide," God said and then dropped his robes.

Mary stared in awe at the perfection of his form, felt her tongue thaw as the muscles rippled across his belly and thighs, the cone of his penis stirred in an arch of thickening flesh that promised her heaven. Her body yearned to feel him against her once more, a yearning so strong her eyes began to close and her lips pursed just to suck the hint of his presence from the air itself.

And then rage swept through her as she recalled the unwanted child at her chest and the stable she lay in and the horrible man she now called husband, all because of the taste of that perfect body before her.

"No," she nearly screamed. "You will not."

God smiled on her, but his lips were not drawn in humor. He was not a god who accepted rejection from his creations and he would waste no more time on this one. In a flash, he pronounced his justice.

"Then you shall have to work for it, from others. My son *shall* have his due."

He turned and motioned at the doors. They sprang inwards, a gust of cold wind swept through the stable. The screams of wailing spirits whipped through the air over her and Mary's flesh prickled in terror. She could see the smoky scowls of abandoned souls hovering in a tornado above God's head.

"Joseph," he called. The old man stirred, looked confused a moment. Then when he saw the glowing figure before him, crawled to kneel at God's feet.

God pulled him close, then raised him to his feet. "She is yours to sell as you will Joseph. You will never have her love and she will not take mine. Therefore, I wash my hands of her. Make her provide for my son. Her body is young and strong and desireable. It will earn all that is needed. Tonight you shall begin. You will receive three visitors. Make them pay for her favors, and so will she buy the kingdom of my son."

Joseph nodded, then God pushed him to his knees once more.

Presently, God smiled and waved at the girl cowering on the hay. Her face twisted with a war of wanton need and crazy hatred for her God. She struggled to keep her hands in fists when they only wished to push Joseph aside and take her Lord into her mouth and arms.

"Enjoy your desert kings, Mary," he spoke. "They will never fill you as I did. Remember, but for your stubborn pride, you could have been the concubine of *God*."

With that, he was gone, and the screeching of forlorn souls with him. Moments later, three sand-covered men entered the stable.

The darkest one spoke, his accent a wild turn of desert and far east.

"The star has led us to this place," he said. "The glowing angel promised us respite here, the warmth of a bed and a woman for the night in exchange for our gifts."

Joseph nodded and pointed at Mary. He accepted their gifts of gold, frankincense and myrrh and placed each in his saddlebags. Then he collected the babe and smiled crazily as one by one the three kings dropped their robes and joined Mary in the hay.

From his cradle in the sheep's manger, the baby watched and listened to the crying, moaning play, and the powerful amber of his endless eyes soon lit to life for the first time. His gaze filled the stable with a heavenly light and Joseph smiled dimly in the corner as he watched the bodies in the hay, musing at the glorious play of music in his head that there was a harpist nearby, perhaps. With the help of the rising light and its strangely comforting heat, Mary and the three kings gripped tighter and harder; fingers traced wet slides of pleasure and pain in the hay and the orgy of celebration brought its own flavor to scent the already thick air of the stable.

Afterwards, the men rose, dripping and dirty from the wreck of the hay to stand bewildered by source of the orgasmic light—the halo of the babe. Each knelt naked before him, holding hands trembling with fear and wonder and want and whispering, they each proclaimed, "Blessed be thy name."

Green Green Glass

The grass moves ahead of me in waves, each knee-high stalk shaking and shimmering in the dying light of a summer afternoon. My feet are bare, each step tentative, negotiating with the ground rather than dominating it. I'd already gouged my soles on rocks and barbed sticks lying hidden beneath the amber sea. A sea that seemed to go on forever all around me. To my left, the golden-green-flecked ocean slid without breaking into the cobalt edge of the sky. To my right, the horizon lightened as it faded into the fiery glow of a sunset. Only I hadn't seen the sun today. The sky above was unbroken blue, and to the right, it was simply red. Sunset without the sun; a murder scene without the body—but rich in blood.

There's no way of telling what direction I'm headed, but I trudge forward anyway, trying to keep to a straight line. Sooner or later, I have to come to something, if I don't double back on myself. In the far distance, it seems as if the drought-burned field must meet a body of water of some kind; there's a hint of green ahead. I glance over my shoulder and there's no trace in the grass that I've disturbed it. It's as if I've never been anywhere but in this one spot, a lone man in the midst of forever.

I keep walking.

The blades of dry, brittle grass slip against my thighs, sometimes tickling me like the tip of a feather, other times drawing across my legs like the paper thin edge of a razor, slicing and stinging me with a thousand tiny cuts. Slice and caress, caress and slice. Pleasure leading to pain, like the dance of love. I could stop, but then I would still be lost in the middle of an endless field. A field I don't remember driving to. Or walking in. Before today.

I woke up this morning naked on a mound of grass. Didn't know where I was or how I got here. After that, what could I do but start to walk?

The sweat runs down my back, and my legs are smeared with blood. I've walked for hours and the view never seems to change. Sheaves and sheaves of grass. Dead brown. My stomach rumbles with hunger, and my lips are parched with thirst. I have to find my way out of this field.

Ahead, the sea of parched death seems to thin, a hint of green showing through. Maybe I am near a river. An oasis of some kind. I step up my pace, hopeful for respite, at last.

Something bites me.

Stabs me in the foot.

I jump back, crying out, and balancing on one leg, hold my ankle in my hands to get a look at the already throbbing slash in the bottom of the sole of my foot. Blood sluices across my hand and I'm helpless to staunch the flow. Crimson drips across my thigh and smears the pale head of my naked cock, and I look away into the frozen sky, injured and confused in the midst of a silent, endless stand of grass. I look down at the ground, my body swaying uncertainly from side to side, and finally see the villain. The sharp edge of a green bottle extrudes from the dark ground. I know the logo, half broken as it was.

Rolling Rock. I haven't touched a Rolling Rock in years. Not since Amy.

I can still see the shard of glass, hanging like a green tear from her eye. A tear that slid out of her socket, lay close to her cheek and transubstantiated a communion of fatal blood from its jagged edge. It didn't mar her porcelain white beauty too badly, and in an instant, my sanity slid from my soul along with my jeans. In that brutal haze of blood and lust, I dropped my jeans quickly, before she got cold. If I was gonna pay for killing her, I might as well enjoy it.

Amy had been a good time girl ‘til I told her about the bottle. Let’s face it, you don’t know where a groupie tramp’s been, and a little alcohol is always a safe sterilizer. I didn’t want the carpet wet and Jack, our bassist, had been in the bathroom with a brunette who barely looked sixteen, let alone legal, for the last hour. So I gave her the Rolling Rock and told her to douche on the balcony before we went to bed.

Amy laughed at first, and shook her waist-long mane of peroxide blond at me, no way. I didn’t laugh, and her previously endearing doe eyes took on a slant I didn’t like one bit as it dawned on her that this was no joke, this fuckin’ creep was serious as hell and she either stuck a fizzing bottle up her crack and made it act like an angry soda pop or she wasn’t going to get fucked by the rock star.

The rock star, that was me. Jamie Turret. Singer of Serenading Sonia. I had more hair than she did back then, and I flipped it over my shoulder and gave one of those trademark half-sad grins and shrugged. “Fizz or fly,” I said. “Your choice.

That’s when she made her mistake. Her fatal mistake, as it were.

She punched me. Actually slammed both hands into my chest and then suckered me in the gut. I’d had groupies walk before, but they’d never laid a hand on me. I shoved her right back, and she stumbled in those two-inch fuck-me heels until her shoulders were perpendicular to the concrete walk by the pool below and her ribs were getting bruised by the iron of the rail. There was nobody below us in the electric blue reflection at that point, just the oscillating waves of the pump jets, water shivering back and forth across the pool, nervously waiting for a diver.

She bent backwards, hair flying in the midnight breeze and hissed “fuck you, asshole.”

That's when I took the bottle out of her hand and slapped her across the face. Part of me hoped she'd go over the edge and be out of my life, *now*. She didn't. It probably still would have ended there, me half drunk in my bed five minutes later and her staggering down the street outside the hotel looking for a cab, except that she didn't stop there. She kneed me in the groin and shoved me back into the room.

A white hot tire iron shot up my belly and my stomach threatened to lose its load of beer, but I was more pissed than hurt. "You bitch," I screamed, and slammed the bottle against the desk for emphasis. Its end shattered, a million tiny emerald blades flying up to cut the air. But I didn't stop there.

No. I had to bring my arm forward to club her with the bottle, in my drunken haze not yet realizing that its lower half had disintegrated around us.

She hardly made a sound after the makeshift emerald knife slipped past that beautiful baby blue eyeball, and lodged in the back of her brain, permanently severing any synaptic intelligence. Something between a squeak and a grunt came from her throat and then, as the blood began to stream down the glass in rhythm with the shocked final pounding of her heart, her entire body spasmed, her knees buckled and she fell to the floor. She twitched a few times, and there was a low moaning gurgle. Then she was still.

All I'd wanted was a few minutes in the sack. Now she was a sack. A dead bag of human lust, ripe to disintegrate into a life sentence of vengeance.

I stared at her, my brain a buzz of alcohol and barbituates. I could almost see her skin shimmer as her spirit took flight, and the warmth promised by her heavy lips faded like the sunset in Hawaii. Quick, silent and beautiful. Live fast, get killed young.

My pants hit the floor without a conscious thought, and I took what I thought was mine. It was difficult to maintain my concentration as that bottle waved back and forth from the ruptured hole that once was her beautiful blue eye, blood leaking out in time with my motions against her body. I plunged the life out of her, and I got what she came for, though without any fireworks to mark the momentous nature of the event. There should have been something more than that, I thought, as I wiped myself off and wondered if that was the last fuck I'd ever have with a woman. Tomorrow, I thought, as I staggered to the bed, I'd be arrested.

But I wasn't.

Jack found me in the morning, huddled by the body, sobbing more in fear of consequence than for the loss of the groupie's life. I'd always been a self-centered bastard. Came with the territory of lead singer, and if it got bad the more famous we got, it got worse when we slipped back into obscurity. Looking back, I have to admit that maybe that was the cause of our ultimate decline.

We wrapped her in a sheet, stuffed her in a canvas keyboard case, and simply walked out of the hotel with her. After driving a couple hours out of the city, we pulled over, Nick and I, and took the body into a deserted stretch of prairie land. We dug a hole in the middle of a grassy field and buried her in the case, figuring that its enclosure would keep the body from stinking up the field and drawing animals. Nick looked at me a couple times as I tore at the earth with a new Ace Hardware spade bought just for Amy, but never said a word.

After she was six feet under, we got back in the car and headed back the way we'd come, three hours now behind the band and the bus, but plenty of time to make our gig that night in Des Moines. We never spoke of it again.

And I never drank Rolling Rock again.

So it made a cruel bit of sense that I was lost somewhere, in the middle of a field, being bitten by the teeth of a green bottle. I wiped more of the wet blood off my hand and onto my thigh, and gingerly put my toes back to the ground, limping forward slowly, and peering more intently at the ground between the dead shoots of grass.

It was well that I did…just a couple feet away, I narrowly missed planting my heel on another broken green bottle. And then just beyond that, I saw another just in time. I could feel a warm slick of blood cover my heel, leaving a trail on the ground as I navigated a crooked path between the bottles, expecting the maze of glass to diminish once the remains of the frat boy or high school delinquent party was behind, but instead, the teeth of glass only grew more frequent. My eyes now fixated soley on the ground, as I played a cruel game of twister to avoid a growing mash of jagged, angry glass.

The ground became easier and easier to see, and then it occurred to me that the grass had completely stopped its incessant slicing and itching against my bare thighs, and I looked up to see before me, not a field, but a sea of liquid green.

Glass.

As far as I could see, the ground overflowed with bottles, white labels jeering at me like vampiric teeth, begging me to walk this way. And they weren't just lying about on the ground. They were stacked on each other, deep and dangerous as the eye could see. The bones of my sin. A narrow dirt path continued from the edge of the field through the maze of broken bottles.

I stood still, looking around me for the first time in an hour, and taking in the change in scenery. Ahead of me, the ground glittered in the waiting fangs of Rolling Rock; behind me stemmed suffocating sheaves of death. To my right, the meeting line of death and murder, weaved an uneven, but mostly barren path through the glass.

I walked on.

It was surreal, I thought. The stillness. It seemed as if I hadn't heard a noise in hours. Not even a whisper of breeze across the endless expanses of grass and glass. I tried to remember how I'd come to be here, but nothing came. The past few days were a foggy blur of rowdy concerts at falling down dive bars and late night after show parties. I shook my head to clear the cobwebs, but there was no clarity. And oddly, no hangover.

The trail led crookedly up one hill and down the next. At each peak I prayed to find a new scene on the other side—a valley. A river. Something. But every hill seemed to lead into another vista filled with broken green glass. And the thin dirt path through the center. My foot throbbed, and I didn't dare to look at how much mud I'd ground into the wound. There'd be time for disinfectant later. Now, I just needed to find water. And food. My stomach strangled in pain, and my legs felt heavier with every step. Everything seemed to have taken on the sickening emerald green sheen of Rolling Rock. The glass stretched to the horizon, and even the stagnant blue of the sky seemed to be leaching its color.

Alex is going to be pissed, I thought, imagining our tour manager going from hotel room to hotel room and asking the guys where I was. Unless he was in on it. Maybe the bunch of them had drugged me and dropped me here. And the path was my only way out…I'd *kill* them.

A flash of Amy's face at that thought, green dagger twisting out of her ruined eyeball, mouth hanging open in shock at my betrayal, blood coating the purity of that soft face…

I shook my head and staggered on, determined not to think of her. I had managed to almost forget about that night, at times. A steady diet of alcohol helped. Still, her ghost whispered in my lyrics and what could I do about that? She haunted my soul and always would. I couldn't deny my damnation, so I celebrated it, flaunted it in song. And the hits kept coming…for awhile.

Another hill and I weaved up its face, careful not to step off the steep path and gouge another wound in my aching feet. My body felt light, almost ethereal. I'd stopped sweating. I was walking on air. I was probably about to collapse, I thought.

And then I reached the top. I looked out over the next valley, and gasped.

In the distance, I could see a town. Or, more specifically, the entry to a street lined with buildings. I let out a cheer, but nothing broke the stillness of the landscape. I was so dry and worn that I couldn't utter a sound. I staggered down the path towards this oasis, almost falling down the far side of the hill before staggering to an abrupt stop.

The path was interrupted.

It simply stopped at the bottom of the hill, and picked up again at the beginning of the next, where it led to the street above.

In between were thousands of broken bottles, stacked one on top of the other, all of them leering at me, jagged ends pointing toward the sky.

All of them green. Without a trace of earth to be seen.

I fell to the ground, but no tears came. I was too dehydrated to cry.

After awhile, I stood again, and stared out across the deadly sea of glass. It was only 15 or 20 yards to the other side, but it looked like a mile. How could I cross it? I had no clothes to bind my feet in, and nothing around for miles that I could use to create steppingstones through the abyss. I couldn't go back; I wasn't sure I had the strength left to climb the hill ahead to the town, let alone walk for hours back to the middle-of-nowhere place I'd awoken, only to begin a trek in the other direction that could prove equally as endless.

I had only two choices: Step gingerly across the glass, letting each blade sink slowly into my feet as I crossed. Or take a running start and hurl myself across the glass, with each step gouging rougher, deeper wounds. But I would probably have to take fewer steps that way.

My shoulders shook in empty cries with the horror of my choices. If I lost my balance from the pain, my entire body would be slashed and I might not be able to get back up. If I ran, the worst pain would be over sooner, but my feet might be shredded beyond repair. If I didn't run, they still might be ruined, unless I could find a path across stepping only on the most shallow of pieces.

I forced myself to stop thinking about it and walked back the way I had come. I wouldn't think about it. I wouldn't imagine the blood blossoming from my feet, the green knives hungrily puncturing my skin, skewering my entire foot until the razor tips peeked through the other side, drenched in shavings of bone and awash in my blood. I wouldn't…

I turned and ran full force at the glass, stretching my legs to long strides, leaping at the very edge of the boundary between grey baked earth and broken blades of deadly glass.

The pain exploded through my right foot, and then the white-hot stabbing took my left. I screamed, opening my mouth in a cry to heaven that echoed like an explosion in my brain, but made no sound. The world remained strangely silent, and I was a hurtling body of unheard pain. I couldn't look down, but forced myself to lift and stomp my right foot again, my knees threatening to buckle beneath me in fear rather than move again. I could feel the glass slicing easily through the soft soles of my feet, first as a warm burst of slippery heat, then as an excruciating stab. It was worst when I lifted my foot off the blade, feeling the jagged glass slip out, leaving a screaming vacuum in its wake that vomited blood and torn flesh.

The first steps were bad, but with the fourth and fifth time, my feet came down on knives that chewed and tore the skin and muscle relentlessly. I was in agony. My mouth opened in a silent, ghastly scream that I couldn't stop and I thrust my arms forward, yearning for the other side.

I closed my eyes in pain and forced myself to lift my left foot again, and felt a shard of glass snap, leaving a piece of itself lodged in the ball of my foot. When I set my foot down, glass ground against glass against bone and I choked in horror. The pain shot up and down my calves, and I stumbled at last, falling to impale my thigh and left hand on broken bottles. Darts of fire pained every inch of the left side of my body.

"Why?" I cried as the green glass slipped out through the back of my hand, and the pain swam wetly through my belly like a shark's bite. Something hot spread across my ribs and side, and I could feel more teeth sinking into my thigh and calf, but I didn't look down.

I stared at my hand; the green glass looked surreal married to the sickly pale caste of my skin. Strange how there was no blood. No blood at all. I was a sculpture of flesh and bone and glass. A twisted crucifixion of man and bottle. I swam above the pain for a moment, marveling.

And then the blood came, seeping out along the jagged edge of glass like the ocean through sand at high tide. It pooled in my hand, rising up slowly to drip over my palm and down the edge of a green knife. As I watched it drool down the broken bottle out of sight, a glint of something that wasn't glass caught my eye from below. I pushed the bottle to the side and gingerly reached down to pry it up. It felt hard and rounded between my fingers, dry as a chalky stick. I pulled and bottles shifted to set it free. Part of it rose above the surface of the glass but it did not break free; some bit was still connected to something below the bottles.

Stretched out from the deadly green sea was a skeletal hand. A silver dragon ring hung loosely on its fourth finger, matching the jewelry on my own. We were mirror images of life and death shaking hands between two realms. Was this, then, where I was to end?

The pain came back full force, and I dropped the bones. Burning fire singed my hand and arm and leg and feet and I looked ahead of me, gauging the distance to the last of the broken bottles. Just a few more steps. I had to get up and move now, and I had to sacrifice my feet to get there or I would sacrifice myself.

I levered myself upright, ignoring the new shards that carved whatever flesh was left on my feet, and put one foot down on a broken bottle. It shifted beneath me, slipping away from my step as another rolled up from beneath it to stab me again. And so it went.

When I collapsed to the ground on the far side of the sea of bottles, my body was shaking in shock, and covered with gaping, ugly wounds. I gasped for breath that wouldn't come and wiped my bloody hand across the hair of my chest to clean it enough to see the size of the puncture through my palm. The center of my hand manifested the stigmata. My lifeline had been gouged into two raw lips an inch long that gleamed with the acid spit of blood. Already it had swollen to twice its normal size, but I could still move my fingers, so nothing crucial had been severed. It might heal.

My feet were another story. There was no skin that I could see left on the bottoms; several stab wounds had pierced through the flesh and bone to come out the other side. They looked like raw meat. I could see the white of bone when the blood flowed right.

I could not stand. Leaning on my right side, I began to crawl up the hill towards the city street so far above. I tried to call for help, but no sound came. I was mute, and the world leered back, unspeaking.

The temptation to lie still grew overpowering but I kept moving. If I stopped, I'd never move again. I looked back, and saw the evidence of my passage. A bony arm, grasping for purchase from the depths of the white-flecked green sea. The bottles glittered red across the center of the glass river, and the dirt nearby was streaked with damp spots and crimson pools where I'd rested briefly. How much more blood could I lose? I wondered.

How long I climbed, I couldn't say. Every inch was a struggle, every yard left a piece of me behind. But finally, beneath the unheeding cloudless blue of the sky, I reached the top of the hill. I took in a deep breath, willing the fire of my body to cool, and stared down a street I knew so well.

Hartford Street. Newfordville.

My home town.

The band had started out here, a bunch of cocky high school kids we were, with bad hair, acne and a thirst for coke and vodka. And an all-encompassing love of music. Jack and Chuck played bass and drums in the marching band, and I played keys and fancied myself a poet. We found Randy through Chuck's older brother. He was a dropout, working the stock room at the supermarket every night and jamming away on his guitar to Led Zeppelin CDs during the day.

There, a few doors down, was the Guitar Shack we'd spent hours at, drooling over the latest amps and effects pedals. There was The Hole, a narrow bar with a stage about the size of a dining room table. We'd played there every month for a year before packing everything into Randy's van and doing our first "regional tour" which basically meant playing a hundred dives just like The Hole for little more to show for it than gas money to get to the next place. We had slept in the van and lived on McDonald's.

Nobody was out on the street, though it was the middle of the afternoon, and I began to inchworm my way down the cement sidewalk, heading towards The Hole. Nick ought to have the place opened by now, and he'd get me some help fast. And a drink.

I pulled myself up to kneel at his door, and turned the knob. It fell open.

The floor was clean from last night's excesses, but the chairs were all still upside down on the bar's tiny round tables.

"Nick," I called out, but my voice was still gone.

"Fuck it," I said to myself, and dragged my body inside, heading behind the bar. I needed water and I needed it *now*.
The sink was just below the top of the long wood bar, and I pulled myself up to it with my good hand, cranking the cold faucet to high. A stream sluiced out, and I plunged my face in, sucking the water into my throat with greedy gulps. When I couldn't drink anymore, I put my wounded hand in the spray, leaving it there until the flow turned back from pink to clear. Steeling my nerves, I put both hands on the bar and pulled myself up until I could drag my feet into the sink. Leaning

across the bar I let the water wash away the blood and dirt and flecks of glass. I could still feel the long shard lodged in my left foot like a fiery brand.

When cold water had sucked almost all the feeling from my feet, I let myself down to the floor, pulled a bottle of whiskey from the "well drinks" shelf, and took a heavy swig. Then I went to work on my left foot, searching in the ragged flesh with my fingers for the glass. I forced my breathing to remain shallow, found its edge, and pushed my fingers up into the raw meat of my sole to flank the glass. Grasping it tight, I pulled, and screamed silently as it came out, a blinding wave of pain and blood following in its wake. I poured the rest of the whiskey over my feet, crying in vain at the burning pain that threatened to stop my heart. Certainly it stopped my breath.

I don't know how long I laid there. When I finally crawled back outside, the light was fading. Still, nobody was around. My stomach was cramping and my kidneys felt swollen. My entire body throbbed with pain. I crawled my way up the street, marking the pavement with dull streaks of red. I stopped at Karol's Kitchen, praying that someone would be there, that someone would give me a french fry, a crust of bread, something. I was desperate.

There was nobody inside the restaurant. But I could smell food. My stomach lurched at the scent of scorched hamburger, and on a table near the door I saw its source. Steam rose from a plate of fries and a burger glistening with grease. I clawed my way into the chair and stuffed half the burger into my mouth. The taste was overpowering. I grew lightheaded with the ecstasy of food, and gorged myself without stopping for breath. Every fry, every bit of bun, every drop of grease I licked from the plate, until my belly felt like it would burst. For those few moments, the hideous pain in my body subsided, and I was in heaven.

But then it all came rushing back.

I pulled napkins off the table and bound the wreckage of my

feet in white linen that quickly bloomed pink. Using the back of a chair as a crutch, I stood, and then moved the chair ahead of me like a walker. Slowly, painfully, I made my way down the street.

Inside the Guitar Shack, the real horror of my situation finally hit me.

I picked up a Stratocaster knock-off, clumsily held the neck and, ignoring the pain, pressed down three strings with my injured hand and strummed.

There was no familiar twang of an E chord, the beginning of almost any classic rocker.

I couldn't hear a thing. I hadn't heard a thing all day.

I'd been so preoccupied by the pain, that I'd ignored the silence of the world, even when I couldn't hear my own screams. Part of me had thought I'd just lost my voice. I'd seen no one, so there was no reason I should have heard any sound.

Angrily I brought my hand across the strings again and again, banging out the riffs to "Can't You See Her," my biggest hit with Serenading Sonia, and then "Rock and Roll" from Zeppelin. Then the bass riff to "Smoke on the Water."

Nothing.

I was trapped in a wall of silence with pain as my only friend.

I opened my mouth and screamed again and again, straining to hear the slightest squeak of sound until I could feel my throat closing raw and angry.

There was nothing for me to hear.

I left the store with the guitar anyway, abandoning the chair and using the guitar as a walking cane. I staggered down my old street, the last place in my life where everything had felt right. There was promise when I lived here. It had all started here, on this street. Fitting that it should end here, after all the wrong roads I'd travelled.

This was my hell, I realized. To be here, alone, stripped of my clothes, of my voice, of my music. To face all the places I'd betrayed. And to walk the path of my unrepented murder. That blackest night of my life had been my final chance at redemption, I realized. To face what I had become and turn back. Instead, I had only fallen farther, drowning the spark. Killing the only thing I had ever really loved.

As I slowly passed the old hair salon, and the VFW hall, I began to see a glow at the top of the hill. The light was fading behind me, but ahead the sky oozed a sickly green. I pulled myself up the last sidewalk square to the top of the hill and looked out. Behind me, the comfortable street I'd come from so many years ago slid into twilight. Ahead of me, a sea of green glass awaited. Just before the glass began, the last outpost before oblivion, stood a hotel.

The hotel. I would never forget the fake stucco pink walls and black wrought iron balconies.

I didn't hesitate. Wrapping my fingers tighter in the tuning pins of my guitar, I lurched inside, and walked to the elevator. I knew without trying that there was only one button that would work. Still, I pressed floors 2 and 3. They did not light up. When I hit the button for the 4th floor, the door closed, and the elevator lurched upwards, lights flickering. Just the way they had when we'd lugged Amy's body down in it, sweating over the idea that those creaks and flickering lights might mean the elevator would stall before we got to ground, and when we were finally rescued the police would check our bags, or see a spot of blood that had somehow leaked through the sheet to make its way through the keyboard case.

It didn't stall then, and it didn't stall now. When I stepped off the elevator into the empty corridor, the door to Room 414 was open.

I hesitated at the threshold, remembering the last time I'd stood here. Setting down the body concealed in the black canvas bag to take one last look inside before closing the door. Making sure there was no evidence of the night before.

There was plenty of evidence now.

Inside, the carpet was covered with blackened pools of blood.

In the bathroom, Angela, a groupie I'd drugged, boned and left behind in a nameless hotel room in Iowa was kneeling on the tile, head resting on the toilet seat. Her eyes were closed, and a spew of dried vomit caked the edges of the bowl.

Lying on the floor behind her, half in the tub, head on the floor, was Rochelle. I would never forget the hair, which was fanned across the tile, hiding her eyes. "Electric blue to match my panties," she had laughed. I had gotten Rochelle high enough to blow all the guys in the crew before telling her that I didn't want their leftovers. I was too drunk to fuck by then anyway. The dye of her blue hair had run and dried in swirling pools across the white tile of the floor with the flow of her tears. She looked stiff.

There would be no rest for me here tonight.

The bed had my choice of brunettes, blondes and redheads. Seven women in all, in varying degrees of decay. Ragged slices ripped across their abdomens; blood had spilled from each of their naked bellies to stain the bed and pool on the floor below. Flies rose in a cloud as I stepped closer, recognizing Melinda, purple-painted toenails hanging over the bed's edge. She had painted those a new color almost every day.

Something jutted out from the black and green sludge oozing from the tear in her stomach and as I peered closer, I made out the tiny pale skeleton of a hand. It looked like a doll was reaching out to free itself from inside her. She'd been pregnant when she'd been slaughtered. The baby must have smothered in her blood trying to claw its way free. A dessicated veil of skin hung from its forearm, translucent as snakeskin. I grimaced and pulled away, but not before recognizing Cassie and Barb and Gin. They were all women I'd taken for rides on the Serenading Sonia tour bus. Some for a month, some for more.

I'd left them all about the time they said they were going to have my baby. I'd bought the abortions and left them strung out in some hotel room somewhere, without a word of goodbye. I wasn't ready to be a father. When they woke up, the bus was gone.

"I didn't do *this* to you," I complained. "I was an asshole, but…"

On the other side of the bed on the floor, the girls were stacked five high, and four rows deep. All were naked. All were rotting, viscous sludge oozing down from one blue-white breast to another purpled thigh to stain the carpet in bright rainbow colors of death. I couldn't recognize most of them. But I knew I had used and thrown them all away; none had ever been enough. None filled that place in my soul that only the scream of an electric guitar had ever touched. I could never bring myself to care enough.

There was a broken bottle of Rolling Rock on the desk.

I stepped to the small balcony, where the curtains waved in a silent breeze, and took a deep breath. Then I pulled the plastic drawstring pole.

Amy was waiting, just as I knew she would be.

A green icicle in her eye. Blood drenched her tight white shirt. She would win the goth version of a wet t-shirt contest for sure. Her nipples protruded through the bloody cotton, as she lounged against the outer rail.

"I didn't kill them," I complained silently again.

"No," she said, pushing off from the rail to step towards me. She was alive! And I could hear her!

"You didn't kill them. These are just the marks you left on their souls."

She stood in front of me, boring deep into my heart with her one good eye.

"I'm sorry," I said.

"That's the first step," she said, "but not the most painful one."

And then she vanished.

I sat down on the bloodied floor and looked at the girls surrounding me. The castoffs of a life spent running from myself.

They had all led up to Amy. I'd tried to forget their faces, moving from one warm drunken kiss to the next, never looking behind their eyes, never seeing what they were after, or what dreams I crushed in my wake.

I curled up on the floor with my pain and dreamed of Amy, alive again. Of Amy saying yes. Of Amy as my wife.

In those last moments before fully waking, I held the image in my mind of her in my house, casual in jeans and a black t-shirt, wearing my dragon ring. It made me wonder. Had I really killed the woman who would have been my wife, my salvation? Had I killed my only chance for redemption?

When I opened my eyes, there was grass all around me. My feet were healed, my hand whole. Had it all been a dream? A prescient vision?

I walked naked, randomly choosing a direction, just as I had the day before. I walked for hours, until I stabbed my foot on a broken bottle of Rolling Rock.

Driven by hunger and thirst, again I bled in agony on the river of broken glass and found brief solace in a heavenly hamburger. I smiled in bitter understanding, as I gorged myself on the meat. Only through a respite in pleasure can one really appreciate the depth of pain.

Once again the dead girls awaited me in the hotel, faces purple with accusation. But this time Amy wasn't there.

I didn't stay in the room, but instead tried all of the other doors in the hotel. None would open. At last, I slept on a chair in the lobby.

And woke in a field of dead grass.

I've gotten used to the glass. And I've thought about the last words Amy spoke to me. The only thing I've heard in the days I've repeated this vicious, bloody cycle. I could walk this same hellish road every day, forever. Being sorry is only the first step, not the most painful one, she said.

Pain is transitory, and while each day, the fresh slice of glass on my heels is beyond description, and the visceral guilt of what I did to all of those women a choking burden, I've discovered that there is an inner pain that is much worse.

Every night I stop at Guitar Shack and strum the silent strings of a Fender or an Ovation, hoping against hope that the music will be there. Music was the only thing I ever loved in life, though I betrayed it as I betrayed myself and countless others.

I strum and pound on the guitar until my hands bleed and my face is wet with yearning.

The music never comes.

Hell is the green, green glass of bone.

Hell sings silent of my sin.

The Devil's Platoon

The devil was on our side.

I wish now that it had not been the case, or that what I just said was only a figurative expression.

But in the darkest shadows of winter, in the coldest desperation of the Black Forest, we called upon the forces of evil to save our cause. And in the calling, we forfeited our fatherland, as well as our immortal souls.

The year was 1945. It was a new year, but to us, it felt old as bare bones. We had been on the frontline for months, each day falling farther and farther back, it seemed. As the winter moved in and blanketed the deep, narrow valleys of the Black Forest in wraith mists and desperation, we ran shorter on fuel, and our spirits thirsted for hope that flowed ever thinner. Some men swore they heard the seductive call of the legendary Lorelei and ran off after the siren into the swirl of the cold earthbound clouds. Generally, a spat of machine gun fire moments later told us of the outcome of such delusions. The magic of the deepest reaches of this place were legendary, but they did not help us. The rest of us held on, as best we could.

Der Fuhrer had a plan, we all knew it. We trusted his genius as much as we trusted our mothers. What the plan was, we were not sure, but the word among the men was that it had been delivered in a sealed envelope to the front weeks before, and all units had subsequently shifted their positions. From the view on the ground, nothing much had changed. We were no longer moving forward, but slipping back. Himmler was behind us, and the Allies in front. As we held our line near the borders of the Black Forest, the River Rhine provided the divider of both comfort and fear; if we had to guard our lines so hard here…here where it had all begun…what had become of the Reich? We sensed that the winds had shifted forever, and Germany would never rule the world. But we would not speak of such things aloud. Nor would we admit that we feared we would soon no longer rule even Germany. Nobody could mouth the thought that in trying to conquer Europe, we would lose our fatherland.

The war for Germany had changed from a victory march to a protective retreat. And then our own ragged company was pressed against our own private wall of desperation.

"Enemy at 4 o'clock!" Schmitt yelled, and we dove for cover. Not fast enough. Around my head the shells sang like dinosaur hornets, loud as thunder yet small as November hail. A scream sprayed the air in blood and I dropped to my chest, gun at the ready and instantly moving along the dusk of the horizon, searching for a target. I couldn't even look back to see who had been hit. There was no time. This was the most dangerous hour; trapped and pinned without any knowledge of where the attacker was holed up. Any move could open you to death; any inaction could leave your back exposed to a bullet. I pivoted on my belly like a cannon, looking for airborne death.

Fire exploded in tiny flashes from the woods all around, and it only took me seconds to realize we were surrounded. With every staccato bang-bang-bang-bang fire of a machine gun blast I heard another comrade scream bloody horrible death into the funeral of the day.

We were dropping with the lead and somewhere, Colonel Cullen bellowed for the company to fall back. Peter and Fritz clapped my thighs and began to shimmy backwards in the fallen dust of leaves. I pushed back with my hands and tried to follow, never taking my eyes off the shadows of the woods ahead. Pops and flashes still cascaded from the darkness there, and soon, as the brush began to obscure my view, I caught glimpses of the enemy slipping in and out of the trees like pale green ghosts.

Between my shaking fingers and the stalking ghosts, lay the bloody bodies, Becker and Dannenberg and Klein. Lange gasped and coughed just yards from my grasp, his breath a scarlet mist in the air as he convulsed and shook on the ground, blood spreading around him as if he was but a soda bottle, shattered and broken.

Whispers from behind me, and barks of direction ahead. I scrabbled backwards through the forest, slipping into the shadows and hopefully following close behind my comrades. They had hit us from three out of four sides; it wouldn't be hard to discover where the remaining soldiers had vanished. When the tap came on my shoulder and it was safe (somewhat) to rise, I stopped scooting like a landbound crab and turned to run, a kraut whisper of vengeance and fear into the blackness of the Black Forest.

There were seven dead (or left for) from our small company, and six remaining. The winter had not been kind to our number. We crouched around a tiny campfire and prayed that the light wouldn't give us away. But the weather gripped us with icy hatred, and we could not survive a night without heat.

We pulled our jackets and blankets close and huddled around the tiny fire until we all coughed from the closeness of the smoke and the foul breath of Kretz, who perhaps had not brushed his teeth since grammar school.

It was Dietz who broke the spell.

"You pussies want to run, or you want to win?" he asked.

The moon shone overhead, and Dietz's face glowed a strange mix of moon-sewn blue and fire-glow orange.

"Win," I remember croaking. From somewhere in the distance, I heard the echo of more gunfire.

"Are you sure?" he asked. Dietz was the ultimate stereotype of a German: shock-white hair, wide glacier eyes, and a granite chin that said, *Don't even think of defying me.*

I met his gaze and nodded. Around me, I felt the other five do the same. We had been cut in half over the past month, and then today, cut in half again. We were tired and cold, hungry and fearful that the end was just a day or an hour away. We bled from a hundred cuts and could have laid down to sleep without waking for 40 hours. We were spent. When the next faraway gunshot hit like a firecracker, three of our number dove for the ground without a thought. We were beaten and broken.

And worst of all, afraid.

Once, we had fought fearsome and fearlessly for the honor and glory of the fatherland. Now, every night Kretz lay awake in his sleeping bag, holding the photo of his girl above his eyes as his cries echoed throughout the camp without restraint. Nobody dared say anything. We may not all have cried openly, but we were all dying inside.

The war was lost, we felt it, but we were still on the front, left to kill or be killed. We kept our ammunition ready and prayed that the sour, ancient ghosts of the forest wouldn't steal our lives before the enemy. Spirits were still more frightful than bullets.

At times I felt completely alone among our company; I had no family to return to, no girl crying in her pillow with my name salty wet on her lips. If I died here in the mud and ice, nobody would really care.

Still…I didn't relish the idea of dying, for der Fuhrer, or anyone else. I believed in the Fatherland, but I didn't honestly want to die for it. I think that set me apart from the others as well; they seemed to talk of Germany with a prayer of worship on their lips. Maybe their family and friends and *fraulines* made the land more solid in their hearts. In mine, it was just where I had lived. Where I had lived but never found happiness.

I fingered the symbol of the Third Reich on my breast and nodded at Dietz. He grinned, a wide, white flash of bone.

"I know of a way," he repeated. His eyes glowed in the dark shadow of the Black Forest. Perhaps it was just the reflection of the fire.

Or perhaps it was really something more. Something preternaturally evil. I'll never know. But we stood there, encamped at the edge of an ancient place. A place that housed the Lorelei, and ghosts of legend that harbored no pleasant dreams for mortal men. The Black Forest sheltered dark things that most men had never seen, and never hoped to see.

When Dietz began to whisper there, above the fire, and beneath the moon, we all leaned in to listen.

I never wanted to have anything to do with killing a child. When we marched into the tiny village of Kunstler, it was the farthest thing from my mind. Actually, the only thing close to my mind at this point was sleep. We'd talked most of the night about Dietz's plan, and argued about the potential for its failure or success. I was skeptical, never having had a great faith in god or man. Or devil. But Schuster seemed completely sold. I saw him whispering in Dietz's ear as we trudged through the dawn of the forest, searching for a place to safely rest. And Lichtmann, all wan and thin and fragile-looking; his eyes had sparked at the description of the ritual. In the end, we were hungry, and scared and lost in every possible soul-searing way. We would have grasped at anything to leave our patrol on the ragged border of the Black Forest. Every moment we blinked betrayed a glint of light to the enemy and opened us to death. Sometimes, death was preferable to the fear of its finality. With such a dark weight on our shoulders, and hopelessness in our hearts, we'd agreed to give Dietz's magic a go. We broke camp and marched as silently as we could through the forest, feet crunching like relentless vengeance through the snow.

Angels of death on the road to war were we.

The destination, turned out to be Kunstler.

Winter dawned for the hundredth time over a rime of crusty

snow beneath frozen feet. And with crunching and cracking and gasping and moaning, we pushed through. Lichtmann's breath came like the reports of battle through clenched lips, and Schuster murmured something with almost every step. I relied on numbers to get me through. With every step I counted, focusing not on the cold or the murder that trailed behind our necks, ready to blast at any moment. I focused on 39 and 40 and 41. And 52 and 54. And 88. When I reached 100, I put hands to my knees, drew a clean cold breath, and with a knife of air in my lungs, began the count from 1 again.

So we passed the morning. Me counting, Lichtmann gasping.

Dietz found the clearing of Kunstler long before we saw it.

"Do you smell that?" he asked.

Five noses sniffed loudly in the air. A pack of dogs.

"Bacon!" Kretz whispered.

We took off on a jog towards the smell.

Kunstler was a town without a population.

The Black Forest slipped away beneath our feet from a crust of snow to a dirt-path road that led in a wavering snake path to a small circle of three buildings. One of them exhibited a sign of occupation; the white smoke of habitation slid silently from a chimney to the sky and a flame of light beamed from a wood-crossed window. The other buildings looked as cold and dark as the forest we'd just left behind. Apparently you could number the denizens of Kunstler on one hand. We knew where to run.

I will hear the voice of the woman in my head until the day that I die.

"Guten Tag," she beamed, obviously relieved to see countrymen as she answered our knocks. "Has the war come to our doorstep?"

"To your very home," Dietz said, and without another word, slammed his gun against her head, knocking her to the floor like a broken pot. Lichtmann gasped. "What the hell are you doing!"

he screamed. Dietz cuffed him and the private fell back like a wounded cur.

"In war there are victims and victories," Dietz declared. "It is time for us to make both."

In the dark of the hopeless night, we had agreed to find a victim; a sacrifice for the Reich. It already seemed oddly remote. The plan a foolish dream of darkness.

But Dietz had not given up.

"She is a countryman," Lictmann cried. "She is who we are here to protect."

"Her name will be etched on the wall of heroes," Dietz said, and kicked the door open, waiving his gun ahead to dissuade any who would resist him. There were no takers.

We filed into the tiny shack in the woods, and just as we were almost all inside, the gunfire began.

"Oh damn!" screamed Peter, and I knew from the pitch of his voice that he'd been hit. He fell hard to the threshold.

Dietz motioned us inside and out of the way, and then reached out to grab Peter's hands. He pulled the youth inside, and we all saw the reason for his cries. Peter's thigh bled like a stuck pig—fountains of crimson were spurting to pool in the wake of his body with every heartbeat.

"Tourniquet!" screamed Schuster and Dietz shook his head. "No shit," he growled, and ripped off his own shirt to tear its tail into ribbons. Someone shut the door, and I helped Dietz hold Peter's leg down so that he could tie off the leg and staunch the bleed of the artery.

The others mumbled and paced nervously behind us.

We had fought together, most of us, for the past 18 months. And over the past 18 days, we had lost twice as many friends as now stood here in this tiny wood shack. We were cold and tired. Most of all, our souls were broken. We wanted the war to be over. We wanted Germany to win. But mostly, we wanted to be back with our families. Or, in my case, just back to our freedom. I wanted to drink a beer in quiet, and read a book without looking over my shoulder for death. I wanted to feel the hearth at my feet and hear the hum of humanity at my back. I didn't want to save them; I wanted to live among them.

Dietz's shirt was a sopping mess of blood, but the flow was more or less staunched. We stood around Peter and wondered: *What next?*

The woman had not stirred from the floor where Dietz had knocked her. Schuster bent to listen to her chest. When he rose, he shook his head. "She's dead," he said.

From outside, another stream of bullets pecked at the wood of the roof and doors. Splinters showered the floor. Dietz propped a gun at Peter's shoulder and commanded him to keep watch. He didn't move him an inch from the spot where we'd dragged him inside.

"Let's go," Dietz said. "Someone else must be here."

We found her upstairs. They were creaky, rickety, do-it-yourself planks of stairs, but they rose from the rough planks of the kitchen up to a small loft above the family room and hearth. Dietz led the way as bullets continued to ping sporadically outside. We ignored the distraction and took the stairs up to the loft with him. At least we were *doing* something for a change.

As I neared the top, something shuffled in the darkness, and Dietz flipped off the stair to crouch on the plank floor.

"Show yourself," he demanded. He held the gun up for emphasis, but did not shoot. That would only alert the enemy to our presence.

We flung ourselves around the ladder to land on the floor beside him, guns at the ready. Again a rustle from the back of the loft. "Put your hands in the air or we will shoot," Dietz screamed.

The hands went up then.

Tiny hands.

Pale and small. Nervously trembling in the dim light. She stepped out of the shadow behind a small, unmade bed.

They were the hands of a child. And the face of an angel. Ice-blue eyes beamed through the murk like Northern Lights. She was scared, but stepped forward.

"You are friends?" she said in a voice smaller than a doll's. "Momma said Der Fuhrer would send soldiers who would protect us."

"We're here to protect everyone," Dietz said. I could hear the lie poisoning the gentleness of his words. I wondered if the girl could. His falseness seemed so blatantly obvious to me.

But she only smiled. "Did you talk to mama?" she asked.

"Yes," Dietz said. "She said for us to come up and keep you safe."

"I heard guns outside," the girl said.

Dietz nodded. "It would be best for you to get into bed and stay there, so we can take care of it," he said.

The little girl picked up the hem of her long, pink nightgown and did just that, slipping under the thin covers to lie down in her bed. As she did so, five German soldiers moved closer to the mattress, knowing but not saying what they knew they had to do.

Dietz's plan called for a sacrifice. An innocent.

"I don't think that we should…" Lichtmann began to say. And then he doubled over with a grunt, as Dietz's rifle butt met the lower portion of Lichtmann's gut.

"This is war," Dietz hissed. "And you'll do what has to be done."

I felt the tears brimming to the surface as I stepped near enough to the bed to touch the child's foot.

"We're here to take care of it," Dietz told the child again. His voice was as chilling as a reptile's hiss. "We're here to save the motherland. To support Der Fuhrer," he said.

"You're good then," she said, in that tiny little voice that only little girls can have.

"We try," he breathed, just before he slipped a hand over the little girl's mouth.

She only struggled for a little while.

In short, sharp commands Dietz told us how to tie her and how to set up the candles and then place the cross upside down above her bed.

When we dedicated her soul as a gift to Satan, we were all near tears.

But nobody shed as many as the little girl, whose glowing eyes threatened to explode from her tiny head with every horrible word that Dietz pronounced.

He never even said, "I'm sorry."

Dietz never said how he knew the words to say, and nobody questioned him. We did as he told us and held the girl down. We dipped our fingers in the blood from her neck and painted our faces with her life. We licked our fingers and professed our allegiance to Satan, if he would only support our cause. And when she screamed that last, awful cry, I swear I felt the cold kiss of the devil brush my lips and neck.

When we descended the ladder, each of us holding a piece of the girl in our hands, I believe we were all shaking. We'd seen plenty of horrors on the front, and far more blood. Yet, this was the worst atrocity.

Certainly the ladder trembled as I descended, rung by rung, until I stood again on the rough plank floor and looked at the broken body of the woman on one side of the door, and the still form of Peter, who had apparently bled to death on the other.

"Peter," I whispered.

Dietz bent to nudge him. "It's ok," he said. "We have the devil on our side now."

Again I felt the chill in the air as he spoke, and I stifled an urge to run. I knew that no matter how far I ran from this spot, it would always be with me. I was now a prisoner of the ultimate sin. Upside down crosses and the murder of a young girl didn't make my heart feel victorious and positive, despite having pledged with the rest of them. I said nothing. I wondered who else felt duped by Dietz.

He didn't show an ounce of fear…or compassion. With hooded eyes and a too-wide grin, he flipped his thatch of jet-black hair towards the door.

"The power is ours," he professed, and stepped outside.

When Dietz stepped outside of the slaughterhouse, he was only followed by two. I think of them now as the Devil's Trinity. They fully bought into his plan, without reservation. They believed.

Dietz had slid his knife across the poor trusting girl's neck, as Kretz plunged a dagger into her heart. And Schuster had taken the direction to split that poor thing from breastbone to pubis. Her poor wool nightgown changed from a protection of purity to a blossom of gore in seconds. We all listened to Dietz then, to get it over with quickly if nothing else, as her cries echoed through the dark attic space. At his direction, we numbly reached inside the steaming cavity of her body—on the devil's behalf—and harvested her heart, her liver, her kidneys. I held one organ, something small in my pocket, now. Its death warmed my breast with guilt.

Somewhere I could hear laughter in the back of my head that would not stop.

Bullets rang again outside.

But moments after Dietz, Schuster and Kretz stepped out of the slaughterhouse and into the fire—the fire stopped. In the silence, Private Lichtmann and I slipped out of the door of the house and dove for the ground to evade bullets. But none came. Instead, standing in the center of the dirt path in front of the old house, Dietz held his hands to the sky and called out something in a foreign tongue. Maybe Latin. Next to him, Schuster and Kretz stood at the ready. But there was no need. Somewhere in the brush gunfire erupted again, but this time the enemy was not the threat but the victim.

An American exploded from the bushes and ran toward Dietz, but not to attack. "Please, no!" the soldier screamed, his face a rictus of terror, before a machine gun erupted again and the soldier's back suddenly exploded before us into a confetti of red rain.

When he collapsed, another soldier emerged from the bushes, with a muzzle still trained on the fallen man. Lichtmann and I grabbed for our guns but a motion from Dietz stilled us. Our comrade returned his hands to the air and whispered something guttural and dark. The American responded with a gale of laughter, just before he raised the automatic weapon to point back at his own face, and pulled the trigger. His face sprayed the trees with gore.

"What the hell?" Lichtmann gasped, when the echoes subsided.

Dietz put his hands down from the sky finally and grinned at us. "You can get up now," he said. The derision bled from his lips like vinegar. "I told you, the devil is on our side."

Dietz wasn't lying.

Over the next several hours, we worked our way back through the forest, back to the place where our full-scale retreat had begun. All around us, gunfire erupted, seemingly at random. We all flinched and dove to the ground the first few times the deadly noise broke the silence. All of us but Dietz. With every sound of war he only smiled and raised his hands in the air, as if advertising himself as a target. But the bullets never came close. Or if they did, they didn't touch him. Instead, screams followed our march. Sometimes I saw the enemy, from yards and yards away, chasing each other through the brush. Brother stabbing brother. Friend killing friend.

They all wore American green. There were no Germans attacking the Americans. They were eliminating themselves, inexplicably.

They killed each other violently, without remorse. Whenever we were in range, the enemy turned instead on themselves. A strange, but effective curse Dietz had wrought. The enemy became our weapons.

We camped for the night in the same field where, just the day before, half our company had died, mowed down by merciless shrapnel and vindictive lead. But we returned as if guarded by an invisible shield.

Before we turned in, Dietz called for us to place hands on each other's fists near a small campfire—a sign of brotherhood and allegiance. "Tomorrow," he promised. "Tomorrow we will take back what is ours."

I slid into the musty cold fabric of my sleeping bag and despite the evidence of the past hours, I doubted. I had seen strange events today, there was no question. But the visions of men gunning down their brothers failed to sway my heart from a new singular obsession. Every American soldier's death replayed itself in my mind as I lay in the dark on the cold, hard ground. In my mind I saw them running through the Black Forest, desperate for victory. Desperate for life. They found neither as their own countrymen gunned them down. At the climax of every murder, I saw neither victim nor executioner. Instead, I saw the innocent face of a young German girl, pinned for sacrifice by five desperate German soldiers. I saw fragile, wide blue eyes.

I saw my damnation.

I rolled and kicked on the ground for hours before sleep finally took me. Nearby, I heard the telltale snores of Dietz and Schuster. It was a miracle they hadn't gotten us killed by now simply because of their nasal passages. But tonight, those sounds ultimately lulled me to sleep. At least for awhile.

Until she came.

For awhile, as my conscience taunted me, there was blackness, and a cool breeze. The empty air felt pregnant with abandoned hope. And then a hand touched my shoulder. And then my cheek.

I opened my eyes and rolled fast to the side, reaching for my gun. From the corner of my eye, I saw a flash of pink flesh. And the round curve of a rosy cheek. Then she was there, right in front of me, frowning as if about to cry.

"I don't want to stay here," she whispered, as a tear did finally begin to trail down that perfect face. "Please let me go."

I stopped feeling around in the bag for my gun and instead asked "Stay where? How can I let you go?"

"It's dark," she whispered. "And he keeps hurting me."

"Who?" I asked. "Who is hurting you?"

"I want momma!" she cried, and then someone was punching me in the shoulder. I looked over and Kretz was there, a scowl on his face. "The devil may be on our side, but you don't have to invite the enemy to test it," he hissed. "Shut the hell up."

"Was I snoring?" I asked.

"No, you idiot, you were talking in your sleep. Keep it down."

After he left, all I could see in the dark was the afterimage of the sad eyes of the sacrificial girl's face.

The next day, we broke camp and headed out of the dark embrace of the Black Forest. We followed Dietz, whose gestures alone seemed to bring the enemy to a strange and divisive end. Again and again the soldiers on the line turned on each other as we stalked by, shooting their comrades instead of ever training a gun on us, their true enemy.

I wondered if the situation was only an ironic metaphor for our own plight. In my heart of hearts, I suspected the devil would not be content with the soul of a sad little girl for long.

Gunfire mixed with screams and the smoke of the front lines floated heavy with the iron reek of blood as we stole through clouds to kill and kill again, never once lifting our own guns.

At midday, Dietz signaled a break to our march, and we camped near the cool fishy musk of the Rhine. As I chewed the rations from my pack, I tasted sawdust, and heard the continued cries of dying men in the distance. Near a small green-barked tree, the face of the murdered girl slipped from nowhere to here. I had found no Lorelei in the Black Forest, but I had gained a haunt.

"Let me go?" she implored. She shimmered in the air just a

couple feet away. I could see her clearly, yet, I could still see the forest beyond.

I closed my eyes and let my head slump, wishing her guilt away from my heart. When I looked up, the girl was gone, but the guilt still hung heavy as a boat anchor from my soul.

"What are we doing?" I asked Dietz. He looked at me in complete incomprehension.

"There are five of us," I said. "We can march around the Black Forest and up and down the River Rhine all we want. And maybe every soldier we see will shoot their comrades and the air for miles will be thick with the smell and flicker of meat flies. But we *cannot* turn the tide of a war waged by thousands and thousands of men in theatres from here to Japan. What are we doing?" I repeated.

Dietz's lips raised in a quiet sneer. "Do you think this is about killing a man at a time?" he whispered. "Do you think we are doling out drops of death?"

He laughed, and slapped me on the shoulder. "The devil is on our side now. We cannot be defeated. And these drops of death that we sprinkle will soon grow to a tide and then a tidal wave. Our march has only begun…and when it is ended, the blood of Americans and English and Russians will coat every trail, every street we pass in red rivers. The power of demons has just begun to grow and manifest through us. In days, we will be more deadly than any company you have ever known. Our rage will loosen the guts of the enemy like cannon fire in a stadium of civilians. Believe," he said. "Believe in the power of the devil."

I wanted to ask him about the girl, but something told me to let it be. The glow in his eyes said any answer I received would not be helpful.

We camped that night in a perverse calm in the eye of a bloodbath. During the last hour of sunset, squadrons of the enemy had charged our position, but we only sat there, complacent and mute as they advanced. Score by score, they shifted their guns from aiming at us to pointing at each other. Dietz only sat there, thin pale lips drawn in a dismissive smile of derision that never wavered. When the last shots finally stopped ringing, and the last dying American bludgeoned his captain before turning a knife on himself, we built a small fire to cook dinner. Dietz claimed the meat came from a freshly killed deer he'd found nearby, but I didn't believe him. There was too much meat piled all around us on the ground for him to have gone game-hunting. This was American meat, I knew. His *coup d'état*. Murder your enemy without lifting a finger, and then devour him as the ultimate victory. I stifled the urge to taunt him with the cliche "you are what you eat" and instead chewed on my bar of rations and turned in early. I heard him whispering to the others outside, but I didn't care. I knew he was talking about me. No doubt setting me up as the next victim for his altar. Inwardly, I shrugged. I would kill the enemy. But I would not *eat* him in a perverse communion.

When the voices outside had stilled, she came to me a third time.

"It hurts," she whispered. "Every time they die, he hurts me."

"Who?" I whispered. I knew the others might hear. "Who hurts you?"

"The mean man," she said. Tears flowed down her cheeks and she rubbed her eyes with pudgy unsoiled fists. "I just want to go home. Please let me go home. I can hear momma calling, but I can't find her."

"How?" I asked. "Just tell me how."

She leaned in close, and did. I was resigned, but not at all surprised to find out that it required more blood. My life revolved around death.

The next morning at dawn, Dietz marshaled our little company to march. We headed straight into the thickest line of the enemy. He didn't care. "The more souls we take early, the faster our wave will grow," he explained. "Long live the Reich!" he added, and automatically, ten fists rose in the air.

We marched.

It didn't take long for the screams to start.

There is no way of explaining the horror of the next hour. The act of murder is a terrible, life-altering moment. It was an act we, as soldiers, were conditioned to enact, again and again. Our own lives shivered in the balance each time like hung laundry shaking in the wind. But there is something different in the murder our tiny company brought. The act of combat entails a horrible price, but somehow it is honorable. Both warriors risk death in the support of their side. But we....we didn't risk anything. We only stood there, gleeful, for the most part, in our assured victory. Meanwhile, our enemy rushed us only to inexplicably slow as victory was in their grasp, stop and finally turn upon themselves. I could see the change in their eyes as the scopes of their battle bloodlust switched from us to their countrymen as targets. A part of their gaze froze, appalled and anguished, as the rest of their faces turned without remorse to fratricide. I turned away after the first men bludgeoned their friends with the stocks of their rifles. Brains joined kidneys on the ground in a broken stew as they beat and stabbed their way into hell.

This was not war. It was a mockery. There were no winners in this scenario. Only evil.

And Dietz's thin grin grew and grew with every act of maniacal murder. His prophecy about growing power was coming true. Now he merely waved an arm at a group of men and they instantly turned their rifles from us to each other. And the range of his influence grew farther and farther afield, just as its breadth widened. By noon he was leading us across a battle field that had been trenched and dug in by the enemy for months. We had been unable to break the line just days before. But now, within moments of our walking near, there were screams from a mile away and echoes of gunfire that only destroyed brothers. As we walked, untouched through bloody mud while all around us men stabbed and beat and shot each other with insane intensity, my stomach sickened.

It had to end before his power grew any further. It had to end before there would be no one left to fight him. It had to end to set an innocent German girl free. Maybe the first girl who'd ever counted on me.

We walked for miles on that day, and killed hundreds of soldiers just by our mere presence. The devil was on our side, and he took great glee in threshing the weak souls and flesh of men.

"At this rate," Dietz said, "We will give the Fuhrer all of Europe within the month."

"We can't walk from here to the English Channel in a month," I complained.

"We won't need to," he said. "Our power precedes us. Watch this!"

Dietz pointed the horizon, and I shrugged. "Do you see the man?" he asked.

I looked harder, and this time saw the form slinking up and around bushes and trees to keep himself hidden from the German forces. He was but an ant on the farthest field.

"Ahhh, you see him now," Dietz confirmed. Then he raised his hand and pointed and the black dot suddenly disappeared. Then it reappeared. And then, I heard a faint single retort of a gun. And the black dot disappeared for good. The soldier had shot himself.

Kretz laughed. "Now *that*, is warfare!" he said.

Under my breath, I whispered otherwise. "No," I said. "That is murder."

We camped that night under the eerie canopy of the Black Forest yet again. I felt a calming balm in its leafy embrace, and longed for another time. A time when I believed in our war, and believed if I killed the men in uniforms that were not German, that God would support us and keep us strong until we took what was ours. What we wanted.

I don't think it would ever have been enough. And perhaps I'm kidding myself about ever feeling that way.

We found another small village on the edge of the forest that night, and stayed in a tiny, broken down inn. I don't think anyone other than us had stayed there in weeks. The owners seemed pleased to help us. Unusally so.

The owner was a fat, greasy man who bowed after every sentence. You would have thought he was from the Orient, but he was just another sycophant, who would suck up to any coin. And it looked like it had been awhile since he'd hosted paying guests.

His daughter pranced about the rough planked dining room, pigtails flying like nascent wings. She seemed a happy thing for one living in such obvious poverty. The soup her father served was barely more than water and salt.

Dietz watched the girl, and I could see the ideas blooming beneath that pallid evil skin. It didn't take long for them to crystallize.

"We need another sacrifice," he said as the girl ran up to him and he ruffled her hair with cold fingers.

"I think we made several hundred today," I pointed out.

"No, not kills," he corrected. "A sacrifice. Innocent blood."

Again he smiled at the little girl.

"Our allegiance to Satan must constantly be re-stated. Soldiers would likely be his at the end of their lives anyway, we're just sending them early. But children… They make him very pleased."

"May I show you something," Dietz asked the little girl, Emmie, after dinner. Her father grinned at us from the kitchen. He was probably used to any strangers making a fuss over his little daughter. And soldiers were no doubt lonely for their families back home. She would remind them of a kid sister. He thought nothing of the advance. But I knew.

One by one we faded from the table and followed the two up hard plank stairs to our rooms. Dietz took the girl to the corner where our gear was stowed. She giggled as he showed her his rifle, and jumped up and down when he offered to take the weapon apart. She giggled more as he poured bullets into her hand, and then loosed the stabbing knife from the gun's tip.

"This is for Germany," he whispered for our benefit, and motioned for us to gather around. Then he said some ancient words as Kretz stroked the girl's head. She rolled the bullets in her hand like marbles, ignorant of her plight, and Schuster and I stepped in to close the dark circle.

"Do we really have to…" Lichtmann said, and the look Dietz gave him could have curdled milk.

"Do you want to win the war for our fatherland?" he hissed. "This is the only way. Our borders have fallen, our troops collapsed and retreated. Der Fuhrer is in hiding and our Reich is in ruins. This is for Germany," he repeated, and raised the knife.

"Cover her eyes at least," I begged. Dietz nodded, and Kretz pulled out a hankerchief.

"Let's play a game," Dietz said, and the girl grinned, cheeks blushing in excitement, eyes alight with energy. We may have been the first guests to play with her in weeks. She couldn't restrain her happiness. And we were here to kill her.

"First we close your eyes," Dietz said, honey oozing lightly through his tone. "Then we lay you here on the bed…"

She followed his instruction like a lamb, and my eyes teared as I saw her straw-bright hair spread out across the pillow. Killing men sworn to war is hard, but acceptable. We all donned our uniforms knowing the price was life—ours or our enemy's. It's a very different thing to take the life of a child who lays down to play a game.

Again Dietz spoke in an ancient tongue and raised the knife.

He may have had the power of Satan, but that did not include omniscience. He looked very surprised when the blood suddenly exploded like a cloud from his chest, and the report of my pistol echoed like God's own fury through the tiny inn. From down below, I heard the fat innkeeper calling Emmie's name in panic.

"*This* is for Germany…" I said, and shot him again as he raised a hand to hex me. This time his head disintegrated in a spray of blood and eyes and bone to paint the room in a gruesome spatter.

"...the Germany I once loved," I whispered, as the hands of Kretz and Schuster grabbed me and began to beat me down to the ground in hatred.

"What have you done?" Kretz screamed just as the innkeeper burst through the door and ran, stepping over the fallen remains of Dietz to lift his daughter from the bed. His eyes went wide as he saw the blood and the body and the men battering me with fists and rifle stocks. But when his baby was in his arms, tiny hands clinging to his neck, he left us to our own disintegration and ran from the room. His departure gave me the chance I needed, and I rolled away from the beating. Just then, Lichtmann opened fire on Kretz and Schuster. Blood sprayed from their chests and faces, and in that moment time suspended, and the air was filled with suspended wet rubies.

The little girl bent down from heaven to kiss my lips with ghostly warmth. In my ear she whispered one thing as Lichtmann continued to fire again and again into the jerking, jittering corpses of the Devil's Trinity. My face and hands warmed with the splatter of their death.

"Thank you," the waif whispered. "I won't forget you. I found momma."

Before the bodies had fully stilled on the planks, Lichtmann dropped the smoking gun and ran for the door. I was quick to follow, but by the time I rolled from the floor, leapt down the stairs and passed the cowering innkeeper in the dining room on my way out, the private was already lost in the fog. I looked around for him a bit, hoping to thank him for saving my life, and then stumbled myself into the black shadows of the forest once more.

I lived on berries and streamwater for days. I don't know where Lichtmann went. I didn't stick around to thank him, I only knew I had to get as far from Dietz and the devil as I could. When I finally found my way back to a tiny village five days later, I learned that Der Fuhrer had shot himself. Five days before.

The Reich was done. The troops retreating faster than ever. Ironically, Dietz, and the devil, had apparently been our only hope. Thanks to me, thanks to my weak heart, Germany was now, without any doubt, losing the war.

But I couldn't believe that winning a war was worth the life of a child. I pray to God that he agrees. And I pray that he'll forgive me for my moment of desperation.

The devil was on our side. And I never want to stand next to him again. Every night I kneel and pray, as the Germany I once knew collapses all around me. I know they'll never talk about the hundreds of Allied troops who for a couple days, near the dark entrance to the Black Forest, slaughtered each other mercilessly. Nobody will ever talk about the week that Germany almost turned the war around in a fit of blackest magic.

But now I wonder…what if God was the one on our side, and wanted Hitler to win? How could God have forsaken us so badly that our only hope was Satan? All I can do is pray. Pray that he'll forgive me for helping to kill the girl. Pray that he'll forgive me for murdering Dietz. But sometimes, I'm not sure which of my actions to apologize for. The girl is still dead, and despite her sacrifice, and because of Dietz's, Germany now falls.

All I can do now is hide here, in the sheltering valleys of endless trees. Perhaps the Lorelei will call to me, at last. Until then, I kneel, and pray.

"Oh my God, I am heartily sorry, for having offended thee…"

Mutilation Street

Here we are.

Be patient. Wait a moment, and it will all become clear to you.

It's 6:30 p.m. and the golden glow of kitchen lights are clicking off one by one as the men are slipping home after long days at the stockyards and the insurance companies and the morgues. Those long days at work are heaven compared to the long nights at home.

The sweet perfume of burning flesh slinks in a fog through the heavy summer air, accompanied by the clatter of pots and the ringing tinkle of crashing glass. The casual walker might traverse this street thinking he heard and smelled the echoes of dinner in the wind.

Of course, any casual walker here would likely never taste dinner again.

On the west side of the street, a washing machine repairman staggers drunkenly forward, tool kit dipping dangerously close to the earth with each step. As he teeters onto the roadway, a Dodge Neon revs around the corner and clips him on the hip with its ever-smiling headlights ("Hi," it seems to say). He cries out, just a despairing bark, really, and spins like a top on the curb before moving on once again, this time back in the direction he'd just left.

He nears the bend at Mrs. Jacob's house and trips on the folded slabs of topsy turvy sidewalk there. The gnarled elm has dredged the concrete up from the earth in its own scrabbling attempt to remain upright—or perhaps it moves the walkway to escape the rotting bodies festering beneath its trunk. But despite the desperate nails of its roots against the cement, its upper limbs remain bent low, and scrape painfully on the ground. Deep in the night, you can hear it clearly behind any of the windows facing the street…*screeeach, scraaatch, screeeach, scraaatch.*

In the alley, there's a cat with three legs that sometimes answers the cries of the tree. If there weren't so many grey spots on the animal, you'd call it a black cat. As it stands, the cigarette burns give it more of a salt and pepper look as it shambles with its own lamed gait towards the crooked entrydoor cut into the Jone's back door. The tiny door hits the feline where its tail would be, if it had one, as the poor animal drags itself through.

The cat's name is Stupid Bitch.

At least, that's what it answers to most often.

Back on the street, the repairman reaches the end of the block once more, and begins to cross the intersection. Again, the cheerful Neon comes roaring around the corner to bash him in the thigh (two points). After moaning for a few moments on the asphalt, the man staggers back to the relative safety of the sidewalk, and half-walks, half-falls toward Mrs. Jacob's twisted elm. His grey uniform is discolored in a startling number of places, smudges of grease and road tar here and there, but mostly wide swatches of blood, much of it already dry. There's a long strip of scalp hanging from the back of his head like a grisly ponytail, but he doesn't seem to notice it, despite the ever-lengthening map of gore down his back.

He has been trying to leave this block since early afternoon. Makes you wonder what kind of mischief a roving repairman could have gotten into with his sack of tools to have ended up stuck here, doesn't it? I'll give you a clue; I happen to know that his repairman's kit used to include a rusty blade and some other nasty looking looped tools that he'd stolen from an illegal abortionist.

Just a word of caution: there are no knives allowed on Mutilation Street.

Knives are against the law. The use of blades in mutilation is too easy. And generally makes things end too quickly.

There is joy in repetition. Dull, painful repetition.

And usually slow death.

And then it all begins again.

Shall I show you more?

Here's Mrs. [Not Her Real Name] Cleaver's house. Mind the entrails. They may look like sausage but the smell never washes off your shoes.

Every night she finds a new way to rip those grue-ish links from the hairy, obese belly of her husband. It's a fixation she has. The best part is, when she gets really wicked, *she* stuffs chunks of his bloody colon into the fridge after he's passed out and then fries them up for him to eat with his eggs in the morning.

Talk about a breakfast that sticks to your ribs.

What makes it all really tricky is that she only has two stumps to work with.

That was his handiwork.

Yes, he used a cleaver, but it was before they came to Mutilation Street. It was, in fact, what caused them to move here. She didn't die, but she must have lost 10 pounds just from bleeding. They eventually just painted the hardwood floors in the room of the house where they found her, because the stain wouldn't come out, no matter how deep the sandpaper ground.

Tonight she's been especially clever. She met him at the door wearing her most provocative negligee—a red silk number that barely covered her chest and left nearly everything else open to the air.

Too little left to the imagination, if you ask me.

When he grinned and dropped his lunchpail in order to kiss the rounded nub that once ended in a hand, she kneed him in the groin and then pounded his chin and balding scalp with the other arm, the one she'd had half-hidden behind her back, the one that had a steel rod strapped around the knotted mound of flesh at its end.

It echoed through the room when the metal met the bone of his skull.

Once he was out, she dragged him into the weight room in the back of the house, pinned his arms, neck and legs to the floor with a couple heavy barbells and, when he woke choking for air, she sealed his trap with the negligee. Fit the whole thing in his mouth, not that there was that much to it.

Red or not, she decided she didn't want to get blood on it.

Spit washes out.

Then she sat down on his face and began to gut him.

With her feet.

Using the broken edge of one of his empty beer bottles.

You'd be amazed at the sensations of having your belly clumsily sawed open with glass while your mouth was filled with your wife's panties and then sealed from calling out for help with the tender skin they usually protected. The blood doesn't really spurt into the air, like you'd think it would, but it does stream steadily to pool on the floor. It also brings with it some yellow nuggets of fat and the occasional stream of blue-black, foul-smelling refuse nicked from the inside of the intestines.

I'm sure he tried to bite, but with all that lace between his teeth, she probably felt nothing more than a tickle.

The great thing for Mr. Cleaver [Not His Real Name] is that she finds a new way to disembowel him every night.

Variety is the spice of death.

In the rambling colonial on the corner of Mutilation and Divine live the Angels. They seem to feel themselves above the law and often take into each other using razor blades. Of course, these are not strictly against the code, not being "knives" per se, but nobody else on the block has ever dared cut into each other with one. Nobody wants to find out what punishment could be worse than life and death on Mutilation Street.

The Angels moved in about six months ago. Word is, before they came to the neighborhood, she screamed at him for taking the Lord's name in vain and so he stabbed her in the eye with a crucifix and then drove a chalice up her—well—you can guess. Turned her loving cup into a holy cup, you might say.

I don't know what she looks like beneath her robes, but she's definitely missing an eye. It's really quite unnerving to try to have a conversation with her and not stare at the scarred pit in her face that should hold a blue and white orb.

Makes her always look off balance, too.

Nowadays, when he gets home from mass, she's usually waiting with a boiling pot of blessed wax. Some men are greeted with a martini and their slippers, he gets a mug of hot candle oil. Can't argue with her methods; it's hard for a man to swear with a cup or two of that melting down his throat.

I hear they've barred her from worshipping at Resurrection Church given her propensity for leaving the building with vigil candles tucked into her blouse, but she still manages to get in now and then to steal a handful or two of holy candles.

I think one of my favorite stories from the street was of the time he got home late from midnight mass and she just *knew* he'd been fooling around with one of the altar sluts.

He walked in the door at 3 a.m. and she was waiting, armed with a statue of the Virgin Mary and a heavy wooden rosary.

"Where have you been?" she demanded.

"I was at mass, sweetheart," he insisted, putting his palms together as if praying.

"And did they use Obsession as incense tonight?" she replied, ever so sweetly.

His eyebrows wrinkled at that one, and as he stammered for

something to say, she reached into his coat pocket and spilled an array of gum wrappers, change and condoms to the floor.

"Did the priest hand those out for communion?" she smiled, pointing at the rubbers.

"I was only worshipping the goodness that He created," he flailed, which was *really* the wrong answer.

Take a note here. Don't try to link adultery with godliness. The holy types never buy it.

She didn't either.

Instead she smashed the Virgin Mary across his temple, dropping him like a kneeler.

She hung the rosary around his throat as a necklace, and then attached its cross to the ornate golden rope drapery drawstring. It didn't take as much strength using the drape pulleys to hoist him into the air. By the time he came to from the statue-bashing, his face was already blue.

Bet he wished then that he hadn't found the studs when he installed that drape rod.

He didn't last long that night, but from what I hear, he *was* awake long enough to see her using his straight razor to slice off his most unholy of organs and then, on a cutting board right in front of him, she trimmed it into thin, waferlike slices.

She put a couple dozen of these unholy hosts in the oven and served them with a cup of his blood the next day to the neighborhood wives.

Apparently she thought if he was going to give himself to one woman on the block, he ought to give a taste to everyone.

Mrs. MacLean, over on 135 Mutilation, has a real classical cruel streak to her. She's also a firm believer in repetition, sans spice.

Her husband comes home every night at 6:30 from his graveyard shift (not the night shift, he really digs all day in the graveyard.) He changes from his muddy clothes into jeans and a T-shirt and comes to the kitchen table, ready for dinner. Mrs.

MacLean is a knock-out; long blond hair sets off piercing blue eyes, tight waist accentuates nicely rounded hips and she's got cleavage to drown in. Every night she shows it off for him, proud of regaining her figure so soon after birthing their first child.

It's always hot here, so she wears hot pink crop-tops and denim short-shorts a lot. The neighborhood boys are always gawking during the day when she lays out on their deck. She is literally tan *all* over, and loves the attention. But at night, she has different reasons for attracting the attention of her mate.

"Was she good for you?" she asks him, as she finishes up preparing dinner in the kitchen, always reminding her husband of his infidelity during her pregnancy.

"Were her tits nicer than mine? More firm? Was she a gymnast for you?"

She sets the table with a pot of steaming green beans and a wooden bowl of salad, garnished with cucumbers and croutons and little pink fingers and toes.

"Was she worth it?" she asks as she sets his plate in front of him.

It's the same every night.

"I hope he's not too done," she says, as he stares down at the blackened carcass of his firstborn son, steam rising visibly from wide slices through its neck and chest, mouth open to a baby scream, a tiny well-baked tongue lolling grey between shriveled lips.

He puts his face in his hands and cries.

"Was she worth it?" Mrs. MacLean asks again.

Oh, you were worried about Stupid Bitch, the three-legged cat? Don't be, really. The Jones' cat is one of the street's most beloved pets. Everyone in the neighborhood takes time from their own vengeful projects to help it out.

Sometimes they strap a box of rat poison around its neck. Others give it hunks of maggot-ridden meat. Still others send gifts from the sewer, or the laundry tub.

The cat takes them all home. Through the alley, up the rotting wood stairs and through its private door, into the living room where the Jones' lie.

They were paralyzed when they came here, some kind of accident with the stairs when the mister was chasing the cat. Amazing that they could both break their backs like that, chasing a cat that only had three legs. Justice, I suppose, for what they did to the cat. I heard that it was affectionate, even though they both put out their cigarettes on its back.

The story goes, one night when it insisted on purring and snuggling into Mr. Jones' lap, he yelled "Stupid Bitch!" grabbed it in a fit of rage, twisting its back leg until it gave in an audible snap. His wife screamed at him that now they were going to have to pay a vet bill and have the dumb cat hobbling around in a cast for who knows how long. He shrugged, said "Not necessarily," and gripping the cat by its hindquarters and dangling paw, gave a great yank, ripping the broken leg right off the poor pet.

The neighbors heard that animal's yowl three houses away.

They did have a vet bill, but the cat didn't need a cast.

Anyway, since they moved to the street, that cat finds something disgusting to bring home every night for their supper. The Jones' are just lying there on the floor inside, and the cat drops stuff right in their mouths. If the neighbors aren't helpful, it brings home stuff from the back alley—dead rats, bugs, toads, poison… they have some pretty painful cramps 'most every night, I expect.

I think the cat's best one came with the help of Mrs. Alfred, down the block a bit. She has a thing for fire—served her husband his own leg as a pot roast one night, after strapping him down on the floor and holding his leg in the roaring flames of their fireplace for 20 or 30 minutes.

Not sure how much appetite he had left at that point.

But she really put some thought into helping out Stupid Bitch—made that cat a little bucket with reinforced tin foil and some shoelaces. That cat carried and dragged its hot burden all the way down the alley, and into its house. Then he tipped the contents into Mr. and Mrs. Jones' mouths, one hunk a piece.

Must have burnt like hell.

Mrs. Alfred gave the cat a couple of white hot coals from her grill.

Nobody likes people who used to put cigarettes out on their pets.

Here we are at last.

Corner of Mutilation and Hunger Ave. This is it. Says so here on your deed.

182 Mutilation St.

This house probably needs some work—it's been empty for a long time, which is odd, because once people move into this neighborhood, they almost never leave.

Not a lot of people find their way to *this* block, though. Makes you wonder how people can possibly end up here. 'Course, hang around the street long enough, and you get to know everyone's grisly stories.

I'm sure we'll hear about yours soon.

Go on in.

Your daughter's waiting for you.

And…

…Good luck.

LOVE & ROPE & SEX & SCREAMS

A Circus in Five Acts

BARNETT
& STALEY
CIRCUS
AND ASTOUNDING
FREAK S

And Then Some

"Stand tall, stand tall," the barker cried.

Ramsey didn't know how he could do otherwise, what with all the naughty bits of his anatomy struggling to escape the confines of his clothes.

"See the Three-Breasted Woman!" the barker continued. "Is she a freak of nature? Is she the next stage of evolution? Imagine if she was your mother…" the barker twirled one side of his black handlebar mustache and sneered with exaggerated slowness "…or your girlfriend."

Ramsey strained his neck above the other eager patrons of the tent and squinted as the curtain lifted behind the stage.

Four long white fingers gripped the dirty canvas, and then slowly pulled the material aside, revealing inch by delicate inch of Yvette, the ace in the hole of Barnett & Staley's Circus—a real live, honest-to-goodness three-breasted woman.

One black fishnet leg stepped inside the tent, followed by her left sequined breast. A tendril of long black hair followed, then a rouged cheek.

"She is everything you've dreamed of," the barker continued, drawing out the moment. "And then some…"

The dark pit of her belly followed, and then a thin nose and her eyes, emerald green and piercing.

Ramsey trembled, and stretched taller. His mid-section seemed tauter, the rest of him should be, too.

She materialized fully then. First one swell of flesh, then another, and then, indeed, another until she stood, white teeth grinning, two eyes daring, three breasts beckoning…

The spotlight shone.

And she stood still, at last, fully, undeniably, revealed.

Ramsey shifted his hips, but felt no more comfortable than before. He could see her flesh pressing against the paper-thin red, sequined fabric. His eyes squinted hard…was it really three nipples playing against the outfit, or only two and a sock…or some other augmentation device?

"Who will volunteer to test our Yvette?" the barker cooed. "Who will handle breasts one and two and…th-reeee to verify that she is all woman. And more?"

The hands poked high among the nearly all-male audience, but a more delicate finger or two protruded from the crowd as well. Lesbians, or merely curious? Ramsey wondered at the painted nails.

His hand joined the rest, and perhaps he looked more desperate than most. Or more normal. His belly didn't protrude six inches beyond his belt and his face wasn't marred by a dozen pockmarks or mangy tufts of hair. He looked like Joe-average. Sandy haired and blue-eyed, 155 pounds and five-foot-ten.

The barker picked him.

Heart pounding, mouth dry, Ramsey broke out of the standing-room-only crowd and approached the stage. She met his eye immediately, her gaze piercing and black, unblinking. He paused.

"Go on, son, feel them," the barker prodded.

"Tell the rest—there are no implants or other chicaneries here…she is all woman. Plus one."

Yvette didn't twitch or nod or even break into a small grin. She only stood there, watching him, invisibly daring him to reach out and feel her up in front of an audience of hundreds. Okay, maybe tens. But it felt like a mob.

Ramsey blanched.

"C'mon, boy," the barker said again, annoyance creeping into his tone. "Don't tell me you haven't always wished for more. Yvette IS more. That she is. More than you could ever dream of."

Ramsey shook himself out of his frozen stance and moved closer, his heart beating in his chest like a crazed metronome. And then he was next to her, sweat beading across his brow and dripping down his ribs to moisten his belt. He hated to be the center of attention, always had. Why had he volunteered for this?

But then he looked at her, really looked at her for the first time. She was pale.

Thin.

Scared.

Those unblinking black eyes met his with a look that said, *Be quick. Be gentle.*

He felt a chill flash down his spine, though he didn't know why.

"Go ahead," the barker growled. "Feel her up. And then do it again. And AGAIN!"

He laughed and the crowd followed, a cackle of horny jealous caws. They wanted her, and couldn't believe this twit had gained the privilege.

An almost-invisible nod from Yvette, and Ramsey felt his hands rise. It would be worse if he didn't.

He reached out, touching her shoulder and then trailing his fingers down, first cupping her left breast, feeling its heavy weight resting in his hand, then with light but visible squeezing, holding her right. He let his fingers drop slightly, to trail across the pendulous flesh that hung just beneath and between the other two, feeling and seeing her nipple rise against the cotton T-shirt as he brought his palm together in a light squeeze.

Then a firm hand gripped his shoulder and moved him away from the girl, who stood stock-still before the crowd.

"Is she real, or is she real?" the barker asked. Ramsey could feel the fingers on his arm tighten with each word.

He nodded.

"Definitely the real deal," he found himself saying.

It was just what the crowd wanted to hear.

"Let's hear it for our volunteer—and Yvette, The Three-Breasted Woman," the barker begged, and they responded, clapping and hooting and hollering as Ramsey made his way back into the crowd. A sallow-faced man stopped him with a hand on his chest and stared hard at his eyes.

"You really think she had three? It wasn't just a put-on?" the man mumbled.

Ramsey nodded. "They felt real. Honest."

The man dipped his head once, and faded back into the mob.

Ramsey eased out the tent, before he had to field any other embarrassing questions, but as he slid through the mildewed canvas flap, he hesitated, looking back to the "stage."

The barker stood behind his star attraction, pretending to do a jiggly juggling act with the three "balls" anchored to Yvette's chest, much to the delight of the mostly male audience.

"She's more than you can handle," he joked, letting her center breast bounce down out of sequence.

Yvette didn't smile. Frown. Or blink.

He met her gaze, or thought he did. For one electric instant, her eyes seemed to connect with his own. "Go on," she seemed to say. "Forget about me."

Ramsey let the flap slide shut behind him, and moved on to sample the cloying sweetness of cotton candy and to lose a handful of dollars in games of "chance."

He figured he had more of a chance to score with a three-breasted woman than he had of winning at one of the rigged booth games—like tossing a basketball into a too-small hoop, or launching rubber frogs into the air with a slingshot and successfully having them land atop plastic lily pads. Eventually he gave up and went home, but not without stopping to look back at the freak show tent.

Her tent.

He couldn't forget about her.

Not that night, or the next.

««—»»

Visions of the barker's hands performing his rude juggling act kept leaping through Ramsey's mind instead of sheep. And as he rubbed his eyes at work, the sensation of her firm, warm breasts kept tingling in his palms.

He went back to the circus.

This time he stood in the back of the tent as the mustacchioed man pushed and prodded and purloined his prize to another man in the audience, who approached his opportunity at triple nipple massage with more gusto than Ramsey had.

Ramsey ignored the macho antics of the barker and his lusty volunteer and watched Yvette.

She showed no expression through it all. She might as well have been a mannequin. He wondered if the circus kept her drugged in order to deal with the humiliation. The barker never went far from her side, prodding her to stand in the center of the stage, and never missing a chance to paw her overly-ample bosom with his beefy hairy hands. He seemed to hold her with an invisible leash.

Ramsey saw the show winding towards its lewd juggling end, and then heard the barker offer something he hadn't before.

Something that made perfect sense.

Something that made Ramsey's heart swell to bursting with empathy and then, implode with sadness.

"Now," the barker said. "You've seen all that I can show you at a family show. But if you're over 18…" He twirled his mustache and grinned. "…see me after this for our mature audiences-only show."

Ramsey slipped out of the tent. The lights gave off enough brilliance to mark the path towards the next tent, but not so much that he couldn't slip out of their cones of spotlit earth to skulk, unnoticed, to the back of the freak show tent. Eventually, she had to come out this way, he figured.

But once in back, he saw that this was not the case. A maze of hastily hung wires and lines followed a length of stained canvas that led from the freak show tent to broaden into another tent hidden from the view of circus goers behind. There must be a hidden exit behind the stage. An exit that led quickly and privately away to another tent shielding a sleeping trailer.

Her trailer.

Ramsey stole quickly across the grass to where the canvas-covered corridor met the fabric of the rear tent. With his hands, he felt along the surface, searching for a seam.

It wasn't hard to identify. His fingers found the steel-lined holes and heavy laces, then began to slip between the pieces, seeking a gap big enough for him to slip through. He didn't think he'd be able to work on the laces to untie knots in the dark.

The tent fabric was laced at the very bottom, and then again a couple feet off the ground. But it was another three feet after that before more laces knit the two flaps together. Ramsey softly spread the hole with his arms, and lifted a leg up and through the resulting gap. The rest of his body followed.

And then he was inside.

He realized he'd been holding his breath, and suddenly gasped to get air. The smells of the carnival had vanished with the close of the flap; the buttery scent of popcorn and tangy aftershave of old baking hotdog grease were gone. Now, Ramsey smelled something different. The nose-watering spice of mildew, mixed with the toxicity of varnish and the vinegar of old apples. He stifled the urge to sneeze, and squinted into the gloom.

A sleeping trailer stood dark and quiet in the center of the shadows, and Ramsey stepped up to its battered doorway, trying the knob. Somewhere not too far away he heard an explosion of hands, and guessed that her show was over. He pulled the door open, but then stopped at the faint sound of a deep male voice talking in muffled tones somewhere behind him.

Ramsey shut the door and stepped back, looking back and forth in the narrow confines between the tent and the trailer for a spot to hide. He ran to the head of the trailer and crouched in the shadows watching. Seconds later, two shadowy figures moved from the interconnecting canvas to the door he'd just touched to disappear inside the trailer.

He could hear the mumbling of voices again from inside, but couldn't make out the words over the crashing, caterwauling sounds breaking through the barrier of the tent from the Midway. When it appeared that the conversation inside the trailer was going to continue for some time, he left his tenuous hiding place and slipped back out of the slit in the tent to wait outside, lying down on the cool grass out of sight of the dirt thoroughfares of the circus.

Eventually, he heard the slight squeak of the door opening and closing, and risked a look just in time to see an elongated shadowy figure disappear down the canvas corridor. Minutes later, inside the tent, the light shut off, and then Ramsey could see nothing but shadow before him, and stars above.

Still, Ramsey lay on the ground. He thought he should wait until things quieted down before venturing back into the tent. After awhile, he rolled over on his back and stared up at the night sky. Despite the glare from the nearby tents, the eastern sky was dark as black velvet, and just as plush. A scattering of pinpoints cut through its shield, and a half moon burned through the horizon. Ramsey thought of Yvette, and of her daily indignities. How could she go on? What must her heart feel, to see so many men wanting, not *her*, but only to see the deformity of her body? To entertain crude fantasies and laugh at obscene jokes at her expense. What was it like to grow up as a freak? What was it like to live as a woman in a circus?

The screams and laughter and background chatter of voices slowly dwindled, and Ramsey dozed. When he awoke, the night was quiet, and the lights from the rest of the circus dimmed. Shaking himself awake, he tiptoed around the musty tent canvas and with his hands explored until he found the slit between the laces again.

The calliope music now played only in his mind as he eased the fabric apart and slipped a leg inside. Then he was turning the knob and stepping inside the trailer of The Three-Breasted Woman!

He worried she would hear the legs of his jeans rub together, or his heart beating. It pounded so hard he could feel the blood pumping like angry surf in his ears. But nothing stirred in the silent, dark space. His eyes were already adjusted to the thickness of the night. Outside, at least, there was starlight. Here, there was only blackness. He stepped forward, and a clatter rang out. Something had fallen over.

Ramsey dropped to a crouch and listened. If she was here, he must have woken her. And if the barker was nearby…

Seconds passed, then minutes. He barely dared to breathe. But no one came. Presently he could make out the shadows of a cot in the far corner, and square shapes on either side of him. Boxes and trunks. He moved quietly, careful not to step on the pieces he'd knocked to the ground.

On his fourth step, he found her cot. And her.

He could still barely see in the darkness, but her skin seemed to lighten the room on its own near where she lay. She was nude, and lying on her back. Ramsey stifled a gasp as he saw the third breast, uncovered, lolling below her normal bosom. It was almost as if she had a second stomach. Or a huge tumor. With a pink cap. The rest of her torso was marked by a handful of other, undeveloped breasts. He could see the reverse pocks of unrisen nipples dotting her ribcage.

The barker hadn't lied. His own *hands* hadn't lied.

It was sick. Perverse. A bit sad. But she had three full teats.

And two wide open eyes.

"I won't hurt you," he whispered.

She didn't respond.

He touched her hand.

"Are you okay?" he asked.

Still she lay there. Looking at him. Eyes open. Lips tight.

"I felt bad after seeing you in the show," he explained. "I wondered how you could let them do this to you. Then I thought, 'maybe she's drugged, or a prisoner.' I had to come see you when no one else was around. I had to make sure you were all right."

Her lips seemed to move but she did not speak. Her hand, however, gripped his own.

"Are you okay?" he asked again.

She lifted her free hand and gripped his shoulder. Then she pulled him closer. Ramsey put his ear to her lips, thinking she was going to whisper some secret.

Instead, her hand went to his head, and pressed his face lower. He smelled the faint hint of lilac on her skin and the tang of sweat-salt. And then his lips were brushing across the silk of nipples. One and two…and three. She guided him like a bee to each, stopping him briefly at each cone to sip and then pressing him on, a perfect circle of silken flesh to sample and taste. He hadn't even meant to open his mouth but suddenly Ramsey realized he'd not only opened it, he was suckling.

He struggled to pull back, and looked up at her eyes. All he saw were contented slits of lids, her mouth trembling and purring in a satisfied O. Her fingers wrestled in his hair, twining like playful snakes, and then pulled him close again. He was drowning in her subtle scent, thirsting for the taste of her skin again. It was dark and close, and everything in the world seemed to come back to her. He couldn't struggle. Why would he want to?

He woke at dawn and disentangled himself from the warm nest of her arms and legs. His left arm was numb, buried beneath her head.

"Hey," he murmured, trying to pull himself away.

Her eyes opened. In the light, he could see they were pale, and green as sea foam. They seemed bottomless.

"I came here last night to talk to you," he began, but her hand stopped his lips. She sat up quickly, her eyes darting side to side.

“I worried…” he said, but her fingers trapped his lips, and with a jolt, she pushed him upright. Pins and needles began pricking his arm as she nabbed his clothes from the floor with calculated attacks. In a flash, he was cradling his jeans and shirt with his good arm, and she was pacing in the far corner of the trailer, near the door leading to the tented passageway to the freak show stage. He took the hint and dressed.

He had to sit on her cot to pull his shoes on. The tingling in his arm still burned, but he shook it out, and forced his fingers to work on his laces. Before he was finished, a hand gripped his arm and pulled him upright. She faced him, chest jutting proud and strange. Her lips met his for just a moment, and then she pushed him out the door. Sensing her urgency, he hurricd to the hole in the outer tent that he’d found the night before. He fell through, landing on the other side on his knees. Behind him he heard a good reason for her haste.

“Yvette?” It was the barker.

He crept away from the tent, slipping from one just-waking attraction to the next, until he’d made his way to the edge of the circus. The sun was burning orange on the horizon as he started back down the road to home. His body was satisfied. And sore.

And he’d left her exactly as he’d found her. Well, not exactly. But he hadn’t rescued her.

She was with him throughout the day. With every shadow that fell across his person, he felt her gaze on him. With every touch—of a comb, of a chair, of a doorknob—he felt the cool balm of her flesh against his. When he drank from a can from the vending machine, he tasted, just beyond the sparkle of carbonation, the sweetness of her breasts.

When he got off work, he didn’t go home.

He went straight to the circus.

««—»»

"Is she a freak of nature? Is she the next stage of evolution?" The barker grinned and winked. Imagine if she was your mother…or your girlfriend."

Ramsey stayed at the back of the tent, but still the barker's gaze seemed to find him. Those black eyes lingered on his as the barker continued his patter.

"She is everything you've dreamed of," he said, pausing to twirl one end of his mustache, "And then some…"

Ramsey slipped back outside and waited behind the tent, hoping that tonight, he'd be able to talk to her. He heard the clapping from Yvette's last show of the night, and the burbling murmur of the men filing out and back to the main venues of the circus. And then he felt a hand on his shoulder.

"Got a thing for our little Yvette, do ya?" The barker's teeth gleamed against the growing gloom of night.

"She took care of you last night, don't you think that's enough?"

Ramsey started, and his captor laughed.

"You think I don't know everything that goes on in her tent? I can't afford to let anything happen to my star attraction."

With that, the barker pushed him forward, steering him towards her tent. "I let her take care of her needs. But don't get the wrong idea."

The man gripped him by both arms and stuck a reddened, wrinkling face close to his own. "She doesn't need you."

They pushed through the loose canvas and Ramsey entered the tent of the three-breasted woman for the second time. She had removed the costume from her performance and sat, as if waiting for him, naked on her cot.

The barker shoved him forward, and Ramsey fell to his knees at her feet.

He looked up at her, hoping for a sign. Hoping for a word. Something. "Are you okay?" he asked for the third time that day.

She twisted her lips up, showing her teeth in a hungry grin. And hissed.

He jumped back, and looked at the barker. "What did you do to her?"

The barker laughed, and patted his head like a dog.

"Nothing, I assure you. The question is, what did you do to her?"

She stood slowly, moving toward them in a feral crouch.

"Nothing," Ramsey cried, backpedaling until his shoulders were hemmed in by the barker's thighs. The woman moved closer, green eyes glowing in the fading light. He was suddenly reminded of the glare of the lioness in the Big Top's animal taming act.

"I'd say you two did a little business last night," the barker laughed, seemingly unconcerned by the strange bchavior of his attraction. "I'd say you took advantage of the poor girl."

"I didn't," Ramsey protested. "I came here to help her and she, she…"

"She forced you into her bed, did she?"

"Not forced," Ramsey said.

"Hmmm."

Yvette hissed again and launched herself at Ramsey, nails raking at his face. He felt her breath an inch away, hot against his neck. He threw his arms up to protect himself from her attack and heard something snap in the air next to his ear. The crack of a whip.

The barker was holding a long strap, and Yvette retreated to the bed.

"What the…"

"Can it," the barker said, dropping his exaggerated crowd-pleasing demeanor. He suddenly sounded like a tired cab driver. "You had to see and now you have. She's done with you. She only uses men once and if you're lucky…she doesn't touch you again."

"How did you make her this way; what have you done to her?" Ramsey protested. The barker just shook his head.

"We didn't make her any way, and we did nothing to her.

She came to *us* when she was just a girl. We give her a home and food and a way to find mates. We take her away before anyone asks too many questions. And if you did what she wanted last night, my guess is, at our next town we'll be billing her as the four-breasted woman."

On the bed, Yvette began to growl.

"Come on, you'd better not stay here anymore."

Ramsey backed away from the cot, his eyes drawn to the three heavy teats hanging from the woman's torso.

When they got outside, Ramsey pulled the barker to a stop before they reached the midway.

"What did you mean about her becoming a four-breasted woman?"

The barker grinned.

"When she mates, and conceives, she grows a new tit. I've seen her with as many as eight! A few weeks ago, she was as flat as a boy—we had no freak show at all. Thank god for that kid in Albany. You'd be surprised at how hard it is to find her a guy that sticks around for a night. They all come out to see the freak, but do you think any of them *want* her? 'Course, some of them want her a little too much and wear out their welcome with her…then I've got to clean up and we've got to leave town in a hurry."

He stared knowingly at Ramsey, who shivered at the implication.

"She has kids?" he asked, after a moment.

"Kids, litters… call 'em what you want."

The barker pushed him towards a mob of people congregating around a juggler in green leotards and a red jester's cap outside the Big Top.

"But… where are they? What happened to them?"

"Where do you think we get the tightrope walkers and animal trainers? Not to mention all those twisted tots for the formaldehyde jars of the freak show display."

With a slap on the back and a throaty laugh, the barker suddenly left him, and disappeared into the crowd.

Laughter and screams rang out all around him, as children ran past with sticky pink cotton candy, parents chasing after them. By the Big Top, teenage girls giggled in groups and flaunted their midriffs for the boys slouching against the painted canvas. Ramsey stood lost in the middle of it all.

His heart ached to go back, to ask her if it was really true. Would he be a father? His belly froze at the thought. He wasn't ready. He'd never meant… After a moment, he found himself swept along with the crowd, moving towards the fairground exit. It was closing time.

He could still taste the ghost of the velvet smooth crush of her skin against his lips. The smell of lilac in her hair. But as he moved away from her tent, he could also hear the angry snarl of her teeth at his neck.

There was a lump in his throat that felt thicker than all the lumps of caramel the vendors were selling at the fairground gates. Ramsey let the crowd carry him towards home. He brushed a finger softly across his lips and didn't look back.

After the Fifth Step

After the fifth step, it was mundane.

Ah…but getting to the fifth step. That was the trick. That was what it was all about. The crowds below, they thought the tough part was in the center, once the safety net was removed. "Oh, such danger," the ringmaster would cry. "Such daring-do."

Such malarky, Reind thought. Once you were moving, in the groove, you didn't *need* a net. The difficult part was in placing one step in front of the other when leaving behind the wooden platform. The first step was like a switch between stepping on sandpaper and high-gloss ice—with a slight movement, his foot left behind the immobile, grainy plywood to slip down a quivering, thin decline of twined, worn fibers. It was stepping through the door from plane cargo bay to open, unparachuted air. That step was the first trick. And the second, bringing your anchor with you.

The hardest was the step after the first. That's where you gained or lost your balance. That's where it became a walk or a fall. After the second step, there was no going back. You didn't turn around on the highwire.

The third step was a beginning. The first complete motion forward on a new course. The fourth step was an affirmation.

After the fifth step, it was just walking.

««—»»

Reind put his first foot down on the tightrope and felt the horsehair-thin fibers catch on the Lycra net of his tights. Comforting feeling, that. While an unpracticed person would simply feel his foot slip down on a waving thread of uncertainty, Reind could feel his sole wrap and grip on the tightly-wound fibers of the rope. It wasn't like stepping on air. It was solid to him. Different than earth, maybe, but solid. If you were in tune.

Maybe that was the best simile. Walking the tightrope was like performing a violin solo. Long, elegant strokes across thin strands of fiber.

Of course, if you flubbed a note on a fiddle, you didn't end up so much dog food in front of an audience of hundreds. Usually. He thought of a spider, stepping without thought across skeins and splinters of web.

Tarantula, sang a dirge in his mind from a long-ago album by This Mortal Coil. That's what he tread across. This Mortal Coil. A skein of filigree and shadow. The web of a "Tarantula." He smiled and hummed.

The second step fell true. He sighed, an invisible breath of success. The audience didn't know the peril of those first two steps. It was the job of the ringmaster to keep them from focusing on that while the tightrope walker gained his composure and rhythm.

Down there, past the round red-and-yellow painted elephant step in the second ring. That's where the megaphone man made his plays. That's where the man with the handlebar mustache barked his exaggerated cries of, "Can you believe it, he's about to step out on the wire without a net beneath him…quiet ladies and gentlemen, this is very dangerous…"

That was exactly when Reind didn't care anymore. That's where the danger became safe. Sleight of hand and misdirection were the calling cards of the circus.

After the first few steps, he was home free. The adjustment zone at the intro; that's where the tough stuff was. It was the job of the ringmaster to keep the audience focused on the center and the false bravado, where it was easy.

The third step was good, and Reind's heart slowed.

Oh yes. Even after all these years of walking, his heart still kicked with a mule's petulant anger when he put that first toe to the wire. His mind may have been stubborn, but his body wasn't stupid. He knew that every walk could be his last.

But with step four, he knew that this was just another day. His bearings found, Reind moved steadily across the rope, one foot in front of the other, each step bearing down lower on the ever-so-slightly sloping rope, until he reached the center, and the object of the ringmaster's over-exaggerated cries of excitement. Once he started that upward incline on the far side of center (over the spot where there was no net) it was like walking up a hill. From the ground, it actually looked fairly level. But it wasn't, not quite. The second half of the walk was work, but it was easy. He began to think of Melienda, the night before. The way her fringed gold lame top had slipped from his fingers to the floor, a bouquet of tinsel. The way she'd shown him how a girl could really appreciate the controlled reflexes of a tightrope walker. She didn't care if his mother was the "three-breasted woman" of the freak show tent.

She loved his surety of self. She loved his lips for their deceiving softness.

He loved her eyes for their kaleidoscopic play of spark and dark and mystery. He loved her dimples for their expressive blushes.

God, he hoped she didn't tell. This was a dangerous game. All of their other meetings had been during the break between their acts. They'd seen each other on the sly for weeks, but never had a night date before. When he slipped back into his tent to face Erin after midnight, he'd had to make up an excuse about helping Raymond with a faulty rope pulley. She'd yawned and shrugged, and turned away back to sleep. Did she suspect?

It was one thing for a man of the circus to love a woman of

the same. It was another for a man of the circus to *cheat* on a woman of the circus with a woman of the same. He knew it was only a matter of time before someone talked to the wrong someone else. No matter how careful he was, tongues would wag. A circus was a family, and like any family, nothing stayed secret for very long.

Erin, Reind's wife, was a ticket-taker at the front gate.

She had no "talents," but she'd loved the smell of the damp bales of hay and the heat of popcorn in the air and the sticky promises that pink cotton candy gave and the front gate cries of, "Step right up ladies and gentlemen! Welcome to Barnett & Staley's Amazing, Mysterious, Phantasmagorical, Traveling Circus. Hear the mighty trumpet of the elephants and the happy horns of the clowns. Taste the taffy of our apples and caramel of our corn. Twist your body in the house of illusions. And for the truly terrifying, visit our freak show. Come and see the frightening Mr. Lee. Dare to meet the stare of Felina of the Five Eyes!"

That greeted the guests a dozen times a day in every town. They stepped past the ticket-taker girls and oohed and ahhed at the brightly colored, massive tents, at the fire engine red signs in the shape of giant hands that pointed this way and that, noting in daisy yellow script: "This way to the Freak Show. See the three-breasted woman! Hear the tiny voice of the Midget Man!" And another: "This way to the Center Ring, the site of the Show of Shows."

The people streamed inside the tent to see what they could never see at home. Sometimes, to breathe sighs of relief that they did not have such freakishness at home. But mostly to lose themselves in the strangeness and warped talent of it all. The circus was ultimately about the people who came to see it. It reflected them. And the people wanted to taste the salt of the corn and the sugar of the cotton and live the vicarious danger of a man on a tightrope and a woman in a skimpy top sticking her head inside the deadly lion's mouth. They wouldn't do it themselves, mind you. But somehow, seeing another person tread the wire or brave the teeth gave them satisfaction in their own lives. That was what Reind did… he gave satisfaction. He made life worth living for hundreds of folks every day.

Erin had been one of those people, once. She'd come to see him walk, and hung around after the show to talk. She'd ended up in his bed. She'd asked if he minded, the next morning. How could he have minded? She stayed with him through the next town, helping out as they struck the tents and pulled up the pitons and rewound the ropes. She'd shown up in a "God Left Me for Another Man" T-shirt on the third day with a backpack on her shoulder blades and said, "I hope you've got room in your bunk in Cincinnati," because that's where they were going. He'd said sure. Aside from the occasional fleas he ended up sharing it with (thanks to the lions), he'd always give up space for a girl like Erin.

Cincinnati, Dayton, Cleveland, Minneapolis, Detroit, Chicago… she'd been in his bed at the end of every show, challenging him to walk a different thin rope than the one he slid across in the air. This tightrope was wrapped in a scrim of emotion… and she was weaving it as they went. He was trapped before they left Ohio.

She began to earn her keep at the ticket-takers' booths.

"I'll not have you carry me," she said, on the day that she applied for the job. It's not like she had a lot of competition. Most of the people who traveled with the circus had talents and skills to show off. Or oddities. All Erin had were her looks and a lover. And free time on her hands.

So she worked the booth.

Reind worked a tent.

They made the circus money, and moved from town to town.

Until, in Peotone, Illinois, Reind met a girl with dark, curly locks that stretched down to tease at the creamy cleft between her purple crop top and the low-slung faded denim of her jeans. And he slept with her in the tall grass just beyond the recently-mowed parking lot. And he found that there was more than a wire, and a ticket-taker, and a suitcase to life. At least, that's what he thought, as her heavy, forceful tongue invaded his lips.

Reind thought he could quit the circus for Melienda, if that's what she wanted. He'd never thought that way when he met Erin. But for now, at least, he wouldn't have to consider it. Melienda had joined Barnett & Staley's Circus a few months before. She was the newest member of the family and was working in the Big Tent, ushering the animals and clowns and kids on and off the floor. Her name proved she didn't know how to spell, but she knew a whole lot else. In particular, she knew what made him feel real good. He'd found that out in between shows while Erin was still out at the front gate selling $3.75 tickets.

"Will you see me again?" she asked after, zipping up her jeans across bare pale flesh at eye level with him as he lounged on her wide cot.

"Yes," he smiled. "I'll do more than see you!"

Reind reached the middle of the rope walk and smiled, both at his memories of Melienda and his hearing… the barker was bragging of how this was "the most dangerous fifteen feet ever attempted by man…a twenty-five-foot high walk with no net across the deadly center floor of a Big Top." He could hear the audience take in a collective breath. Oooh. Ahhhhh.

His mind was far from the plodding step of toes to rope. His mind was on the deep, brown eyes and wide, pink lips of Melienda. And on what they might do for him tomorrow.

He almost didn't even hear the ear-crushing applause when he stepped up on the board on the other side and turned to bow to his audience, perfunctorily, before climbing down the ladder as a lion tamer came running across the dusty dirt floor to take his place in the public's eye. His private eye had other concerns.

Reind feigned sleep when Erin came in. He couldn't face her, tonight. He was a terrible liar. And, truth be told, despite his feats on the tightrope, a coward. He lay in bed with his eyes locked shut, wondering if he could convince Melienda to stay in Springfield with him. The circus could pack itself up and hit the road, and when it arrived in St. Louis, it would just be short one tightrope walker and one glitter girl. They could hitch onto another circus easily enough… He didn't really believe the last part, and he doubted Melienda would either; she'd just finally ended a job search. How many traveling bands of multitalented gypsies were there in middle America? And how many needed performers?

He rolled on his side as Erin kicked her shoes into her trunk with two muted thuds, and slipped off her heavy, gold-lined, red jacket, draping it over a folding chair with a hollow clang of metal beads meeting metal back. As she did every night. He heard her jewelry hit the pressboard of her thin shelving unit. She insisted on keeping one light piece of furniture in their portable "home."

She slipped beside him under the covers, cool silk brushing his thigh. Reind could feel her eyes burrowing into his neck.

"You wanna talk about it?" she said finally. He didn't stir.

"Yeah, didn't think so," she whispered.

They both lay there, faces to the canvas ceiling, each knowing the other was awake, as somewhere a clock ticked through the hour, click-stop, click-stop, click-stop, click-stop, click…

When Reind woke up, Erin was already gone. Part of him was relieved, but another was frightened. What did she know? What would she say, when he finally came clean? He shook away the visions of her screaming and beating at his chest with clenched fists. He dressed quickly, and went out to meet the crowds. He had a show to do.

He passed his mother, Yvette, "The Three-Breasted Woman" outside of the freak show tent. Her arms were crossed over the objects of her attraction, and she shook her head at him and tsked.

"Behave," was all she said— though that was a volume for her—and vanished behind the flap of canvas.

Great, Reind thought. *Did everyone already know?*

The first step was harder than usual.

The second, almost impossible.

He couldn't focus. He kept hearing Erin ask in the darkness, "You wanna talk about it?"

She knew.

She *knew,* damnit. Maybe his mother did too! Shit, maybe the whole goddamned circus knew. But how? It hadn't been that long. And they'd been careful…Or was he just being paranoid?

He could feel a change in texture to the rope beneath his foot at step three, but didn't look down. When you were on the wire, you didn't turn back, and you didn't look down.

But then he felt it again. His foot seemed to slide, just a bit.

Reind didn't move his head, but his eyes slid down, staring at the event horizon of the long rope below him. He saw the cause of the disturbance. If he hadn't been so preoccupied with his infidelity when climbing the ladder and starting out across the rope by rote, he couldn't have missed it.

Someone had wound strands of golden tinsel every few inches, all down the length of rope.

Cute, he thought, and refocused his gaze. Irritating, but not dangerous. He was already past step five and the rest of the way was just a walk in the park, really. He and Rafe, the tentmaster, would be having a long talk when he got down for this little stunt. You don't mess with a guy's tightrope to "pretty it up" without telling him!

Down on the main floor, the ringmaster was just winding up, getting into his act.

"Shh, ladies and gentlemen, be very quiet now," the man in the red- and white-striped suit intoned, holding a finger to his lips. "He is coming up to the most dangerous part. A walk of intense peril. The most dangerous fifteen feet ever attempted by man… Look as he steps out over the ground fifty feet below… without a net!"

Reind hardly smiled at those familiar words. Old hat. He'd heard them too many times. He stepped, slipped a little again on tinsel, stepped again and stepped…

"Shit," he hissed. Something bit into his foot. He hurriedly stepped again and almost fell.

The rope felt as if it had disappeared and he was treading on a razor. The thin fabric covering the soles of his feet barely shielded them from the rope, allowing him to feel the texture of the strands beneath him. And right now, all he was feeling was pain and a growing heat down the center of his feet.

His arms struck out and waved for balance as his walk slowed, and the crowd took in its breath with a perceptible gasp. The whole world seemed to creak to a slow motion crawl.

He stepped again, and this time, cried out.

And again. The pain was growing, but Reind could not go back. He could not stop. On the wire, there was only going forward, or going down.

Reind looked down, afraid of losing his focus completely, but unable to stop himself from seeing what had been done to his rope.

His rope had been taken away.

Across the fifteen-foot gap above where the nets were withdrawn—the "dangerous" part of his walk—a single, heavy steel wire extended. He had stepped, without seeing, from thick rope onto thin, slicing wire. Ahead, where the protective nets again began below, the wire rejoined the treadable thickness of rope.

He would not be safe until he'd truly "walked the wire."

Tears were already slipping down his cheeks from the pain, but he would not, could not stop. To stop now would mean death. Or at the very least, a broken back.

Another step, and the skin of his feet was separating, slipping down in a wet, bloody kiss around the wire. He lifted his right foot, feeling the skin sucking at the steel as he pulled it up and away, only to place it down again.

He screamed.

And stepped.

Cried, "Oh my god, my god."

And stepped.

The audience was aware that something wasn't right, and the background noise grew in volume as people pointed and chattered and a thousand voices whispered, "Oh dear, oh my."

He could feel the web between the second and third toes of his left foot give way with a painful tear and he nearly fell again, wobbling off balance, arms akimbo, waving from side to side but still his legs not stopping, not slowing, no. He put his right foot down, bloody, shredded and fire-hot to the razoring foot-garrote and swore every curse he knew in a foul blue stream, no longer caring if the audience heard or saw his moment of weakness. Now it was life or death for him.

This wasn't a performance.

This was a survival test.

This was a punishment.

At last the filleted remnant of his right foot came down on what seemed to be a foot-wide support of rope, and he pulled his left forward to match.

He'd made it. Whoever had done this, he'd beaten them. He'd survived.

He looked down at the familiar surface, checking to see if more foot irritants lurked in the last third of his journey across the sky of the big top.

The rope was free of exposed wire, and golden tinsel. In their place, was a new decoration.

Every remaining foot of his walk was marked off with what looked like raven-smooth ribbons. Ribbons made of long, black twists of hair. The slippery, red blood of his foot was dripping down the satiny locks of one curl even now.

Reind knew whose hair had been shorn to decorate his rope.

Reind knew whose costume the golden tassels had been ripped and clipped from.

And when he finally reached the platform at the end of his faltering walk, when he slumped down on his knees to cry and shake with relief on the plywood surface, and saw the glass jar with a fist-sized, bloody organ floating inside, Reind knew whose heart had been cut out.

The doctor cleaned and stitched and dressed his feet, and assured him that he would be able to walk the ropes again. If he wanted to. Reind didn't ask about the new jar perched on the doctor's medicine shelf. The jar with something kidney-shaped floating inside.

Back at his trailer, Erin waited.

"They said you had some trouble with your walk today," she cooed, one eyebrow raised in an innocent question. "Oh my, what happened to your feet?"

He set the crutches aside and collapsed on the bed next to her, where she kissed his forehead, and stroked his hair.

"My poor baby," she said. "Do you want to talk about it?"

Reind shivered and shook his head. "I don't think so. Some things, just can't be said."

She stood up, shaking her head in agreement. "I'm glad you think so. I feel the same way."

She walked over to her shelves, and pulled a jar from the top. "Your mother gave me this today," she said, holding it out in front of her, as if to catch the light to see something hidden inside.

"She asked me what I thought about adding it to the display of two-headed calves and conjoined twins and all the rest of the twisted mutants they have jarred up over there in the freak show. I told her I thought so, but I said I'd ask you. What do you think?"

Reind took the proffered jar and stared deep within its

yellow, formaldehyde waters. Inside, a tiny Tom Thumb floated, umbilical waving like a wrinkled, severed worm. Its eyes, barely the size of a pinhead, were black, and open. Despite its size, Reind could make out every finger and toe. It was perfect.

"Some things just can't be said," she murmured. "And some things just shouldn't be born."

Reind could see a tiny drop of blood hanging like smog near the tiny cord, drifting in the preservative solution. He choked, and nearly dropped the glass.

Erin rescued it from him, and flashed a sad, weary smile. "So what do you think?"

"I think it's going to be hard to walk for awhile," he said.

"Yeah," she answered. "Yeah, it looks that way. But you've got me to take care of you. We'll all take care of you."

She paused and met his gaze, her eyes hard. "We're all family, remember? The circus takes care of its own."

Then she took the tiny child, and left the tent, leaving Reind to cry in dry, empty sobs over the loss of his son, and his lover, as he stared into the other jar left behind on Erin's traveling shelves. Reind stared for hours into the deep, brown, floating eyes of Melienda, who would never see again.

Birth and Death

Erin knelt at the foot of the bed, steam beading in tiny pearls on her neck from the bucket of hot water on the trailer floor by her thigh. In front of her, writhing silently on the damp sheets, lay her mother-in-law. Every inch of the woman seemed in motion—eight breasts shivering like a glass of water in the early tremors of an earthquake, hands grasping at the bed frame like an electrocution victim, toes clenching and releasing like a spastic row of misfiring pistons.

Erin worried that Yvette was dying. The Freak Show Tent's main attraction had been in labor all night, and so far had introduced no new mutated stillborn wonders to the empty mason jars at her left, or new future circus performers to the cribs at her right. Her face was pinched and white, and her breathing erratic. This description was perhaps not unusual for a normal woman in labor, but Yvette was no normal woman. She was the Eight-Breasted Woman (or the Three- or the Four- or the Six-Breasted Woman, depending on how pregnant she was), and after giving birth to dozens and dozens of freaks and fellow performers over the past two decades, childbirth was normally a fairly painless process for her. But her last couple pregnancies had not turned out any viable children, and now, this one seemed to have some major complication…

A cool draught suddenly chilled the steam on her neck, and behind her, the barker trod with a heavy foot into the room.

"How is she?" his low whisper growled.

Erin glanced backwards, taking in the uncontrolled tousle of the barker's normally pristinely coiffed locks and the red tint to his habitually sharp, glinting brown eyes. He'd been pacing outside the trailer all night.

"Still the same," she said.

"Reind is waiting outside," he murmured. "And Felina. And Andrese. And Skyy has been here. And the dwarf twins. And some of the others. They all want to help."

"There is nothing to do," Erin sighed. "It is all up to her."

They both stared at the sweat-sheened face lying close-eyed on the bed and grew silent. They both thought the same thing; what would the circus be without Yvette?

Talman was 17 years old and cocky as hell. He had every reason to be. He was *there*, man. *Part* of it. *Into* it. His jeans were five sizes too large, and bagged at his ankles as they revealed the white band of his Jockey briefs. Anyone would envy his look—he had it *going on*. He wore a gold chain around his neck and a black Kid Rock T-shirt around his middle. He'd shaved his hair in an oblong pattern that suggested a football that had been cut in half and snapped on top of his head. His arms boasted an intricate, complex purple and red and turquoise swirl of ink. Talman had spent a lot of hours hiding out and helping out and tasting the pain of the needle in the back of his uncle's tattoo parlor. A finely scaled serpent constricted in waves around his biceps twice before its crimson-forked tongue kissed the lips of a well-bosomed, barely clad babe clutched in the claws of a glowing green dragon. On his forearm, a garden of roses decayed into the sneer of a bloody demon. On his shoulder, a skull winked as smoke curled from the cigar between its bare, bone teeth.

Talman's back was a more disturbing canvas, but that art he didn't show off. The tattoos there were the work of his stepfather—a crisscross network of bruises and scars and half-healed scabs. His stepfather Larry had a habit of taking out the frustrations of his pathetic, go-nowhere life on Talman after the lights went out and his mom passed out. But Talman swallowed the blows, and lay still on the bed beneath the belts and punches and eventual callused caresses that signaled a guilty end to the beatings. Talman survived. Nobody was going to stop him.

He was cocky as hell.

Today, he felt so cocky he'd ditched his L-with-a-capital-thumb-and-forefinger Loser job at the Dairy Queen (DQ to the regulars) and turned up with 16 bucks in pocket at the circus. It was only in town for the weekend, and how often did a circus come to an out-of-it backwoods like Liberty, Illinois anyway?

He was gonna see some shit today, goddamn. Hell with the endless litanies at school and work about when and where he should spend his time. Hell with Larry and his beatings. Hell with Uncle Pete and mopping up the back room floor dotted by spots of anxious, mistaken blood and angered, broken needles.

Talman hit the circus with attitude. Not a little of it desperation, though he'd never have put it that way. Talman was on the rail. Hell, his back wasn't even too sore today.

««—»»

The two-headed boy cried four trails of tears as the audience threw the usual, unimaginative jeers and jokes his way.

"How would you like to have to think the same thing twice all the time?" the barker called out, accusing the crowd with a long shaking finger and stifling the urge to hug the poor child in public. All of the circus performers were worried about Yvette, and an easy audience dig of "So tell me freak, are two heads better than one?" which would normally have rolled right off Andrese's twisted back, had brought tears. The insults were all part of the act, but neither the barker nor Andrese had the strength to go on today.

"All right," the barker crowed, a lump in his gravelly throat.

"Let's say good day to the boy who proves that two heads are better than one and hello to the girl who proves that spiders aren't the only ones to get around quickly on eight legs.

He fled to the shadows of the freak show tent and wiped away tears as Yvonne, the spindly girl with four legs leaving her hips, and four arms dangling from her shoulders (two of them as disproportionate as Tyrannosaurus limbs) shambled like an arachnoid across the stage.

Yvette's last truly successful freak creation was in tears before she pirouetted across the center boards of the stage. The circus was not a happy place today, as its mother and soul lay gasping for breath in her trailer. Everyone—from ticket-takers to clowns to freak show paraders—knew that Yvette was in a bad way. And there was nothing that could be done.

The makeup of Wen and Wong, her dwarf children who served as keystone cop clowns in the Big Top, was being touched up every hour, and the skintight red costume of Skyy, the three-eyed fortune teller, was purple with sweat, as the grieving child sought to tell fortunes for her clients while thinking incessantly of the pain of her mother just a few tents away.

She would find herself tracing the lines of an innocent's palm and saying "You will die" without hesitation, and then, seeing the shaking, quailing fear in the eyes and hands of her clients, she would backtrack and pat their shoulders.

"I'm sorry, I'm sorry," she begged as they pushed away from her to scurry from the tent. "My mother is very ill…it was her fortune I was channeling. I am so sorry."

Skyy would think of those words as her clients ducked through the canvas back to the sun of the Midway and cry.

Her mother ought to be living to enjoy the circus, now that it was beginning to become wildly successful. Of course, with Yvette sick, maybe this was the beginning of the end, and not the beginning of the beginning.

Outside she could hear her brother Reind, filling in briefly for her usual ticket-taker Matthew, urging passersby to stop in to her tent to "sneak a glance behind the shadowy veil of the future." He wasn't as mysterious as Matthew, but he was persistent. And suddenly, the flap of her tent moved, and the iridescent strings of beads and bells rattled and chimed, and the most colorful man Skyy had seen in weeks stepped up to her table.

"Good day," she intoned softly.

"Hey," he said. And then, "Fuck."

He stood before her, arm half raised to his head, mouth locked open in an O for seconds.

"You've *really* got three eyes," he gasped finally, staring at the offending orb that blinked calmly in the center of her forehead.

She nodded.

"That's fucked up."

She shrugged and pointed to the chair in front of her. "Please, sit. Relax."

He pulled the chair back cautiously, his eyes never leaving hers. Never leaving her forehead, really. Finally, he eased his long body into the seat, and was soon slumped back, one arm anchored on the table, the other hanging listlessly off the edge of the chair to dangle pointing at the floor.

"So you're a fortune teller, huh?"

"I'm Skyy, and I will tell you your future," she said, warming up to her usual spiel.

"Whatever," he said, stopping her cold. "Just don't lie to me, okay?"

"The future doesn't lie," she said. "It just *is*."

"Well, if it's like the present, it probably sucks," he said. "But lay it on me. I wanna know."

"Come now," she crooned, her triple gaze tracing the beautiful lines of the art on his arm, and lingering on the shadowed wells of his deep brown eyes. "Could it really be that bad?"

"You tell me," he said, and offered her his palms. She accepted them into hers, and with a purple painted nail, traced the long seven of his right hand, and then the tributaries and creases extending from it towards his thumb. This didn't tell her anything, but it was one of the expected tricks of the trade.

Skyy really did tell fortunes. It was a gift of the third eye, or a fluke of nature. But what she needed to catch the scattered glimpses of a person's future wasn't the slant and flail of their wrinkles, it was the touch of their aura. And this she gained from holding Talman's hands.

As one finger traced the soft lines in his palm, behind her eyes a vision built, and then broke, plunging her consciousness into another place. Her eyes unconsciously shut as she absorbed the waking dream, and suddenly she *was* Talman, lying in a darkened room, face buried in pillow, fists clenched and pounding uselessly on a mattress, as a machine gun swift hail of piercing, painful slugs sliced into his back.

"I'm through with talking," a heavy, slurred voice said, and then another red-hot pain sliced through her vision. Something warm and wet was dripping down her ribs, and without warning, she suddenly felt nothing at all below her neck, though she could feel her body rocking with the blows.

"Fuck you," she heard herself say, and then something sharp and pointed hit the back of her head and she kissed the pillow, suddenly not feeling able to speak or move or…live. The world was a mass of black and red spiders, skittering and weaving a criss-cross pattern of pain around her until the strength ebbed, and she felt her very self slipping down a dark rabbit hole, a well of existence, and the life above became a light that glowed bright and then ebbed as she fell farther and farther…

Skyy snapped back to reality and opened all three eyes to stare without mercy at Talman, whose hands remained clasped in her own.

"You will die," she said, and this time she wasn't mistakenly channeling the future of her mother. She was serious.

"No shit," the boy said, unflinching. "The question is, 'when.' Everyone will die. That's not much of a fortune."

Skyy met his eyes with a trace of fear. She'd only seen the moment of someone's death a handful of times in her life, and her mother's imminent demise was one of them. She'd never seen the death of someone so young. And from the glimpses she'd seen of Talman's body in the seconds she'd "been" him, his murder was not far in the future.

"I'm sorry," she said, searching for the way out of her admission. Telling the tale of someone's death was not good form for a circus fortune teller. It didn't exactly increase business.

"You're right. Everybody dies eventually, and you don't need to know the method of yours. Let's try a different reading."

She reached out to touch his forehead, but instead he grabbed her palm and pushed it against his own.

"I don't care," he insisted. "Tell me exactly what you saw. Exactly."

Skyy looked down, avoiding his eyes.

"Straight-up," he urged, and tugged on her hand.

"You were lying on a bed," she whispered, "and someone was beating you from behind. With a knife I think. It really hurt. At the end…I think you died."

"Figured that sooner or later fists wouldn't be enough," Talman said, releasing her hand. "Thanks," he nodded, lips drawn tight. "Thanks."

He rose to go and Skyy stood to stop him.

"Don't go yet," she said. "Let me try to see something else. The future is a changing path."

"If I go home, I'm dead," he said. "That's pretty clear. And when it comes to it, I didn't really need a fortune teller to tell me."

Talman turned and walked without pausing through the opening in her tent, and Skyy slumped back to her chair and cried.

"Reind," she called out after a minute, and the blonde tightrope-walker's head popped inside the flap.

"Don't let anyone else in for a few, okay?"

His face clouded, but he nodded and stepped back outside.

She put her face in her hands and cried on the table, her eyes still seeing the shadowed fabric of the pillows, her chest feeling the pressure of the threads of the sheets as someone behind her sunk piercing blade after blade into her back and neck and legs…

Talman walked away from the fortune teller's tent with speed. He had no destination, but he didn't need to be reminded that going home meant eventually dying under the misguided wrath of his stepfather. He passed the games of chance (read, rip-off) and then the Big Top, where he could hear the echo of the barker's microphone, and the bleating trumpet of an elephant.

At last he came to the Freak Show tent. Outside, the entrance was empty, and a sign hung from a lone post that said "Closed, please come back in an hour."

"Fuck that," Talman said, and, looking around to see that no one was watching him (they weren't), he stepped up to the tent and found the opening. With a nod and a step, he was inside.

The tent was dark, but it wasn't hard to tell what the rows of jars just beyond the ticket-taker's podium were.

"Shit," Talman pronounced, and stepped closer to see the contents of the seemingly endless rows of jars. There were five rows, stacked in front of a gold curtain. They lined the passage that led inside to a main stage where freak show performers did their thing. But the first thing you saw upon filing into the tent was the jars. Inside each one floated a small body—or in some cases, two small bodies, which happened to share a common organ—like a chest or a groin. There were babies with six eyes ranged across their skulls, and unborn abortions of six and eight limbs, or two heads, or three legs. Talman stared at the array in disbelief, and peered closely into the yellowed water to see if he could tell whether the bodies were plastic, or if they were real bodies that some fucked up death artist had taken and sewn together in warped and wicked ways. It was dark, but he swore he could see the intricate whorls of fingerprints on the seven fingers of one larger body. Its eyes were like black pools of tar, and Talman drew back suddenly, the hair prickling on the back of his neck. He felt as if he was being watched, as if all the dozens of dead things were silently turning and twisting in their transparent crypts to stare at him.

He backed away from the wall of babies and moved into the main area of the tent, where empty metal folding chairs waited in lines for an audience and a performer to take the empty stage.

"I thought that was you," a voice said from behind him.

Talman whirled to face the newcomer, a tall, heavyset man with thick lips, a wide nose and hairy arms. A man Talman knew well. Terry. The scars on his back burned at the sound of his voice.

"Yeah, so what?" Talman said.

His stepfather moved closer, his steps menacing.

"You're supposed to be at work," he said.

"You're supposed to be finding a job," Talman retorted.

The blow landed before the boy could lift his foot to move, and he fell backwards, the explosion in his head quickly whited out by the spears of pain from the backs and legs and seats of chairs meeting his body between ribs, behind his knee, cracking against his neck. He'd barely touched the ground when his stepfather was lifting him by the front of his shirt and slapping him across the face again.

"Don't fuckin' give me mouth, punk. You want to go a round, we'll do it. And you'll lose."

Talman didn't say a thing, still trying to focus past the stars in front of his eyes.

"We're gonna go home now, I think. And maybe you and I will have a little more discussion once we get to your room."

Talman remembered the vision of Skyy, and wondered if today was the day. Certainly Terry looked mean enough to do some major damage if they were truly left alone. Fear chilled his belly and Talman knew that he couldn't go home. Didn't dare.

"Little fuckin' prick," Terry was going on. "I shoulda fed it to you a long time ago and gotten you into line when you were younger. Now it's only gonna hurt more."

Talman knew what that meant, and his back and legs throbbed with the memories. No, he decided. He wasn't going. Not this time. With a sudden lunge, he brought his knee up to slam into Terry's crotch and then ripped away from the bigger man as his fingers relaxed for a moment and he screamed in anger and pain.

Talman ran for the exit, but just as he rounded the bend to the hallway of fetal jars, a blow struck him in the back and he went down, tasting dirt and grass.

"Now you're gonna really get it," Terry growled, pulling him off the ground by his hair. Talman saw the murder in those steely blue eyes and screamed for help.

"Shut it," Terry yelled, clamping one hand over Talman's mouth, and then doubling over just a little and gritting his teeth. The knee had done a good job.

Talman thought frantically about how to extricate himself from the man. Today was the day for sure if he ended up on his bed back home. He wasn't strong enough to punch his way out of this, and Terry was guarding his crotch with his left hand. Talman looked into the black eyes of the dead baby with seven fingers. It seemed to speak to him. A quiet urgent voice in his head told him exactly what to do. And he did.

The crack of the glass against Terry's temple caught his stepfather by surprise, dropping him instantly to the earth as a stinking rain of yellow liquid and glass covered his chest and shoulder. As he rolled over on the ground, Terry's face mashed into the soft, buttery skin of the dead child, ripping a tissue-thin veil of flesh from the baby and bending its arm backwards with an almost inaudible snap. A darker but still almost clear fluid trickled from the pale insides of the baby to drool on Terry's lips, but he didn't flinch. The man was out cold.

Talman dropped the lid and the glass mouth still connected in shards to it, and started for the tent flap leading outside. But then at the last minute he turned. If Terry came to in the next couple minutes, the first place he would look would be outside in the sun, where Talman would be easy to spot. He needed to hide.

Stepping over his stepfather and the broken baby, Talman ran through the exhibition area and across the stage. In the back he found a passage leading away from the crowds and the entrance, and he took it, stopping just before rounding a bend where he heard voices.

Cautiously he peeked around the canvas and saw a dark-haired man in a red suit with a long mustache pacing outside of a trailer. Two dwarves chattered nearby. He waited, wondering if he was trapped now. He couldn't go back; he didn't think Terry would stay out for long. But he was too exposed to stay here. What could he do? He looked around but saw no place to secret himself, until the area cleared. Then he could hide behind the trailer if he wanted. Or duck out the back of the tent and continue across the grounds. But he was probably safer hidden in a back tent for a couple hours than wandering around in the open.

The door of the trailer opened, and Talman saw a pretty girl poke her head out and call to the three waiting.

"Get Skyy," she said.

The door closed and both the man and the dwarves hurried out of the tent through a flap a few yards away. They were heading back out towards the Midway. As soon as they were gone, Talman ran to the back of the trailer, and sat against its walls, arms hugging his legs close to his body. How long could he stay here?

"She wants you," the barker said, and a chill spiked through Skyy's belly. The time was here. Taking a deep breath and blinking back a tear, she hurried after him and Wen and Wong to her mother's trailer.

Inside, Reind stood against one wall as Erin mopped Yvette's brow with a rag. The others were there too, Felina, Yvonne, Andrese, Helena. Nobody said a word as she entered, and she went straight to the head of the bed. Erin stepped away and Skyy knelt in her place, immediately feeling the awful pain of her mother through the strange sight of her third eye. All pain was bad, but this pain felt truly…wrong. Terminal.

"Mama," she whispered. The older woman smiled weakly and nodded.

There was a thud from the far corner of the trailer and Andrese turned his blonde head to look out the back window.

"Someone's outside," he announced. His brunette side never stopped staring at Yvette.

"Who?" Skyy asked.

"Kid. Big hair and tattoos. He's leaning against the wall over here."

"I'll shag him," Reind said, and moved to the door.

Skyy watched him leave, but then called him back just as the door was closing.

"Reind," she said. "Don't send him away. Bring him in here."

"You can't be serious!" he said. "She's dying, you can't…"

"Trust me," Skyy said. It felt right.

The door closed and she looked at her mother's white face. Despite the shaking, wracking pain, Yvette's eyes met hers with a strange calmness, searching her daughter's soul.

"I'm not ready," Skyy whispered.

Yvette met her gaze and hissed. "Ready," she said. "You must. You'll find help."

The trailer door opened, and Reind pushed a struggling Talman into the room.

"I wasn't doing anything," the boy protested.

"Shhhh," Skyy said, looking his way. Talman was instantly silent.

Talman saw the room was filled with freaks. A two-headed guy. A girl with too many arms. Dwarves. Skyy and her three eyes. But the strangest, he thought, was on the bed, where a half naked woman lay gasping and shaking with an exposed and ridiculous number of breasts. He suddenly knew why the Freak Show tent had been empty in the middle of the day. They were all here.

"Is she having a baby?" he asked, noting the bulge of her belly and the cribs and jars.

"Several," the girl with four arms answered.

At that, the woman on the bed suddenly cried out loud, a hideous, toe-curling scream that seemed to cut off as quickly as it began. She rose from the pillow, and then fell back to the bed, and Talman saw the woman at the foot of the bed reach forward, and rescue a red, wriggling thing from between the woman's legs.

"It's a boy," Erin said and handed the child to Andrese who immediately began wiping it clean.

"It has three heads!" Andrese announced. "And it's still living!"

And then Yvette screeched again, and another bloody bundle fell into Erin's hands. This one made no noise. Erin shook her head and handed the stillborn child to one of the dwarves.

"Too many testicles," Wen said, and sponged the baby off before placing it in a jar to be worked on later.

Again Yvette cried out with heartstopping volume, and then instantly stopped as deformed child after deformed child was delivered, eight in all.

Talman watched it all silently, keeping to the wall and out of the way as each of the family took a child, dead or alive and cleaned it, readying it for life…or display. A girlchild had eight nipples, just like its mother. A boy had a tail growing from the end of its spine.

The one that chilled him the most though was the child without any sex at all. It was a stillborn, and was smooth between its legs. In the center of its chest was a second mouth. Both of its mouths were wide open, and Talman imagined it inside Yvette, soundlessly screaming in stereo as it expired.

At last, with a final expulsion of dark blood and what Talman guessed were the slick organs of "afterbirth," Yvette slumped to the bed, and cried no more.

"Benjamin," Skyy suddenly called, and the door burst open instantly. The ringmaster entered, and rushed to Yvette's side.

"I think it's over," Skyy whispered, and drew back as the man buried his mustache in the crook of Yvette's neck. The woman didn't stir.

Skyy came to stand by Talman, cheeks glistening with the waterfall of tears from three crying eyes. After watching Benjamin cry and whisper to Yvette's body for a few minutes, Skyy finally turned to look at Talman with a long, wet stare.

Finally, she nodded to herself and asked, "You don't want to go home, do you?"

He shook his head.

"Would you like to travel with us for awhile?"

The faces of her sisters and brothers nearby turned towards her with frowns and one of Andrese's mouths whispered, "What do we need him for?"

Skyy smiled. "He needs us right now."

Talman stood up straighter, about to protest. He didn't need anyone.

"And *I* need him," she continued. "If mama's passing things on to me, I need help, and you all already have work enough. And I don't think Benjamin is going to be up to it for awhile."

The ringmaster was now sobbing uncontrollably at the bedside.

Talman relaxed slightly.

"It's been awhile since the circus had a tattooed man," Skyy said thoughtfully, looking again at Talman's garishly decorated arms. "Interested in adding to your collection?"

Talman grinned, just a little.

"Yeah," he said, and moved with Skyy to stand at the side of Yvette's bed. He looked around the room at this bizarre family of freaks and felt something strange inside. Something he hadn't felt since his dad passed away.

Talman finally felt at home.

"Yeah," he whispered again, this time to himself. In his throat he felt a lump of sorrow for the pain of his newfound family, and after a moment, a tear crossed his cheek, for the mother he would never get to know.

You Never Got Used to the Needle

"Let me tell you something about my tattoos," the artist said. "When I draw on you it is not just a picture; with my ink I will scratch into your soul. My art is deeper than skin."

Right now it felt like the needles were penetrating his soul.

You never got used to the needle.

Talman grit his teeth and closed his eyes. It was always difficult, but today it seemed worse than ever. Normally, after the first sting of the needle a warm fuzzy glow spread out across his body from the start of the tattoo. He would close his eyes and the world would become a haze of pain and blood. As the artist worked, he could feel the image growing across his skin, spreading out from its center to embrace him, to own him. He was the artist's canvas, as the needles wove their ink indelibly into his skin. As he grew used to the pain, his mind slipped away. At first he was anchored by the fire in his flesh, but after a while, Talman could see beyond the tiny rooms with their tawdry pictures and dark stained floors.

Every town was the same. Every town had a tattoo parlor that blared its trade in neon screams and called to young and old to decorate the skeins of their lives in garish ink.

There was almost always a girl at the counter with dark hair and painted eyes and arms that spoke of storybook nightmares and whimsical dreams. Sometimes, Talman stared deep into their ocher eyes and marveled at the emptiness there. But mostly, he bypassed the girls and moved straight to the artist and asked if he or she could do something special.

The artists were often cast from a similar mold as well. They wore shirts with sleeves ripped out in order to display both their skills and demons in Technicolor flexing. Sometimes their heads were shaved and sometimes their skulls bore the imprint of another's needle—at least Talman hoped it was another's. He couldn't fathom how somebody could stitch a picture into his own scalp, though he had met artists who claimed to have done every one of their tattoos, from the snakes around their thighs to the dragons on their backs, using their own hands and a mirror. He couldn't imagine. Even after three dozen designs carved in his skin, Talman still squinted back tears and struggled to slip away from the moment of inking.

He would think about the circus, and Skyy. He would think about the children, and pray that they were all right. Ever since the death of Yvette, the circus' eight-breasted woman, he and Skyy had acted as surrogate parents to Yvette's babies, Skyy's siblings. He worried most about Sal, the three-headed hermaphrodite. How could the child ever survive with so many choices to make?

But today he felt far from Sal and the circus and Skyy. He had stalked away from the circus grounds early in the morning, as Skyy still breathed softly in sleep. He'd been awake most of the night again, haunted by the feeling that something wasn't right. The ache in his heart had grown with each passing day for weeks. He couldn't put his finger on the reason, but Talman was troubled. Skyy sensed it, he knew. Each night she tried to lull him to sleep with kisses and caresses, but Talman only rolled away. He wasn't happy anymore, and there was nothing she or anyone else could do about it.

So this morning, he'd done what he always did when he felt lost. He'd taken a long walk that led straight to a tattoo parlor. A place where he could mask pain with art. But with the art, came the agony of the needle. And the needle was doing its work now.

The pain was all-encompassing; it was all he could focus on. It was all that there was. He could feel the artist's needles dipping deeper and deeper into his flesh, injecting their bloody ink closer and closer to his core.

He had covered his body in the past with pictures of snakes, fairies, skulls, dragons and all manner of mythical, colorful creatures. The children loved him to bend and flex and reveal the mysteries beneath his shirt. And when he bared his leg they'd shriek in fear of its wickedly snarling black demon of death. He had thought that the ancient serpent that coiled from his left thigh up around his belly button was the most painful tattoo he could experience. But this latest tattoo struck straight to the heart.

And that was the artist's intention.

Talman could feel the pound in his chest drumming faster and faster as the needles penetrated the flesh just above its cage of bones. This was a new magic; the artist had promised that this tattoo was not of some fictional beast or some mythical god. When Talman had entered the tiny tattoo shop in Parkville, Illinois he had stood alone for many minutes staring at the colorful walls. The pictures here were not the normal sort of tattoo artist showings. Oh, there were the grinning skulls and the burlesque tarts and the snarling dragons and more, but somehow these tattoos, these pictures, seemed more real, more intricate than any he had seen before. Perhaps it was because of the shop's darkness, for there was no girl waiting at the counter to tease and encourage. And Talman saw no artist waiting at the back room. He had been ready to leave, turning towards the door when a voice called out, "Can I help you?"

Talman turned to see an old man with white hair shuffling from a back hall. The man was polishing something with white cloth.

"Maybe," Talman said. "I'm looking for something special,

something really unique. I'm the "tattooed man" for a circus, so I can't get away with the usual blue and red dragons. When our barker introduces me, he tells everyone that my body will 'inspire, and amuse, and frighten.' Is there someone here who has the skill to help me? To give me something truly different?"

The old man slipped the white cloth in his pocket, perched a thin pair of glasses on his nose, looked him over a moment, and then nodded. "I may be able to help you."

The man's hand tremored as he held it out to shake, and Talman raised an eyebrow.

"You can draw well?" he asked.

"I don't just draw on your skin," the old man grinned. "I draw on your soul."

"I ain't got no soul," Talman shook his head and blurted. "I've just got skin. And I need to use it well. You can't be the tattooed man of the circus if you don't have some real art on your parts."

He waved a hand around the shop. "Are these pictures of your work?"

"Pictures only tell a part of the story," the old tattoo artist said, but he rose and walked stiffly to retrieve a black binder tucked beneath a white formica counter.

"The real story is in here," the artist nodded, tapping a gnarled finger to his equally weathered forehead. "And here," he repeated, tapping his chest.

Talman took the binder and paged past its cover, instantly sighing in awe of the intricate twinings, lifelike portraits and bleeds of patterned color displayed on arms and legs and necks via 4x6" photos there.

The old man nodded. "My work is never simple," he said, "and its life stretches beyond its canvas. Sit with me and talk awhile and let's consider the manner of your tattoo."

He gently pulled the binder away from Talman.

"Let's not talk of books or patterns. You said you need something different than the rest, so it won't do to look at things that others already have. Let's talk awhile, and from there your own particular image will grow."

Talman shrugged and humored the old man, following him to the back of the shop to sit in old, cracked red vinyl chairs. They talked about each and every design that covered his body, from the mundane skull grinning amid decaying roses drawn when he was just 16 to the more recent, more elaborate serpents, clowns and mystical symbols. Gradually he told the old man of how it started. Of how he would get tattoos to hide the bruises and scars and cigarette burns left by his stepfather and of how he'd joined the circus to leave that abuse behind. He told the man of how he'd stood at the deathbed of the circus matriarch Yvette and watched as she bore freak after three-headed freak before expiring in the arms of the ringmaster. He told of how he fell in love with the matriarch's daughter Skyy, and how they struggled to keep the circus on the road moving from town to town never stopping, never resting.

"But why?" the artist asked. "Why did you stay with them, why didn't you go to school? Do you really want your whole life to revolve 'round the colors of your skin?"

"It's as good a job as any," Talman said.

"Do you care about your patrons?"

"They pay us." Talman shrugged. "What more do I need to care about?"

"What are you running from now?" the man asked. Talman looked away. A moment passed while neither spoke.

"Take off your shirt."

Talman didn't question. He already had lifted the shirt before to show the serpent and the dragon wings crossing his back. Now he rolled the white T-shirt over the top of his head with a single pull and the old man appraised him slowly, walking around and around him, one finger to his lips, nodding.

"There is room on your chest," the old man said. "You already have heart, but how would like to have some more?"

"What, we're going to put a valentine on my chest?" Talman laughed, but the old man did not smile.

"Let me tell you something about my tattoos," he said. "When I draw on you it is not just a picture; with my ink I will scratch into your soul. My art is deeper than skin."

««—»»

On the way back to the circus grounds, Talman felt weak. Getting a tattoo always left him a little knock-kneed, but this was worse than usual. His entire chest seemed seared. It tingled as if a cascade of blue electric arcs ranged across it. He forced himself not to touch the bruised, angry spot in the center of his chest; he didn't want to ruin the heavy sheen of antibiotic ointment that glistened there.

The main street was lightly trafficked for a sunny midsummer afternoon, but Talman felt oddly clumsy, as if no matter which way he turned, he couldn't get out of people's way. He dodged and weaved at every passerby.

A small boy in a black and yellow striped shirt caught him unaware from behind. As the boy shoved past him and darted away, Talman's chest seemed to burn hotter than before. The tattoo above his heart seemed alive with electricity, and both boy and street faded for a second.

The child ran into the Hobby Shop at the end of the block. The boy threw open the door and raced across stained yellowing tile towards an aisle overflowing with boxes and boxes of model cars and space cruisers. He grabbed at a model of a red Mustang convertible, and held it up. "This one," he cried out to the store.

The vision slipped away and the street was back. Talman could see the yellow and black shirt a block away, still darting in and out of passersby, a zig-zagging Charlie Brown.

What the hell was that? he thought to himself. He shrugged, and checked his step to stare through the window of a pawn shop. Instantly, the warm crush of another shoulder slapped into his own.

"Excuse *me*," a voice rapped sharply.

Talman turned back to see a wizened old woman with silvered hair pulled up in a beehive and horn-rimmed glasses scowling over her shoulder at him, though she didn't slow her march.

The strangest thing happened. The harrumphing woman's back shivered and slipped, as if in mirage. Again the street slipped away. Day faded to night and Talman was in a small, dark room.

An old man in blue pajamas slept peacefully on a bed piled high with blankets and pillows. The old woman stood at the head of the bed, her two gnarled, blue-veined hands poised just above the man's face. They held something that glittered in the dim light of a candle flickering on a dresser.

Her bony hands came down, and he saw what she held. Long silver knitting needles. She brought them down fast to punch with an audible clap into the ears of the old man. Black blood spurted onto the shadowy bed, and the man's body jerked from snores to frenzied spasms.

Talman's heart triple jumped and the vision vanished. He stumbled and fell to the pavement as daylight and the street sprang back to his eyes. The old woman was just a few steps behind him, moving with authority.

Talman scrambled back to his feet. His new tattoo burned like fire and he stepped off of the sidewalk to lean against the building. Nobody seemed to have noticed his spill. He shook his head and stared at the hard white cement at his feet, waiting for it to turn into something or someplace *else*. When he was satisfied that it wouldn't shimmer away into a vision of murder, he began to walk again towards the edge of town. As the blocks slipped by, his step grew faster and faster.

He crossed the open field behind the town's lone grocery store, and at last the gravel of the fairground parking lot crunched underfoot. The dirty canvas of the Big Top beckoned comfort like a well-worn coat; he longed to slip inside its mildewed folds.

Skyy was working the ticket booth. She grinned at his

approach and ran up to give him a quick peck on the cheek. At her light embrace his chest seemed to burn with a sudden blaze of heat.

"Where've you been?" she asked. "I was starting to worry." She stepped back and after a penetrating gaze shook her head. "You got another one, didn't you?"

He nodded.

Skyy rolled her eyes. "You're going to run out of room before you're 25, you know that? What is it this time—a swamp demon? A vampire?" When he didn't answer immediately, she raised an eyebrow and guessed, "a girly-girl?"

"A heart."

She blushed. "With my name in it?"

"Just a heart. I'll show you later."

Skyy stepped back to the booth to deal with the growing line of patrons and made change for a $10 bill.

"Better get to the show tent," she warned. Then with a flash of cheer she nodded to the next customer. "Welcome to the Barnett and Staley Circus, the strangest show on earth!"

Talman changed out of his walking clothes and into his red silk and gold-fringed costume. He buttoned the shirt gingerly, cringing as the fabric stuck and slipped across his wounded skin. He wanted to lie down and sleep for a day. But while the tattoo gave a good excuse for feeling like that today, the fact was, Talman felt like that more and more lately. He was burnt out. When he'd met Skyy, just months before, he was just a kid looking for a way out. He'd seen it in Skyy and the circus. Their life seemed ideal; self-contained, they moved from town to town, never staying long enough to get bored, never falling into the rut of the mundane 9-5 day-in and day-out. Every week they woke up in a different town, and while the show remained the same, the people around them always changed. Endless interest.

What he hadn't foreseen was that constant, tedious packing

and unpacking and the fact that while the faces in the audience changed, those were not the faces he ever interacted with. In some ways, the circus was more isolating than being stuck in a 9-5 rut in an office building. At least when you lived in the same town, at the end of the day you could build new relationships with different friends you could choose to see again and again…or your bartender. But the only relationship that Talman could build was here, in his closed community. His work was his home and his town. After a while, it all got stale.

Talman stabbed his shirt tail into his pants and clenched his teeth, willing the feeling away. The circus was his life now, and his family. They had taken him in, and Skyy had taken his heart. He should need no more than this, want no more than this. He blew his nose and forced the moisture from the corner of his eye to dry in the tissue. Need and want knew no boundaries, listened to no leash. Taking a deep breath he fled the changing room to take his place on the wings of the stage.

The show must go on.

"And for your artistic pleasure, we bring to you the man of mystery, the man of art, a man illustrated with your dreams and terrors. He collects your secret thoughts and wears them proudly on his skin. We bring you, 'the tattooed man.'"

Talman took his cue and strode proudly onto the stage, bowing at the proffered hand of the ringmaster.

This was a more intimate audience than the center stage, and the performer moved from face to face at the tiny stage's edge, flexing his leaping biceps skull, and stretching to allow them a glimpse of the deadly shivering snake that wound 'round his torso. The ringmaster called the shots, telling Talman when to allow the paying crowd to see the hidden dragon at his thigh and begging their attention as the tattooed man shed his shirt and long pants to display the full breadth of his well-inked body. His skin glowed in the narrowed spotlight, dragons and snakes and deadly teeth laughing and prowling across his skin for the patrons who *oohed* when expected and *aahed* when suggested.

Talman had thrived on the attention at first, but now he only went through the motions. He knew that it didn't matter that it was *him* on the stage. All the crowd wanted was a garishly painted man; someone whose excess would make them feel secure in themselves. They didn't care about the beauty of the illustrations, or their meaning. They only reveled in the freakishness of it all, and walked out saying, "thank God, I don't look like that." Talman's tattoos set him farther apart than he already was, and that gulf made his audience feel good. But for Talman, it only accentuated the realization that he was alone.

Even with Skyy, and his newfound family of performers and fellow freaks, he was alone.

Sometimes, after his shows, he would stand behind the tent as the chattering patrons filed away to lose money on the watergun and frog-leaping "games of chance" on the Midway, and cry.

When he was a kid, his stepdad had beaten him, literally, and he'd hoped that attention meant he was loved. Now, he was surrounded by people who loved him, and he felt completely isolated.

Talman finished displaying his tattoos and smiled and bowed his way off the stage to applause. He slipped behind the tent to crouch down until the grass tickled his thigh like feather kisses. A salty flow quickly kissed his lips with heat, and with the back of a hand he roughly brushed aside the wetness his eyes betrayed.

"Mister, are you okay?" a tiny voice asked at his elbow.

Talman flinched, and roughed a hand across his eyes once more.

A young boy stared at him from around the edge of the sideshow tent. He looked about six, and was dressed in stiff blue jeans and a too-old-for-him striped button shirt. His head was covered in freckles and fiery orange hair.

Talman shook his head and tried to stand, fumbling forward in surprise. He started to fall, but the young boy grabbed at his elbow to steady the performer.

"Careful, mister," he said.

Talman's chest suddenly burned hot orange like a forge, and he grabbed at the boy's arm to steady himself. The circus faded away.

The boy lay in the dark, tears wetting his pillow. A damp curl of fiery hair was plastered to his cheek.

"But what about mom?" the boy cried.

"Mom isn't going to help you anymore."

The air shuddered with the crack of a hand on skin. The boy winced and shook with every strike, but he didn't make another sound.

Crack, crack, slap.

The sound of fingers slapping flesh seemed to echo louder and louder as a brutal voice screamed, "you will never, ever, speak to me like that again."

"What did you say?" Talman whispered.

"I just asked if you were okay," the boy said. "Are you?"

He opened his eyes and the room was gone, the sounds faded. They stood, a querulous boy and a young melancholy man, behind the freak show tent, hands gripping each other. The grass rippled in a soft summer breeze.

"Yeah," Talman said, ruffling the boy's head with shaking fingers. The image of that head being struck with a fist again and again entered his mind, and as he parted the boy's hair he noticed a purpled spot deep beneath the carrot twists. "I'm just fine."

"Did you get spanked?" the boy asked. His eyes were wide.

"Not today," Talman smiled. He held out his hand, and the boy looked confused. After a moment, he pressed smooth, porcelain white fingers to Talman's own weathered ones.

"I'm Talman. What's your name?"

"I'm Jimmy Jenkins."

"Pleased to meet you, Jimmy Jenkins. Did you see the show?"

"No, but my dad did."

"Where is he now?"

The boy pointed through the aisle of tent posts and taut wires to a couple several yards away. A tall, gaunt man and a plump middle-aged woman engaged in heated conversation, and as Talman watched, the man shook a long finger at the woman, who only turned her back on him to stalk away.

Talman felt a familiar frisson at the scene, and looked closer at the small boy.

"Not a good day?" he ventured.

"Never is," the boy said. Then Jimmy Jenkins turned and ran away.

"Wait," Talman called, but by the time he'd rounded the edge of tent, the youth was gone.

That night, in their trailer, Skyy stepped up behind him to press a cheek to his shoulder. Talman's chest burned at her touch.

"Can I see?"

He peeled off his shirt and let it drop to the floor before turning around.

"Always," he grinned.

Skyy pressed a soft finger to his sternum and delicately traced the edges of the wound. It had burned, at least a little, ever since Talman had left the tattoo shop. Now he looked down at it with her, and saw the blood-red stain of the illustrated heart matched the throb of the pain it caused.

"It looks so real," she whispered, staring up into his eyes. "Does it hurt?"

"Kind of," he downplayed.

"Let me kiss it and make it better," she promised.

The lights in their tent were soon out, sight replaced by sighs.

Over the next few days, the ache in Talman's chest stilled, as the new tattoo healed. The circus packed up and left Parkville, spending three hours on the road to get through an endless stand of knee-high-by-the-fourth-of-July cornstalks.

At last they arrived at the site of their new beds—for the next few days anyway. Ivanhoe, Indiana.

"Aye, aye," the circus roadies joked, as they pounded in the stakes and hoisted the tents. "Aye, aye I., I."

Talman had been strangely silent as they traveled away from Parkville. He heard strange sounds in his heart, and begged it to be still. When Skyy touched him, he felt edgy, but alive. But when he hugged and shook hands with his fellow circus workers, he felt bizarre mixes of hatred and love, often in oscillating measures. The world shook. He was constantly uneasy.

That first night in Ivanhoe passed slowly. He tossed and turned in their bed that felt both strange and familiar in its new home. Skyy slipped into slumber quickly, worn out from the day of moving and paperwork. She'd gone into town without him to make sure all the permits were in order before the first stake was struck, and then made sure the tickets and receipts and all the other hidden business that runs a traveling town were in order before they opened the next day.

As she snored beside him, Talman felt a familiar empty ache begin anew in his chest. This feeling, he knew, had nothing to do with the tattoo. This was the start of another sleepless night. "God, just let me sleep," he whispered, and then leaned in to smell the warm musk of Skyy's hair, for comfort. His ache was instantly replaced with fire.

Skyy sat in her nightgown on the edge of their bed. There was a bundle in her arms, and as she turned, he saw that she nursed a tiny infant, rocking it slowly back and forth. Her hair was knotted and tangled, her face pale. But her smile was radiant.

"Whose is that?" Talman stammered in the dream, and reached out to touch the black down of its soft red-blotched head.

"He's a little me," she said. "And a little you."

Talman's heart jumped. He rolled away from Skyy and the vision was gone. His eyes shot open and he only saw the blackness of their trailer at midnight, and heard the soft breathing of Skyy, deep in sleep.

What was happening to him? For a second, as he had touched her hair, the whole world had changed. It was as if he really was there, with her, in some future place while she held their child. Was it really the future? A wish? A delusion?

He remembered the vision of the old woman, plugging her needles into the old man's head. And of the boy running into the aisle of a hobby shop that Talman had never before seen. And of Jimmy Jenkins, *Crack, Crack, Slap* who cringed in the dark as his father's hand came down. Ever since he'd gotten the tattoo, he'd been seeing things. He ran a finger over the bare, damp skin of his newest tattoo. "What are you doing to me?"

"I don't just draw on your skin," the old man had said. *"I draw on your soul."*

"But what did you draw?" he wondered.

Sleep, strangely, then came easy.

Talman woke to the coughing, painful sound of retching. He reached for Skyy, but she wasn't in bed. He lay there, listening for a moment to the hollow deep gasps, followed by thick chokes, and the splash of something liquid. It was coming from just behind their trailer; he could hear it through the thin aluminum wall as if it were in the room with him. His stomach turned at the sound, and then it finally clicked through his bleary mind. It was Skyy.

Rolling out of bed and pulling on a pair of shorts, he stepped out into the dim glow of dawn and found her kneeling in the mud. He put an arm around her shoulder, just as the last wracking chokes slowed.

"What's the matter?" he whispered.

"Something I ate?" She looked up at him, red-eyed and face damp. "I just woke up and … ew. I didn't want to wake you. I had to run so I didn't get it on you."

He grimaced at the thought. "Glad you did! C'mon, let's get you inside and cleaned up."

Talman helped her back to the trailer and laid her down in bed. He sat beside her, mopping her forehead with a damp cloth.

"Better?"

"Mmm-hmm," she said, her face beaming at him.

"Want some 7-Up to settle your tummy?"

She shook her head. A look of hesitation crossed her brow.

"I was going to wait until I was sure to tell you," she began. "But… I think I'm pregnant."

Talman bent to kiss her. As their lips touched, his heart caught fire once more, and the vision of the night before blurred his eyes again.

Skyy rocked the child gently, hugging it close to her breast. "Do you want to hold him?" she asked.

"It's a boy," he said, and put his arms around her. They hugged for a long time.

That day during his performances, Talman thought of Skyy holding their son, and his soul leapt. But as he stared out at his audiences, his eyes kept lighting on small children. Every kid seemed, for a moment, to have red hair and eyes filled with emotion that ran deeper than a mineshaft.

Jimmy Jenkins was every boy.

Talman was haunted by that wounded gaze. His brief vision from days before in Parkville kept returning, and he could hear the slaps of rage landing on Jimmy's face and back. *Crack, Crack, Slap.*

"I have to go back," he told Skyy that night in their trailer.

"Go back where?"

"To Parkville. There's something I need to do there."

"What's going on?" Alarm crossed her face. Talman kissed her, and scooted closer on the bed. "It's about the tattoo…"

««—»»

The road passed quickly in a blur of dotted yellow lines. Talman drove one of the circus pickup trucks, and pedaled the gas with the goal of cutting the three-hour drive to two.

He'd gotten up early, so that if things went well, he might be back at the circus for his nighttime performances. He arrived in Parkville long before lunchtime, and headed straight for the tattoo shop.

The place wasn't open yet, but Talman put his palm to the glass and peered inside. The shop was dark, but he could see the dim images of the artist's work on the walls. He stepped back from the door and looked up, noting the 2nd floor curtains. The old man probably lived here, above the shop, he thought. He looked for a doorbell. Finding none, he began to pound on the glass of the door.

A car passed him on the street and Talman looked around in sudden fear. What if the police slowed down and asked for him to leave?

But it was just a car, not a cop, and it passed by. The street was quiet again. And again Talman rapped on the door. Something stirred within, and he saw the flash of something at the back of the store.

And then the lock on the door clicked and the face of the old man greeted him, white hair wild and tousled.

"You've found your heart," the man stated. Talman stepped inside.

"What did you do to me?"

"I gave you a tattoo," the old man said and turned to walk back into the murky shadows of the store.

"I'm seeing things," Talman said, following. "Strange things."

"And you've come back to me because…"

"I want to know what they are!" Talman shouted.

The old man turned. "Do you want some coffee?"

"Sure. But first, I want to know what you gave me."

"I gave you nothing you didn't already have," the artist said, and disappeared into a doorway. Talman followed and found himself in a black and white tiled kitchen. He heard the choking cough of a coffeemaker and tasted the scent of fresh brew on the air.

"Is it the future I'm seeing? Or possibilities? Or…what?"

The tattoo artist didn't answer at first. He pulled a white mug from a hook on the wall above the sink and set it next to the coffeemaker, and then a mauve mug. Talman recognized a "Far Side" cartoon of scheming cows on one. He had to grin in spite of himself at their plot against the farmer.

"Cream or sugar?"

"Black."

The artist handed him the mauve mug, steaming with pure caffeine, and gestured to a small table with two chairs. "Sit," he said.

Talman took a seat, never taking his eyes off the old man.

"You gave me a gift," he began. "And I just want to know what it means."

"I gave you nothing you didn't already have," the artist said, knotting two bushy white eyebrows above the "Far Side" cows.

"I never saw visions of old men getting murdered before I came to you," Talman countered.

"Perhaps you weren't open to seeing them?"

"What the hell does that mean?"

"Your heart was strong before you came to me," the old man said. His eyes seemed to twinkle with starlight in the morning air. "But it was wounded. Hiding. Your new heart…allowed you to see those things you had, perhaps, ignored before."

"Is it the future?" Talman whispered.

"Only you can say," the old man said. With a loud slurp, he downed the last of his mug.

"Follow your heart," he pronounced. "Trust your vision. I think you will find it true."

They held each other's gaze for a moment, each silent.

"Can I borrow your phone book?" Talman asked.

There had been two Jenkins' in the phone book, but only one of them was "James Jenkins" and Talman had no doubt about which address to pick. "Where is this?" he asked, showing the old man the address. In moments, he was on the road to the outskirts of the small town.

He pulled into a gravel driveway outside a small, isolated house, and put the truck in park. The day seemed extraordinarily still, as the car door echoed its closure and he walked down the crunching path to knock at the front door of the small, blue-framed ranch.

There was no answer at first.

And then, from somewhere deep within the shadows of the morning, a voice announced, "We don't want none. Kiss off."

"I ain't selling none," Talman said, and tried the doorknob. It moved, but not enough. The door was locked.

"Not gonna tell ya again," the voice said, closer this time. The wooden door opened and a familiar face owned the space. The man from the carnival. The man who'd been arguing heatedly with the woman.

"Can I talk a minute with your son?" Talman asked.

"Piss off," the man answered, and began to shut the door. But from somewhere within, Talman found a strength and a stubbornness he didn't know he had. He pulled open the screen and shoved his foot in the gap of the wooden door, and stopped the other man from shutting him out.

"I'd like to talk to Jimmy, if I could," he said.

"He's busy," the man said and tried harder to shut the door. Talman threw his shoulder against the wood and forced it open.

"Now," he insisted.

Talman forced his way past the man, who looked shocked at the intrusion.

"I'll call the police," he threatened. But the threat sounded hollow.

Talman turned and looked at the flustered man. "Where is he?"

"You have to leave now," the man said, and grabbed Talman's shoulder.

Later, he couldn't have said why he did it. But he knew

something was wrong. It was in the air. Talman didn't question his heart; instead, he threw a hard left to the jaw of the older man, who fell back in shock and surprise.

Talman didn't waste a second. He ran through the murk into the house, turning left at a hallway outside the living room.

"Jimmy?" he called. There was no answer, but he thought he heard something thump from deeper in the house.

He poked his head into the first room on the right, and flipped the light switch on. It was a small bathroom, lime green porcelain tub and toilet accented by a mauve shower curtain. There were dark spots dotting the edges of the snot-green sink. Talman thought they might be blood.

"Jimmy?" he called again, and pushed open the door of the next room, this time on the left of the hall. Again he flipped on a light, and saw posters of Batman on the walls, and a small desk littered with comic books and a catcher's mitt next to the unmade bed. A child's room, but no child.

He moved to the last room, on the right. This time he didn't need to turn on the light, or call for the boy.

Jimmy was there. He knelt on the floor in the middle of the room. He was crying, holding his hands to his eyes. Talman could see the boy's arms were slick with blood.

His mother's.

She lay on the floor in front of Jimmy. Talman guessed that she had been dead for a while already. There were bloody footsteps fading across the carpet that led towards the hall, and the murder weapon was missing. But Talman had no doubt of what it had been. Jimmy's mother looked as if she had been torn open by a hacksaw. Her t-shirt, which once might have been white, was slitted and slashed with a dozen tears, and blood had streamed out of each to pool on her belly, darkening the brown shag carpet beneath her.

Mrs. Jenkins had been stabbed. Over and over again.

"Dad, no," Jimmy cried.

Talman turned just in time to catch a glimpse of silver in the air. He started to dodge, but the blade caught him on the arm, and he screamed as he rolled to the floor.

"Shoulda minded your own business," James Jenkins said. "Now I'll have to do you, too. Can't letcha just walk outta here, can I?"

"Whoa," Talman said, crabwalking backwards, hands and feet treading through the blood of Jimmy's mom, until he was trapped against the bedroom wall. The older man followed, calmly, as if he had all the time in the world.

Jimmy still sat next to his mother's body. "Dad please," he cried. "No more. I'll be good, I promise."

Talman could see the blue of a fresh bruise covering the boy's right cheek.

"Shut up, boy, or you'll get more of the same," the man spat, then moved in on Talman. One corner of his lip raised in a sneer. "Stay still and I'll make this quick for ya. I got enough mess to clean up as it is."

He leaned closer and aimed the butcher knife at Talman's throat.

"I remember you," he grinned. "Shoulda stayed at the circus, freak."

Then he struck.

Talman struck at the same moment, bringing an arm up to shield his face while kicking out at the man's stomach with his feet. Something hot sheared his forearm, but the other man fell back, and Talman leapt up from the floor. Before he could take a step, Jimmy's father was on him again, knocking him back to the ground with a tackle. Talman's face slammed into the carpet, and he felt something sticky on his forehead. He lifted his face off the ground and found himself at eye level with the glazed eyes of the dead woman.

Her husband straddled him from behind and yanked both of his wrists together, holding them with a steel grip to the small of Talman's back.

This is it, a voice in the back of his mind said. *You escaped from this kind of shit, found a nice girl, made a baby...and you had to come back for more.*

"Why did you do it?" Talman found himself asking, still staring at the quiet glaze of the dead woman's eyes.

"She didn't know when to mind her own business either," James Jenkins answered, pressing cold steel to the back of Talman's neck. Suddenly the voice got closer, and hot, sour breath whispered in his ear.

"I give the boy a little discipline and she can't keep her trap shut. Boy needs discipline to be a man, you know. Or didn't your father teach ya that?"

Suddenly Talman was 10 years old again, and in his old bedroom, in the dark. He smelled stale cigarettes and beer, and felt the sting of leather crack across his rear end. His father had pulled his pants down and bent him over the mattress for a whuppin'.

"You need discipline, Talman," his father said, voice slurring ever so slightly. "I'll teach ya." The belt cracked down again, and Talman's whole body screamed.

"No more," the older Talman whispered, a tear forming in his eye. It rolled to the carpet, slipping into the blood of a dead woman, and the fight seemed to leak out of him with the saltwater. His whole body relaxed, and he waited for the last stroke of the knife.

"I'll take care of you," James Jenkins promised, still leaning in close. "And then I'll teach the boy a thing or two about listening to his father."

"Leave him alone," Jimmy yelled. The boy shoved his father, trying to dislodge him from Talman, but the man only laughed. With a backhanded slap, he pushed the boy away. Talman heard a thump as Jimmy lost his balance and hit the floor behind them.

Talman felt the ghosts of cigarette butts burning his bare arms, and saw the purple of bruises on the face and back of poor Jimmy Jenkins.

Are you going to just lie down and die?

He let out a fierce scream and put all of his heart into flipping the bigger man off him. Twisting around, he caught James off balance, and punched the man in the jaw.

"Ugh," the older man gulped in surprise, and then his eyes lit with anger.

"Shoulda let me do you easy," James said, and belted Talman in the face with a fist that left the buzz of bees singing in his ears.

But Talman didn't slow. He'd always been fast and nimble, and now he twisted and shimmied his way loose from the knees of the other man, punching at him again, this time in the gut.

James yelled in fury and raised the knife to plunge it into Talman's chest. But just as its blade nicked the skin, Talman was sliding sideways. The blade slit his shirt, and caught with a *thunk* in the floor. As the other man wrestled it out of the wood beneath the carpet, Talman grabbed the haft with both hands, and wrested it away from the other man.

"No ya don't," Jimmy's father grinned, and backhanded the younger man with his free palm. But Talman didn't let go. His grip held James' hand to the knife, and they strained against each other in a deadly game of arm wrestling. Talman was quickly on the losing end.

"Yes I do," he whispered, and threw all his weight against the knife. He prayed it would be enough, because if it wasn't, he would be lying on the floor beneath the blade again in a heartbeat, and this time, there wouldn't be a reprieve.

It was enough.

The older man fell sideways at Talman's attack, and before James could regain his balance, Talman screamed a whoop of fury and thrust both hands forward, still holding tight to the knife.

"Ugh," James said again, and this time, his surprise was terminal.

A wash of white-hot heat burned Talman's chest as the knife sunk deep into James Jenkins' heart.

The older man slumped backwards, falling to the floor next to his wife, holding the haft of the knife with both hands. He stared in surprise at the wooden stub for just a moment. And then he lay down, eyes blinking as he gasped for air.

"Fucker," he hissed.

And was still.

"Oh my god," Talman murmured, staring at the blood quickly soaking James' shirt. "What have I done?"

He staggered to his feet, and stepped back from the bodies. All of a sudden, he could see the whole room at once, as if from the air. A brutally butchered woman. A murdered man clutching in death at the knife in his chest. A young, beat-up boy, cowering and crying in the corner, head between his knees. And his own hands, smeared with the blood of both of the dead. Talman started moving towards the door. "Shit, shit, shit," he said aloud.

For a split second, as he looked at Jimmy, he saw the father's heavy, dark-haired hand balling into a fist and connecting hard with that small, freckled face. And then he just saw the boy, alone now, and scared, rocking back and forth.

Talman took a deep breath, shivered, and moved back into the room, stepping carefully around the bodies to put his arm around the hysterical child.

"Shhh," he whispered in the boy's ear. "You're going to hyperventilate that way. C'mon, and let's get out of here, okay?"

The boy nodded, and Talman guided him out of the room and back to the toy-strewn bedroom.

"I just wanted to watch cartoons," Jimmy said finally. "Dad said no but mom said okay."

Talman nodded. It was always something simple. Something stupid. He'd lived through it himself. And escaped.

"I know," he said. "It's not your fault."

The boy hugged him, then looked up, tears streaming down his face.

"Can I go with you?"

"I don't know," Talman said. "We need to find your grandma… or your aunt or uncle."

Jimmy shook his head. "Don't have a grandma. Or aunt. Don't have anyone now."

That brought a fresh bout of tears, and Talman pulled the boy close.

"Don't worry," he promised. "I won't let anything bad happen to you."

"Then you'll take me with you?"

Talman thought for a second. If he went to the police, the kid would end up in an orphanage, and he himself might end up behind bars. If Jimmy really didn't have any other family…

««—»»

Skyy grinned at him from behind the ticket booth.

"'Bout time you got back," she said. "You missed all your afternoon shows!"

"I know," Talman answered. "Couldn't help it."

"And who's this?" she asked, smiling at the pale, red-haired boy clenching Talman's hand.

"This is Jimmy," Talman said. "He's going to be staying with us awhile."

A frown crossed her brow, and Skyy looked at him suspiciously. "Talman, what did you do?"

He ruffled a hand through Jimmy's hair, and then patted it to her tummy. His heart instantly burned. But it felt good.

…In the field behind the elephant's pen, a toddler struggled to throw a baseball. He pushed the ball out into the air with his hands, but instead of flying across the field, the ball fell to the ground, just a couple feet away. An older boy with a thatch of sun-red hair reached down and picked it from the dirt. "How bout you *try to catch instead?" the red-haired boy said, and the younger child grinned and held out his hands…*

"I think I just found our baby an older brother."

He knelt down next to the boy. “Welcome to the circus, Jimmy Jenkins.”

A grin spread across the Jimmy’s face for the first time that day. Talman felt his own emptiness melt away as he spread his hand out towards the chaos of the big top, the animal trailers and the mobs of people laughing and talking and clutching stuffed animal prizes under their arms.

“Welcome home.”

Irrelephant in Anathzebra

I shot the zebra right between the eyes. It didn't die quickly. Its feet bucked, and the mouth shuddered, shivering open and closed, open and closed as it fell. Didn't make much sound though. It lay on the floor kicking for a minute or two, one drop of blood greasing the way across its white and black stripes for more. Soon there was a pool of it on the hay-strewn floor beneath the zebra's head, and after a while its eyes stopped accusing me. All its life, I had brought it carrots and a pat on the head. Now, I made it hurt. And die. I had gone from its saint to its anathema. Anathzebra, I thought, in a crazed moment of foolish mindplay. My chest, which over the past weeks had grown strangely cold and numb, suddenly burned in scorching pain.

Have you ever killed someone that you loved?

It could drive you more than a little crazy, I thought.

My eyes misted as I stared at that beautiful animal, resplendent and grand even in defeated death. Its stillness screamed injustice. I looked at the empty iron cages to the left of me and shrugged. The lions were performing right now, so I'd have to come back for them. Instead, I turned toward the chimpanzees. They screamed and threw themselves away from the cage door when I approached; they'd seen what I had done to Angla.

In a minute, though, the animal tent was quiet.

Quiet, but filled with the scents of metal and gunpowder. Blood and shit. The elements always win over the flesh.

Slipping out the front flap of the tent, I confirmed that nobody was around to hear the sounds; barely anyone had come to opening night besides the circus performers, and they were all at the Big Top. Which was my next destination.

Skyy watched the ringmaster announce the lion act with a rising surge of panic. You could count the audience by the handclaps. You could be blind and figure out attendance, but she had three eyes; so it was especially hard not to notice. Her stomach twisted and threatened to upchuck right there. She put a hand to her mouth and turned from the words she had heard ten thousand times.

"Ladies and Gentlemen, your attention please. These lions are some of the fiercest beasts to ever inhabit the earth. With one snap, those jaws can take off your arm or your leg, or…if someone was so foolish as to put it near them, your head. And that's just what the lovely Ms. Katrina is about to do. Please be absolutely quiet now, as she lowers her head into the mouth of our lion king…"

Skyy ran from the tent to her trailer. It was too much. The tears let go, and the summer night turned a blurry mess of black velvet sky and running reds and yellows. The circus was a maze of primary colored signs and tents, and they all turned to a viscous swirl as she ran. Somewhere, she heard the chimps screaming in irritation, but she couldn't go check on them now. Her breath came in great hitching gasps, and she needed to lie down. She needed to let it out. She needed Talman to hold her.

But he was working the ticket counter out front. The ticket booth that nobody was visiting. That nobody had visited in the last dozen towns.

Skyy threw herself on the bed and cried. She and Talman had been running the Barnett & Staley Circus now on their own for a few years, but every season had brought fewer and fewer patrons. Every town brought her stronger premonitions of empty stands and starving performing animals. And Talman's heart—which once found empathy in the visions of others' hurts—had grown hard from the insistent defeat as each town brought fewer patrons. And even those that came seemed as if they came out of duty. Perfunctory. The circus seemed to have no place in today's world.

Ms. Katrina was amazing at what she did with the lions…but nobody cared enough to come see the act anymore.

And ever since Yvette, the three-breasted woman had died, the circus had lost its top-drawing "naughty" freak show. Talman's "illustrated man" act simply didn't draw that many people anymore; what interest is there in an Illustrated Man when tattoos were all the rage these days among regular people? You could see guys and girls with more tatts than Talman had managed to accumulate on the pages of magazines in any bookstore…and sometimes just walking down any street. In a culture obsessed with body modification, he simply wasn't that much of an oddity anymore. And as for Tonya, the smallest woman, and Yvette's kids, Wen and Wong well… lots of people had met and seen dwarves. They just weren't that unique.

Media killed the circus star.

Barnett & Staley's had plenty of things you don't see in the average subdivision of Beloit, Wisconsin or Loveland, Colorado. But the fact was, that didn't matter anymore. You could see weirder things on 500 channels of cable than you would ever assemble in the circus, and with HD TV, you could actually see most of them better from the comfort of your couch than if you came, parked your car in a rutty field, paid your ticket price, bought your popcorn and sat on the bleachers behind some fool with B.O. and an unwieldy collick.

Kids went to the mall and played sports and battled addictions to X-Box and Nintendo. They didn't go to see lions and monkeys and musclemen and dwarf women at the circus. It was passé. Their fathers might have gone to see a three-breasted woman and dragged them along…but those days were gone. And Yvette's always mutated children had never seemed to live long enough to take her place as a centerstage attraction that could have truly brought in some spectators for the freakshow.

She'd had some doozies, that was for sure. Her daughter Yvonne still showed off her extra set of legs and arms… but…somehow, it wasn't enough.

And so Skyy and Talman had continued to take the circus from city to town to village, first following a long-travelled route, and then gradually moving to less traveled markets as the old venues found reasons not to have the circus come back.

The towns, and the attendance shrank and shrank until now, she and Talman had had to dip into their savings to pay the performers after recent shows. And they didn't have much themselves. It would only take another bad date or two to bankrupt both them *and* the circus.

Skyy clutched her pillow and pressed it to her face, a swollen mask of heat and painful tears. She had grown up in this circus and had no other skills if the bigtop stopped putting down spikes and putting up marquees.

She opened her lips against the wet pillowcase and let out a long, drawn out sob. Her cries drowned out the sounds of bullets just a few yards away.

««—»»

Desperation is an insidious thing. You can live with it for a long time, and probably not call it desperation. You'll say, "yeah, I'm kinda down today," or "it'll get better" when someone asks you how you are. You'll tell yourself for a long time that the blackness that gnaws at your neck and threatens to engulf every word you try to utter before it can get out is just a phantasm. Ephemeric pathos. You'll drink a lot, and think a lot. You'll consider how long it might really take for the blood to leave your body if you draw a sharp object across your wrists.

You might consult physics texts and arithmetic to arrive at a formula to determine how long it will actually take your heart to bleed your body dry with open veins. And when that seems a pointlessly extended option, you'll consider the odds of surviving should you somehow manage to find yourself standing in the path of an oncoming train. Is a 5% chance of survival as a quadriplegic worth the risk?

Throwing out these uncertainties as foolishness, you'll instead concentrate on first making your surroundings better…and then you'll convince yourself in resignation that the world you inhabit is certainly better by far than that of many and you have no right, no fuckin' right to complain.

And then you'll drink again.

Mind you…the world did not change. It stayed the same as it ever was. But somewhere along the line, you came face to face, not with a bit of "oh bummer" depression. You came face to face with desperation.

And it haunted you because you refused to acknowledge it head-on.

But when you did, you didn't take the pussy-boy way out. You didn't finally drag the blade or stand in front of the iron horse for release. You decided to change your world. You were going to get out…but still stay. And you bought a gun.

Okay, maybe *you* didn't. But I did.

Because I knew in my heart that the circus was dying. I could feel its horrible gasping breaths struggling for intake and release every day. But I was a merciful guy. As much as it was going to hurt me, I knew what I had to do. I had to put it out of its misery. Euthanasia.

The zebra was only the first in a long line of mercy killings on my agenda tonight. Biting back the tears, I started towards the elephant tent. I could almost feel the fuzzy hide of Emily slipping between my fingers from the last time I'd given her baggy neck a hug.

««—»»

Jimmy slipped out of the trailer with his stepbrother when he heard Skyy crying. The baby opened a fist and pointed at the moon as Jimmy stepped onto the dark path that led to the midway. Something popped and popped again in the distance, and Carl jumped.

"Shhh," Jimmy soothed the child, stroking the wispy dark down on its head. "We'll go see the lions. You know you like lions."

The baby made a roaring sound at the word "lion" and grinned, showing all four of its teeth.

"That'a boy," Jimmy said, and moved faster down the path. The night was quiet, but for the occasional cheers from the Big Top. Quiet and cool. He shivered at the goosebumps that rippled up his arms, and hugged the baby closer, enjoying its burning warmth, and sweet baby smell.

In answer, the child wrapped a chubby arm around his neck and pulled at a lock of the hair by his ear.

"Luv ya, buddy," Jimmy whispered and slipped into the Big Top from the side. He carried the baby up the rows of weathered wooden planks, and sat high in the tent, away from the paying customers.

Above the center ring, Reind walked the tightrope, his mouth a tense line of pink concentration, as sweat beaded in glinting lights on his forehead. The small crowd drew in a breath as one and exhaled, as the performer wavered on a step, threatening dramatically to fall to the nets below, but then recovered his equilibrium.

"You can do it, Reind," Jimmy whispered, scratching the baby's back to calm it as it fidgeted. "Steady as she goes…"

And then the tent erupted in ragged, meager applause to celebrate Reind's final step from the rope to the platform. The tightrope walker bowed, and quickly slipped down the ladder to disappear out the back of the tent. Reind always left a show and went straight home these days, ever since that nasty business his wife had caught him in with Melienda. There was still evidence of Reind's deadly affair floating in formaldehyde in the freak show. Not that anyone ever visited that tent these days.

Jimmy held the baby close and tried to stop the fluttering in his stomach. Talman had rescued him from a horrible place and brought him to the circus to live with Skyy. And then they'd had a baby, Carl. But lately…for quite awhile now actually, the circus had felt thin as a leaf in fall. As if it might all blow away leaving Jimmy with the taste of cotton candy and an empty cardboard cone. Or maybe not thin. Maybe it felt heavy. As if it could collapse in upon itself at any moment, a towering construct of concrete supported by a frame of kite string.

Skyy sometimes cried about it with Talman at night when she thought he couldn't hear the two of them talking, but he could. That's why he'd taken Carl out of the trailer tonight when she'd started letting go in the other room. She needed her time, and he needed to find a place where there were no tears. For awhile, he'd found it here at the circus. But then his bad luck had caught up with him, and his newfound parents were suffering because of it.

"It's all my fault," Jimmy whispered, rubbing a tear into the baby's soft shoulder.

"And in this corner, we bring you the exotic safari tricks of Angla, our magical Zebra!" the ringmaster was promising. He pointed towards the tentflap at the end of the Big Top, but nothing came through.

Jimmy tried to pull himself from his funk, and pointed at the animal entryway.

"Look Carl, here comes Angla," he said.

But the tent didn't open. No zebra trotted through. The ringmaster gestured again, and then, with a slight rustle, Perry came running in, eyes so wide you could almost see the veins in them from the top of the stands. He ran to the ringmaster and whispered something, then tripped and sprawled headlong on the dusty ground as he tried to run back the way he'd come.

"Angla isn't feeling well tonight," the ringmaster covered,

and pointed at the far stage. "So instead, we'll bring out Concertina, and her amazing Band of Monkeys!"

"Here come the monkeys," Jimmy grinned at the baby, whose eyes opened wide at the word. The baby loved the monkeys and together the two boys bopped up and down on the bleacher and imitated the monkey sound, "ee-ee-ee."

But moments later, Jeffrey from the stables came running into the center ring and whispered to the ringmaster, and again the flustered director in his gaudy sequined red cape had to announce a delay.

"It looks like our monkeys won't be joining us tonight either. But that's ok, because Emily, the most talented elephant ever to takc the stage in a circus is on her way, and she's going to show you all what it really means to move a trunk.

The tent grew silent in anticipation, as the crowd waited for the next act to arrive. But no elephant was forthcoming.

As all eyes trained on the tent flap at the north end of the Big Top, nothing could be heard but for the occasional sniff and sneeze of a child. The ringmaster stood helpless in front of the vacant stages, waiting for someone, anyone, to come help him entertain the meager crowd.

But when the tentflap finally moved, it wasn't entertainment that entered.

It was a man. With a gun.

««—»»

The elephant was hard. She'd kissed my neck with the wet ridges of her trunk a thousand times. Truth be told, I hated the fuckin' monkeys, so that was easy. They were like shooting clowns in a barrel. Good riddance. Fur puree. Whip 'em up and coat the cake.

But Emily…damn it was hard to hold the gun to her grey hide. She looked at me with complete incomprehension as I whispered in that gigantic ear that it was all over, it was time to bring down the curtain.

One beady eye looked over at me as her trunk dragged a load of hay to her mouth. She was comfortable with me, completely at ease.

"Irrelevant elephant," I said. "Just like the rest of us. We're all irrelevant."

I whispered "Irrelephant "as I pulled the trigger and sent a hunk of lead straight to her stupid, trusting brain.

She didn't struggle like the zebra. She fell hard. And fast.

I was glad.

After I wiped the tears from my face, I slipped out of the tent and started down the path to the center of the circus.

To the Big Top.

««—»»

Skyy stared at the black tears on her sheets and knew she had to lift her head. The show must go on. And it was…right now…without her. Talman was working. Jimmy had taken Carl somewhere…and she was here, crying in her bed. She had to stand up and pull it together.

And that's when her third eye chose to open.

It was unpredictable, her secret sight. But when it did show her visions, they were always true.

And as Skyy pushed herself up from the sheets tonight, she felt a veil lift in her mind, and suddenly, she saw, not the dark shadows of her rhinestone costumes hanging in the corner, but the heavy flow of fatal blood. She saw Angla's black and white stripes turned ragged and gory, and the troop of screeching monkeys lying still at the floor of their pen. She saw people too, and she screamed, struggling to close the sight of her third eye. Her vision ran red, and her stomach threatened to release itself on her bed as she realized the import of her sight.

Blood, blood everywhere. And her best friends' bodies dead upon the floor.

She could have named them all, those white faces with red

spattered upon their dead cheeks…but Skyy was afraid to name them in her head, as if naming them legitimized their deaths…made them real. She refused to recognize the deaths that her sight showed her.

Instead, she forced them out of her brain and rolled off the bed. She stood, rubbed hands across her face in a vicious effort to clear her brain, and headed towards the Big Top. She had to find Talman and Jimmy and Carl. Something wicked this way came. Something bad for all of them.

««—»»

"Ladies and gentlemen, your attention please!" the ringmaster exclaimed, when he saw the newcomer. "In this corner, we present the most amazing of…"

The gun coughed, and the ringmaster fell to the dirt floor, a blossom of cherry growing fast across his white-vested chest.

A woman in the stands screamed, and the crowd leapt to their feet, frantically looking for the fastest way down from the stands and out of the tent.

But the man didn't stay on the boundaries of the Big Top. He strode fast toward the center, and with a deft hand plucked the wireless microphone from the corpse of the ringmaster. He yelled so loud into its tiny face that the speakers crackled in a lightning storm of static: "Sit the fuck down," his command echoed.

The audience gasped, and then almost as one, plunked jean pockets down on the rough-hewn plank seats. Parents held their hands over the mouths of young children who opened wide to cry. And wives clutched the waists and shoulders of their husbands and pleaded in their mind's eye for this crazy man to look somewhere, anywhere, but at them.

"What's wrong with you people?" the man asked. His voice was quiet now. Now that the tent had become still as a tomb.

"Why are you here at a dusty, smelly circus, when you could

be at home watching TIVO? You could be running the kids over to a football game or a piano lesson, or maybe you could be off on your own, having a nice steak and bottle of wine while your kids are giving their babysitter a headache for once instead of you?"

The man waved the dark barrel of a revolver in the air, pointing at the hidden sky and then trailing its barrel along the line of petrified faces in the woefully populated stands.

"Are you fools?" he asked. "Don't you understand? The circus is done. It's over. We don't matter anymore. None of this…matters. There is no sense of community to be found here, because there is no community, anywhere. There is no frivolity in the freakshow tent. There is only sadness. We don't entertain…"

Behind the man, a tent flap moved, and a white-faced clown tiptoed into the Big Top. The clown's clothes were almost blinding—silver and red in the intense light of the centerstage spots. His mouth was outlined in a wide river of electric crimson limned in black; an exaggeration of the river of speech. His eyes were raccoon-rings. And a silver hat perched forgotten on his head. The clown put a finger to his lips, urging the crowd to be silent, to ignore him.

But it didn't matter. Maybe he saw the cloud's reflection in a child's eye. Maybe he heard the crunch of a foot on a loose bit of gravel. Somehow the gunman knew. And when he turned in mid-sentence, he didn't hesitate to fire.

The clown's whiteface turned ghastly red, and he fell to the dust, a cloud of grim humor lost like woken dreams or surprised lust.

"Why are you here?" the gunman asked, waving his weapon again. "Why do you sit here to watch the animals stand on two legs when they'd rather walk on four? Why do you want to see a woman struggling through life with four arms, or the smallest man in the world climb a ladder so that he can be seen? Do you think any of them are *happy* to demonstrate their deformities to you? Would you enjoy showing us all your darkest shame, night after night? Would you be able to live with yourself if you had to get up each day to show off your weakness and pray for applause for your deformity each time, because maybe just maybe that would mean that you still have an income and could eat this week?

"Would you work to make your freakishness worse? Maybe if you cut off your arm, people would pay more to see you?"

The man laughed, and stared down his arm at the tattoo of a skull. "Maybe you could degrade yourself more, and make more money…Maybe if you were the ultimate freak, you could make enough money as a main attraction that you could leave the circus entirely, eh?

"Well, look around folks. Do you see enough paying customers to send any pathetic clown or freak to Easy Street? Cuz I sure don't. I see a bunch of pathetic losers who don't realize that the circus is the *last stop* for pathetic losers, and you and your kind have been keeping us here year after year with your pity money.

"You don't love the circus. You're drawn to it. You come to the circus to show that you're better than all this. But you know what? You're not. Most of the world has moved on. Look at the empty seats next to you. People don't need this shit anymore. There's no need to train a bear to wear an apron to make you feel good. Why do you want to torture the bear that way? Why do you want to laugh at the world's Fattest Woman? Do you think she wanted to be that way? Do you suppose she said "hmmm…well, I could have big tits and a tight waist and wear some rouge so I get paid lots of money to pose in *Penthouse* and *Maxim*, or I could gorge myself with chicken fat and doughnuts for years because I'm miserable, until I'm so big I can't move without help so that the rubes in bumfuck Iowa can pay a quarter to look at the rolls under my chin?"

The man scowled at the crowd and waved the gun in the air. "Well, what do you fuckin' think?"

In the front row, a blonde-headed boy opened his mouth and began to cry. His mother, a cherry-red bomb leaned down to kiss the boy's head and whisper something in his ear.

The boy only opened his mouth to scream louder as she pressed two thick lips against his head. Her lipstick left trails on his scalp, but it didn't matter. A second later, the boy's head exploded, as the man fired one bullet upwards. The redhead screamed as her son's blood dripped from her forehead, and the ragged gore of his head jerked away from her lips to slop in her lap.

"Damn," the gunman hissed. "I meant to take out the bitch." He grinned and looked out at the crowd. "The kid thought he'd whine and the world would just fall in his lap. He was a spoiled brat, let me tell you." He pounded his chest. "I could feel it."

He raised the gun again, this time sighting the cherry-red head more exactly. "Like I can feel that his bitch of a mother is a slut who looks down on everyone she fucks just as much as everyone she doesn't."

He pulled the trigger and the tent echoed with the sound of a chamber explosion that spattered the audience with the crimson rain of Cherry-Red brains. The people all around the woman screamed and shrank away as her body fell backward between the bleachers. Her leg caught underneath the seat in front of her and so her body dangled and hung there, raining blood to the grass below…still nobody dared stand up and run for fear that they'd be the next target. The stands grew moist with secret stains of piss and sweat as the adults wrestled their fear and struggled to stay hidden while in full view, and children's cries of fear were smothered by parents' trembling hands.

"Let it go," the gunman whispered. His weapon hung low at his thigh, and with a tear trailing down his cheek, the man shook his head at the crowd.

"Don't you see?" he said. "Our time is over. So Let. Us. Go. Sometimes the hardest thing is to say goodbye. And sometimes, the meanest thing is not to."

The curtain at his right suddenly shivered, and a woman stepped into the Big Top. She wore an iridescent uniform of eye-piercing ocean blue, and her hair stood up in a tower of brunette ice. A silver comb glimmered in the light like a beacon, but it was her eye that the crowd fastened their attention on.

Her third eye. Right there, in the center of her forehead like a garish tattoo.

Only, unlike the drawings on the arm of the gunman, her tattoo shimmered, and teared as it opened and closed. It was no representation.

Her eye was real.

"Talman," she cried out, tears streaming from all three eyes. "Why are you doing this?"

The circus' Tattooed Man shook his head and pointed the barrel of the gun at his wife. "No," he deflected. "Why are YOU doing this? Why don't you let this die? Let everyone rest. Our time is over. You just refuse to let it go. Don't you get it? We're not relevant anymore. The world has moved on. We're a footnote."

Skyy walked into the Big Top. She held out her hand for Talman's gun.

"We're not a footnote," she said. "We're an attraction. A diversion. Entertainment. We never were *relevant*. We were only a place for people to forget, for awhile. A place where people might leave their troubles at the popcorn stand and forget about life for awhile. And now you brought all that trouble back in. You've ruined it."

Talman raised his gun to Skyy's third eye. The crosshairs in the sight trembled, but he didn't bring his hand down. "Sometimes you have to kill the thing you love to set it free."

Talman's finger drew back on the trigger of the gun, priming the bullet for release.

"Dad, no!" a voice behind him screamed.

A frown flickered across Talman's face and his attention wavered and he turned to see Jimmy standing a few yards away, baby Carl in his arms.

"Listen to your heart," Jimmy begged, tears streaming down his face. "It used to show you things. The right things. You promised me that life would be better here. You promised me that other people weren't as mean as my real dad."

Talman turned his gun on Jimmy's face, and then shifted it slightly, until its barrel pointed at the bald head of the toddler in Jimmy's thin arms. "Dada," the baby grinned, oblivious to the danger.

"It isn't, and they are," Talman said gripping one hand on his chest. "Life isn't better, and people are horribly mean. My heart doesn't lie. But I did."

Behind him, a horrible shriek erupted as Skyy broke into a dash across the dusty floor of the Big Top while a ragged audience looked on, too stunned and afraid to interfere in the drama below.

But before Skyy could reach him, Talman's gun went off. Blood sprayed up in the air like a geyser of hopeless mist. The audience didn't wait any longer to see what happened. They grabbed their children and ran towards the exit.

Skyy reached Talman, but she didn't stop; instead she kept going to take Jimmy and Carl in her arms.

"Oh my boys," she cried, holding them close. In the dust behind her, Talman's head spasmed rapidly twice, and then again, sending a gout of dark blood pulsing into the ground as his life left him in a rush. Brains and defeat leaked in equal measure through the holes he'd blasted from his jaw through his tortured skull.

The baby pointed to the ground and grinned at the gory prank. "Dada," it said.

««—»»

Skyy brushed a lock of hair across the sight of her third eye and pushed the last roll of sideshow tent into the rocky crevice. She had played in these caves once a year every season when she was a kid and the circus came to play here, in Northern Kentucky for a week each summer.

After burying Angla and Emily and the monkeys and Talman, she had decided that this was as good a place as any to bury the circus. At least for now. Skyy disagreed with his method, but had to admit that Talman's heart, in its tortured, insane way, was right. Their time was over. The world didn't need a circus or a sideshow.

"That's the end of it," she breathed, pushing the last of a fabric fold onto the rocky shelf.

Jimmy nodded but said nothing. He walked out of the cave without looking back. The circus, in its celebration of outcasts, had failed him in offering a safe refuge. But still, it had given him Skyy. In the glare of the day ahead, he followed Carl who ran clumsily ahead, every step threatening to let his body fall. Yet he pressed on, as only toddlers can. Carl chased a bright red and green beach ball.

"Dada" the baby squealed, still not understanding that Dada's day was dead.

How could he understand the end of what had gone before, when his day was just beginning?

Skyy stepped out of the cave behind the boys and took a breath.

And then another. And another. Her third eye began to open with a glimpse of the future but she poked a thumb at it, blinding its vision.

And then she opened her lungs and breathed a sigh of relief.

John Everson is the Bram Stoker Award-winning author of the novels *Covenant* (Delirium Books, 2004) and *Sacrifice* (Delirium Books, 2007) which will both be released in mass market paperback from Leisure Books in 2008/2009. A Polish translation of *Covenant* was issued by Poland's Red Horse Books as *Demoniczne Przymierze* in late summer 2007.

His short fiction has appeared in magazines like *Space and Time, Dark Discoveries, Wicked Karnival, Red Scream, Black October* and *Grue,* and in the anthologies *A Dark and Deadly Valley, Kolchak: The Night Stalker Casebook, Dark Doorways, Cold Flesh, Damned: An Anthology of the Lost, In Delirium* and the CD-ROM anthology *Bloodtype,* which includes an Everson-composed techno theme song. His short stories have also been translated and published in Polish and French. Much of his short fiction has been collected in three short story collections - *Needles & Sins* (Necro Publications, 2007), *Vigilantes of Love* (Twilight Tales, 2003) and *Cage of Bones & Other Deadly Obsessions* (Delirium Books, 2000). He is also the co-editor of the *Spooks!* ghost story anthology (Twilight Tales, 2004), and the founder of Dark Arts Books: www.darkartsbooks.com.

John lives near Chicago with his wife Geri, son Shaun, and Kiwi and Lem, his two avian "editorial assistants."

For information on his fiction, art and music, visit John Everson: Dark Arts at www.johneverson.com.